BORDER DOGS

ALSO BY KAREN PALMER

All Saints

BORDER DOGS

a novel

KAREN PALMER

ISBN: 1-56947-315-3

Library of Congress Cataloging-in-Publication Data

Palmer, Karen, 1961–
Border dogs / Karen Palmer.
p. cm.
ISBN 1-56947-315-3 (alk. paper)
1. Border patrols—Fiction. 2. Mexican American Border
Region—Fiction. 3. California, Southern—Fiction.
4. Mexican Americans—Fiction. 5. Birthmothers—Fiction.
6. Adoptees—Fiction. I. Title.
PS3566.A526 B67 2002
813'.54—dc21   2002072754

For J—
XXX

ACKNOWLEDGMENTS

Thanks to my wonderful agent, Susan Ramer, for her patience and advice and, especially, her friendship; thanks also to Michael Congdon, Cristina Concepcion, Don Congdon and Christine Larsen. I am indebted to the good people at Soho Press: Juris Jurjevics, Laura Hruska, Bryan Devendorf and Aileen Lujo. Thanks to Margaret Wolf for diligent copyediting, to James Reyman for his superb designs, to Teresa Carbajal Ravet and Melinda Gonzalez for vetting my Spanish, to Ellen Zweibel for a physics tutorial, and to Clay Evans for cowboy lore. (Any errors are mine alone.) For careful readings and/or a sympathetic ear, I owe: David Sheppard, Nan Goodman, Karin Lazarus, Amy Knox Brown, John McNally, Marilyn Krysl, Daniel Salazar, Beth Robertson, Janis Hallowell, Tom Jones, Tim Hilmer, Robert McBrearty and Juliet Wittman. Special thanks to Mimi Wesson (aka PDB), whose warmth and intelligence are unparalleled. The National Endowment for the Arts supplied financial support for the completion of this project—may this organization retain congressional goodwill into the next millennium.

Last but not least, love and gratitude to my family: E! and A and Mr. V.

Mexican proverb:

Si quieres vivir en paz, lo que sabes no dirás y lo
que ves no juzgarás.

If you want to live in peace, what you know you
will not tell and what you see you will not judge.

CHAPTER ONE

The patrol rode his quarterhorse over land that looked like the sea, the night-vision goggles turning the 2 a.m. desert green, a dream of liquid hills and shifting sands, tumbleweeds, arroyos, dried riverbeds. He was working a desolate stretch of the southern U.S. border, nearly a hundred miles in from the Pacific Ocean, a place where there were no substations, no checkpoints, and no twelve-foot-high steel fence, only the hard-won knowledge of where one country stopped and another began.

A shredded cloud drifted clear of the moon and James saw wild mustard blooming in the roots of a stunted scrub oak, lacy flowers the goggles colored a dazzling nuclear lime. The sparse vegetation rustled with creatures: snakes and birds, lizards, rodents. Slowing his horse, he passed the reins from right hand to left, then reached up to fasten the goggles' harness more securely at the back of his head. The whistling March wind stung the tips of his ears. He brought both hands to his mouth and blew into his palms; he'd forgotten his gloves. Beneath him, the horse snorted and tossed its head, its flanks quivering. The shank of the bit glittered in its black mouth.

A quarter-mile ahead his partner broke into a trot as the illegals they'd been tracking charged through the scrub.

The radio at James's hip hummed with static and Leo's excited voice crackled out at him, "Hey, old man . . . I've got 'em now! Pinches pollos . . . gotcha!" James heard muffled shouting, the snap of branches. Leo's voice came again, "Gotcha!" and three men tumbled free, followed quickly by a fourth. The pollos fell to their knees, hands crossed on top of their heads.

Leo cried, "Where the fuck are you, James!"

But a green blur had caught his attention, a lone figure scurrying east toward the canyon. The figure ran upright and sure-footed, as if certain of both course and destination.

Coyote, thought James—the pollos' guide, paid to shepherd illegals over the line. The smuggling of human beings was a federal beef, an automatic ten years. James *had* to get him. But the only way was to cut the guy off before he reached the canyon.

He slapped the reins and jabbed his boot heels, urging the quarterhorse into a canter. He rode with hips dropped deeply into the saddle, loins and waist kept supple to absorb the horse's movement. The sound of hooves hitting the sand was like a muffled drum roll. Through the goggles, he saw a green bounce of terrain, and the coyote, running hard, arms and legs pumping wildly. But James on the quarterhorse quickly gained ground.

Within twenty yards of his prey, the rocky lip of the canyon became visible, the chasm gaping darkly beyond. The horse thundered forward. "¡Inmigración!" James shouted. "¡Párate, la migra!" *Stop! Immigration!* But the man ran all the harder. James took up the rope coiled on the saddle horn. He fed the looped end into the palm of his right hand. Closer, closer . . . he shook out the loop, raised his arm high and swung counterclockwise. Spiraling his wrist, he accelerated the spin, then leaned from the saddle and threw. But the coyote had inexplicably stopped dead in his tracks.

When he turned to run back the way that he'd come, the loop whizzed harmlessly past, dropping onto a clump of thick brush. The branches emptied of angry birds.

As James veered away, the rope, hung up more than he'd realized, buzzed from his left hand, burning him. Cursing, he reined up hard. The quarterhorse skidded into a halt, its hind legs sliding underneath it. James trotted back around. He yanked repeatedly on the rope, attempting to free it. But the brush was captured and fully secured.

Goddamnit! James dismounted.

He raced in front of the horse, where his legs got tangled up in the line; it nearly decked him. Circling the brush, he swiveled his head—the goggles impaired his peripheral vision—searching for a telltale green glow. But he saw nothing. He hurried back to the spot where he'd seen the coyote stop, and there he found a kicked-up pile of sand, tracks zigzagging away. He followed them just far enough to determine that, in spite of the about-face, the coyote was still headed toward the canyon. James jogged to the horse. With some difficulty, he freed the caught rope. He wound it into a coil and mounted again. He sat in the saddle a moment, catching his breath.

He felt an ooze of blood in his palm.

In the distance, a small white object lifted and spun in the air. From the radio, Leo's voice came again: "Where the fuck are you, James?" And then the coyote disappeared over the edge.

James stared into the canyon. Fifteen sheer feet led down to bedrock obscured by dried scrub, an undercurrent of jagged stones and discarded clothing, broken bottles, burned tires. To his right, a small green figure swam through the debris. The coyote was aimed at Mexico.

James knew he'd never catch up on foot. Useless, too, to follow on horseback from up on the ridge. Southward, the canyon deepened impossibly. He'd never have an opportunity to get down.

He should just let the guy go.

But watching the coyote's frantic progress, he thought: No one ran that hard, not without a reason.

And then he remembered a diagonal cut in the rock, a narrow path down. The cut was a short distance north, and initially, would take him in the wrong direction, but once on the canyon floor, he could make up the time.

He rode to the cut and turned the horse in. Leaned back in the saddle, he loosened the reins. Down they went. At bottom, the animal nickered and James bent forward and stroked its hot neck, breathing in a smell of rawhide and sweat. The radio fizzed at his hip; rock interfered with the signal. Even with the goggles, the canyon was dark. Rivers of shadow poured from the steep sides. James was acutely conscious of the horse's gait, a blunt clopping against the hard floor.

He squeezed his legs and took the horse up into a trot, high-stepping it around obstacles. Minutes passed, and still he saw nothing. He hated like hell to give up. But he was about to when, rounding a bend, he sighted a white shirt thrashing in the bushes, legs that waded through the tangled undergrowth. Trotting forward, James again readied the rope, feeding the looped end into his palm.

But something diverted his attention, something wriggling, down low. A creature darted out from the brush. Before James could register what he was looking at, the quarterhorse spooked, whinnying and bucking, rearing on its hind legs—and then James was sliding, shooting down from the saddle, the rope still in his hands. He landed on his hip, a bone-jarring thump. The goggles flew. James rolled away from the horse, afraid of being trampled. Pain shot up his side. But a surge of adrenaline brought him instantly to his feet. Blinded, he could still hear the coyote, rustling in the brush, panting, and moaning softly.

The coyote cried out and James hurtled forward. Branches tore at his face and his hands. Now he saw the white shirt; he could almost touch the man's back. His pounding heart felt ready to burst. Diving, he closed the gap between them.

He went down face-first, but on the way, managed to wrap his arms around the coyote's left leg—a padded stick. The coyote dragged him several yards, branches snapping. James's knees and shins bumped over rocks. He couldn't believe the guy's strength! He was losing equipment all over the place: shield, pistol, flashlight, canteen. Worse, his hold was slipping. In desperation, he hauled back hard on the leg. A heel thumped him in the chest as the man staggered and fell. The coyote crawled a few feet, then collapsed.

James scrambled on top of him. He dropped all his weight, panting into the coyote's ear, "Motherfucker!" He waited for the man to squirm or lash out, but the fight seemed to have gone out of him. James rolled off. Up on one knee, he flipped the coyote onto his back.

He blinked the sweat from his eyes.

And now, at last, he realized his mistake.

What he'd taken for a white shirt was the man's naked skin, ivory over his torso and arms, darker at the neck and wrists. A campesino's coloring. The man's chest was slight, and womanish, the ribs sharply defined. His breath came in fluttering gasps. He smelled badly of diesel fuel. James noted three pairs of pants, one on top of the other, and no shoes. The man's bare feet were bloody.

Goddamnit! Caught, coyotes often posed as just another pollo—but no coyote would ever travel barefoot.

An unexpected flash, and the man heaved upward. A blade drew down across James's left shin. His pantleg parted and flapped. He felt a sharp sting, blood dripping, and his stomach plunged—he'd been cut!—and then he was on his feet and kicking. His heel met the side of the man's flailing arm. The pollo grunted, and dropped his arm to the ground, the knife still clutched in his fist. James lifted his boot and stomped once. He heard a sickening crunch.

A gurgling sounded deep in the pollo's throat. He lifted his head, vomited a watery stream down his chest, then lay back.

James swooped down for the knife.

"Shouldn't've done that," he said.

The pollo stared up at him, breath wheezing and whistling. His eyes watered, washing into the lines of his face. He turned his cheek to the ground, muttering.

"Say what?" James peeled the fabric of his pantleg. He inspected the wound to his shin. A long slash, but shallow. He'd live.

"Coco," the pollo said.

Coconut. Brown on the outside, white where it counts.

"Fuck that," James said. He'd heard it before. But he wasn't the first, and he would not be the last. More than half the Patrol was Latino these days.

He examined the knife, an everyday, folding implement, with steel rivets and a plastic handle scored to look like ivory. He closed it and buried it in his pocket.

Clumsily, the pollo rose into a crouch. James tensed, but allowed it, knowing that this was the stance of submission: head down, fingers limp against the groin. The damaged hand was already swollen; the pollo had likely suffered a few broken bones. Stone-faced, he hunched forward, as if ashamed of his nakedness. Or maybe he was only cold.

James stood.

He pulled the pollo to his feet, then seized him by a skinny bicep. The man tucked his wounded hand up against his chest, like a bird with a broken wing.

James walked him back to the quarterhorse, gathering his lost equipment on the way. He slid the pistol into its holster, hung the goggles from a loop on his belt. Two thousand dollars a pop, he thought mournfully. The boss was going to flip.

They found the horse nosing in a pile of rocks. James dragged the pollo over, but when he indicated the stirrups, the man shook his head.

James hunkered down, twining his fingers together. "¡Ahora!" he commanded. *Now*. The pollo hesitated, then executed a feeble hop. Skidding a bare heel into James's cupped palms, he lunged for the saddle horn. Suddenly, James appreciated how vulnerable he was. One good kick could snap his neck. He jerked away. But the man sat the horse calmly, seemingly indifferent. Relieved, James instructed him to move forward. No response. He prodded the pollo's hip and the pollo wriggled awkwardly against the saddle horn.

James poked a boot into the stirrup. He hoisted up and slid in behind, groaning at the lightning bolt of pain in his hip. Though the pollo was small, two in the saddle was a tight fit. James unlocked the cuffs from his belt. Circling his arms about the man's waist, he snapped the bracelets onto his wrists. He nudged the quarterhorse into a trot.

The pollo shivered. A bead of sweat rolled down his neck.

James twisted in the saddle. He loosened a bungee cord and pulled at a folded square of brown wool and shook it to one side. He draped the blanket over the pollo's shoulders.

They came to the cut in the rock, and James walked the horse up, the pollo pressed against him. Gradually, the desert opened before them, a vista that never failed to take James's breath. The few trees swayed in the breeze, leaves fluttering. Sand swirled like fog about the horse's ankles.

The radio came crackling to life. James raised it to his lips.

"Leonardo," he said.

"James," his partner replied. "Where the fuck've you been?"

"In the canyon, looking for coyote."

"For glory, I'd say. You see your name in lights." A staticky pause. "You shoot him?"

"I did not." Patrols used their guns only if directly attacked. But what about the knife? Well, James had gotten even for that.

"You let him go?" Leo said.

"No, Goddamnit, I have him right here." James added reluctantly, "But he's no coyote." He could hear Leo laughing.

"Maybe, old man, you ought to retire."

"Fuck you." James hated that old man stuff. He wasn't even forty; soon, yes, but not yet.

Leo snorted. "And where the fuck're you now?"

Without the goggles, the desert seemed a vast bowl tipped to spill its contents against the night sky. A multitude of stars pulsed behind clouds. James felt their hidden weight. He had a sense of portent, of warning—but he pushed it away. There was comfort, after all, in human insignificance. He drank in the hallowed silence in this, the one place in the world he felt most at home.

He said to Leo, "I'm here."

"And what the fuck does that mean?"

James removed the goggles from his belt. He held them to his eyes. Nothing. He gave the casing a gentle shake, and the image came in. Christ, he thought. He was a lucky man. Because there was Leo in hot green miniature, slouched in the saddle, head cocked to one side. The captured illegals were tied together in a scooped-out crater of sand.

Leo raised a gloved hand. He danced his black mare.

James felt the pollo's spine go rigid as steel.

Then and there he decided the broken hand was payback enough. He would say nothing regarding the knife. A medic would set the pollo's hand at the station before sending him home; and if the pollo was smart, he would not fuss about his injury, much less explain.

"Fuck." Leo's drawl floated over the wire. The living voice followed an instant later, an echo carried on the thin desert air. "You mean *here*."

Grimly mute, nine men sat with their backs to the van's inside walls. Several were shirtless, shoeless, and empty-handed, relieved in advance of whatever goods they'd tried to bring north.

Leo and James stood out on the highway's blacktop, horses tied to a steel guardrail.

"Looks like Anteater took 'em all for a ride." Leo grinned.

James peered into the rear of the van. "Señores," he addressed the pollos, "who was it led you over the line?"

Silence.

"¿Sus cosas," James said, "quién se las robó?" *Who stole your things?*

More silence.

"¿El Oso Hormiguero?"

El Oso Hormiguero—Anteater. A coyote new to this stretch of the line, but famous already for his long snoutlike nose, a sticky reach that could locate possessions wherever hidden. Within weeks, it seemed, he'd built a lucrative practice smuggling Mexican nationals across the border, then abandoning them to bandidos for a prearranged cut.

"I'd like to get that bastard," James said.

"Guy must have a stash," Leo said. "Whole lotta polyester and dead radios. Didn't grab it all, though. Here . . . catch." He tossed something at James, a thin chain with an oval-shaped medal attached, silver inlaid with mother-of-pearl. James ran a thumb over the etching. Our Lady of Guadalupe, beloved patroness of Mexico.

"Where'd you get this?"

"Found it," Leo smirked, "in the sand." Which meant he'd taken it off one of the prisoners.

A gust of wind pushed at James's back. He said to Leo, "You might at least look ashamed."

Leo stared, unperturbed. A faint bruise still darkened the skin beneath his left eye, and James acknowledged to himself that he'd put it there. Well, they'd both been drinking after the shift—a bad idea, beer in the a.m.—and they'd scuffled stupidly in James's front yard, with James the victor, and James's wife the only witness. Though he couldn't have said now what it was they'd been fighting about, he remembered perfectly his satisfaction that Mercedes had seen.

Idly, the van's driver revved the engine.

James flipped the medal over and squinted at the microscopic lettering: *Blessed Virgin In Heaven Pray For Us Sinners On Earth.* "I hate that religious shit," Leo said. "Speaking of which, get a load of this." He reached into the van, grabbed a young pollo with lips plumped beneath a mustache like a curl of black smoke. Leo pulled the boy forward, turning him so that his naked back was displayed. The flesh was crisscrossed with scars.

Lash marks by the dozens, James realized. And underneath, the Seal of Obligation. He counted six long cuts: three down, three across.

"They're baaack," Leo sang.

James said, "Be Holy Week soon." He asked the pollo, "You a Penitente?"

With his cuffed hands, the pollo made the sign of the cross.

"¿Vienen a la morada?" asked James, and the boy dropped his chin to his chest.

The Penitentes—what remained of the sect—were supposedly confined to the mountains of northern New Mexico and southern Colorado. But James knew it wasn't entirely so. During the Lenten season, he'd seen La Hermandad on the square in El Pilón, walking barefooted, dressed in their white trousers and black hoods. Self-scourging, to suffer as Christ had suffered. James didn't get it, though he supposed he understood guilt well enough. The morada, their chapel, was rumored to be somewhere out east. In seventeen years he'd never once come upon it. It was buried in one of the canyons, maybe, tucked under a jagged outcropping of rock. Impossible to find unless you knew where to look. That land, he thought, was owned by the rattlesnakes and scorpions.

Leo said, "Mercedes'll go for it."

James stared at his partner, who tipped his chin, indicating the medal in James's hand.

"Stuff." Leo winked. "That's what our girl wants. Take my word for it, old man."

Leo had a funny attitude about Mercedes sometimes. He'd dated her first, and that made for tension with James. But two men would always want the same girl, one would always lose.

As far as the job was concerned, they did well enough, though James didn't really like the guy, and he didn't trust him, either, not entirely. Leo was the youngest partner he'd ever had, all hard, reflective surface, and who knew what lay underneath. Too often he behaved as if the world had been created for his personal entertainment. There was something dangerous about that. James might've complained. He might've requested another partner. He might've dug deeper, or, God knows, sympathized. What he'd done instead was cut the guy out. Small things; but that was dangerous, too.

James felt his own jealousy there. Leo was such a healthy handsome animal, so clearly at the beginning of things. Less than two years out of Patrol School, he'd been in the elite Horse Patrol from the start. Unlike James, who'd walked the streets for ten years.

"And with what this job pays . . ." Leo left it hanging.

The standard lament. And Leo, he'd observed, had expensive tastes. Leo wore nice clothes, he took fancy vacations, he drove a new Jeep. He liked to talk about getting rich quick. The Internet, maybe, or the lottery.

James considered his own check, woefully slim, and never enough. It all went for—what? Food, he supposed. Insurance. The mortgage on the house, the loan on the truck. At home, unpaid bills sat on the kitchen counter: MasterCard and Sears and Montgomery Ward. Because he and Mercedes had to have furniture, they had to have appliances. There was also the matter of the ten thousand he'd borrowed last year from his folks. He'd gotten into a scrape on the job and needed the money for legal fees. James had promised to pay it all back, with interest, and he tried, giving a little each month. But it was a token, and he knew it and they knew it. Mercedes, too.

He leaned into the van, swung the silver chain from a crooked forefinger. He asked the pollos, "¿De quién es esto?"

Averted faces meant no one was willing to admit ownership. James shook his head. Nothing left to lose, and still these people were reluctant to draw attention to themselves. He wondered whose sister or mother would cry.

A light flashed in the sky, followed by the faint whopping of chopper blades. James lifted a hand to his eyes. An INS helicopter was flying in low from the west, its search beam tracking the desert floor. White glare, a deafening mechanical wail. The wind raised a cloud of biting sand and the horses reared, snorting and whinnying. The pollos covered their ears as the chopper passed overhead, aiming eastward to the glow of Corville. Across the border, the lights of El Pilón flickered, the Mexican town all but invisible.

The chopper circled back, again flying low. The van's driver shouted into his radio, "Goddamn you, Fred! You hot-dog fuck!"

The pilot whooped. "I'm bringin' her in!"

"Aren't you supposed to be in Yuma tonight?"

"Yes, I am! But hell, a man's got to take a break sometime. I'm going to park her at the station and head on over the line, down to Efraín's. I'm in the mood for huevos."

Leo said to James, "Chichis, more like." He cupped his hands in front of his chest. "I hear there's a young goddess works the graveyard at Efraín's."

A burst of static, and the pilot said, ". . . Reese around?"

James shouted up to the driver, "Tell Fred I'll catch up with him tomorrow. Same place, same time. Tell him I plan on taking *all* his money."

But the driver yelled back, "Sensors are picking up footfalls. South-southeast, Sector Forty-nine." Above them, the chopper dipped and swung away.

James reached for the door handles. A dusty foot thrust forward.

"What the fuck?" Leo said.

One of the pollos scuttled forward on his ass. "Mi sombrero, señor."

Leo's arm shot out. He cracked the man on the side of the head. The pollo fell back, but immediately crept up again, now staring balefully at James. He held a fat limp hand to his chest. Christ. It was the man who'd cut him, the one he'd ridden in on his horse. "Mi sombrero," the pollo insisted. Leo lifted his arm to strike him again. "Wait a goddamn second!" James said. Over Leo's protests he asked, "¿Qué quiere?"

The pollo rubbed his cuffed hands over his hair.

Suddenly, James remembered the white thing twirling as the pollo had disappeared down into the canyon. *A hat.* With all this campesino had endured, he still cared about a hat. "Lo siento," James said. "Ya voló, señor." *I'm sorry. It's gone now.*

The driver shouted back, "You guys ready yet? Sensors're goin' nuts here."

"Fuck," Leo said. "I hate Forty-nine." Several miles east, the sector folded in against a round hill, where a trickling creek fattened the scrub and the hiding places of the pollos were hard to get at. "But hey," Leo said, "you heard yet when we're going to get to that fire? Smoke the vermin!" INS had been trying to schedule a controlled burn for days. "What's the word from Danny Patillo?"

Patillo was Corville Station's fireboss, one of James's poker buddies.

"He's waiting," James said, "for the wind to die down."

He slammed the van's doors.

The driver flashed his turn signal and pulled out. The two lanes wore a fresh coat of blacktop, split by a broken white line that wiggled just past the turnout, as if the paint truck had gone out of control. For a few seconds, the van straddled the line, then it drifted back into its lane. The tail lights receded, parallel sets of staring red eyes. The pollos were headed home. James felt a momentary tightness in his chest.

Leo untied his horse. He climbed into the saddle and looked down on James. "Pinches pollos," he said.

James heard a challenge in this, one he saw neither point nor profit in answering. Sand had worked its way under his uniform and he plucked his shirt from his chest, lifted his feet, and shook out his legs.

Leo gave him a disgusted look.

James scrubbed his hands over his face. There was a smell on his skin, something he didn't like but couldn't quite identify.

Abruptly, Leo pulled on the reins. He turned his horse, high-stepped it off the highway. A trot became a canter, and then a gallop. Sand flew from the animal's hooves.

Silence fell like a blanket thrown from the sky.

James watched his partner ride, Leo on the black mare growing smaller and smaller—another grain, another star—until at last he was indistinguishable from the landscape that surrounded him.

CHAPTER TWO

D awn, and James walked his horse across the stationhouse parking lot, past the chopper still detoured from its destination of Yuma, Arizona. The sky was just starting to pale, the moon and stars fading. But the air was already dry, with a burnt-rubber feel. The day promised to be hot.

He cut around a couple of brand new 4 x 4's, turned a corner and came up on the stable's double Dutch doors. Eagerly, the horse pushed on through. It trotted down the barn bay and into its stall, James following.

He lifted a bucket from a hole built into the ledge, and headed back to the tap. He smelled tobacco, heard coughing: Gordon Jenks was in with Leo's black mare. A man in his early sixties, with knobby bones and long feet made longer by pointy silver-tipped boots, Jenks had been hired part-time to see to the horses' grooming and feed. But if James wasn't too tired he preferred to do these tasks himself.

KAREN PALMER

He saw Jenks down on one knee, working a metal pick at a
stone caught in the mare's left rear hoof. Ash dropped onto his
shirt from a cigarette, but he didn't seem to notice.

James filled the bucket with cold water, returned to the stall,
and dropped the bucket into the hole. He removed the bit and
bridle and the horse stepped forward. James watched the animal
drink, the muscles of its throat moving rhythmically under the
skin. He thought of the half-naked pollo he'd chased down into
the canyon. With the coyotes charging a thousand dollars and
more, likely the man had spent his life savings to cross, traveling
hundreds of miles to the border on foot. Up from Oaxaca, Zacate-
cas, Chiapas, maybe.

Finished, the horse raised its muzzle. James slipped a halter over
its head. In his mind's eye, he saw the pollo flat on his back, narrow
rib cage fluttering. Afraid—afraid of James. Years on the job, and still
he fought the temptation to feed on that fear. He told himself there
were dangers far worse than Immigration. Blazing heat and breath-
less cold, dope runners, vatos and cholos, white supremacist gangs.
James unbuckled the saddle and pulled it free, then lugged everything back to the tack room where he set it on a rack. The feed
grain was kept in garbage cans with tops clamped tight against rats.
He filled a cardboard box and returned to the stall.

The quarterhorse ate with steady concentration.

Jenks called out, "So, Jimbo. How many'd you bring in tonight?"

"Eighteen, maybe nineteen total."

"See any bandidos?"

"Not a one."

Jenks hawked deep in his throat, then spit.

James went to the mare's stall, where Jenks now sat hunched on
a three-legged stool, legs crossed, fingers fishing in his shirt pocket
for smokes. He took the pack out and slid one loose, lit it off the
butt in his mouth. When James asked, "You got a currycomb?"
Jenks lifted his chin. Eyeing the rafters, he blew a perfect smoke
ring. "Help yourself."

16

Back at the stall, James's horse had finished eating. James set the feedbox aside. He began to curry the animal's neck.

Jenks appeared in the stall's opening. "You look like you been in a tornado, my friend."

James felt it. He was bone sore, grimy from head to toe, his uniform torn and twisted, buttons missing, belt scuffed.

"Rough night?" Jenks asked.

"I've had better," James said.

"You ever wonder, what is the point? Of the job, I mean to say. 'Cause they just come right back. Over and over again."

They'd had this conversation too many times.

"You're going to do it," James said, "you might as well *do* it." And he'd caught more illegals than anyone in the history of Corville Station. He'd also pissed more people off. Which explained why, after seventeen years, he was still a field agent instead of the boss. That suited him fine. He moved the currycomb down the horse's chest, then the forelegs. "The point is the law," he said. Sometimes he believed that, sometimes not. Sometimes he thought the point was the game.

"And what is the law? I mean, what, precisely, does the law signify?"

Christ. James hated it when Jenks got philosophical.

He worked the currycomb over the horse's back and along its belly, the outside of the hind legs and under the tail. The horse's hide rippled in response. Switching to a stiff brush and short lifting strokes, James removed loose dirt and hair. He polished away the remaining dust with a cloth. The horse graciously lifted a hoof and James checked for injuries and stones.

Jenks said, "They want in that bad, we should just let 'em come. You're pulling 'em out of gas tanks and wheel wells."

"They take our jobs."

"Only the ones no one wants anyway. Your own people, too. You're Mexican—"

"Half," James corrected.

"In the South, used to be any black blood made you black. One drop, even."

Where did Jenks get this stuff? James said, "I was born in L.A."

"Last I heard, they got Mexicans there."

"Fuck that," James said.

Jenks dropped his cigarette, ground it out beneath his boot heel. He threaded his fingers and cracked his knuckles, all in a row, a musical sound. "Face it, Jimbo," he said. "You keep 'em out, keep 'em down."

Coconut, thought James. He'd had about enough.

He decided the horse's hoof was perfectly clean, the crevices dark and smooth as candle wax. "See how pretty," he said.

Originally a storefront, the stationhouse still looked like a cheap five-and-dime, with empty display counters lined with black felt and a row of out-of-date automotive calendars tacked to a wall. Corville was so small that Immigration shared quarters with the local police. But it was a busy place. Since '95, Operation Gate-keeper had driven the coyotes and pollos ever eastward, and the increased traffic triggered a jump in overall crime: murder, drug smuggling, gun running, and thievery.

This morning, however, all was quiet. A uniformed desk sergeant sat in the window, his wide blue back to the street, a sitting duck if anyone cared.

A group of cops coming off duty gossiped in a doorway.

James said his good mornings and shouldered through. He started off down the hall. Leo was approaching from the opposite direction, a loose-hipped strut, as if his joints had been packed with grease. Already on his way out, he was showered and shaved, dressed in blue jeans and a tight short-sleeved black shirt.

"You reek, buddy," said James.

Leo smiled, his teeth so white in his tanned face they might have been false. He smoothed the cropped sides of his hair with his palms.

"Got a hot date," he said.

"You ought to give up that cheap-ass cologne."

"You're just jealous."

"Of what?"

"My youth and power."

James laughed.

He ducked into the head. At the sink, he soaped face and hands, then rinsed his mouth. He put some salve and a bandage on his left palm. Then he combed the dust from his hair. There were scratches on his neck and his chin, but James thought he looked mostly okay. Nevertheless, in the locker room he traded the wrecked uniform for a clean extra. No point in scaring Mercedes to death. He gathered the night's paperwork and took it into the lounge.

Recently remodeled, the room sported white Formica tables and putty-colored carpeting. A rectangular window framed the armored trunk of an ancient date palm. Over by the coffee machine, three patrols were debating the outcome of last year's election. James helped himself to a stale jellyroll and a cup of coffee he knew would taste like boiled dirt. Half-listening to the patrols' argument, he sat at a table and filled out his reports. He wrote a narrative about the pollo captured in the canyon, keeping it short and honest in the particulars, but leaving out the business with the knife, and the pollo's broken hand. A quick once-over, and he was aggravated anew at how stupid he'd been. Meanwhile, another part of his mind worked on Leo. That smart mouth, that stolen medal, which *our* girl would want . . .

James downed the dregs of his coffee. He signed the reports, and left the lounge, stopping by the INS office to drop everything off. The boss, Tommie Yard, loomed behind his cluttered desk, tethered as usual to the telephone, lips tight and brow creased, fat cheeks swinging as he motioned for James to come in. But the person on the other end of the line said something Yard must not have liked, and he erupted in a string of expletives and spun his chair away. James was happy enough to escape.

Continuing on down the hall, he came to the police photography lab. The front room was empty, but a red light blinked over a second, interior door. The darkroom. Which meant Charlotte Murray was here.

James stepped inside, sniffing the familiar chemical smell, strips of damp negatives clothespinned to a rope strung over the sink. Police film was usually mailed to San Diego for developing, but in a crunch, Charlotte processed the photographs here herself. Occasionally, she used the lab to do her own work.

From the look of things, she'd been here for hours. An overnight bag sat on a chair, the bag's zipper undone. James resisted peeking inside. He walked to the drafting table and inventoried the items: light box, X-acto knife, rubber mat, printer's loupe. A single negative was attached to the light box with masking tape, and he'd just begun to study the image when Charlotte emerged from the darkroom. Her yellow rubber gloves were wet to the elbows. Two eight-by-ten prints dripped in her hands. If she was surprised to see him, she didn't let on. Skirting past, she pinned the prints to the clothesline, then peeled the gloves and rinsed her hands at the sink. James stared at the back of her head. Charlotte's hair was longer these days, captured in a loose knot. She'd always spent a lot of time in the sun, but the skin at her nape remained pale as pearls.

Without turning, she said, "So, Jamie. How's your dad? We sure miss Des around here. How's he enjoying life on the farm?"

Two summers ago, when Desmond Reese had retired, his first civilian act had been the purchase of a flower farm up near Marquette. There he grew daffodils, tulips, and gladioli. Having worked Homicide his entire career—gangs and jealous husbands and drunken disagreements—Des intended to spend the remainder of his allotted time surrounded by nature's beauty. He almost never drove down to visit the squad, yet a week couldn't pass without someone cornering James, asking after his father's health and well-being.

"He's all right," James said. "His arthritis drives him crazy. Rains more up there."

"And Marie?"

"She's okay."

"Sometimes I think about making a call."

"You should. Marie's lonely. No one to talk to but Des, it must get old."

"Oh, I don't know." Charlotte shut the tap. She dried her hands on a paper towel.

"What about you?" James cleared his throat. "What've you been up to?"

"This and that," Charlotte said.

She turned and leaned against the sink. As always, James was struck by how pretty she was, in spite of the lavender shadows under her eyes, the lines etched between her brows. He'd known Charlotte since high school; they'd dated for years. Since his marriage last year, he'd had a hard time settling on how to treat her. He wanted to be friendly. But he understood that Charlotte wasn't his friend.

This and that. James had heard she was seeing a cop—what else?—a new hire in Robbery with hair that looked oiled from a can and five o'clock shadow darkening his cheeks before lunch.

"And you?" she asked politely.

"Fine and dandy."

Charlotte raised an eyebrow.

She unpinned a strip of negatives from the clothesline. At the drafting table, she cut the film into strips. She placed one on the light box, bending to inspect the images.

She slid the loupe across the row, then returned to the first.

"This one, Jamie," she said, moving aside.

James stepped forward. He put his eye to the loupe. Time spent with Charlotte had taught him how to interpret a negative; experience with the night-vision equipment helped as well. Still, at first sight, he was always disoriented at viewing the world in reverse.

This picture was, as so often with Charlotte's work, a full-faced portrait. An old man's features filled the frame, a landscape of angles and gullies, bristled whiskers like treetrunks stripped of branches and leaves, and all black for white, white for black. The irises of the eyes shone like silver marbles.

Charlotte asked, "Can you read it?"

An old game, and James seldom won. In any case, he knew he shouldn't play.

He straightened. "I don't think so." He stared over her head at a spot on the wall. James had never been much for exposing himself, a fatal problem between them. The time to speak frankly was now surely past. Charlotte had been flabbergasted, and disbelieving, and, finally, furious when he'd married Mercedes Ramirez. After years of professing he wasn't the marrying kind.

But Mercedes was *it* for James, had been from the moment they met. He hadn't been looking for a Mexican wife, would've sworn up and down it didn't matter. But he recognized her. And she understood him in ways he'd never thought possible.

"It's been a long night," he said. "I've had it, Char."

"Yeah, you look beat," she said, letting him have his out. "Go on home." She gave James a small push. Her hands on his chest made him swallow hard.

"A married man," she scolded. "What will people think?"

It was a mile and a half from the stationhouse to the Reeses' front door, and since Mercedes had the truck for the day, James had no choice but to walk. He minded some—he'd been a foot patrol so long he objected purely on principle. But his heels hitting the pavement sounded a familiar rhythm, and he hummed to himself as he left the station behind.

The morning's faint chill had vanished and bright sunlight reflected off parked cars and plate-glass storefronts, new meters placed every ten feet on the way to the square. James reached into his breast pocket and pulled out his mirrored Vuarnets and set them on his face.

A few blocks and he came to the center of town, a park filled with crabgrass and bottlebrush and tangled ivy. In the corners, a quartet of date palms stood like sentinels. The focal point of the square was a concrete fountain, bone dry. The city turned the pipes off for all but the few weeks before and after Christmas, when colored lights made a display of the dancing waters.

This morning the square's sole inhabitant was an old woman in a navy-blue pea coat who sat on a bench, dipping into a supermarket bag and tossing bread at a flock of greedy pigeons. Flipping the bag upside down, she shook out the last of the crumbs, and the birds rushed her in a wild flap of wings.

James scanned the swath of grass at the old woman's back, sweeping the square's perimeter. He searched for shadows in doorways, in the lee of parked automobiles. But all was as it should be. At this hour there were few people about, the businesses lining the square not yet open. Some of the shops were still boarded up, victims of the last recession, but the barber and the stationer and the hardware store, all long-time merchants on the square, had recently been joined by Japanese and Thai restaurants, a computer store, a retirement home, a couple of antiques dealers and beauty salons. Even the former post office had been converted to a lingerie shop, the windows filled with bustiers and crotchless panties. That stuff made James laugh, naked being the only thing he'd ever really cared about.

The old woman stood, stuffed the empty bag under her coat, and waddled off, grumbling.

James left the square. He walked east on Lincoln Avenue. Apartment houses and bail bondsmen, a laundromat, a used-carpet

store. Charlotte lived on this block, a two-story, third from the end.
On a whim, he ducked into the alley to have a look at the building's parking stalls. A Harley sat in Charlotte's space. The boy-
friend's, he assumed. James was tempted to give it a push. But
then he heard creaking from a window above, and embarrassed,
hurried out of the alley. He crossed the street and right-turned
onto Seventh. Here bungalows crowded shoulder to shoulder, the
tiny yards fenced with chainlink. Formerly a district of white working class, the area was now almost entirely Latino, eight and ten to
a house, cousins from over the border hidden in the garage. Por-
tions of the sidewalk were covered in gang graffiti. The occasional
broken window gaped.

But James saw homey touches as well, painted trim, pots of red
and white geraniums. In a yard filled with toys, a girl lazed in a tire
swing, a curly-headed baby plopped on the ground at her feet. The
girl dipped a plastic wand into a jar, pursed her lips, and blew a string
of soap bubbles through the hoop. The baby stared, open-mouthed,
while a spotted mutt loped along the chainlink, tracking James.

He slowed, nearing the corner house. *Yes.* There was the white
picket fence, the spreading ash tree. The clapboards had once
been painted yellow, but the desert sun could peel a place clean,
and the color was indeterminate now.

This was where James had landed after leaving L.A., sullen and
raging, a nine-year-old prepared to hate his new foster family on
sight. The Reeses were his third placement in as many years, and
he'd hated them, all right. Then again, he'd hated everyone. He'd
long since given up expecting anybody from home to come and
get him, but he knew he didn't belong here, in this place, with
these people. Within a month, he'd fought every kid on the block.
There were three grammar schools in Corville, one junior and one
senior high, and over the years he'd been kicked out of them all.
Vandalism and truancy, fights in the schoolyard. In the classroom,
he'd had trouble concentrating. All those letters and numbers and
words. Up at the blackboard, the teacher looked as if he were see-

24

ing her through backwards binoculars, her voice dimming all at once, like shutting the volume on the TV. God, it made him mad. Poor Desmond, poor Marie. He'd been more trouble, probably, than he was worth. James figured he was lucky he hadn't wound up in jail. It could so easily have gone that way. In the end, it was the Navy that saved him, time in the service succeeding where Desmond could not, the anonymity and the routine allowing James to channel his anger into something that felt like doing right. When he returned to Corville after his tour—sick to death of water, he never thought he'd be so happy to see sand and rock— he'd been surprised to find himself in possession of a small but significant measure of self-control. It was in no way reliable, not then, not now. But it was *his*.

He stopped at the gate. Checked curtains hung in the windows and James pictured the two bedrooms inside, the modest living and dining rooms, a hallway papered with hunting scenes. In the bathroom, the toilet had run continually. James remembered Des heading out to the hardware store every few weeks. Mr. Fix-it, the eternal optimist.

A rusted red bicycle leaned against the ash tree. James smiled. At nine, two wheels had been his favored mode of transportation.

Up on the porch, two teenage boys were draped across an old couch. A third straddled the rail, a boombox balanced between his knees. He had a beer can in one hand. The kid stared boldly at James, then dropped his head down inside the porch. He came up grinning, exhaling white smoke. A twirl of the volume on the boombox and conjunto music blared. The boys on the couch looked vaguely alarmed. And then James caught it, the sweet scent of marijuana.

He adjusted his sunglasses. He puffed out his chest, playing, allowing himself to feel the uniform. Still grinning, the boy raised a leg and brought his knee to his chin. He wore denim shorts, several sizes too big, and his thin brown thigh showed through the open leg hole.

The boy wiped his mouth with the back of his hand. But the other two slid off the couch. Heads down, they shuffled sideways and melted into the house, la migra being one thing, a drug bust something else.

James wasn't interested. He was off duty now.

Across the street, a screen door banged shut, and a middle-aged woman hurried out to her yard. She carried a laundry basket to a clothesline. Plastic pins in her teeth, she reached for a wet sheet. The spotted mutt started to bark, not at the woman, but at James, throwing itself witlessly into the fence. The curly-headed baby wailed, and the girl in the tire swing jumped down. She scooped the child into her arms.

Finished with the sheet, the woman called over the top of her clothesline, "Pinche pendejo."

The boy on the railing laughed, and clapped his hands.

James sighed.

He allowed himself one last look at the red bicycle. Then he left it behind.

Five blocks shy of his current residence, he took a detour into a brand-new development. He crossed a gravel-paved road, climbed a low stucco wall. A sign announced his arrival at Sandpiper Point. But there were no sandpipers here, and for that matter no point, though James had seen the architectural renderings and knew a black-bottomed pond would eventually grace the development's entry. Of the four houses proposed, only the model was complete. The remainder languished in various stages of partial construction.

Two trucks were parked at the site, an old Chevy and a candy-apple-red Ford, which bore the legend RAMIREZ & SON. A large black dog slept in the back, surrounded by dusty cardboard boxes. James said, "How you doin', boy? You guardin' the place?" The dog lifted its sleek head and yawned.

Up on the foundation, the builders were in the process of raising a wall. Two-by-six studs had been nailed at sixteen-inch intervals to a sill plate, the wall propped at a forty-five-degree angle and braced temporarily by shorter beams. Two men stood at either end; a woman in a yellow hardhat took the middle position. All three wedged their shoulders against the wall and heaved. The wall wobbled, then straightened. The workers scrambled to secure the frame, the air filling with the rapid-fire *bang!phoot* of nail guns.

The woman stepped back to survey the results. She wore a tank top and jeans, heavy steel-toed boots, kneepads, and gloves. When she raised her arms, a dark braid tickled the small of her back.

One of the workers looked up and saw James and shouted over, "Ese! Ain't you got nothing better to do? We're all legal here, man."

Mercedes turned and set her hands on her hips. She said something to her brothers that James couldn't hear, then clanked down the driveway. His wife looked like a gunslinger to him, muy macha, the leather tool belt sagging provocatively to one side. Even with the heavy equipment, she had a graceful long-legged walk.

At the foot of the drive, Mercedes stopped and leaned against the red Ford. She stripped off the gloves and tucked them into her belt, removed the hardhat, and tilted her face to the sun. A crescent-shaped scar rode her right cheek, souvenir of a childhood spill into a glass-strewn gully. Mercedes's features were too bone-sharp to be considered beautiful in any conventional sense, but her skin was smooth, her mouth wide, her lips full. Her eyes held the clean clear light of intelligence. James liked that, even if it cost him sometimes.

"You're hiding," she said. "Lose the shades, corazón."

"My eyeballs hurt."

Mercedes granted a smile, her teeth like white stones. "It's this vampire shift. When you going to go back to days?"

"Not my call, honey."

"Uh-huh." Mercedes knew he liked working nights, his midnight rides through the cooling desert. She looked him up and down. "That's a mighty clean uniform, James."

He shrugged, and she said, "Jesus. That *job*."

"I know, I know—how 'bout a break?"

"We only just started."

"So what. Come home with me. Just for a little while." James raised his eyebrows suggestively. God, he wanted his wife, and wanted her now—but then, how was *now* different from any other moment in time? He always wanted her, her body, of course, but that wasn't all, and it wasn't ever enough. Mercedes eyed him frankly, appraisingly, then glanced up at the site. Her brothers stood at either end of a whining table saw, feeding two-by-sixes past the spinning blade. At twenty-eight, she was eldest, but Carlos had been the head of both family and business since their father had died. Rubén was seventeen, a senior in high school. Without actually ever having known them, James had seen both boys around town for years, wiry smart-eyed kids running the streets. Now they were businessmen. In-laws. Family.

Carlos shouted something and Rubén lifted the studs. His pants hung low on his slim hips, the waistband of his boxers showing. James wondered why he was here instead of in class.

Reading his mind, Mercedes said, "Spring vacation. They're all off. And we really need him right now, we're so far behind."

"Then an hour isn't going to make a difference. Come home with me."

"Don't you have *ears*? I told you, I can't."

James stuck out his tongue and Mercedes laughed. "So very persuasive," she said. "There's a thermos of coffee out back. We can sit in the yard."

She led him around stacks of lumber and scattered tools, saltillos piled under a tarp weighted with rocks. A row of pink plastic pennants snapped in the breeze. Sand sifted in under a fence, a yawn of desert visible through the green mesh.

Someone had fashioned an awning from cardboard seamed with duct tape. In the trapezoid of shade was a thermos and a paper bag stained with grease. They sat cross-legged in the dirt. Mercedes poured black coffee into a metal cup and handed it to James. She opened the paper bag and took out two yellow pastries. Pan dulce: baked rounds topped with clumps of sugared flour. The soft dough crumbled in James's mouth. He sipped at the coffee. Beside him, Mercedes chewed purposefully. Another thing he admired, his wife's single-minded devotion to the task at hand. "Delicioso," she said, and licked her fingers clean.

The black dog had abandoned the Ford to join them. Sad-eyed and slavering, he sat as close as he dared. "Beggar," Mercedes said. The dog wriggled his hindquarters, inching in. "Garbage belly." But she dipped into the bag for a sweet and passed it to the dog. With a frenzy of tail whapping, he swallowed it whole.

"Last night," James said. "How'd the meeting go?"

Mercedes frowned. "Kansas didn't bite."

She'd shown the model home to a couple in from Wichita. Retired military, which usually meant San Diego, but the wife preferred the dry desert air. "They complained the house is too small," Mercedes said. "Two old people, no kids, and three thousand square feet isn't enough? The lady made me run all the faucets and flush the toilets. She bitched about water pressure." Mercedes wrapped her arms around her knees, brooding. "We're *behind*, corazón. The bank's been calling. They're going to cut off the credit line. The VISA, too."

James wasn't surprised. None of the homes had been purchased yet. The project was a stretch to begin with, the Ramirezes more used to small commercial projects, single-story cinderblock, or stucco, offices for accountants and chiropractors.

The brothers were nail-gunning another line of two-by-sixes to a plate. They started at the outer edge of the sill, moved in on their haunches to meet in the center. It looked like a kind of choreography, all rhythm and footwork. A small miracle, James thought, the way their labor turned the raw materials into an actual house.

Mercedes said, "Carlos asked Mama for money last night. While he was mowing the lawn."

James could just picture it. "And what did Cruz say?"

"'Ten cuidado, m'ijo,'" she mimicked, "'there is a wasp nest over by the garage.'"

Black clad, silver-haired, traditional housekeeper and cook, Cruz Ramirez often gave an impression of inattention. A useful disguise. When James had first talked to her about him and Mercedes getting married, Cruz had seemed to ignore the question implied, telling him instead about how all through fourth grade, her girl spent every lunch hour in church, face down in the aisle, praying for the stigmata and waiting to be called as a martyr for Jesus Cristo. James couldn't picture it. The Mercedes he loved bowed down to no one. She had appetites. She wielded a hammer and wrote letters to the editor. So he'd laughed. And Cruz's eyes had narrowed to shining slits. *You don't know,* she said. *The body isn't everything, James.*

"¡Cabrón!" Up on the site, Carlos jumped up and down, his right hand stuck into the opposite armpit. "You want to nail my goddamn finger!" He cuffed Rubén on the side of the head. The boy tossed a sheaf of hair from his eyes.

"Pobrecito," Mercedes said affectionately. "Rubén's got no sense of timing."

"I wish him better luck with Yolie," James said.

Rubén was getting married in a couple of weeks. Holy Redeemer Church, a catered reception in the parish hall. Yolie— Yolanda—was his fiancée, a girl with the sweetest roundest face James had ever seen.

"Luck isn't the word," Mercedes said. "Not with her expecting. Maybe the boy's got some rhythm, after all." She looked suddenly wistful.

James stood. He swiped industriously at the seat of his pants. She gazed up at him. "A *baby*, corazón."

James felt his face growing hot.

Married less than a year and it was already between them: her desire for a child, his reluctance to oblige. James liked kids, it wasn't that. He even enjoyed infants, their tiny fingers and toes, soft round skulls, the perfume of milk and powder and piss. The idea of creating his own—it was a chance to make up for everything that had happened to him. He wanted that. And he wanted to make Mercedes happy. But he was afraid of his history, and so his excuses got tangled up in his lies: they hadn't enough money; the house was too small; they needed more time alone. He'd allowed his wife to see his fear without grasping the source.

"Listen," he said, "I've got to get going. Okay if I steal your wheels?"

"Of course," she said.

James put down a hand and helped her to her feet. They walked back to the truck, the black dog trailing. James leaned against the driver's side door. He removed his sunglasses.

"Ah, finally," she said. "There you are. Eyes the color of money, but where did you get those Indian bones?"

A joke. Mercedes knew he was adopted. Everyone did. That much, at least, could never be kept secret in a town the size of Corville.

James pulled her into his arms. He played his fingertips down the length of her spine.

The brothers had stopped working to watch them. "Hey!" Carlos yelled. "Migra! Stop bothering my *seester*." But he was smiling, and so was Rubén.

James was never quite sure where he stood with Mercedes's family. They were so easy with each other, so careful with him.

He whispered into her ear, "I'll see you later."

"Oh, yes," she said. "You certainly will."

He climbed into the Ford. The seat was so hot he could feel it through his uniform. Mercedes shut the door on him, and he started the engine, and she stepped away. He looked over his shoulder and backed down the drive.

Glancing a final time at the site, he saw his wife still standing where he'd left her, backlit, the sky a hot blue. James got out his sunglasses and put them back on, hoping to kill the worst of the glare.

CHAPTER THREE

The plan was to shower, then catch some much-needed shut-eye, and then run errands in the late afternoon. But when James got home, the light was blinking on his answering machine. Marie, requesting that he come up to the farm. *Immediately.* She didn't say why. He played the message again, to verify the tightness in his mother's voice, and then he called back. But the phone rang and rang. Reluctantly, he decided he'd better drive right on up.

Forty-five minutes on a two-lane through open desert brought him to the edge of humped green foothills. The truck gently climbed. James took a series of hairpin turns a little too fast, pine trees closing in either side of the road, followed by an open meadow filled with wildflowers, and then he rolled through the town of Marquette. General store, dry cleaner, pizza parlor. A small stone house on his left—the neon sign in the window advertised psychic readings—and then a minimart marked the turnoff to his parents' farm. James glanced at the gas gauge. The tank's needle hovered below empty, so he pulled into the station, got out, and pumped twelve gallons of unleaded. All the while he stared through a picture window at the girl behind the counter, a teenager with thin shoulders and red hair that hung down her back. The girl wore a blouse with a row of ruffles at the neck and James allowed himself a moment or two of fantasy, where the girl was willing and he was unknown, desired for being unknown. When he went in to pay, he was glad she had her nose buried in a tabloid. Quickly, he skimmed the news rack, picking out a car magazine for Desmond, a pamphlet on rose care for Marie. For himself he got a *San Diego Union*, a cup of coffee, and a bag of sour-cream-and-onion potato chips. The purchases all went on the soon-to-be-canceled VISA card. The girl ran it through a slot in the register, handing it back without looking at James or checking his signature.

Outside, a wooden bench had been placed to catch the western view. James settled himself on the boards, the newspaper unopened in his lap. He ripped the bag of chips with his teeth, ate a handful, took a sip of coffee. From here he could see flower fields scattered downslope, solid blocks of color he imagined rolling all the way to the Pacific Ocean. The surrounding hills were thick with new growth, but in a matter of weeks the land would dry and turn dull, dust kicked up from the fields to veil the sky. In other parts of the country, he knew, summer was the season of green.

He watched a lizard dart across the cement. A breeze rustled the pines.

James thought about his adoptive parents, Desmond and Marie. As newlyweds, they'd traded the Ohio Valley for California, Los Angeles first, and then Corville and the house on Seventh Street. James had heard Des remark often enough how long it had taken them to get used to it here, how long it was before they began to think of this place as home. He couldn't remember ever having asked what his father meant. What was it they'd missed—their families? their hometown? the solid white of snowfall? the taste of humid air? And why had they chosen this part of the world? The border's loyalties and grudges felt ancient to James, and yet the place reeked of impermanence. All that shifting sand. He took another sip of coffee, cooled now past drinkable, and finished the chips. He swiped oily fingers down the sides of his pants. He set the newspaper to one side, pondering his long lack of curiosity. Well, he thought, any normal child believes his parents to have had no life before his own; but in his case, that consolation had been turned on its head. He'd come to them so late. He'd been so angry, so afraid of questions. He was the one who'd lived an entire life before joining theirs.

James stood, suddenly unnerved by the quiet. He glanced back at the girl, motionless in the window, her head bowed to the page. James's reflection floated beside her, insubstantial as air. When he stepped forward, the image disappeared. He collected his trash and tossed it into a can. The neon sign in the psychic's house winked twice and went out.

Back in the truck, he took the remaining mile at a leisurely pace, rounding the curves with care enough to guarantee the road beneath his wheels.

He saw at once that Desmond's pickup was gone, though the tail end of Marie's green Chevette poked as usual from under the half-closed garage door, forced out by stacked cartons and haphazardly piled furniture, items that after the move from Corville his parents had deemed too worn to serve, too good to throw away.

Clay pots planted with red geraniums lined the path of pine needles that led to the porch. The branches of a spruce overhung the old shingled roof, a mosaic of green and brown in the filtered sunlight. At the top of the steps, Des had stacked freshly cut firewood. A corn broom leaned against a watering can. It was cool in the shade and James rubbed his arms, watching a spider drop down to the can's spout.

He pressed his face to the front window. The curtains were drawn, but a slit in the fabric allowed him to view the darkened living room. He made out the backside of the couch, an end table, a lamp. A television was pushed against the far wall, useless up here without cable, for which service Desmond refused to pay. A yellow glow shone through an open doorway. The kitchen, the only sunny room in the house.

James called out for Marie. No response.

He tried the door and found it unlocked. He stuck his head in and called again. And now he heard running water, his mother doing the breakfast dishes. He'd just started for the kitchen when a voice behind him said, "Strange."

Marie was sunk into an armchair. Her hands rested in her lap; her feet crossed primly at the ankle. Reaching to brush at a shelf of straight-cut gray bangs, her arm quavered, the loose flesh at her elbow hanging. Since the move, Marie had given up dyeing her hair, given up the once careful makeup. Without lipstick, her mouth looked colorless.

"What is it, Mom?" James asked.

"I phoned you," Marie said, "not five minutes ago." She ran her palms along her thighs and the faint scritching sound made James think of mice in a drawer. Marie's blouse had been tucked neatly into her slacks, but several of the top buttons were undone. He glimpsed the patterned lace of her bra, the blanched fold of skin beneath the band, and this scared him more than he would've thought possible.

"Why's the water running?" he asked.

When she didn't answer, he ducked into the kitchen.

At first he could see nothing wrong; nothing felt out of place. Then he realized there was no sign of his father's breakfast, no smell of bacon, no pot of oatmeal congealing on the stove. A teakettle was balanced at the edge of the sink, as if his mother had been interrupted while filling it. It gave James the creeps. He crossed the linoleum and shut off the tap and stared out the window at Desmond's vegetable plot. The earth there was dark with manure, green shoots pushed up through the soil. A dozen fruit trees formed a small grove, white blossoms clinging to the branches like snow.

He returned to the living room. "What's happened here, Mom?"

"Your father told me to stay in the house. But it's no one's fault."

"*What's* no one's fault?"

"There's a dead child in the east field, Jamie . . . a little boy. At first I thought it was you. Isn't that ridiculous? I'm supposed to stay in the house."

James knelt at Marie's feet. He took her hands in his own. He studied the wrinkled cheeks, the hooded eyes. Up close, Marie smelled musty and sour. It bothered him; he hoped it didn't show. As always, he had to remind himself how much he owed her, this woman who'd seen him through the worst of his childhood, the aftermath of abandonment. Sometimes, he knew, he forgot to love her as he should. Because where Desmond was forceful and open, Marie was private and still. In thirty years, he'd never once heard her voice raised. His first day in Corville, she'd greeted him at the end of the driveway of the house on Seventh Street, straight-backed and composed, hands tucked into her sleeves. They'd regarded each other in silence, a lost boy and a woman who thought she'd never have a child. Marie had known enough not to touch him, offering only a jelly sandwich and a glass of cold milk. He was well out of the Navy before he appreciated that kind of self-possession.

"Do you remember," she said, "how you used to lie all the time? About anything, anything at all. What day it was, whether you'd eaten your lunch or put your toys away."

James nodded.

"You had a way of holding yourself. So ungodly stiff. I wanted to ask why you couldn't just tell me the truth. But I never did. I think I was afraid of what you might say." She drew her hands free of his and folded them in her lap. "All children lie," she said. "But your father never saw. All those years as a cop . . . it really is funny. And I

37

could never bring myself to tattle. Desmond would have insisted on a punishment."

James said, "He wanted me to fly right."

Marie's mouth collapsed. "Such a little boy."

"I was never a little boy."

As soon as he'd said it, James realized she was talking about the dead child.

"Your father's in the east field," Marie said. "The gladiolas."

James waited for something more.

Her pale lips tightened. "You'd better go."

He walked the service road for a third of a mile, a dirt track that paralleled the eastern edge of the tulip fields, flat acreage nestled between the hills. The flower stalks had been cut back, and the remaining foliage was yellow and brown, collapsed like long-armed soldiers prostrate with heat.

The road narrowed, looping around the side of a hill, and then he was into the gladiolas, row upon row of juicy green, rounded buds like fists closed over a prize.

Desmond's pickup was parked alongside a police car that fish-tailed into the field. Red lights flashed, a warning weakened by the sunshine. James lengthened his stride, then started to jog. Coming up behind the vehicles, he saw that both were empty, though his father's truck idled, the key still in the ignition. A dispatcher's voice droned from the police radio.

James leaned against the black-and-white. The sun was hot on his head and he pushed his fingers through his hair, damp with sweat. He swept his gaze over the field. Pale green stems, brick-colored earth. The irrigation pipes looked like snakes hidden under the leaves. Another pass and he saw four figures huddled at the end of a row. A strip of yellow crime scene tape.

James followed several sets of footprints, careful not to disturb them with his own.

Closer, he saw Desmond down on his knees, bent over something laid out in the flowers. Des's shoulders strained against his shirt; a damp spot traced the length of his spine. His bald pate was deeply tanned, furrowed like the fields. A few paces away, two uniformed officers stood at attention, while a third man in a cream-colored suit squatted, trying to avoid muddying his knees.

From behind the yellow tape, a farmworker looked on. He wore jeans and a long-sleeved flannel shirt. A Dodgers cap obscured the upper half of his face.

The man in the suit leaned and a yellow necktie danced. He said something to Desmond. With gloved hands, he fed the tip of his tie between his shirt's middle buttons. One of the uniforms tucked a clipboard under his arm. A measuring tape swung from the second cop's wrist. Someone said, "Fruit of the Loom," and James saw a splash of red.

He pulled up short.

Desmond swiveled from the waist. "You got here fast."

The man in the cream-colored suit rose, eyeing James. "And you are . . . ?"

James stepped forward, hand outstretched. "James Reese."

"Detective Raymond Fricke. Elbert P.D."

The uniform with the clipboard glanced at his watch. "Same spelling?" he asked.

"This is my son," Desmond said.

The uniform made a quick notation.

And now James spotted a bare leg, very small. Ah, no, he thought. He moved in, the uniforms parting reflexively to make room.

A boy lay on his side, knees bent. His arms were drawn in against his chest, his fingers tightly curled. A pink plastic rosary wound about his left wrist. The boy's head rested on a small mound of dirt, surrounded by scratchings, as if someone had fashioned a pillow of earth. Recently shaved, an eighth-inch of black plush clung to his skull. James forced himself to look at the face.

He heard Marie saying, *I thought it was you,* and for an irrational moment he expected . . . well, he didn't know what. But the features registered simply as dead. Mottled skin, lips and ears tinged a faint blue. The open eyes bulged. James ran his gaze down the child's torso. Red T-shirt, ragged shorts. The fronts of the legs were stained a deep purplish red, thin white creases about the knees. Bare feet, filthy, the bottoms thick with calluses.

Four or five, thought James. No more than that.

Over the years he'd run across his share of bodies, of course, murders, suicides, acts of God. It came with the job, and the landscape, too. But the *kids.* Working a sector thirty miles outside of Corville, he'd once ridden up on five skeletons lying atop a flat rock. Small white bones: pollitos who'd run first out of water, and then out of time. James couldn't get over it, the way they were laid out like that, all in a row, like cigars in a box. The ME claimed the bodies had been there for years. James couldn't get over that, either, how many times he must've ridden on past.

Desmond, still on his knees, moved his face inches from the boy's. Detective Fricke started to object, but Des ran right over him. "Asphyxia," he pronounced. "Petechia in the eyes, that tells the tale. Broken capillaries, that's what that is."

Dryly, Fricke said, "I know the term."

"Coroner'll find it in his heart and lungs, too."

Des in full cop mode, thought James.

"But he wasn't strangled," Fricke said. He put a hand in a pocket and jangled his keys. "And I'll tell you what else—you can get up, Mr. Reese."

Mister. There were apparently limits to professional courtesy. Desmond, James noted, remained on his knees. But Fricke was right, the boy hadn't been strangled. There were no signs of assault, no marks on the neck, no telltale bruise.

"He was smothered," Desmond said, "but not here." He pointed at the mottled purple on the boy's legs. "The lividity—when he died, it was face down. Later, he was moved."

"That boy was *placed*," Fricke said. "Deliberately. Right here, right on this property. And why would someone want to do that?"

"I have no idea," Desmond said.

Fricke said, "Somebody doesn't love you."

James was studying the tangle of tracks leading up to the boy. The prints crossed and recrossed, mixed in with others that were fresher, likely belonging to the farmworker and the two uniforms. He glanced around at everyone's shoes: huaraches, police oxfords, Italian loafers—these last on Detective Fricke. Desmond wore beat-up hikers. The rest of the prints had been made by smallish feet. Running shoes, and one pair of high-heeled shit-kicker boots. The boot tracks were scuffed with fresh dirt, as if the wearer had attempted to kick them away.

"Four guys," he said.

Fricke switched his attention to James. "What's that?"

"It was four guys brought the kid in."

"Yeah?" Fricke said. "And who the fuck are *you*, to be instructing *me*." Scowling, he nonetheless ordered one of the uniforms back to the car for casting materials. "And get the goddamn camera." Fricke patted down his jacket, located pen and notepad in an inside pocket, then gestured at Desmond's worker. "Yours, I presume."

Grunting, Desmond pushed to his feet.

"Legal?" Fricke asked.

Des shook his head and Fricke smiled.

James looked away. He rocked on his heels, fists shoved down deep into his pockets. That smile made him mad. More to the point, however, was just how thoroughly Desmond's answer had caught him off guard. A lot of the farms in this area employed illegal aliens—once safely across, a pollo could almost count on la migra having neither the manpower nor the inclination to crack down on every last working man—and yet he would've bet the house against Desmond's having anything to do with it. Des believed in Law and Order. Right and Wrong. Capital letters carved

41

in stone. In principle, James admired this. In actuality, it could be hard to take. He remembered how, when he was a kid, Des used to talk about his cases sometimes, in unnerving detail and often at the dinner table. The man knew how to make a moral and then drive it home, chest heaving, his pounding fists making the cutlery jump. James had always assumed that these performances were intended as object lessons for himself. But, no, he allowed now; probably not. All the same, he'd held it against Des for years.

"Shorts are worn out," Desmond said, "but that shirt looks brand new. And just the right size. Somebody cared."

Fricke was not to be diverted. "Are there others?" he asked. "And I don't mean dead boys."

Desmond said evenly, "Yes, there are others."

"How many?"

"Three or four."

"And where might they be now?"

"Took off, I'd say."

Fricke looked at Desmond's worker. "Why didn't this one go, too?"

"He found the body." Desmond ran a hand over his naked scalp. "Came and got me and I asked him to stay."

"Does 'he' have a name?"

"Rafael." Desmond glanced at his worker. "Rafael Noyez."

Rafael Noyez gave a barely perceptible nod.

Fricke said to him, "You hablas any inglés?" No response. "English," Fricke said. Again, no response. Fricke asked Desmond, "How's your Spanish?"

"He's a good worker," Desmond said. "The best."

Fricke said, "That's not what I asked."

"Mine's fluent," James said.

The uniform was back with the camera, a bulky old Polaroid. He passed it to Fricke, who threw the strap over his neck and raised the camera to his face. The shutter clicked and a square print shot out. Fricke snapped, "Do your goddamn *job*," and the uniform set

42

the tape measure on the ground beside the boy's head, then stretched it to his feet. Fricke moved the viewer an inch to the right and took another photograph. He eased in for a close-up of the head. He held the developing prints between the fingers of his left hand, and James recalled a card trick he'd once seen, in a restaurant with Mercedes on Valentine's Day, where the magician had with a flick of the wrist turned each of four different cards into a queen of hearts.

The uniform jotted numbers.

Fricke looked a question at James.

"Border Patrol," James supplied. "Out of Corville Station."

Fricke stared. "Well, well. That's mighty interesting. All things considered." The camera fell against his chest. "Okay, why don't we give your Spanish a go. Ask Rafael here if he knows who this kid is."

James did as requested. Once again, Noyez made no reply.

"Ask him," Fricke said, "if he knows the parents."

James asked. No answer.

Fricke folded his arms. "Tell him he's going to be deported. Unless I arrest him for murder instead."

"For God's sake," Desmond said.

"Stay out of it!" Fricke said. Then to James, "Go on, now. Translate."

At this point, Rafael Noyez found his tongue. He began to yell and kick at the dirt. In a flash the uniform jumped the row, grabbed Noyez's arms and thrust them roughly behind his back.

Disgusted, Desmond said, "You don't need to do that."

But Fricke barked at Noyez, "Get rid of the goddamn *hat*." To the cop he said, "Let him loose."

Noyez whipped his arms forward. He took off the cap and held it against his waist, bowing his head as if in church. His black hair shone, iridescent in the sunlight.

A skidding noise sounded from the service road. Everyone turned as an ambulance lurched to a stop. Three emergency techs in white jumpsuits hopped out and ran around to the back. They rolled out a stretcher and trotted into the field.

Desmond said sadly, "I'd hoped never to see a dead human being again."

James felt a clanking groan inside his rib cage, as if his heart were turning over. Then he realized it was the irrigation sprinklers chugging to life. The first drops fell, soft peltings that gave him a chill.

"Goddamnit!" Fricke jumped in an attempt to dodge the water. The techs had already retreated back to the road. "Camera's going to be ruined. And my goddamn *suit!*" He tried to stuff the Polaroid beneath his jacket, but it wouldn't fit, so he gave up and sprinted away, the uniform following, Rafael Noyez in tow.

Desmond and James remained in the field.

James had to ask. "You got kids working out here?"

"No. Of course not."

"The rest I can almost understand. But kids. That's something else."

Desmond shook his head.

"I'm not sure I believe you."

"Don't say that, son. Some things should never be said."

"But where'd the boy come from?"

Again Desmond shook his head. Water fell over him, soaking his pants and his shirt. James could see the musculature of Desmond's chest. He'd been a powerful man. He was powerful still.

James was wet, too, but he couldn't feel it.

"Illegals," he said. "How come you never told me?"

"You know why."

James crouched awkwardly in the mud beside the dead boy. A rainbow arced through the wet field, the colors dropping behind a green hill.

The footprints were filling with water, making small pools.

James said, "Who'd want to hurt him?"

"This wasn't a homicide, son."

"What makes you say so?"

"Experience. Intuition."

Wishful thinking. That seemed much more likely to James.

"You're sure you've never seen him before?"

"Never," said Des.

"So why do you think he was brought here? Because Fricke's right about that. Someone deliberately placed the body."

"I don't know, son."

For several seconds James watched clear rivulets run across the child's face, and it looked as if the water were traveling up, rather than down, a controversion of gravity. He reached out a hand.

"Don't," Desmond said.

But James ignored him and closed the boy's eyes.

Hours later, after Fricke and Company had finally quit his parents' property, James found himself alone in the kitchen with Marie, Desmond having disappeared into the bedroom for a nap. A nap. Never had James known Des to lie down in daylight.

He washed his hands and face at the sink, pulled paper towels from the roll, and dried off. Fingers of light reached through the windows, the walls stained the exact color of the honey Marie had pulled from a shelf.

James put the water on to boil with a sense of déjà vu—and he recognized where the feeling came from: this morning's kettle, balanced on the edge of the sink. While Marie settled into a chair, he got a blue ceramic teapot down from the cupboard. The shelves were lined with flavored teas.

"You choose," he said.

"Chamomile," said Marie.

James scooped leaves into a metal basket set into the teapot's neck. The kettle whistled and he turned off the gas. Pouring, he smelled flowers.

A cup for Marie, and one for himself. Two saucers. Two spoons. He brought it all to the table.

They sat in silence for a while. Then James lifted the cover on the pot. Judging the tea sufficiently brewed, he poured. He unscrewed the lid on the jar of honey, dipped in a spoon, and dribbled a little into Marie's cup. He knew she didn't like it too sweet.

Marie stirred her tea, the spoon tinkling against the side of the cup. "Drink up, Jamie," she said.

Marie sat straight in the hard kitchen chair. Her jawline, which had struck James earlier as doughy and soft, now appeared firm. All afternoon, he'd watched his mother put herself together again, while Desmond went progressively weak and scattered. When Fricke had asked for the phone number at the farm, Desmond had had to turn to James.

He wrapped a hand around his cup, and blew on the hot tea. The surface rippled, a tiny ocean.

"It's been a long day," Marie said. "I'm glad everyone's gone. We can relax."

But the objects around them—walls and windows, teacups and towels—all seemed to James to be charged with expectation, weighted with meaning beyond their function.

"Don't be too hard on your father," Marie said. "He's a good man."

James agreed. But goodness wasn't the point.

Marie said again, "A *good* man."

James could feel his mother wanting him to confirm that everything was all right, that he wouldn't hold the day's business against Des, against them. And he wouldn't; he didn't even want to. All the same, he'd suffered his parents' disapproval for too many years. When against all reckoning he'd stepped into the life they'd always wanted for him, it turned out to be a little like dropping down the rabbit hole. At bottom, they'd all changed places somehow. He should've been pleased, but it hadn't quite worked out that way.

Marie peered at him over the cup's rim. "There's a letter for you."

"What letter?" he asked.

"It came last week."

"Here? Why didn't you call?"

Marie said only, "It's on the table, by the front door."

James went to retrieve the envelope. Cream-colored stock, heavy weight. It looked important; it looked official. The original postmark was two months old. Apparently, the letter had been sent first to the old address on Seventh Street, then forwarded to the farm.

Back in the kitchen, James studied the return address: Wyatt, Seward & May, Attorneys at Law. Santa Monica Boulevard, West Los Angeles.

A premonitory fear plucked at him. He glanced at Marie.

"Go on," she said. "Open it."

He ran a forefinger under the flap, pulled the single page and scanned the contents. Hands shaking, he went back to the beginning of the letter and read it again, more slowly this time.

In a single short paragraph, Alexander May, Esq., informed James that his birth mother, Lara Shipp Santana, had recently died. What's more, she'd named him sole heir. But Diego Santana— James's uncle on his father's side—was contesting the will. The attorney concluded with a request that James phone the office at his earliest convenience, to set up an appointment to discuss the matter in further detail.

Impossible, thought James. Another part of him felt he'd been waiting for this for years.

"Trouble?" Marie asked.

Wordlessly he passed the letter.

There was something else in the envelope. Upended, a photograph fell to the table. An attached sticky note read: *Lara wanted me to send this to you.*

James peeled the yellow square.

The photo underneath was an old black and white, curling edges, shades of gray. Two young men posed in front of a gate.

Thick bushes loomed on either side, the hint of a small house behind.

With a shock, James realized that one of the men was Emilio Santana—his other father, his first father—dead and gone for thirty years. Heart thudding, he brought the snapshot closer.

Here Emilio looked to be about twenty, eerily similar to James at that age. The same shock of hair, the same broad cheeks and sturdy shoulders. Emilio wore loose chinos and a tank shirt, tattoos climbing his muscled arms. Smiling, he cradled a baby wrapped in a blanket. And that *would* be James. Eerie. As if three generations of the same person were here in the room, because James was old enough now to be the father of the father in this photograph. All ghosts, he thought.

He looked now at the second young man. Emilio's brother—the same Diego who was contesting the will—here a skinny teenager dressed in identical chinos and tank. Diego leaned into Emilio, while also reaching toward the baby. The thin arm was blurred, caught midmotion. It gave James a chill. He thought of Charlotte saying, *Read it for me*, and concentrated. Was the arm coming up? Coming down? Given the angle of descent, the arm's trajectory, wouldn't it have struck the baby? Was that even possible? There was no way of knowing, because frozen, the intention behind the movement was lost.

James contemplated his infant self: fat-faced and peaceful. Asleep, probably.

He flipped the picture. On the back, written in wobbly script, were three words enclosed in quotes: "Guilt and Innocence." A title, as if the snapshot hung in a museum.

Below that was the line: "Dearest J, it is my fault—"

The ink was dark enough that James thought this might have been penned fairly recently. "J" could be only himself. The handwriting was Lara's, he was certain of that, even if it was decades since he'd seen it last.

His mother. Blond hair, and green eyes, like jewels. The smell of cigarettes and oranges.

But Lara was always upstairs in her room. In bed, alone. Her body under the covers had curved and humped like sand piled on the beach. Any old wave might wash it away. James remembered standing in the doorway with Emilio, the room dim, the air salty and stale, thick curtains drawn against the sunlight. He remembered the rivets down the seam of Emilio's jeans, and the scratchy feel of his father's palm closed around his. Emilio saying, Querida, you must not sleep your life away.

James had loved his mother once—he must have, all little boys did—but he couldn't think now what that had felt like.

"Fuck this," he said.

Marie's eyes welled. James handed her the photo. She barely looked before setting it down.

"Did you know this was coming?" he asked.

"Of course not, Jamie. How could I?"

"Why didn't you call?"

"I don't know . . . I was afraid."

James sat forward intently. He was sweating, his shirt glued to his back. "Of what?"

Marie shook her head.

"So." His voice croaked. "What do you make of it?"

Marie hesitated. "You ought to talk to the lawyer."

"Yeah." James flopped back in the chair, thinking hotly that he'd do no such thing. Because this letter was poison to him, what it represented, what it said and what it did not. The past was the past. He intended to keep it that way.

In fact, he was tempted to toss the letter into the can, right now. The photograph, too. But Marie was watching him, too carefully. So he took the items and folded them back into the envelope, then slipped it into the pocket of his jeans.

"We're a family," Marie said. "Don't you forget."

"Hey," James said, rising. "I need to call home."

Marie made a sour face. And Christ, James thought, even now. Marie didn't like Mercedes; she never had. For no reason that he could ever discern, except that she wasn't Charlotte Murray.

"Mom, that's beneath you," he said. "Don't talk to me about good."

The phone was in the living room and he went in and sat in Desmond's easy chair and dialed. He could hear Marie crying in the kitchen. He was sorry, but he also thought, Let her cry. Mercedes's voice came on the machine, then the beep. James stared at the phone. He didn't know what sort of message to leave, so he said only that it was after four now, that he was leaving, that he'd see her soon.

In the kitchen doorway, he slapped a hand against the frame.

"What will you do?" Marie asked.

"I'm going to head out." But he knew she meant the letter.

"Your father's ashamed," Marie said. "That little boy . . . Desmond would never ever do this to you."

"To me?" James didn't understand. And then he thought that maybe he did. It wasn't just a matter of illegal aliens, of whether he approved of what Des had going out here. No. Desmond didn't want James to have to contend once again with a murder so close to home. Because Emilio Santana—that smiling father, baby in arms—had killed a young woman when James was just four. Two years into his prison term, he'd been murdered himself. Shanked in his bunk. James wasn't supposed to know that, but he did. Crouched unseen at the top of the stairs, he'd heard his mother and uncle talking about it. His mother's voice, he remembered, had sounded so weird, the words swallowed and released, rising like balloons from the hallway below.

For weeks afterward, he'd had dreams of sleeping in blood. He'd wake up crying, the sheets warm and soaking wet. Urine, of course, and not blood at all. And somewhere in there, Lara Shipp Santana had given him up. A six-year-old boy. Teeth chattering, eyes burning, skin tender, bones sore. Goddamnit. Who gives away a six-year-old boy?

Goddamnit! He wasn't going to think about this. He hadn't in years. Whatever else they'd intended, his adoptive parents had made that easy for him. From his first day in town neither had ever spoken about his old life. It wasn't their way. He'd come to them so late. He'd been so afraid of questions.

In any case, that kid, he didn't exist anymore. He was as dead as the child found in Desmond's field, as dead as Emilio Santana himself, as dead as the girl his father had drowned.

Up and down the block, automobiles sat cooling in driveways, surrounded by tricycles and lawn mowers, abandoned toys. Yellow light shined on James's neighbors as they moved in their windows, fixing dinner, helping children with homework, attending to the tasks of a weekday evening.

James nudged the truck's bumper up against the garage, then killed the engine. Next door, a sprinkler gyrated rhythmically. He rolled down the window and hung out his arm. A cold mist settled onto his skin. Then his own front door opened and Mercedes came out and sat on the step. Her hair was wet from the shower, the front of her white T-shirt darkened by the dripping ends. At the sight of her, the mad drained right out of James. He climbed out of the truck and walked around to the step.

Looking up at him, Mercedes said, "Your mother left a bunch of crazy messages. What happened up there?"

"Okay if I sit?" he asked. She scooted to make room and he lowered down. He said, "They found a dead kid out in the field."

Mercedes sighed. She leaned against him, and James rested a hand on her thigh.

"Kid's illegal," he said. "Five years old, maybe. No parents in sight. The body was dumped. And all of Desmond's workers took off, except this one guy. But he says he doesn't know who the boy is."

"You believe him?"

James thought a moment. "No, not really."

"How did he die?"

"Looked like suffocation." James closed his eyes. He saw the boy laid out on his side, arms drawn to his chest, the purple markings down the front of his legs.

"Was he murdered?" she asked.

"I don't know. Maybe. It's too soon to tell."

She got up and came around to stand in front of him. James opened his knees so that she could step inside. Lightly, he kissed her between the legs. She smelled of laundry detergent, clean skin. Mercedes took his head in her hands.

He shifted a little under her scrutiny, aware of that photograph in his pocket. He'd thrown the letter away—torn scraps flying from the truck's driver's-side window—but kept the picture, after all. No point in trying to figure out why.

Unexpectedly, Mercedes said, "Why don't we put that tree in the ground?"

The last time James had been up to see Des, his father had given him a young orange tree, roots wrapped in burlap and set in a pot. He'd driven straight home, only to stash the thing in the back yard, under the eaves, in a ribbon of shade. He gave it a little water when he remembered, which wasn't anywhere near often enough.

"Okay," James said. "Let's do that now."

Out back, they stood on dried grass.

"Where do you want it?" he asked.

Mercedes paced back and forth, glancing at the sky occasionally as if she might find an answer there.

"We need sun to make fruit," she explained.

James said, "We got nothing but sun."

He went into the garage and brought out the shovel, then returned for a forty-pound sack of fertilizer. When he came out again, Mercedes was gone. James wrapped his arms around the bag, as if wrestling a man. He lugged it over the grass.

His wife's face appeared at the bedroom window. She lifted the screen and pointed. "How about there?"

"Good a place as any," James said. He dropped the fertilizer, dragging it the final few feet, then went back for the tree. It weighed less than he expected, the branches brittle, the soil at the roots hard and dry.

He took up the shovel and started to dig. The first couple of inches were easy enough, but after that the dirt was packed solid. Soon sweat was pouring off him. James stripped his shirt. By the time he finished, his heart was racing. He threw the shovel down.

Mercedes was outside now, unwinding the hose from its coil. James mixed a little of the fertilizer with loose dirt and shoveled it into the hole. On his knees, he planted the stiffened mass. He pushed the soil into place with his hands. Mercedes brought him the hose, then ran back to turn the spigot. A thin trickle spilled onto the ground. James got to his feet.

"We'll see it from the bed," Mercedes said. "Orange blossoms."

James squinted at the tree. "That's one sad-lookin' stick."

"It's lonely. We should put flowers around it." Mercedes linked her arm in his. "Want to know a secret?" she asked.

"I do if you want to tell me."

"When I was a girl, I used to be in a gang."

James leaned forward to look at her.

"Tenth Street," she said.

"I'll be *god*damned." Tenth Street were the badasses in town, responsible for more mayhem than all the other gangs put together.

"I was jumped in at twelve, out again at thirteen. Quick tour, eh? I liked it for a while, though. Us against them. It was another kind of family. A way to be somebody, you know?"

James nodded, thinking, like the Navy, like the Patrol.

"Mostly," she said, "we were there for the guys. To love 'em up good. We had to wait on the vatos, bring or do or be. All for them. That rubbed me the wrong way. You know how I hate taking orders."

James smiled. There was a difference between them. Not that he enjoyed being told what to do. But a part of him wanted it and needed it, the relief from decisions he might make on his own. The irony there being that there was no relief, because the job demanded he think for himself.

"I had to fight all the girls," Mercedes said. "Both times. Getting jumped out was the worst. Some of those cholas will rip your tongue out. It was the insult, I guess. Like my wanting to go meant something bad about them."

"It did," James said.

"They let me know it." Mercedes sighed. "Carlos had to pull them off of me. He heard it was going down on the square—it was supposed to be some big secret, but secrets are made for someone to tell—and he came running. Little brother. Bless his motherfucking interference. I was down on the ground, bleeding so bad. I recognized his shoes. Carlos said later he thought I was dead. . . . But guess what? I wasn't that happy to see him. I didn't want to give up. I wanted to finish it by myself."

In the dark plane of her cheek, the scar beneath Mercedes's eye looked like a slivered moon. James watched the rise and fall of her chest. Half-consciously, he timed his breathing to hers.

"That tree might not make it," he said. "Some transplants never take. Even when everything's right."

Mercedes said softly, "What was it like? Going to live with Des and Marie?"

He hadn't realized he was talking about himself.

He said, "It's like being starved. There is the food spread out in front of you. You can have it, it's yours. But then you discover you don't know how to eat."

Later, when they made love, James looked down into Mercedes's face, wanting desperately to read anything and everything that he might see there. But he couldn't get close enough. Even now, she seemed a stranger, the pulse at her temple beating like a separate heart, her closed lids a fluttering veil. It made him sad, and it excited him, too. He licked Mercedes's lips and then he kissed her, deeply, moving his tongue in her mouth. Her legs circled his hips and she flung her arms overhead, hands palms up upon the pillow. James worked his fingers in her hair. He wanted to peel back her skin. He wanted to swallow her whole. And then the top of his head was coming off, and he felt Mercedes gathering beneath him, and it was a struggle for both of them. It felt like they were fighting toward something rather than riding their desire to its natural end. Mercedes jerked her head and arched her back, and then, Christ, it was over and James was already dissatisfied, wishing he could begin again and this time do it right.

Mercedes placed her hands on his chest and pushed. She said hoarsely, "You want too much!"

James rolled onto his back. Closing his eyes, he saw stars, and flashes of color, and he imagined himself as a cartoon character, someone who always appears with empty bubbles above his head, never words.

Mercedes turned over and pulled the sheet up her hip. Dark hair tumbled down her shoulder. James touched the soft strands with his fingertips.

Time passed and her breathing slowed and he felt her slip away.

James lay very still, his mind quiet on the surface, alert underneath. The graveyard shift had long since thrown his body's rhythms, but the inability to let go was something he'd suffered with since childhood. Watching and waiting.

Light and shadow swept across the ceiling, two cars driving past. His heart was a terrible weight in his chest.

Why, he wondered, had Lara Shipp Santana sent him that photograph? What was the message and why should he care? And why had the woman named him in her will? After everything she'd done. Giving him away, just another donation to charity.

Why would Tío Diego contest?

Then it hit him: There was real money involved.

But . . . but what? But . . . it came from the Shipps, and not Emilio. And so—he followed the thought—what claim did his uncle have? He was no relative of Lara's, not anymore; he wasn't entitled to anything. James squeezed his eyes shut and pictures flashed like a slide show. The house on the cliff, the ocean below. The dark blue Cadillac in the garage. Lara in a green dress. Emilio clipping flowers out by the pool. And Diego—Diego with his telescope, and schoolbooks. Diego watching TV. Sketching, or swimming laps, or riding a skateboard down to the beach. Down, and down. The wheels rolled on asphalt.

And suddenly James was sinking fast. Water lapped, waves at his throat. He tried to rouse himself, but it was no use. A door slammed, a curtain dropped. He slept like the dead.

CHAPTER FOUR

J ames awoke with a shout. He was alone in the bed, sweating
in a blade of sunlight that sliced through the open window.
He rolled onto his side and out of the heat, out of the glare
that was like a watching eye. But whatever the images that had so
frightened him, they were gone now. The room was eerie with
quiet. He regarded the squatty pine dresser, the brass floor lamp,
the overstuffed chair layered with Mercedes's discarded clothing.
On the wall behind the dresser, a small oil painting showed a hawk
circling a lemon grove, clouds alight with the threat of dawn, and
something in the spread of the hawk's wings, or perhaps the angle
of flight, tugged at his memory, and he was again afraid.

He tossed the covers and climbed out of bed. In the bathroom,
he splashed his face with water. He threw on an old pair of jeans
and a frayed cotton shirt, tied on work boots, and fastened his
watch. One thirty. He was more than an hour late for his regular
poker game.

He checked his wallet, found almost two hundred in cash. Keys jangled in his fist. The truck, he knew, waited for him in the drive. Silently, he blessed Mercedes for that. Ten minutes and he hit the border gate. The patrol on duty waved him over with barely a glance. The truck lurched, James's foot too heavy on the gas, but as soon as he'd crossed, he felt lighter than air. He passed six abandoned cars, hoses spilling like entrails from under the hoods, a Pemex station and a mercado, a nondescript building made of corrugated tin. A long empty stretch, the road rough and rutted, and then a steady rise. He crested a hill tinged green from the rains. He pulled over and stopped. From here he could see straight down into El Pilón. Short streets, some no more than a single block long, spoked from the central plaza. At one end the Catholic church sat like a patriarch at the head of the table; at the other, a cantina was the disgraced and unrepentant relative. In between, ramshackle shops ringed the sparse grass. A group of old men congregated at a picnic table, motionless beneath a jacaranda that wore the last of its drooping blooms, the flowers a delicate violet haze. A child walked a burro along the back of the church.

El Pilón was smaller than Corville, and infinitely sleepier, but James wasn't fooled: concealment was the essence of Mexico. Nothing here was ever quite what it seemed. He loved that, the way his perceptions slipped and skewed, until he almost believed that in this country he could be someone other than who he was.

On the way out of town, he encountered a Mixtec woman roosted on a blanket in the middle of the road. She wore a crushed velvet hat, colorful wide skirts that hid her crossed legs. A pile of rag dolls filled her lap. She appeared to be sound asleep. James slowed, steering cautiously around her, but the woman never opened her eyes.

* * *

Three miles farther south he came up on 24-Hour Efraín's, a small cinderblock rectangle painted dead black, with no sign, no electric lights, no front door or front-facing windows. Five vehicles were nosed into the weeds, three with Mexican plates, one from Arizona, one from California. Everyone was welcome at Efraín's, and that included patrols—so long as they came with cash and behaved.

Of the five vehicles, the only one James failed to recognize was a late-model van, tan-colored, large tires. The body sat high off the ground, with beefed-up suspension, in anticipation of a heavy load. CHOOSE LIFE, a bumper sticker advised. Tinfoil blocked the rear windows.

James walked around to the driver's side and peeked in. Sheepskin seats, a steering wheel wrapped in leather. A statue of the Virgin of Guadalupe was glued to the dash. A metal wall divided the front seats from a cargo area, and through a square of wire mesh, he saw heaped plastic bags. He saw spilled tapes and CDs and a Hula Hoop, shirts and dresses and shoes, an embroidered tablecloth. A collector, he thought.

He followed the flattened dirt path around back to the patio, made of poured concrete mixed with eggshells. An iron rail bordered a trickling creek, and cottonwoods clung to the far embankment, their branches filled with sparrows. Beyond the trees, a few dilapidated buildings were fenced with barbed wire. La Boom: the fireworks factory.

A rooster strutted at James's ankles, pecking combatively, its red comb wobbling.

James watched two men roll a barrel down La Boom's loading dock.

He heard a high-pitched babbling behind him. A child's voice. He turned to see a little boy planted in a bucket of water, enthusiastically lathering himself with a chunk of yellow soap. James flashed on the dead child in Desmond's field. But this one was alive, and lively, rubbing his fists over his arms and shoulders, legs like twigs, a belly round as a beach ball. The boy scratched furiously at his scalp, then bent to grab a cup which he dipped into a second bucket. Lifting his arm, he dumped the water. Bubbles rolled down his neck.

James went to him and said, "Here, let me do that." He put out a hand and the child passed him the cup.

"Shut 'em," James said. The boy squeezed his eyes and James poured, working his fingers through the soapy tangles.

A young woman stepped out onto the patio. Teresa: Efraín's oldest girl, a tiny thing with auburn hair curling around a thin face.

"Buenas tardes, señora. ¿Cómo está?" Always, with Teresa, James used the formal address, though he'd known her since she was herself a child.

"Bien," Teresa said, "¿y usted?"

"Bien."

"And me, too!" the boy piped up in English.

James reached down and tickled his belly. "¿Dónde están sus pantalones, señor?" *Where are your pants?*

"No sé." The boy dropped his head to gaze between his legs. He gave his penis a friendly tug.

Teresa let loose a stream of scolding Spanish. She disappeared into the cantina, reemerging with a towel and a pair of blue shorts. She dried the boy and handed the damp towel to James. Teresa held the shorts for the boy to step into, while James worked on his hair till it stood straight up. Then she lifted her son and carried him, protesting, inside.

And now James heard familiar voices, raised in mild argument, plates crashing in the kitchen, the clink of forks and knives. He smelled fried eggs and tomatoes, fresh tortillas, the vinegar bite of jalapeños. A radio played a ranchera ballad, guitar and ocarina, the singer liquid and languid and sad.

Blinded by the dark, James navigated between the tables by feel.

He slapped his palms on the bar. He climbed onto a stool, nodding at the shadow behind the register. As his eyes adjusted, the shadow acquired substance and form: a man, very small, with wiry arms and lean hips, dark hair shot with silver, a thin expressionless face. He wore a white butcher's apron over black pants and a red short-sleeved shirt.

James said, "Efraín."

Efraín lowered the volume on the radio. "Jaime."

"What's up, buddy?"

"Eh," Efraín waved a hand. The middle three fingers were missing, a consequence of his prior employment at La Boom.

"Business good?"

Efraín shrugged.

"How's the family?"

Another shrug. But after a moment, Efraín asked, "And you?"

Images strobed in James's head. The half-naked pollo on his back in the sand; the nape of Charlotte's pale neck; Mercedes licking sugar from her fingers. That old photograph: Emilio, and Diego, and James.

"I'm okay," he said.

"¿Tienes hambre?" Efraín said. "The eggs are fresh."

James surveyed the shelf behind the bar, a line of dusty liquor bottles. Two wooden santos stood at either end, statues with painted faces, human teeth, human hair. A third dangled from the ceiling, a skeleton cloaked in black, hatchet in hand.

"I see you've brought out La Muerte," James said.

Efraín nodded. "For Semana Santa." *Holy Week*.

The skeleton's lower jaw was missing, a disturbing effect. James rubbed at his own chin. "Nomás cerveza," he said. *Beer*. "Cold, por favor."

Efraín reached under the bar and brought up a bottle. He set it down, pulled an opener from his breast pocket, and flipped the cap. Foam bubbled over the lip. The bottle slid across the bartop to James. The glass was icy, wet with condensation. The beer tasted even better than he'd expected it to. Their conversation over, Efraín turned up the music, and James swung his seat around to observe the other patrons, homing in on a table in back, a quartet of cowboy hats. The table was covered with dirty plates, bottles of Cuervo and shakers of salt, dishes filled with sliced limes. Shot glasses stood at every elbow. An upended hat held a pile of dollar bills, American. With pleasure, James noted that the regulars were all in attendance: Fred, the helicopter pilot from Arizona; Danny Patillo, Corville's fireboss; Mako, one of the old-timers from La Boom.

The fourth guy he didn't know. He had a long nose and black hair gathered into a stringy ponytail.

"Deal," Fred directed, and all four hats leaned. Each man pulled a dollar from the pot and studied it.

Liar's Poker. The usual warm-up for seven-card stud.

And now James saw a fifth player, bareheaded, his hat the pot: James was looking at the back of Leo's buzz cut.

"Four fours." With a flourish, Leo stuffed a dollar into the hat.

And what, James wondered, was he doing down here? What was he doing at James's table? The younger patrols usually kept to their own; and what's more, generally speaking, this game was closed. Generally speaking, James liked it that way.

Danny Patillo countered, "Four fives," leaning in to make his contribution, as did Mako, who raised him with, "Cinco nueves."

Fred, the pilot, shook his head. "I pass."

The unknown player examined his bill. He took a drag off a cigarette, then dipped his chin in an odd gobbling motion. Tucking his bottom lip behind his front teeth, he blew the smoke down rather than up, so that it clouded around his hands. The tip of his long nose drooped. "Seven eights, señores," he said. He held out a palm and Leo pressed in a dollar which was then transferred to the hat.

Efraín said darkly, "Eh, those two."

James asked, "Who is that guy?"

"Ese malvado—" Efraín said.

"Seven nines," Leo said.

Patillo passed. Mako passed and then Fred. The bidding returned to the long-nosed player who said, "Eight nines, señores."

"Fuck." Leo threw up his hands. "That's it for me."

Fred the pilot looked up. He called over to James, "About time you showed, Reese!"

Danny Patillo raised a hand in greeting.

Leo glanced over his shoulder. "Hey there, old man."

"Hey, buddy," James said. "Didn't expect to see you."

"Came down to take your money. Yeah, James. Yours."

"Kid's a player," Patillo said.

"Got a real gift," Fred agreed.

"Is that so," said James. The long-nosed player sucked on his teeth and James asked Leo, "Who's your friend?"

From behind the counter, Efraín clucked in disapproval.

But Leo said amiably, "This is Richard Serrano. Richie to you and me."

Without looking up, the long-nosed player lifted his hat.

"Guachen, compadres," Mako grumbled. *Pay attention*. "Eight nines was the bid."

James polished off the last of his beer. "Tell the truth, Leonardo," he said. "Some chick stood you up."

"Not a chance," Leo said. "But even I can't fuck all fucking day. In spite of reports to the fucking contrary." Leo looked around at the others. "That it? Okay, let's count 'em." All the players laid their bills flat. They inspected the various serial numbers, adding, checking to see if the final bid was present or merely a bluff. The count took longer than it should have, what with restarts and challenges and tequila-impaired arithmetic. Efraín got James another beer. The door to the kitchen swung open and he saw Teresa bent over the stove, the boy chattering at her side.

Finally the hand was decided and Richie Serrano scooped bills from the pot. He turned in his seat and stared baldly at James. He pushed his tongue against the inside of his cheek, and smiled— gapped yellow teeth.

James slid off the stool. The others were throwing bills in the hat. James plunked his beer onto the table, got himself a chair, and pushed in between Leo and the long-nosed player.

James turned to his partner. "At this rate," he said, "you're never going to get rich. What do you say we break out the cards?"

A straight dozen hands took them into late afternoon—five- and seven-card stud, anaconda, spit-in-the-ocean, deuces wild— with James playing as badly as he ever had in his life. He upped the ante when he had nothing to show, folded when his cards promised more than half a chance. But when they switched to draw poker, he suddenly hit a lucky streak. He won several hands in a row, adding three hundred dollars to his opening stash. By this time, the cantina had mostly cleared out, the workers headed back to La Boom. The five remaining players hunched around the table, the only sounds Efraín's radio, Richie Serrano sucking at the gaps in his teeth, and piles of money sliding, over and over, toward James.

"Ante up," Patillo said, and they each threw a fiver into the pot.

James helped himself to more tequila. He fanned out his cards. Queen of spades and four diamonds, which he arranged in descending order: king, queen, ten, nine. Tantalizing. But the odds of getting that jack were piss-poor.

With Mako gone back to work, Fred, the pilot, started off the betting. A fast round, everyone in. Then a second, and a third. Nobody folded. The pot grew by five dollars, and ten.

When it came time to draw, Fred turned in three cards.

Patillo dealt replacements. "How 'bout you, Serrano?" he asked. "How many you want?"

"Dos, por favor."

"James?" Patillo said.

James thought a moment. He had his two queens. He could throw in the rest and see what turned up. Or he could try for the straight. "Just the one," he said, discarding the extra queen. Patillo dealt him a card and James stuck it in the middle of his hand. He squinted. The right corner of the new card showed red and white, the J sitting above a pretty diamond. *Goddamnit.* And why wasn't he in Vegas, betting the ranch?

Leo drew a single, as did Danny Patillo.

James looked from one man to the other. Two pair, he thought. Or a full house. Or one of them might have a straight. But it would have to be a royal to beat his hand. How likely was that?

"You're up, Freddy," Patillo said.

Fred folded his cards. "Up and out."

Richie Serrano bet a ten-spot. James saw it and raised ten. Leo raised another twenty. And now Patillo took himself out. The next round, Serrano folded as well. That left Leo and James.

The room went quiet with expectation.

"I see you—" Leo used two fingers to push the bills toward the pot, "—and raise you ten more."

James matched the bet. He threw in another twenty.

"You're bluffing, old man," Leo said. He saw James's bet and put in thirty more.

James called, and raised again. Peering at the pot over the top of his cards, he figured it for about two-fifty now.

Leo rubbed a hand over his buzz cut.

James loosened his jaw. His eyelids drooped. He shifted his cards around.

Richie Serrano said, "¡Chingao! This one's a sly dog."

"My *partner*," Leo said.

"Not right now," said James. "You should've folded, buddy. Live to fight another day. 'Cause I'm going to kill you here."

"You're full of shit," Leo said.

"Put your money down and find out."

Leo threw in two bills. "Call."

James said, "You're not going to raise?"

"Call," Leo said. "I—"

"All right!" Patillo interrupted. "That's it! Let's have a look."

James fanned his cards on the table. Straight flush, queen high. Just about the best hand possible. James grinned. He knew he was gloating, but it felt good to win.

Patillo said to Leo, "Let's see yours—"

But Leo was up on his feet. "You're a fucking cheat, James!"

"Hey!" said Fred the pilot.

James stretched his arms forward to gather the pot. "And you're a sore loser, buddy."

"A fucking thief!"

"Hey! Hey!" said Patillo.

"It's okay," James said. To Leo he said, "I'm just lucky."

"But you make your luck. Don't you?"

"The more reason it's mine."

Leo put both palms on the table and addressed Serrano: "What'd I tell you?"

Richie Serrano was laughing, a silent shaking of the shoulders.

James downed a quick shot, the tequila an improving fire in his gut. He went hot all over. He turned to Serrano, and in a moment of complete and unexpected clarity said, "You're Anteater, aren't you? El Oso Hormiguero." He pictured the tan-colored van parked out front, all the crap that was piled in the back. Shirts and dresses and shoes. "You take their fucking *shoes*."

Fred the pilot whistled.

Patillo said, "C'mon, now!"

Serrano shrugged. "I was a barefoot boy. I can't never have too many shoes." He tugged at the brim of his hat. There was a crude tattoo on his forearm: red roses, black thorns. Three drops of inked blood dripped toward his wrist.

James froze. The back of his neck crawled. That tattoo . . . *that tattoo* . . . it meant something to him. His mind's eye scanned, searching for the reference. But he couldn't get it.

He stood then, too fast, knees knocking up beneath the table. Glasses tipped and skated, plates and bottles, money and cards, and Danny Patillo said, "Jesus, Reese!" At that moment, a huge, percussive rumble split the air. Everyone jumped up at once, kicking chairs aside and scrambling out onto the patio. The rooster ran in as James was running out, and he had an impression of wild flapping before he tripped. He threw out his hands. All the same, his chin hit the concrete, the impact setting off an explosion behind his closed lids. Gingerly, he turned his face to one side. He rested his cheek against the cold floor, as sober as he'd ever been. The rooster pecked at a damp spot near his mouth. Then Efraín was helping him to his feet.

"Fireworks," Efraín said. "The hens won't lay for three days."

In the shadowed cantina, Teresa stood with her son in her arms. Another boom cracked.

"Hurry." Efraín gave James a push. "If you want to see."

The second rocket flowered high in the sky, red, white and blue, a patriot's dream. Streams of shivering light fell, the arc of descent so graceful that James caught his breath; and he thought about how this wasn't his country, how these weren't the colors of Mexico. Across the creek, La Boom's workers were gathered out in the yard. Laughter, and shoving, but no one seemed hurt. Except for James, who fingered his chin. His jawbone throbbed, an egg already rising.

Leo removed a Colt pistol from his ankle strap, sighted down the barrel and squeezed the trigger. *Pop pop pop*. Sparrows flew up from the cottonwood trees.

The workers at La Boom hooted and howled.

"Fuck," Leo said. "I missed."

The sparrows circled, then settled in the branches again.

Leo passed the gun to James. "You try, old man."

The Colt was light in James's hand. He brought it up and sighted and fired once. A thrill went through him, and then he felt sick as the tiny body toppled down through the green. Leo whooped. He ran to the iron rail and vaulted over.

Fred whistled. "Nice shot."

"And that's our cue," Danny Patillo said. He was looking strangely at James. Poker aside, the two didn't see each other that much, but James had known Danny a long time—since high school, anyway—and he felt his friend's reproach.

Patillo was lingering. He said, finally, "The weather holds, we'll burn tonight. You up for it, Reese?"

"I could use a good fire," James said. "Clear everything out." He thought of the pollo he'd chased down in there yesterday, the one who'd cut him. "No more hiding in that fucking canyon."

"Too bad it's just the one."

"Yeah, well. We could burn till kingdom come and not get it all."

Patillo nodded. He touched his fingertips to his brow.

James turned to Anteater, who was grinning like a maniac.

"Old man," Anteater said. "Sunlight don't lie."

James squinted. "I could say the same about you." The guy was in his fifties, at least. The black ponytail was dyed. But in spite of that, in spite of the teeth and the nose, he was a handsome man. Copper-skinned, a whippet frame, cords in his neck like steel cable.

Anteater said, "An enemy of the people, that's what you are. Migra fuck. I know you better than you know yourself."

"You don't know me," said James.

The grin widened.

James said, "At least I don't steal."

"Don't you?"

"You leave them with nothing—"

"And you leave them with less. All the poor fuckers want is out of Mexico. And you're the one thing stands in their way. Admit it, you get off on that. But don't be ashamed. I'm not. And you and me, we are the same." Anteater spit on the ground. "I know you from way back."

James said tightly, "We're not the same."

Inside the cantina, Efraín pushed a broom against broken glass.

Leo's voice floated up from the creek, "You took its fucking head off!"

James went to the rail. He leaned over, his throat gurgly and loose. On the bank below, Leo crouched to inspect the dead bird. James swallowed a nasty taste in his mouth. Then someone was tugging urgently on his belt. Teresa's boy. James tried to hold the child back, but with a wriggle the kid was under his arm, pressing his face to the rail. James set his hands firmly on the boy's shoulders, thinking, little bird bones. The boy twisted to look up at him.

"Está muerto?" he asked.

James nodded. "Sí."

The boy's eyes were shining.

Out front, an engine roared to life. "Hey, Leonardo," James said. "How'd you get here? Where's your Cherokee?" Leo kicked the sparrow into the creek, and the boy's shoulders jumped. From inside the cantina, Efraín said, "Roberto. Ven acá." *Come here*. The boy twisted free of James. He ran to his mother, who was moving table to table, clearing dishes.

James said to Leo, "Your buddy seems to have left without you."

Leo scrambled up the bank. "What the fuck—" He swung his legs over the rail. He trotted around the side of the building, but returned within seconds. Now he headed for their table inside. He searched through the mess on the floor, thrusting the chairs in and out. He said to Teresa, "Hey, señorita, where'd my money go?"

Teresa added another plate to the stack.

Leo said, "Hey, I'm talkin' to you!"

Wordlessly, Teresa set the plates down. She took her boy by the hand and led him off to the kitchen. "*Hey!*" Leo started after them, but now Efraín was rapping his broom handle on the bartop. "¡Mira! ¡Mira!" Leo turned. Efraín leaned the broom against the counter and stepped back and dipped his hands into his apron pocket. He scooped the bills up for display, then pushed them down again.

"Hey, that's fucked!" Leo said. "That money's mine. By rights, I should've won that hand."

Efraín said, "I am not keeping it." He lifted the broom handle and poked at La Muerte. The statue swung; the hatchet in its hand rose and fell. "Semana Santa," Efraín said. "A time to give to the poor."

"*I'm* the poor," Leo said. "I give to *me*."

Efraín said, "You will leave now. And you won't show your face here again."

"Fine!" Leo walked out onto the patio, then turned around and came back and kicked at a chair. Then he left for good.

The room was empty but for James and Efraín.

"Más mejor," Efraín said. *Much better*.

The tables stood half-cleared, half-piled with dirty dishes. The floor was crusted with broken glass and spilled food, cigarette butts strewn everywhere. Efraín saw James looking. "You eat, and you drink. So later, we clean." He turned the radio up on yet another love song, a woman's voice snaking around a guitar. Te quiero. *I love you*. So sweet, thought James. He could hear Efraín's wife and daughter singing along, the voices coming through the closed kitchen door.

Outside, a blue light washed the creek and the trees, the iron tables, the sky. Dusk. The sparrows on their branches looked like tiny pinecones.

Efraín swiped a damp rag across the bartop. "Ese malvado," he said. "Your partner needs to pick his friends more carefully."

James said, "Leo's young."

"He's a worthless fuck. Greedy."

"Everybody's greedy." James thought about Anteater and the pollos' stolen shoes. Then he thought about Lara Shipp Santana's will. He dug into his pocket, pulled out the bills, counted two hundred, and set the cash on the bar—only to have Efraín ignore it. "For Holy Week, buddy," James said. "Okay," Efraín said, but he didn't pick up the money. Gratuitously James added, "Another contribution from INS." He didn't know why he was defending Leo. Almost everything the guy did set him on edge. But it bothered him to hear Leo called bad.

And so, twenty minutes later, when he drove up on his partner slogging along the side of the road, instead of passing by, he slowed the truck and threw the passenger door open and yelled, "Get in. I'll give you a lift." Leo set his hands on his hips. His face was flushed, his eyes very blue. For just a moment his expression was so calculating, James considered that in stopping he'd made a mistake. But Leo was already climbing into the seat. He slammed the door, lifted his legs and settled his feet on the dash. The smell of his aftershave permeated the cab.

James said, "You didn't have be such an ass."

"Wanted my money, is all," Leo said.

"It was *my* money."

"You're a fucking cheat."

"It's only a game." James reached over and pushed at Leo's head. "What goes on in that thick skull."

Leo jerked away. "Don't touch me, okay?"

James said, "What're you up to, buddy?"

"What do you mean?"

"You know exactly."

Leo sighed. "Let me tell you a little story. How once was a guy wanted more than anything in the world to get the baddies. Chase 'em down, bring 'em to justice, make 'em pay. So this guy went into law enforcement and it was a pretty good gig for him. The job used his best abilities. And *fuck*, it was fun, too. Big wide world. Guy sure liked the taste of the gun.

"But came a day when he ran up against—well, let's call it an opportunity. And suddenly the baddies didn't look quite so bad. Nothing's ever just black and white, James, there are all those nice shades of gray. You can appreciate that, can't you? How a little dirt never hurt anyone."

"Don't kid yourself," James said. "You're taking advantage."

"Of who? The pollos?"

"Yeah, the pollos."

Leo laughed. "You forget, I've seen you in action. Push comes to shove, you look out for number one. No, you're just trying to bust my balls here. . . . You know how much money that fucking coyote makes?"

"You're not on that side."

"What side is that?"

"I don't believe it!"

"*What?* What don't you believe? That it's money makes the world go round?"

"Stay away from that guy! You're an officer of the law." Desmond's words and Desmond's tone. James didn't like that. He felt goaded and put-upon. He asked now, "Why'd you bring him to Efraín's? Why'd you stick it right in my face?"

"Richie wanted to meet you."

"Me? What for!"

"You're such a stiff, James. Just forget it. It's none of your fucking business."

"I'm your partner—"

"Change that if you want to."

"I can make it my business."

"Well, I should've known you'd say that." Leo snorted. "'Cause you always act like everything's yours. Like that's the way it should be."

A half-mile of silence, and then James felt obliged to point out, "I can make it Tommie Yard's business, too."

"That, old man, would be a mistake."

"Meaning what?" James tightened his hands on the wheel.

"You figure it out."

Leo told James to drop him in El Pilón.

James braked at the top of the hill. Leo got out and James watched him lope off down toward the square, where in the last hours nothing had changed but the angle of light. Purple blooms still drifted from the jacarandas. The same viejos sat motionless at the picnic table. And there was Leo, striding into the scene, his elongated shadow slanted behind him, following.

CHAPTER FIVE

At midnight the stationhouse parking lot was lit like a stage, crawling with firefighters, patrols, and uniformed cops. Jeeps and Explorers were parked willy nilly, lights flashing, and someone, somewhere, tested a siren—an operatic yowl.

Drawn by the commotion, a number of citizens had gathered on the sidewalk in front of the house. They booed as patrols marched in and out, until one agent finally turned to the crowd, showed his teeth, and waved like a movie star at a premiere. The spectators broke into enthusiastic applause.

James pushed on through.

The boss was passing out equipment at the back of the locker room. Yard sat at a card table, baggy-eyed and bloodshot. His hands shook like maracas.

Holding an imaginary phone to his ear, James said, "Withdrawal, boss?"

"Eighteen hours I been in this shithole," Yard said. "You missed muster, Reese."

"Sorry, boss."

Yard shoved a pile of gear at him: Nomex jumpsuit, heavy fire-proof gloves, steel-reinforced rubber boots. "Air-paks are already checked and loaded. Go get yourself dressed."

James found Leo on the bench in front of his locker, suited up, a helmet laid in his lap. His right leg jiggled, enough energy there to power half of Corville.

"Nervous, buddy?" James asked.

"Fuck, no." Metal doors banging shut echoed around them. "The fire ants say they want us to bust a move. You notice," Leo consulted his watch, "here I sit."

James placed the firesuit on the bench. He stripped off his uniform.

"So," Leo drawled. "You make up with the little woman?"

For a second, James didn't know whom he meant—no one referred to Mercedes that way—then the gist of the question sunk in.

He said into his locker, "Why would I need to?"

"Well," Leo said, "she seemed a little ticked off."

James slammed the door. "When'd you talk to my wife?"

Leo shrugged.

This was news. Mercedes had said not a word. James shook out the firesuit and stepped into the legs.

"Don't worry," Leo said, "I won't give you away."

And what was that supposed to mean? James yanked the zipper, and closed the Velcro. He bent to snap the legs' cuff adjusters.

"Personally," Leo said, "I don't give a fuck whether you've got something going on the side. But if I'm supposed to lie, you might want to fill me in in advance."

James tugged on his boots. He stamped his feet.

Leo scraped his voice up into a whining falsetto. "You never tell me anything."

Shaking his head, James trudged off to the lounge.

Already, he was roasting like a son-of-a-bitch in the gear. He got a drink of water from the cooler, eavesdropping on a group of patrols who were swapping descriptions of the ugliest girl they'd ever fucked, each account topping the one previous, until the last featured a lady three-hundred pounds, one-eyed, one-legged, pock-marked, and bald. Shotgun laughter burst from the patrols, and James crumpled the paper cup and tossed it into a can. He wiped his lips with the back of his hand.

Why had Leo talked to his wife?

Back down the hall, lights were on in the photography lab. James stuck his head in, saw Charlotte's purse on the floor. A red bulb winked above the closed darkroom door. James went over and raised a hand. He hesitated, then knocked.

"Just a minute," Charlotte called.

He shifted his weight from one leg to the other. The minute came and went. Finally, Charlotte said, "Okay, you can come in."

Entry was on the dry side of the darkroom: enlarger; a plastic drawer filled with tools; a half dozen boxes of photo paper. James swept aside the dividing curtain. He found Charlotte standing at a small sink. She'd submerged a print in a tray filled with developer, and was gently rocking it. As she worked, her shoulderblades moved under her thin cotton shirt. Like wings, he thought. In the amber safelight, her upswept hair shone like polished brass.

She removed the print with plastic tongs, and slipped it into the stop bath. From there it went into fixer, then under running water. She squeegeed the photo on an overturned tray. The finished product was clipped to a clothesline.

"Twice in one week," Charlotte said. "To what do I owe the honor, Jamie?"

Without answering, he stepped forward to inspect the wet photograph: a large dog and a buffed-out cop, that telltale shadow darkening his chin. James felt a little drumbeat of jealousy.

"Ugly mutt you got there," he said.

"Your reading. Mine says he's very friendly. Loyal, too." James opened his mouth, but Charlotte put up a hand. "Don't, please.

Whatever it is, I don't want to hear. I can't help. And it's not fair of you to ask."

James stiffened. "Who says I'm asking?"

Someone was pounding on the darkroom door. "Hey! You in there, old man?"

James went to the darkroom's dry side. He laid his ear to the door.

"Come out, come out, wherever you are!"

The smirk in his partner's voice made James's hands go to fists. Behind him, Charlotte said, "Oh, God. Just let it go."

"I'm sure you're busy," Leo said, "but the troops are hot to trot."

James wanted to throw the fucking door.

"*Jamie*," Charlotte said.

He opened up.

"I knew it!" Leo slicked a hand along the side of his head. "Fuck, you are a sly bastard, James. But we got to burn when we got to burn, never mind that you're already on fire!"

On horseback, they followed the jeeps east along the highway, past the last of the housing developments and into the parking lot of a brand-new supermarket. A silver-bellied water truck had been set up around back, at the foot of a loading dock, the jeeps all nosed in like piglets at a sow.

A dozen firefighters squatted around a field map spread on the ground, while Danny Patillo passed out two-way radios. Unlike the patrols, the firefighters wore full turnout, layers and layers of space-age materials, waterproof, heatproof, and acidproof.

Patillo played a flashlight over the map, following a hairline contour that swept north from the border. "*Here*." He stabbed a finger at a blue-lined canyon, the same canyon where James had captured the half-naked pollo. "Two miles," Patillo slid his finger south, "and here's our baseline. It isn't deep at this point, so we should have no trouble at all getting in. And that bend there. That sharp angle makes for a natural break. We'll start the fire and it should run lickety-split right on up. Walls'll contain it, no problem whatsoever." He gestured at the silver-bellied truck. "Water's waiting here in the lot, ready to kill whatever flames make it this far. Tomorrow, if the arroyo's still on fire, the air corps can come in and douse."

"Good piss oughta do it," somebody said.

Scattered laughter, and Patillo set a proprietary hand on the map. "Pay attention," he said, "while I outline the plan."

They rolled out over the sands, all headlights and engine roar, no need for stealth tonight. A quarter mile south, Patillo gave a signal and the jeeps split apart. Three sets of red lights jounced east across a shallow cut in the canyon, while the other two vehicles, along with James and Leo on horseback, continued on the western side. Over the next mile, the chasm deepened and spread, and then one of the vehicles braked, disgorging two firefighters, men who would monitor the upper fireline.

The second jeep rumbled on.

James rocked in the saddle, the reins loose in his hands. The sky showed thickets of stars, and mountains poked like teeth from the curve of earth's jaw. The air smelled like rain. He watched an eagle drop straight to the sands, then rise again as if pulled by a wire, some kind of small prey dangling from its feet.

Leo, he noted, was skirting the canyon's edge, riding too close and too fast, his yellow suit splashed like a premonition of fire across the mare's back.

Another half-mile. Then James heard the faint grinding of gears. His radio clicked and popped. Patillo said something he couldn't quite catch. Ahead, the jeep swung to the canyon's lip: the designated baseline.

James rode up on the group, everyone gathered again around Patillo's chart, spread this time across the jeep's hood. Patillo raised the rest of the crew by radio, and one by one, they confirmed instructions.

Patillo looked up at James. "We're right on the line, I believe."

James peered into the canyon, five feet deep and forty across, a sharp bend to the east.

"Might even be over," he said.

"We're not supposed to burn old México."

"The Federales don't like smugglers any more than we do."

"Good." Patillo grinned. "Let's clean it out."

While James dismounted, Patillo pulled a rag from his coat and held it over his head. The rag fluttered.

"Five knots, I'd guess," he said. "Out of the south. Let's go!"

The firefighters emptied shovels from the back of the jeep. A gas-powered saw, a pick ax and several extinguishers. Patillo jumped down into the canyon, and the firefighters fed him tools, then followed after. James dropped down, too. Patillo set everyone to clearing a seven-foot swath. The east-angled wall provided a decent break, but the extra buffer would prevent the fire from traveling south.

The crew worked for several minutes, dried branches splintering under the saw and the pick. James shoveled. He tore at the loosened brush, scrape of metal on rock. Soon he was sweating copiously inside the suit.

Stopped to catch his breath, he saw Patillo with hands on his hips, staring up at the canyon's edge. "Hey, Tutrone," he yelled, "get your ass down here now!"

Leo stepped away from the jeep. When he hit bottom, Patillo had a shovel waiting.

When the buffer was finally cleared to Patillo's satisfaction, the firefighters used their extinguishers to soak the scrub on the Mexican side. Then Patillo sent everyone back up the wall. He strode to the middle of the clearing, retrieved the rag from his pocket and held it high. "Still south, southwest," he said into his radio. "It's picked up a little. Seven knots? Just means we'll get to go home early. Everyone ready?"

Yes, *yes*, and *yes*.

"All right. Put on your paks. I'm going to set the headfire now."

Leo handed out air-paks from the back of the jeep. James shrugged into his. He secured his helmet under his chin.

Down in the canyon, Patillo fired up the drip torch. At the edge of the east wall, he addressed the flame to the brush.

James thought: *Fuel, oxygen, heat.* And *flashpoint*: the temperature at which a fire ignites.

A burst of yellow light, a whispered crackling.

A thin column of smoke twisted into the air, like the trailings of a phantom cigar. Walking slowly, Patillo dipped the torch every few yards, then scrambled up the side to join the others.

At first, the fire didn't do much. A little smoke, a lick of flame. A gust of wind blew.

There was a whooshing sound as the brush exploded. The line of fire passed forward and another section caught. Another. The smoke thickened and flames leaped, rising briefly above the canyon walls. The fire was rippling northward, slowly at first, then yards at a time and picking up speed. Within a few minutes, it had generated so much smoke so far ahead that James could no longer pinpoint the advance.

At baseline, the brush had been taken down to the ground. The blackened floor bubbled like a cauldron.

Leo stood beside James. "Wicked," he said.

Patillo raised his eye shield. "Piece of cake. Absolutely textbook." He spoke into the radio. "Anybody up there got it yet?"

A voice returned, "Nosir, but I see it coming."

"All right," said Patillo. "I'm leaving one man here at baseline. The rest of us will follow the blaze."

* * *

But when they caught up, the action had slowed. The canyon ran deepest at this particular point, with less oxygen available to fuel the flames. James walked his horse along the rocky lip. He looked down on a slow boil of orange and red, billows of smoke that erupted like rain clouds from deep underground.

Leo trotted up beside him. "What say we go on ahead? Tell some fortunes, read some lifelines!" Code for a patrol's second sight: the ability to track pollos that had left no trace.

Before James could answer, Leo spurred his mare and charged off, a challenge left hanging. James knew he shouldn't do it, but followed. Leo had the mare in a raging gallop. And why was he in such a goddamned hurry?

Ahead, Leo stopped and dismounted and walked to the canyon's edge. He was waiting near the cut in the rock that served as a path. James reined up with a weird sense of dislocated pursuit, himself on the horse, Leo down on the ground.

Leo looked over a shoulder at him. "Pinche pollos," he said.

The quarterhorse snorted and stamped.

James said, "Are you kidding me?"

"I know they're down there."

"Based on what?"

"The *smell*."

But James smelled only fire, and horseflesh, and his own acrid stink. But he dismounted and joined Leo at the edge. Below were tangles of brush, a wink of broken glass. To the south, the smoke gently rolled, the lights of Patillo's jeep crawling above. To the north, more headlights flashed.

Leo flipped his eye shield.

James said, "There's nothing there."

"What are you—blind?" Leo stepped onto the path.

"You can't go down."

"Watch me, James." And Leo was off.

James raised Patillo on the radio.

"What is it!"

"Leo's gone into the canyon—"

"*What?*"

"He thinks there's pollos."

Leo had made it to the canyon floor and was headed north, thrashing through the brush. James looked past him; he thought he saw a little movement ahead. At the same moment, Leo twisted and stared up the rock wall.

James said into the radio, "I'm going down, too."

"Goddamnit, James!" said Patillo. "You *wait*!"

But James had started down.

The rumble of the fire increased with each step, the sound trapped by the canyon's rock walls. At bottom, the smoke seemed closer than it had from the ridge. James could just see Leo's firesuit through the brush. He plowed after it, aiming for the yellow as if for a raft.

When the branches unexpectedly thinned, he heard a roar behind him. He glanced back and saw flames. *Impossible.* He buckled at a blast of hot air.

Funneled between the steep canyon walls, the fire had leapfrogged ahead of the smoke. Another wave of scalding heat broke. Reeling, James swung his head away. He realized the fire had passed the cut in the rock. That avenue of escape was now lost. His heart thudded. He couldn't think of anything worse. And then he ran out of air.

Disbelieving, he sucked at the mask. Nothing. *Nothing.* He yanked it off, shrugged his shoulders free of the air-pak. Christ. The gauge read empty. *Impossible.* James's eyes burned and teared. He choked on the taste of liquefied sand. He bent over, gasping, and when he straightened, Leo was facing him from a few feet away.

James cried, "I'm out of air!"

Leo stood like a wrestler, knees bent, arms held out from his sides. His eyes behind the shield locked onto James, who saw a flicker of something there. Something that intended him harm. Then Leo's face crumpled. "God almighty, *fuck*!" he cried. "Here it comes!"

The wind pushed a fat wall of smoke. Embers rained. A possum burst squealing from the brush. Then they were engulfed in blackness and staggering heat. The fire shrieked, it was like the mouth of a dragon, and James couldn't move, couldn't think.

Leo grabbed his arm and dragged him forward. The second they'd outrun the smoke, Leo pulled off his mask. He clamped it over James's mouth and nose, and James filled his lungs. Leo took the mask back, and breathed. He threw his arms against the rock wall, seeking handholds and footholds, a way to climb out.

James stared up the fifteen-foot face.

There were firesuits up top, voices blaring through a bullhorn, a dangling rope. Leo swung the rope to James, indicating that he should go first. James started to climb, Leo right behind him. The rock was slippery and twice James slid down, his hands skipping along the rope, his legs banging into Leo's shoulders.

Almost up, the brush below ignited with a howl. James's feet felt seared through the soles of his boots. He was encased in an envelope of scorched air.

A firefighter reached down and tugged at his hands. Someone else gripped him under the arms and dragged him forward. He fell gagging and coughing onto the sand.

A second later, Leo stretched out beside him. In one movement, they rolled onto their backs and gaped at the sky.

James trembled violently; he was cold all over. A firefighter bent over him, asking questions he couldn't understand, let alone answer. Then the firefighter disappeared. James heard Patillo's baritone crackling from a radio. Leo said, "C'mon, old man, let's check it out. See what we missed." Cocky bastard, thought James. But Leo was right: he wanted to *see*. They crawled the few feet to the edge.

The canyon shimmered, filled with an otherworldly red light.

Leo said, "That's what hell looks like, James."

Behind them one of the firefighters said, "Anyone's down there, they're barbecue."

Leo started laughing. James caught it, hilarity bubbling up from his chest. Christ, it hurt. But he was alive. Sputtering and choking, he suddenly needed to stand. He lurched to his feet, weak-kneed, exhilarated, hollowed out at the core.

Leo was standing now, too. He put a hand on James's shoulder, and James, very carefully, stepped back.

B y the time they returned to the supermarket parking lot, the fire had also arrived, short flames leaping from canyon to asphalt. The pumper truck had been moved, and two firefighters aimed thick hoses at the blaze. With nothing left to burn, it was quickly finished. The smoke went from black to gray to white. James couldn't believe it was over, all that apocalyptic power reduced to *hiss* and *spit*.

Inside the EMT vehicle, a medic examined his nose and throat, listened to his chest and took his blood pressure. All were within normal range. "You're lucky," the medic said. "But later, your throat might swell up bad. Or you might get confused. You gotta go to the hospital if you get confused." He gave James some Tylenol with codeine for the pain. Breathing from an oxygen mask, James lay down on a cot and waited for the pills to kick in. The medic filled in his forms. When he'd finished, he reached into a backpack. He brought out a yellow pad, set it on his lap, and started to write.

After a while, James took off the mask. He sat up and said, "I'm okay." The medic frowned, but didn't protest.

Standing, James's vision reddened in pieces, like a jigsaw puzzle breaking apart, then all at once cleared. He climbed down from the ambulance.

While he'd been resting inside, the sun had come up.

He saw Leo at the edge of the lot, stroking the neck of his mare. James's quarterhorse nosed in a patch of grass. He wondered briefly who'd ridden him back.

Danny Patillo came barreling around the side of the ambulance. Head to toe, he was covered in soot.

"Hey!" he said. "There you are, James. How you doing?"

"I've been better." Even with the codeine, it hurt him to speak.

"You gave us a scare." Patillo rubbed his face, smearing the ash. "I know you don't feel up to much now . . . but I've got to ask something. What'd you think you were doing down there?"

"Pollos," James said. It wasn't the whole truth, but Danny didn't have to know that.

"So I heard. But you had no business. I told you to wait."

"I know. I'm sorry. I—" James stopped. He felt Leo staring at him. It made him crazy. And then it made him mad. He started off across the lot. A walk turned into a jog, James weaving in and out of the crowd. "What the fuck, Leonardo!" he cried, pulling up short before his partner. "What happened down there?"

Several firefighters turned to look.

Leo smoothed the mare's neck. "What happened is I saved your bacon, old man."

"What else?" James demanded.

"Bacon. As in: your life."

"But what else!" He knew there was something else.

Leo stuck his chin out. "You got a language problem, James."

"What is it you want?"

"A pad at the beach. And to fuck Cindy Crawford every night of my life."

Somebody laughed.

Leo turned his head and James caught a hint of greenish-yellow through the soot on his partner's cheekbone. Christ. That bruise he'd given the guy was still there. James remembered now why he'd done it. They'd been parked at the curb outside his house, drinking the last of too many beers. That old Beatles song, *Lady Madonna*, had come on the radio and Leo, giggling, had confessed that he'd always thought the words were, *Knee deep in doughnuts*. James watched the curtains flutter in the living room window—Mercedes was there—and he said to Leo, *You're a fucking idiot*. Then he climbed out of the Jeep and over the grass, thinking only of how much he needed to get into bed with his wife. But Leo was right behind him. *Fuck you, old man*, he'd said, *everybody's done that, messed up the words, you've done that, James, I know you have*— and of course, it was true, though now he couldn't ever say so. And then Leo jumped him and they were rolling on the wet grass. The front door opened just as James landed a punch below Leo's left eye. He remembered Mercedes standing on the steps in her night-gown, her hair loose, arms crossed protectively over her breasts. *Shame on you*, she'd mouthed at James. But he didn't care. He'd been glad.

A gust of wind threw scarves of smoke to the east, the sun's glow hidden briefly behind a gray veil. James felt a prickling in back of his lids. His throat ached. Suddenly, he was very sorry.

But then he remembered the look in Leo's eyes—down in the canyon. What did it *mean*?

Patillo had come up beside them. Danny glanced from James to Leo and back again. "Troublemakers," he said.

Unfazed, Leo said, "You going to search for bodies tonight?"

"Karma," Gordon Jenks said to James. They were in the barn, smell of oats, timothy grass, horseshit, and fire. The hand was watering Leo's black mare. He'd already seen to James's quarter-horse. "What goes around comes around, Jimbo," he said.

"Meaning?"

"Meaning the chasers can always become the chasees. You ought to remember that."

The mare tossed her head, throwing the empty bucket.

Jenks grabbed the handle and went to the spigot for a refill. Back in the stall, he set the bucket in the ledge hole, water slopping over the sides.

The mare drank, slowly now, one red eye on James.

Jenks sat on the three-legged stool. He lit a cigarette, took a drag, and blew out a series of perfect smoke rings.

"We went in to save them," James said, finally. "Wasn't anybody chasing us."

"No?"

"No."

"How 'bout that fire?"

James threw up his hands.

Inside, he found the stationhouse crowded again, dozens of sooty footsteps marring the floors. Firefighters and patrols stood in small groups, gulping coffee from Styrofoam cups between bites of a coconut cake someone's wife had brought in. Their voices were raucous as they relived the fire.

Still in a slight codeine haze, James glided past the photography lab, empty now, Charlotte gone home. In the locker room he shed the firesuit. He changed back into his uniform and dumped the suit into a hamper. Then he stopped by the boss's office, intending to have a word with Tommie Yard. But Yard wasn't there. In the hall, James ran into Leo, who said, "There's somebody waiting for you in the lounge. Corner table."

Detective Raymond Fricke. In his ice-cream suit and yellow tie. Sitting alone, Fricke sipped coffee and flipped through a dog-eared magazine. He seemed oblivious to the clamor around him.

Goddamnit, thought James. And what does *he* want?

He stalled at the coffee machine, pouring himself a hot cup. He lifted a slice of coconut cake onto a paper plate and carried it to the table. Dropping into a chair, he pushed the cake at Fricke. The detective looked up from his magazine.

"What a good host," he said.

James stuck his nose in his cup and sniffed. Woodsmoke. The idea of drinking it made his throat close.

"Big night around here," Fricke said. "Looks like quite the celebration."

James sighed. "I'm whipped, Detective. Could you get to the point?"

"All right." Fricke crossed his legs and picked at the knees of his cream-colored pants, and James glimpsed tasseled brown loafers, brown and red argyle socks. "All right," Fricke said again. "About that kid found up at your dad's. Nobody's come forward to claim the body. Don't you think that's a little bit strange?"

"Not really," James said. "The relatives are hiding." Likely, they'd cleared out long before the body was cold.

"They're all wetbacks, of course." Fricke reached for the slice of cake. He brought it to his mouth, but didn't bite. "Wouldn't you think they'd want to give the boy a proper burial? Consecrated ground and all that. He's got to be Catholic, most Mexicans are. Why else put that rosary in his hands?" Fricke set the cake down. "You know, Reese," he said, "for a former cop, your father is pretty goddamn unforthcoming."

James didn't need to hear this.

"He hasn't been any help," Fricke said.

"What, exactly, would you like Desmond to do?"

"Produce *all* his workers. For one."

James shrugged. "You have Rafael Noyez."

"But he isn't the only wet your father's got on that farm. You know that. But god*damn*, the others seem to have up and disappeared. And Noyez isn't talking. I might have to charge him."

"You don't believe he killed that kid."

"No, but I'm pretty goddamn sure he knows what happened."

"Which is what? What'd the coroner say?"

"The boy died of asphyxiation. It's preliminary at this point, but I can't see what else lines up." Fricke finally took a bite of the cake.

He chewed, shreds of coconut stuck to his lips. "No sexual molestation," he said.

James grimaced. "Small favors."

"The only thing in the kid's stomach was a little candy. Tootsie Roll." Fricke licked his fingers, then sighed. "I wish I had a coherent scenario . . . but that's why I'm here. I'd like you to tell me again. That morning, what were you doing up in Marquette?"

"You aren't serious."

"You bet I am. I'd like to find out where your father gets his workers."

"What does that have to do with anything?"

"For one, a truthful answer might bring me closer to knowing why the boy died."

"I imagine," James said tightly, "Desmond gets them the same place as everyone else. The coyotes have a line on what farms are hiring. Probably, the pollos come to Des."

"Probably? Brought by whom?"

James felt the blood in his face. "I don't need this shit!"

"Oh, yeah." Fricke leaned in. "Don't think I wasn't watching. You and Daddy out in that field. Getting soaked, putting your heads together. Made me wonder what you were talking about."

CHAPTER SIX

In bright sunlight, the model home at Sandpiper Point looked like a toy. Baby junipers popped against sand-colored dirt. Pink plastic pennants snapped in the breeze. Both trucks were parked at the house-in-progress, beds loaded with pallets of saltillo tiles; but the site felt deserted. No hammering, James realized. No sawing, no radio, no barking black dog.

He walked up the drive. And there they were, Mercedes and Carlos and Rubén, sitting cross-legged on the foundation, their three heads bowed. Carlos was the first to look up, and James saw that his brother-in-law was annoyed. Clearly, he was interrupting something.

"Loafing so early?" he joked. "It's only seven."

"Ramirezes don't never loaf," Carlos said.

"Oh, c'mon. You loaf *some*times. You—"

"Hey, James!" Rubén interrupted. "How come your face is so red?"

90

Mercedes stood. She came over and placed a cool hand on his cheek. "Been having a moon bath, eh, corazón?" Then, looking more closely, "Jesus, are you all right?"

The fire had singed his lashes and brows, and his features, he knew, looked oddly bald, left to fend for themselves. "Surface damage only," he said. "Though I could use some nursing." He waggled his brows. James had neglected to clean himself up at the station, and he knew he made a less than appealing prospect, but he said anyway, "Come home with me."

Ordinarily this would've elicited catcalls and whistles from the brothers, but both were strangely silent today.

A long moment passed.

Mercedes said, "This is not a good time."

"Obviously." James looked at Carlos. "What's going on here?"

"Just a little family meeting, ese."

The implication being that that did not include James.

Rubén grinned sheepishly.

Mercedes gave James's arm a light squeeze and said, "I'll walk you, okay?"

He let her lead him back down the drive. They stopped between the two trucks, and James chewed the inside of his cheek, looking from one bed to the other. Something was wrong. The last he'd seen these saltillos, they'd been stacked up at the back of the site, waiting to be turned into a kitchen floor and a covered patio.

"You're taking them back?" he asked.

Mercedes nodded.

"Are they the wrong size?"

She folded her arms. "We need money for lumber. We've got to finish framing today. It'll look better for the bank."

"Uh-oh," he said. "The bank?"

"I can't talk now, James. Really. I've got to get back." She turned to go.

"Mercedes, wait." James grabbed her wrist to stop her. "I want to ask you something." He could feel her impatience, and he closed her hand in his own. "Why'd you marry me?" His lips were cracked, sticky on the *m* words.

She gave him a half smile. "What kind of a question is that?"

He didn't know. He hadn't exactly planned to ask it. He suspected it had something to do with Leonardo. But he couldn't say so.

"I was just wondering," he said.

"All right," she said. "I liked it how after you came to dinner that first time you wrote my mother a nice thank-you note. Nobody I went out with ever did that . . . and I liked it that you're ticklish under the arms, like a little boy. I liked it that you ironed your own shirts."

James said, "The bachelor's way."

"You could have sent them out. A lot of guys do."

"Too cheap, I guess."

Mercedes shook her head. "The point is," she said, "you don't fit. I liked that."

It took him by surprise. "I fit," he said.

"You're so quiet," she said. "Everyone in my family talks too damn much."

James thought a moment. "Liked," he said, finally. "Do you still?"

"The quiet part? Not so much," she admitted. She glanced back at her brothers. "But I can't do this now. We'll talk at home, later, okay? Before Mama's party."

He'd clean forgotten the dinner at Cruz's tonight, a celebration for Yolie and Rubén, a last chance for the families to get together before the wedding.

"Do me a favor," Mercedes said. "Go straight to bed. Get some sleep, okay? You look like you need it."

"Okay," said James.

But halfway down the block he thought he heard her calling his name. He turned. Mercedes had her hands cupped to her mouth. "Meet me!" James nodded and waved.

Later, he decided that what she'd actually said was, "Sweet dreams."

James couldn't sleep. He ran a lengthy shower instead and scrubbed himself raw, until the water turned cold. His throat was hurting like a bastard again. When he got out, he chewed four Tylenol, one after the other, then wrapped himself in a towel and lay on the bed. He stared at the ceiling. There were cracks in a corner he'd never noticed before. It bothered him; the house wasn't that old. He shut his eyes and tried to relax. It was noisy inside his head, but he wasn't interested in listening now. After a few minutes, he got up again. He dressed in a T-shirt and jeans and decided to putter around the house for a while. He fixed a leaky faucet, paid bills, ran a load a of laundry. Late afternoon, he crawled beneath the covers again, and this time he overslept, waking groggy and disoriented only when Mercedes returned from the site. By then it was dark, well after eight, and they had to hustle to get over to Cruz's house, where the entire extended family and then some was seated in the tiny dining room. Flushed faces and bright eyes, jewelry and party clothes and salsa on the stereo. The air perfumed with the scent of roast chicken, onions, tortillas, and corn.

Up and down the table candlesticks flickered, the light playing across white dishes and sparkling silver, a brightly embroidered tablecloth, making of it all a scene from a movie, or a painting. Border Supper, maybe, thought James.

Ranged around the table were: Carlos, and Loretta, his girlfriend; Tío Manuel and Tía Alma and their twin daughters, aged about twelve; silver-haired Tío Arturo, the family's long-time bachelor. There was an older couple as well, people James didn't recognize. The man wore a blue pinstriped suit and a red tie, his neck and hands so thin he seemed made of kindling. The woman sat plump and pretty in a green satin suit.

Yolie's folks, James realized.

93

Cruz Ramirez occupied her usual seat, closest to the kitchen. Opposite, Rubén and Yolie reigned in matching armchairs.

The black dog sprawled beneath the buffet, one eye open, hoping for morsels dropped to the floor.

James and Mercedes's entry had prompted a chorus—¡Hola! ¡Buenas Noches! Dios Madre, and here you are at last!—and now Carlos said, "The party started an hour ago."

"The chicken," Cruz said, "is cold."

Rubén toasted James with a bottle of beer. His hair stood weirdly on end. "We're all legal here, man!" he shouted, and Yolie giggled, her round facing shining.

A lollipop of a bride, thought James.

Cruz served him from the buffet. "Sit, *sit*," she said. She piled a plate high with food, kicking absently at the black dog. The animal scrabbled to its feet and slunk to the kitchen entry, where it laid itself out like a rug.

Mercedes dropped into one of two empty chairs. James took the other, between his wife and Yolie's father, who offered a hand: brittle bones, a crushing grip. James smiled around him at the pretty wife, while Carlos called across the table, "What are you drinking, ese? Wine or beer?" His girlfriend Loretta said authoritatively, "He wants wine." James was wondering what it was about him that made her so sure, when Carlos tossed him a beer. James caught the flying bottle just in time. "Gotta watch the reflexes," Carlos said, grinning wickedly. Cruz, returned to her chair, reached out and slapped her son's hand. At the other end of the table, Tía Alma was singing along with the stereo, while Tío Arturo entertained the twins by folding his napkin into animal shapes. And as usual, James felt awkward, all wrong. The Ramirez family always had this effect. He belonged, and he didn't; he wanted their regard, but he also refused to give a goddamn.

He stared through the doorway into the living room, where a marble-topped table displayed the family altar, a photograph of Carlos Senior surrounded by religious statues and votive candles and fresh-cut flowers.

James felt Cruz giving him the fish-eye.

He said, "The food is delicious." He knew he was safe there.

"¡Pobrecito!" Cruz suddenly cried. "What on earth has happened to you?"

Carlos said, "He put his head in a oven."

Mercedes said, "He got caught in the fire."

All eyes were on James as he launched into an account of the burn, complete with unnecessary technical information, a description of turnout, the various pieces of firefighting gear, including his air-pak, which he mentioned had run out on him. There were a few sympathetic noises, a gasp from Yolie's mama. But when he backtracked to say something about the pollos down in the canyon, the atmosphere changed.

Cruz said, "James leaves no stone unturned."

He'd crossed the line here. He would always be la migra, and the son of a cop. The white boy with the Indian bones.

Carlos drawled, "But you rescued them, ese. Didn't you?"

The chill wore off, and the party went on, rise and fall, music and food and plenty to drink. James talked for a long time to Yolie's father, mostly about local politics. In the background, he heard Rubén discussing the band they'd hired for the wedding, Yolie describing her dress for the twins. After a while, Cruz brought out a cake and Carlos opened champagne. Standing, he rapped on a glass with the back of a knife. Over his mother's increasing protests, he told a series of unflattering stories about his little brother, all designed to illustrate Rubén's stupidity: the time Rubén jumped from the roof, using an old umbrella for a parachute; the time he got picked up for shoplifting a comb; the time he ditched school every day for a month. Cruz said huffily, "But he gets A's and B's," and Mercedes chimed in, "Better than you by a long shot, Carlos, eh?" Everyone laughed.

Mercedes had one long leg tucked up under her hip. She wore a red skirt, very short, and James traced the line of her bare foot where it intersected with thigh. He raised his eyes to her throat, that sweet curve of flesh.

Mercedes met his gaze. "We need to talk," she said. "And soon, corazón."

"Yes," he agreed.

"You remember," Carlos cried, "when I broke your arm?"

"You twisted it!" said Rubén. "Because I wouldn't share the Cocoa Crispies."

"You had to go to emergency—"

"—and Papa beat you so bad that you woke me up later and broke my finger, too!"

"We got a Popsicle from the freezer and ate it in bed. You used the stick as a splint." Carlos beamed. He swayed a little, and James realized that his brother-in-law was very drunk. He wasn't feeling so hot himself.

Then Yolie's father got to his feet and raised his glass high. He sucked on his puckered cheeks. "I should break something of Rubén's also, eh? And I don't mean his fucking finger!"

Again, everyone roared.

And then the women were clearing the plates, the men migrating to the living room. James sank into an easy chair, the shrine to Carlos Senior at his elbow, candlelight trembling in the corner of his eye. A serious discussion was well under way, the subject being the current baseball season. After much argument, a grudging consensus was reached that only a brainless fool could root for the Padres this year. Arturo threw out an invitation for any and all to accompany him Sunday to the dog races at Agua Caliente. Carlos said, That's Easter, man, and Arturo said, The dogs don't know that. Then the topic shifted to a local drug bust made earlier in the week and occupying daily column inches in the *Corville Border Call*: cocaine and marijuana and half a million in cash, all confiscated from a ranchito thirty miles west of town. Arturo and Manuel took the position that drugs were the scourge of modern life, the source of everything from teenage pregnancy to racial tensions to AIDS; that the DEA and the ATF and the FBI, etcetera, were all contemptible failures at keeping the poison out. Carlos said that half the guys he'd known in high school were locked up in jail for drug offenses. Rubén agreed; in his class, it was much the same. Yolie's father maintained that drugs were good for the economy. How else will we keep our young people employed? Carlos cried, The downfall of many for the benefit of a few! Arturo said, What else is new. James sat forward then. An interesting part of the proposition, he said, was how the cash got back into Mexico, back into the pockets of the cartels. No one thinks about that, how you have to complete the equation. We watch the borders so carefully. High tech, low tech, strip searches and dogs, all expended in an effort to stop drugs at the point of entry. And still it gets through. And what about the money-laundering schemes? What about the black-market Peso Exchange, where wire transfers and money orders moved dealer cash? One hundred and forty-thousand cars came through San Ysidro each day. It was the busiest gate along the entire border. But the traffic was two-way, product and cash, and who was watching as the money traveled back down?

"The BP, eh?" Manuel said. "You can catch them, James."

"We don't work that side of the line."

Arturo reached into his jacket and produced a handful of individually wrapped cigars. "Cuban," he said. "My drug of choice." There were appreciative murmurs as he passed them around. "A cousin sends them up from Guatemala."

"They're illegal, ese." Carlos winked at James. "Maybe you should make an arrest."

James stripped the cellophane from his cigar. He slid the smooth brown cylinder under his nose. Faint scents of vanilla and dung. He bit the end, and deposited it in an ashtray on the coffee table. He settled back in the chair. "Possession's okay," he said. "You just can't ship or receive." He pointed the cigar at Tío Arturo.

"Remember—you don't receive." A lighter was making the rounds but Arturo couldn't wait and he bent to light his off one of the candles at the altar.

"That's some disrespect there," Carlos complained.

"He was my brother," Arturo said. "He wouldn't mind."

Rubén said, "Just don't let Mama see you."

Arturo held the candle to James's cigar. James inhaled.

"Besides which," Arturo said, "James is too busy keeping undesirables out."

"Getting caught in fires," Carlos said, "and burning off his eyelashes."

James exhaled, his smoke mingling with the communal cloud.

Manuel said, "What do you mean, Arturo, by 'undesirables'?"

"You know perfectly well."

Yolie's father said stiffly, "I have been in this country since World War Two. You couldn't pay me to go back to México."

"Hey," Carlos said. "That's the Motherland you are talking about."

"What Motherland?" Arturo said. "You were born here, and your father, too."

"That doesn't mean I don't have the right loyalty."

"Alma," Manuel said solemnly, "is from Nicaragua. She takes the twins down to see her mother each spring. When she is angry with me she says she will stay."

The men smoked in silence, contemplating this threat.

Then Yolie's father said, "Does anyone know what has happened to Hector Reyes?"

Manuel said, "I heard he went back to Veracruz."

Arturo said, "I heard he opened a restaurant down there. Hector has a gift at the stove. Menudo so sweet it brings tears to the eyes."

There was music coming now from behind the closed kitchen door. Fast music, very loud, and a shriek of laughter that James recognized as belonging to his wife.

Yolie's father folded his kindling arms. "Men," he sniffed, "shouldn't cook."

James stuck his head into the kitchen and discovered a wild scene in progress, waving arms and gyrating hips, the women all dancing to oldies in their bare feet. A Philco radio sat like a fat Buddha on top of the refrigerator, belching music that crackled with interference. The Temptations sang: *Tweedledy-dee, tweedledy-dum, look out baby 'cause here I come!*

James stared in amazement at his mother-in-law. Cruz's shoulders shimmied and her silver hair flew. Every few steps she snapped a blue dishtowel at her daughter's ass. Mercedes, partnering Yolie, more or less, adroitly avoided the towel. The two young women separated and came together again, their movements synchronized.

James couldn't believe his beautiful wife, the color in her cheeks, her eyes shining.

When she saw him she curled an arm, luring him in. "Come, James. Be one of the girls."

He hesitated in the doorway.

"Don't be such a scaredy-cat, eh?"

Manuel and Alma's twins laughed and screamed, "No walking allowed! You have to dance in!"

Shoulders shrugging, James shuffled self-consciously over the floor. But when he reached Mercedes's side, the song stopped. The women froze giggling in place as the announcer's voice erupted in an unintelligible stream. Then opening rhythms were struck, a simple bass line and drum. "Stand by Me." The women paired up again, arms draped languidly around necks and waists.

James reached for his wife, but she slipped from his grasp. Mercedes's temples were beaded with sweat, the high color drained. She said, "I don't feel good, James."

Dishes were piled high in the sink. The room was thick with soapsuds and steam, the smell of burnt onions and chicken and cake. The oven door sat open, expelling volcanic heat.

"What is it?" he asked.

Mercedes put a hand on his elbow. "Do me a favor—dance with Yolie, okay?" She urged the girl at James. He took Yolie's wrist, watching Mercedes vanish out the back door.

He placed his other hand at Yolie's waist, and gathered her up. She tensed, and he was confused, and then offended, and then unsurprised: Yolie was young enough to be his daughter. He loosened his hold, providing a comfortable distance between their bodies. As Ben E. King crooned, they worked a square yard of tile, and gradually, James felt Yolie relax. She rested her head on his chest. Her hair, he noticed, smelled like licorice. The room was pleasantly hot and the music surged around him, and in him, a thumping warmth that spread up from his chest; and then there was a tap on his shoulder. Rubén pressed beer-flumed lips to James's ear. "So tell me, Papi, how does it feel?" Rubén stepped back and set his hands on his hips and tapped his toe in a parody of wifely impatience.

That suit, James thought, is too big on him. This skinny boy is too young by far.

Rubén opened his arms.

And James was just drunk enough that he imagined he was the one with whom his brother-in-law wanted to dance.

He found Mercedes in a corner of the back yard, playing with an old tetherball. The Ramirez brothers' first do-it-yourself project, if he remembered rightly, installed a decade ago, when Carlos Senior was still alive.

The pole, pitted with rust, leaned precariously from its concrete base. The boys' father had apparently encouraged them to make their mistakes. In concrete, thought James.

Mercedes drew back an arm and gave the ball a solid smack, and the chain wrapped clanging around the pole. Involuntarily, James put a hand to his neck. The air seemed to have revived his wife. When he stepped forward to return the serve, she crowed, "Ha! You don't stand a chance! I used to be school champion."

The ball sang past James's ear. But he got it the next time around, and they volleyed, the chain snapping in taut half-circles. And then James aimed high and struck hard. Mercedes ducked, backing away. She was crying—it shocked him. He stopped the ball. "What is it?" He came forward, but she put up a hand, then bent to wipe her eyes on her skirt. Her braid trailed over one shoulder. James could hear her shallow breathing. "I have to tell you," she said, "Ramirez and Son is officially dead. We're flat busted."

James said softly, "I figured. I'm sorry, honey."

"We've lost the building contract. Also—" Mercedes straightened, squaring her shoulders. "I'm pregnant, James."

His heart squeezed, his breath caught. He tasted fear and confusion and a tight-gripping joy.

Then he plucked a random thought: The baby was no accident.

"You just decided by yourself," he said.

"No. Not by myself."

"A big change like that."

"It's what you wanted, isn't it?" Mercedes's eyes glittered. "Tell me that you're happy, James."

He was happy—yes. Wasn't he? But he was also confused. They'd talked about this. Hadn't they? They weren't ready. *He* wasn't ready.

He said, "How long have you known?"

"A couple of weeks," Mercedes said.

"Why didn't you tell me?"

"The little kit, that thing from the drugstore, I just used it today. To be sure. But I already knew. I know when it happened, too. And so do you."

"What are you talking about?"

"Think. You'll remember."

But Christ, his head was spinning. He'd had too much to drink. The taste of cigar was like mud in his mouth, and his throat felt scraped raw, as if along with the liquor he'd drunk broken glass. *A baby*. He couldn't wrap his mind around it.

"I don't know," he said.

"¡Dios Madre!" Mercedes cried. "What is it that you're so afraid of? I know you had a hard time as a kid, and I'm sorry, but thirty years is long enough to suffer. Desmond and Marie have been good to you. Marie's a good mother. Desmond's a good father. Even I can see it. And I *love* you—but it doesn't seem to count for very much."

It does, James wanted to say, but his lips were made of rubber and he couldn't get the words out. He heard laughter and running water, a clatter of plates, and it felt as if these sounds were inside his head; then he turned and saw Loretta and Cruz at the sink, framed in white light. All along the house's back wall, uncurtained windows lined up like dominoes. The corner room was Rubén's. James could see the single bed, the automotive posters tacked on the wall.

So tell me, Papi, how does it feel?

Astonished, he said, "They know, don't they? All of them. You told them first."

"They're my blood, James. And they're happy for me. I wanted someone to be happy for me."

He was outside, looking in. He'd always come last. He felt sick and angry inside.

"How could you not remember?" she said. "You're always so motherfucking hungry. You eat me alive. But okay—okay. Then there's the other James. The one that's sleepwalking, eh? Acting like you don't have to touch anyone, because, hey, why bother, it's only a dream. What I want to know is when you're going to wake up."

Abruptly, James said, "Leo claims he's been talking to you."

Mercedes froze. "Oh, no, not this. Not now. Just because you don't like hearing the truth."

"You got secrets, honey?" James closed his eyes. "Well, you're entitled, I guess." He couldn't stop himself now. "And I can't pretend I haven't enjoyed the mystery. I can't—"

The kitchen door creaked. He opened his eyes. Light flooded the yard for a second before it went dark. He felt the slam in his bones.

CHAPTER SEVEN

A nd then he was standing in his front yard, dampened once again by the neighbor's sprinklers. James didn't mind. The chill felt good, a reminder to pay attention: This day wasn't over yet.

He surveyed his property. Tidy enough, the trim freshly painted, the windows cleaned, the walkway swept. A simple fact: James liked his modest house. He liked the way it sat there under the stars, square and silent and ordinary. Evidence of an ordinary life, one in which he worked hard, kept his head down, loved his wife, and was loved in return—Mercedes was wrong to think he didn't feel it. He knew that tonight he'd been a jerk. It wasn't the first time and would not be the last. The right words at the right time so often eluded him. And sometimes, a black fury rose up inside, and it scared him to think about where it came from and what he might do. But the point was, he tried to take care.

Maybe, he thought now, that wasn't enough. *A baby*, he thought. That changed everything.

A baby deserved—no, required—a rock-solid foundation, a haven, a place where life could safely begin. And James was scared he'd never have what it took to provide. Inside, where it counted. Because even on days when he felt most at home, days when he felt his skin fit and the world was welcoming, there was always something that could trip him up, something lurking in the background. An emptiness that wasn't empty at all, but filled with separate truths that implied an eventual reckoning. Because there were those cracks in the bedroom ceiling, the half-dead orange tree in the back yard. And right here, right now, all the windows in his house were dark. No candy-apple-red Ford sat parked in the drive.

A little spooked, James hurried inside. He headed for the kitchen, got a glass from the cupboard, and poured himself some milk. He sat at the table. It was a relief to think of nothing at all—except that he felt as if he were watching himself *thinking nothing*—and that propelled him up and out of the chair, into the bedroom, searching for the portable phone. He dialed Cruz Ramirez's house, but hung up before anyone had a chance to answer. *Coward.* Because Mercedes was there. Carlos and Loretta. Yolie and Rubén. Maybe even the future in-laws, still, ironing out the wedding's final details. It was less than a week until the ceremony at Holy Redeemer Church, where James and Mercedes had wed. The same priest would serve. Father Michael, who looked more like a model, with his lush lips and chiseled cheekbones. There'd be a nuptial Mass, and the gospel would be Jesus' first miracle, the wedding at Canaan, water turned into wine. A sermon on the sanctity of marriage, God's pleasure at the creation of a new family. Even, thought James, if you started a little early . . . but what did it *mean*? As a boy in L.A., he'd attended Mass just twice a year, Christmas and Easter, and once Emilio went to prison, not even then, Diego having decreed that science canceled out the existence of God.

Desmond and Marie hadn't gone in much for religion, either. Des had witnessed too much human misery to ever credit a merciful God.

James thought about Mercedes in the fourth grade, her lunch hours in church, waiting for visions and longing for martyrdom. What would make her desire such a thing?

And what about the pollo Leo had pulled from the van? The one with the scars down his back, lashes given in the sign of the cross. And La Muerte, that raw vision of death, hanging behind the bar at Efraín's. Santos and hymns, humiliation and suffering. At the cantina, each Saturday, James played cards and drank too much, ate too much and cursed a blue streak, and he was happy to be doing exactly that, and what did God have to do with it, anyway?

He was sweating, furnace-hot. He threw down the phone.

He decided to go out to the back yard.

There, against his skin, the night air drew down soft. The sky was black, the stars wavering as if seen through running water.

He stood on the deck, trying to settle on something to do. His gaze landed on the transplanted orange tree. Most of the leaves had already dropped, a not unexpected defeat. He got the hose out anyway. He pulled it over, went back to the spigot and turned on the water. Liquid pooled blackly around the tree's roots, bubbling as it seeped down into the soil. Maybe he could save the poor thing after all. Maybe, someday, they'd even have oranges. Baby oranges.

A baby, thought James. His and Mercedes's child.

He wished now that he'd asked her why.

Why she'd spoken to Leonardo, and what, exactly, they'd spoken about. And when and how often and was it in person or only on the telephone. Leo had taunted James, in the locker room before the fire. That much was clear, that throwing out the idea of a secret communication. James knew better—though why hadn't Mercedes told him?—and still he felt the bite of jealousy, felt it then and felt it now, teeth sunk and gnawing evilly at his soft gut. He knew he deserved that particular pain. Because the fact of the matter was that he'd stolen his partner's girl. Last summer, at a party at Leo's place, Mercedes had been the hostess and James just a guest. It was Leo's patio upon which they'd danced—once. A hot night, a white moon. Her hips rolling under his hands like a wave that never breaks.

Cold water spilled over his feet. Cursing, he tightened the spigot. As long as the ground had softened a bit, he might as well fertilize. He marched off to the garage, thinking now about Yolie and Rubén.

As far as he knew, the kids hadn't planned a honeymoon. Because Rubén was needed, and badly, on the site. But with the job lost, maybe they were free to head out. Where, James couldn't picture. For their honeymoon, he and Mercedes had driven up to Las Vegas. They'd caught Jay Leno at the Mirage, still in their wedding clothes. Afterward, they'd run the casino gauntlet—ringing bells, the chink of money falling—to the elevators. Their suite was at the top of a tower, with a view of black mountains and flashing candy-colored lights, but the principal feature was the round bed beneath a mirrored ceiling. Normally James didn't go in for that stuff, clichéd sexiness, manufactured delirium. But just the once, he allowed himself to get caught up in it, the sight of this second couple's bare skin and tangled limbs, the woman's hair spilled across the man's thighs. The bodies doubled seemed to be other people entirely, and the displacement excited him. The sexy disorder of it all. It felt good, it looked good. He could taste Mercedes's skin, feel her pulsing under his hands, and he could also watch her respond, watch her coming, watch twice. He could catch this woman at angles never possible before, and most likely, never possible again. Beauty hidden, beauty revealed. Well, from the moment he'd met her, she'd been *it* for him. The surprise was that for just that one night, his wedding night, James felt beautiful, too. His dick, his throat, his tongue and his hands, fingernails, the small of his back, the roots of his hair. He'd never slept so well in his life. The next morning, he and Mercedes had eaten a breakfast fit for truckers on a cross-country haul. Biscuits and eggs, bacon, sausage, waffles, cup after cup of coffee with sugar and cream.

They'd returned to the casino, where they'd lost more than twelve hundred dollars playing roulette, betting it all on the red. The chips swept away. But every loss felt like a gain.

And who, he wondered, were those reckless gamblers? A mirrored reflection of Mercedes and James? Who were they today, tonight, this very minute? More than the sum of their parts, he hoped, more than the individual definitions: husband and wife; construction worker, patrol; mother, daughter, father, son.

In the garage, the fertilizer was nowhere to be seen. Or else he couldn't find it—but hadn't he just had it out? He knew he wouldn't have stashed a forty-pound bag anywhere that required lifting it overhead, but he messed around on the shelves anyway, looking into coffee cans filled with nails, sacks of clothing Mercedes no longer wore. It was scary how much junk they'd acquired. They hadn't been married that long.

Reaching up onto an upper shelf, James's fingers closed on a small cardboard box. He slid it forward and pulled, grabbing at the falling box with two hands. He held it a moment, then turned it over. Ancient cellophane tape secured the box at every corner. He shook it gently and the contents rolled. Though it wasn't heavy, there was something about the weight—it made his spine stiffen, as if faced with a task that required strength—that gave him the idea this was what he'd been looking for all along.

He took a utility knife from a drawer and slit the tape. Then he carried the box out into the yard and sat on the grass beside the orange tree. Licking his lips, he glanced at the house. There was the bag of fertilizer, right where he'd left it, leaning against the kitchen's back wall. It occurred to him that feeding the tree again so soon would probably kill it.

He lifted the box's lid. Inside was a rag doll, a kaleidoscope, a rock.

The doll he had no memory of. But the kaleidoscope—that had been a gift from his father, Emilio. James lifted it from the box. He tilted his head back and peered through the viewing hole. The night was too dark and he couldn't differentiate colors at all, but when he twisted the tube, he got a sense of changing design.

He remembered how, long ago, in a prison visiting room, the child he'd once been had peered through this eyepiece. Startled at what he'd seen, he'd pulled back, flipped the device, and inspected the end, where the magic seemed to be trapped. How was it done? he'd wanted to know. He'd looked across the table, but his parents were busy kissing, Lara's blond head tipped up to Emilio's face. Lips and tongues, a pulse at his mother's neck. It made James feel funny inside. Tío Diego sat beside him, and he was looking, too. Diego let out a breath, a sound like a tire leaking air. He scooted his chair closer to James. There are mirrors inside, he whispered, and bits of colored glass. The possible patterns are nearly infinite. Mirrors? James thought; he didn't believe it. Diego might be the smart one in this family, the college kid, able to add columns of numbers in his head, but he didn't know everything. Go on, Jaime, Diego urged, look again. James looked. Twist it, Diego said. But James still did not understand. Diego reached over and turned the end piece for him and the colors exploded, and collapsed, and exploded again. Diego said, It's different each time, yet the elements are the same. All the pieces are there.

James returned the kaleidoscope to the box.

He reached for the rock. Quartzite. About the size of an egg. Moonrock, he thought.

But no. This was a common specimen, nothing in particular to set it apart.

The rock fit neatly in his cupped palm. He tossed it from one hand to the other. After a while, he got up and paced the yard's perimeter, like a guard dog tracking a presence on the other side of a wall. He could smell it and feel it. But he just couldn't see.

CHAPTER EIGHT

He wound up spending the rest of the night at the station-house, sharing the bunkroom with two other patrols, both of whom snored like tractors climbing a hill. James watched knife-shaped shadows glide over the floor, and then one of the guys was shaking his shoulder, saying, "Boss wants to see you."

James rolled onto his side, facing the wall.

"Wants to see you *now*."

Locker room voices, slam of metal doors. Patrols coming in, going out. A shift change: 6 a.m. James reluctantly lifted his head. The other beds were empty, the blankets pulled taut. He asked the swinging door, "What does Yard want?"

Half-asleep, he trudged off to the head. One of his bunkmates stood at a sink, naked, chin and cheeks covered in pink shaving cream. "Hey, Reese," he said, "your wife ever tell you you're a pain in the ass? To sleep with, I mean."

James yawned. "What'd I do?"

"You were shouting. Woke me up twice."

"What'd I say?"

"Who knows. Sounded cuckoo to me."

James shut his eyes and black squiggles scudded like insects behind his lids. He bent to the sink, splashed cold water onto his face. He rinsed his mouth and spit.

But stepping into the boss's office, he woke up entirely.

Tommie Yard sat with his fat hands folded demurely on the desk. He appeared calm, but overly attentive, a posture James knew meant trouble.

There was no clock and no place to sit, two of Yard's particular twists, intended to keep the guys on his timetable.

"There's a boatload of pollos," Yard said, "in the processing room. Gets worse by the minute 'round here. I haven't been home since day before yesterday." He cleared his throat, his skin reddening across nose and cheeks. "So, Reese," he said, "I understand you've had a busy week."

"That I have, boss."

"What do you say we hit some of the highlights?"

"Okay, boss."

"First off," Yard said, "and I've already talked to Tutrone about this, but I need to hear it from you. Can you tell me why you all went into that canyon yesterday?"

An easy one. James said, "Leo thought there were pollos down there."

"You get a good look yourself?"

"I did not."

"Well, the fire ants been searching for remains since yesterday. So far, they haven't come across one goddamn thing. Not so much as a bite-size scrap of bone. They'll keep at it, though. Hope it's not a waste of their time."

"Me, too," said James.

Yard yanked at the center drawer on his desk. James heard papers rustle and pencils roll, the rasp of something metal on wood. Yard banged the drawer shut without removing anything. He flopped back. The chair squeaked in protest.

"Can you tell me," he said, "what happened with your goddamn air? You check that gauge before you went out?"

James said the only thing that he could. "No, I didn't." And why hadn't he? He couldn't recall. "I didn't think I was going to use it. Other than training exercises, I never have." He added, "Not once in seventeen years."

"I know how long you've been on the job!" Yard pressed his lips together. "Why'd you leave the tank in the canyon?"

"It wasn't working, boss."

"Uh-huh. They found it, you know."

"The Scott-pak?"

"Yeah. It's a mess, all right, melted all to shit, but they're checking it out. As we speak." Swivel, *squeak*. Yard turned in the chair. "Help me get this straight now. Tutrone's the only one saw those pollos?"

"That's right," James said.

"You been having any trouble with him?"

James hesitated. "No more than usual."

"You're the senior man, Reese. You don't work alone . . . I don't like it! Something here stinks."

James thought about Leo calling him into the canyon that night, the look in his eye. Then he thought about Leo sharing his air. Leo talking to Mercedes and making sure that James understood. There was Richie Serrano—Anteater—to consider, as well, that van filled with stolen goods. Christ. It was all so stupid. James knew he should tell Tommie Yard, he had an obligation. But he couldn't bring himself to do it. Because he'd look like he was playing his young partner tit for tat, and Leo would think he'd gotten to James, and James couldn't stand that.

"Goddamnit!" Yard exploded. "What about that business with Detective Raymond Fricke! That little dead boy found on Desmond's farm? Fricke's been sniffing around, and I don't like it one bit." Swivel, *squeak*. "This is some serious stuff, you get that? You know I love Des. We all love Des. But illegals? Right on the old man's property? With you a patrol? We're in the business of throwing the fuckers back, not employing them." Yard slapped a hand on the desk. "The detective implied that you're dirty. That you're smuggling aliens." He glared at James. "Are you?"

James bristled. "You have to ask me that, boss? You have to ask that about Des?"

"It doesn't look right."

"Listen. I'll talk to him about the pollos."

"Yeah, well." Yard's fat red cheeks swung. "Don't bother. I'm making that phone call myself." Yard lifted the receiver from its cradle and dialed with a fat finger. James heard ringing on the other end and then his father saying, "Hello? Hello?"

"Desmond! How the hell have you been?" Yard turned his chair to the wall.

James waited at home for Mercedes for hours, working in the garage and the yard, dozing on and off in front of the tube. His wife was just five blocks away, at Sandpiper Point—busted or not, there was surely work to do there—but he refused to go by. Just as she refused to come home. He wanted her to come home. But by 11 p.m. he understood she wasn't going to. He was disappointed, and sorry, and more than a little angry. With himself as much as with her, he supposed. But it was too late to phone Cruz's house now.

And then he realized he never had talked to Des—he really should have after that business with Tommie Yard—and impulsively, he decided to drive up to the farm. His parents would be sleeping, but he could let himself in. He could crawl into his old bed in the guest room and pull the blanket up over his face. In the morning things might make more sense. But though it was after midnight when he arrived, Desmond and Marie were up and only just sitting down to dinner, Des having been out late in the fields, harvesting gladioli in the cool of the night. His workers, he explained, had never returned. If he didn't get the flowers cut now, the crop would be lost.

There were white candles on the kitchen table, daisies in a jelly jar. A bottle of wine chilled in a silver bucket. James asked Marie if it was a special occasion—was he interrupting something?—but she dodged the question, saying only that she was glad to see him, he'd been on her mind. She set an extra place and served him a thick slice of roast beef, along with mashed potatoes and carrots, corn, and fresh peas.

Afterward, Des suggested they take their peach pie outside. Marie made a pot of decaf and the three of them went out to the patio, settling into a trio of plastic chairs. The pie was juicy and sweet, the coffee hot. In moonlight, the vegetable plot looked mysterious to James, the tips of the plants pushed through the earth. White blossoms littered the grove; they'd fallen since he was here last. Desmond's pickup was parked at the top of the service road, buckets of glads in the back. James offered to go to market with Des in the morning, but Marie cut him off, patting her husband's arm and saying they'd already planned the day together. Suddenly, James was embarrassed. His parents were so rarely demonstrative and their interests had always seemed miles apart. He'd imagined this phase of their lives together as a long final stretch where differences stood out in sharp relief against the reduced obligations of retirement. He sipped at his coffee, had a bite of the pie. Likely, he thought, he'd misunderstood the marriage for years.

Finished with desert, Desmond got up to weed the vegetable plot. Kneeling, he worked a small patch of ground. James heard him softly huffing. Desmond's bald head was bowed, and he seemed a happy monk, praying, or apologizing, maybe, to the weeds. Desmond shook the soil from the roots and tossed them into a plastic pail.

"How can you see what you're doing?" James asked.

"I can't," said Des.

"Then how do you know you've got the weed, not the plant?"

"They feel different to me."

The air was cool now. Marie went inside for a blanket and a couple of sweaters.

Desmond asked James, "You call that attorney yet?"

Alexander May, Esq. In West Los Angeles.

James said, "I haven't exactly had time."

"What're you waiting for?" Desmond knee-walked three paces. He buried his hands in the dirt. "There's money there. You could use it."

"I didn't like the guy's letter," James said. " 'At your earliest convenience,'" he quoted. "I threw it away."

Desmond looked up. "What are you talking about?"

"It's bullshit, that's all."

"Don't be stupid, son. Someday you're going to want your own family."

"I don't need her money."

Desmond sat back on his heels. The whites of his eyes gleamed. "It'll be all right. That Alex May will get you through it. He's a nice man."

That took James by surprise. "You know him?"

"I don't *know* him. He handled the adoption, that's all. Their end of things."

For three long years of foster care, James's only desire had been to go home. He'd believed he'd go home—to Lara and Tío Diego and Los Angeles. But someone on *their end of things* had shut the door forever. And eventually he'd belonged to Des and Marie.

"Back then," he said, "how much were you told? About what you were getting into."

"Enough," Desmond said. "More than enough."

Again, James was surprised. He'd had the idea that adoptive parents weren't provided much in the way of details. He remembered an article he'd once read in the *Corville Border Call*, a piece about a local couple adopting a little girl from an orphanage in Romania. There'd been a photograph, the new parents smiling, the kid's face, round as a dinner plate, held up between theirs. As James recalled, she was a pretty thing. He'd seen her once on the square, out with her mother, tossing pennies into the fountain.

Later, though, he'd heard that the couple had returned the girl. She'd had problems the agency hadn't ever mentioned, medical stuff, and some sort of psychological trouble, too, something that kept her from loving the people who'd taken her in. A consequence, James thought, of how long she'd been in the orphanage. It was like learning a language: If you weren't exposed at the proper time, you never quite got it right.

"Did you ever have any doubts?" he asked Des. "About me."

Desmond shifted his bulk. "Well, I didn't much like it when you got expelled. And the goddamn fights. The shoplifting . . . but none of that stuff made you any kind of born-and-bred juvenile delinquent. Not in my book."

"Or mine," Marie said. She was standing in the doorway, sweaters piled in her arms. Desmond declined, but James took one gratefully. Slipping it over his head, he smelled earth and mothballs and his father's aftershave.

"What about the cat, Mom?"

"Oh, that." She sat in the chair and pulled the blanket to her throat.

"Yes, that," said James.

Shortly after he'd arrived at the house on Seventh Street, Marie had brought him a cat from the pound, an orange tabby of indeterminate age, with a torn ear and a stub of a tail. The cat had clearly had a rough life, and he had to be careful with it or it would scratch. That animal was the first pet James had ever owned, and after school, he couldn't wait to get home and play. He'd take it out into the yard and trail a length of yarn on the grass, trying to make the thing pounce, a brand of fun that made him feel like a boy in a picture book.

But one day, swinging into the yard, he'd found the cat hanged by its neck from the ash tree. The animal's eyes were open, and its mouth. The tongue lolled horribly. Dead cold inside, James had walked into the house. He took a knife from the silverware drawer, then trudged back out to the tree. Mechanically, he'd sawed at the rope, and he tried to catch the cat as it fell, but it slid through his arms, landing with a sickening thud on the grass. That was when he went running for Marie. She'd had a headache and was resting in bed, but at the sound of his voice, she got up at once and came out. She'd looked at the cat, at the dangling rope in the tree, and then she'd looked at James, long and hard.

"It wasn't me," he said now.

"Of course it wasn't," Desmond said. "We know that. I always suspected those damn Hickman kids." Boys next door that gave James a bad time from the day he moved in, until finally he handed the oldest a bright bloody nose.

James looked at Marie, until she said, quietly, "I thought it was you."

"I know you did."

"I'm sorry. It's just that—"

"I'd tell you if I'd done it. I'd tell you now."

He knew Marie was thinking about their conversation the day the dead boy was found. About James's lying, his lies. He said, "I did plenty of other things," and Marie said, "I'm sure you did." But Christ, James thought, they had no idea. The smashed windows, the stolen cars. His thirteenth year, he'd turned into a peeping tom. Creeping around Corville like an angel of death, marking windows: *this* one, and *this*. He'd liked looking at the women, of course, and the girls, preparing for bed, or a bath, those soft forms revealed. But the families, complete, were more interesting. Fathers and daughters, mothers and sons. He'd wanted to see how other people behaved, what they ate and drank and watched on TV. He'd wanted to know what they said to each other, in their presumed privacy.

It was too chilly now and too late for Marie. She said her goodnights and went inside.

Des got up from the vegetable plot. He brushed dirt from his knees. "Take a walk, son?"

"All right," James said.

They followed the service road past the cleared tulip fields, then looped around the side of the hill. What remained of the gladioli stood nearly waist-high, cupped flowers covering the stems. If the buds opened any more, the flowers couldn't be sold.

Out here, in the dark, the colors looked flattened, a uniform gray. James had never been in the fields late at night, and the landscape appeared slightly sinister, as if everything had been shuffled and rearranged.

"I'll get these last tomorrow," Desmond said. "Depending on how hot we go, they might still be okay."

Nearing the place where the dead boy was found, they stopped. It was colder here than it had been by the house. James folded his arms and peered down the row.

Desmond stuck his hands in his pockets. "Your wife called last night. Woke me up."

James sighed.

"You two have a fight?"

"You could say that."

"Well, hell. That's okay, son. Everyone fights. Hope it wasn't important." James shook his head, refusing the bait. But Desmond kept on. "Girl tried to act like she knew where you were. It was obvious she did not."

"I slept at the station," James said.

"I see. Well. . . . You talk to her about this lawyer thing yet?"

"Not exactly."

Desmond gave him a look. "You need to be careful. Don't keep too many secrets from a woman you love. You don't want to lose that one, too." Desmond put up a hand to stop James's protest. "Hiding," he said, "cost you Charlotte. You know that . . . your poor mother never understood what went wrong there. She loves Char.

I know Mercedes has picked up on that, and I'm sorry. But *you*, James. You're getting too old to try it again."

James didn't much like being lectured, so he said, "You know that Raymond Fricke came by the station."

"Yes, I heard," Desmond said.

"He claims you're being uncooperative."

"I don't like what he's done to Rafael. Who's still in jail, by the way."

"Fricke's just trying to find out how the boy died. And he can't seem to get any information from you."

"Rafael's a good guy. Smart as hell. Works hard, sends all his money home to Mexico. He's got a wife and four kids down there."

"He tell you who the boy was?"

Desmond said, "I *know* Rafael."

But James thought Des was deluding himself. With illegals, there was always a wall, even if it seemed made of glass. It was a translation problem, one that had both everything and nothing to do with actual words.

He said, "Fricke thinks I'm supplying you with workers. Using the job to get you people out here."

"He can think what he wants. We know you're not."

"It's illegal." James couldn't believe he was defending Fricke. He couldn't believe his father did not understand.

Desmond stiffened. "You don't have to tell me that, James—but I can't get anyone else. Who's going to come up here and work? College boys? The locals, maybe? Fat chance. The kids all run off to San Diego or L.A. right out of high school. The few left would rather make eight an hour flipping burgers. With air-conditioning."

"You could pay better."

"Don't be stupid. The farm operates so much in the red, I might as well just open a vein. We're going to go under sooner or later."

This was news to James.

Desmond said, "Takes most of my pension to run this place."

"You know," James said, "everything I have is yours."

"And what do you have?"

James bit his lip to keep from saying what he knew he'd regret.

"You make that call," Desmond said, "and the offer might actually mean something, son."

James took a few steps into the field. The earth was damp and sucked at his shoes. Suddenly, he wanted to see the exact spot where the boy had been found. He continued down the row until he thought he saw a scratched mound, that pillow for the boy's head. He squatted and grabbed a handful of dirt, let it sift from an hourglass of fist.

Desmond came up behind him. "Rafael had nothing to do with it."

James looked up. His father's bulk filled all of his sight. But he couldn't see Desmond's face.

"Are you sure?" he asked.

"As sure as I am you didn't hang that damn cat."

"Somebody hung it," said James.

He drove the downsloping hills in the dark, the air pine-scented and cool as ice cream, warming only as he spilled out onto flatlands. The sun had begun its upward crawl; streaks of light painted the sands pink and gold. Windows open, James headed east. He ran the truck up to 95 mph, and no knock or rattle came from the V8 engine, just the smooth rolling of miles under his wheels, all the way into Elbert, a valley town hemmed in by avocado and orange groves. From the highway, the treetrunks lined up no matter which way you looked, acres and acres of precise geometry.

He exited at the sign for the Business Loop, cruised sleepy streets named for flowers that would never grow here. He found the Elbert police station, where Detective Raymond Fricke was a homicide cop and Rafael Noyez sat in the jail.

It was a sleepy stationhouse, too. James had only to flash his shield, and bitch a little about the rigors of the deportation biz, and the crusty-eyed desk sergeant accepted him without question or complaint. They made small talk about the state of Detective Fricke's investigation and James threw the name around as if he were an intimate, *Ray* this and *Ray* that, thinking all the while, *Fuck him*. James said, "I hear he's got squat," and a cop passing by ducked his head to hide his laughter. James said, "There's only that poor illegal bastard. Which brings me to my business here."

Shuffling into the hall, Rafael Noyez said nothing to James, apparently indifferent to this turn of events. James walked him through his release. Noyez signed a few forms. He traded the orange jumpsuit for his jeans, his T-shirt and cap. The clerk handed him a manila envelope through a half-moon opening in bulletproof glass. Noyez halfheartedly picked at the clasp. When he opened the envelope, his wallet fell out. He flipped the billfold: empty. Still, he said nothing. He put on his cap, pulled it low enough to hide his eyes.

James made a show of having forgotten his cuffs, and the crusty-eyed sergeant loaned him a pair. Resigned, Rafael Noyez held out his wrists.

He balked, however, out in the parking lot, when James tried to get him into the truck.

"Por favor, no."

"Desmond Reese would want you to."

Noyez stared at James.

Again, he held out his wrists, expecting now to have the cuffs removed. Job done, they climbed into the truck. James drove to a Denny's he remembered passing on the way to the jail.

They slid into opposite ends of a booth, orange vinyl that crackled with the slightest movement. The restaurant featured striped wallpaper, pink and orange, and James thought of circus tents, ringmasters, and clowns. At this hour, most of the other diners were farmers and day laborers, with a lone blue-suited businessman at the counter. The place smelled strongly of sausage grease and syrup. James ordered Grand Slam breakfasts for them both, bacon and eggs, hash-browns, toast, and pancakes. When the food came, Noyez ate with his head inches from the plate. He drank five cups of coffee, black, no sugar. Finished, he folded his hands on the table and belched.

"What I don't understand," he said, "is why they let me go. If they think I killed that niñito, it doesn't make sense."

So he speaks English, thought James. Noyez's pronunciation, though accented, was excellent.

"You talk to a public defender in there?"

"No," said Noyez. "Only that detective."

"See, right there. They don't think you killed anyone."

"That's not what the detective said."

"You were going to get out anyway. They can't hold you this long, not without evidence." James paused. "Well, not *out*, exactly. Deported. That's a given. Put you on a van for Tijuana. It's going to cost plenty for the coyote to smuggle you back."

Noyez shrugged. James sipped his coffee.

"That detective's gonna fry your migra ass," Noyez said. "Why are you doing this?"

"Because my father thinks highly of you. Because I'm pretty sure you had nothing to do with that kid's death. Because . . ." James left it hanging.

Noyez slumped. While eating, he'd turned the bill of his cap around, but he flipped it back now and pulled it low.

"What do you want?" he asked.

The waitress was moving toward them, coffee pot in her hand. James waved her away.

"I can always run you right back to jail. Maybe Fricke can hang it on you, after all."

Noyez said again, "What do you want?"

James leaned forward. "Tell me how that boy died."

Foothills, grassy slopes, rock, and ravine.

The two-lane road wound ever skyward, hugging a craggy hillside. When they were nearly to the top, they passed a deserted produce stand and a VW bus up on blocks. Then came a narrow turnoff marked with a hand-painted sign: SCHILLER FARMS.

"Turn here," Noyez said.

James pulled onto a dirt road. He followed it into a broad clearing bordered by oak trees and bottlebrush. A bicycle had been thrown into the bushes, along with a rusted grocery cart. There was a sharp drop-off on one end. James looked for a place to park, but Noyez said, "Not here. The work trucks see this, they won't stop." James continued on the dirt road. They passed a narrow brown field, a fence of close-planted cypress trees, and then Noyez said, "Okay, this is good," and James steered to the side and cut the engine. They walked back to the clearing. From there, they dropped into a steep-sided ravine, slipping and sliding on leaves and loose dirt. Branches scraped across the narrow path. Down they went, into an ever-increasing dark; green light filtered weakly through the treetops. There was a sudden smell of meaty rot, something dead, or dying, and James heard trickling water. A creek. He knew what to look for now and he found it: foot trails veering out from the path; camouflaged shacks, plywood and tin patched with plastic sheeting; trip wires strung through the bushes. Trash was piled up everywhere. Tin cans and newspapers and plastic wrappings; liquor bottles, broken tools, dead radios, split and molding sofa cushions. An outboard motor poked from a torn clump of bamboo.

"Private property is safest," Noyez said. "The migra needs a warrant to get in. Or the farmer's permission."

"What's in it for Schiller?" James asked.

"He gets his crops picked for free."

"You trust him?"

"No way." Noyez pointed to a wire that crossed the path at chest level. James ducked underneath.

Now the path opened onto smaller clearing, the bare ground scarred by cooking fires. Below, a creek burbled, silvery water that percolated around yet more garbage. A number of shirts were hung on the branches of a mulberry tree.

A heavy rain, thought James, and that creek would flood.

"How many live here?" he asked.

"Twenty, maybe," Noyez said. "Sometimes less, sometimes more."

He put thumb and forefinger into his mouth and whistled. A lengthy silence, then a dozen or so men floated like phantoms out from the brush. The men were dressed uniformly in dark pants and dark long-sleeved shirts, battered running shoes.

A few nodded at Noyez, but no one spoke.

They all stared at James. Noyez made a brief introduction and, here and there, James saw flickers of interest.

Noyez turned to him expectantly.

After some thought, James began with a general question: "¿De dónde son, señores?" *Where are you from?*

Silence.

"¿De dónde en México?"

Noyez said, "Contéstenle." *Answer him.*

One of the men said, softly, "Michoacán." The speaker had stringy black hair, a drooping mustache. He pressed on the mustache with the pad of his thumb, grooming strays.

Someone else said, "Chihuahua."

Someone else said, "Querétaro."

Then silence again.

James didn't know what to do now. It seemed a mistake to offer much in the way of information about himself—la migra surely being an unwelcome presence here—so he improvised. He talked about his wife, Mercedes, and her job with her two brothers, building houses down in Corville. At this, several of the stilled faces registered disapproval. James thought that maybe these men were jealous; his wife did a man's work and made a man's money. Or maybe, he considered, they saw James as a poor husband for that. Their women worked in restaurants, or as maids or nannies, or more likely, remained with the children back home in Mexico. James decided to change the subject. He told them about Desmond Reese. How hard and how long his father had worked,

how on retiring, he'd bought himself a flower farm. Tulips and daffodils and gladioli.

"Some of you have probably worked for him."

Silence.

He said, "Do any of you know that little boy? The one that was
found on Señor Reese's farm?"

Silence.

Then the man from Michoacán staggered forward, pushed from
behind.

"It's all right," Rafael Noyez said. "You can talk to him."

James dropped down onto his haunches. He lowered his eyes
and hung his hands between his knees: the pollo's stance of submission. He heard uneasy shifting, feet scuffing at loose dirt, and
then the man from Michoacán also squatted. They remained in
position until James's muscles screamed.

Finally, the man said, "El patrón will take good care of him."

James averted his eyes. "Do you know how the boy died?"

The man said nothing.

"I promise," James said, "no one will hurt you. I am only looking
for information. Por favor, where are the boy's parents?"

"He has no parents." The man swallowed, clearly struggling.
"He was at the bottom of the van."

"The boy was?"

"Sí, he was sneaking. And the coyote, he was too greedy. The
trip was too long. The boy was at the bottom."

James looked at the man, at the bead of sweat rolling from his
temple. Again, the man pressed on his mustache with the pad of
his thumb. Then he wiped under his lip, as if crumbs were gathered there.

He said, "We could hear the fenders scraping."

A terrible pressure settled on James. He felt it in his hips, his
back, his ribcage, his hands. All those bodies piled up in the van.
Goddamnit to hell. The kid had been crushed to death.

He asked now, "Why did you leave him on my father's farm?"

"The coyote, he said to put the boy there."

"The coyote." James didn't understand.

"Sí," the man said. "For Señor Reese."

And then someone in the group said, "Ese hombre es la migra."

The clearing filled with whispering.

"La migra."

"La migra, sí."

"¡Sí, es verdad!"

The man from Michoacán got to his feet.

James also stood. He looked into dark faces, dark eyes. In all his years on the job, he'd likely picked up one or another of these men, and likely, more than once; but there was not a single face he recognized. The men stared back at James. Hostile now, whereas before they had seemed merely wary. James realized that he could be hurt here. No one knew where he was.

"How does it feel?" Rafael Noyez asked. "To be in the wrong place at the wrong time."

James said, "I'm not going to harm anyone."

"And that is the one thing that is keeping you safe." Noyez clapped his hands and said to the men, "Enough, eh? He's all right, Señor Reese. Hijo del patrón, okay?"

James heard grumbling. Someone threw a rock out into the creek. Then, from the top of the ravine, came the honking of horns. The men looked up. More honking: *shave and a haircut, two bits.* "Pinches gringos," somebody said. Scattered laughter broke the tension. The men exited the clearing and started to climb.

Rafael Noyez climbed, too. James had no choice but to follow.

Up top, the workers fanned out around two new pickup trucks, the drivers sitting on dusty tailgates. The drivers looked the men over, pointing casually at those they wanted. The designated workers jumped into the stakebeds. When one man pointed at James, he shook his head a little too emphatically, and the driver frowned. Noyez stepped forward, but eyes flickered past.

The selection was over. The trucks started up. They circled the end of the clearing, then came back along the dirt road.

One by one, the men not picked to labor wandered back down the ravine.

When they were alone, James said to Noyez, "You want a ride out to my dad's? I'm sure there's still work."

Rafael Noyez kicked at the dirt. "I can't go back there."

Of course. He should have realized.

"You knew all about it," James said. "That kid, what happened to him. Why didn't you just tell Detective Fricke?"

"I was not in that van. I did not kill that boy."

"But why not say something about the coyote? Get the detective off of your back."

Rafael Noyez shrugged.

James watched a huge crow divebomb the clearing, black wings shining in the sunlight. The bird landed in the dirt and hopped forward, tilting its head.

James said, "So tell me his name."

Noyez shrugged again.

"Tell me what he looks like. Long black hair, maybe? Long nose?"

"I wasn't there."

James shot out a fist. He grabbed the front of Noyez's shirt, twisting hard.

Noyez glared and James tightened his grip.

Finally, Noyez raised his right hand. With his fingertips, he cupped the tip of his nose, then drew the hand down.

At home, the light was blinking on the answering machine. From the way the house looked, James could tell Mercedes still hadn't been back; he thought it might be her on the box. But it was Danny Patillo instead, wanting to know where on earth James had got to, he'd been looking all over for him. It wasn't their regular poker day, but Danny was driving down to 24-Hour Efraín's. If

127

James got the message in time, he should stop by—Danny had something to tell him, something he couldn't trust to the machine.

James was bone tired. But there was a note in Patillo's voice that he didn't like.

And so a half hour later he nosed up against the cantina's screen of tumbleweed. He parked next to the ancient Dodge Colt that belonged to his friend. James squinted up at the sky. Scalloped gray clouds were gathering. It was late in the season, but rain was surely coming. He could smell it.

He walked around back, where a lone campesino squatted on the patio, a striped woolen blanket draped around his shoulders.

The cantina's lights were all out.

"Danny?" James called. He took a deep breath, thinking that he smelled gas. "Danny?" he called again, louder. Patillo answered, "I'm working on the generator." James followed the voice around the side of the building. He skirted the hen house, climbed a pile of broken concrete.

Efraín's generator leaned against the cantina's south wall. The size of an upright piano, it had two wheels, both flat, and a built-in trailer hitch that probably hadn't been used in thirty years. Patillo sat cross-legged in the dirt, a cooking pot full of gasoline in his lap. He had the side-panels off, dozens of parts spread all around on newspapers. He lifted his dripping hands from the pot and scrubbed at the float needle with a paint brush.

James crouched down beside him. "You want some help?"

Patillo nodded at a second brush. James grabbed a gunked-up spring. He dunked it into the gasoline, then worked the bristles into the wire.

"Bastard went out two days ago," Danny said. "Efraín's pissed. But guess what? He threw the fuel filter away months back and forgot to replace it. So I'd say it's his own fault. The carburetor's fucked, completely. Crappy Mexican gas."

"Where is Efraín?"

"Beats me." Danny set the float needle aside. "He didn't leave a note."

He wouldn't, thought James.

Danny selected another piece, dipped it into the pot.

They worked for a while in an efficient silence, setting the cleaned parts to one side. The sky continued to darken. A light breeze ruffled the dirt and disturbed the leaves on the cottonwood trees.

"So, buddy." James said. He inspected the float chamber he'd just finished brushing—all clear—and took up a cap nut. "What'd you want to talk to me about?"

"Couple of things," Patillo said. "First off, the good news. I'm thinking of getting married again."

James grinned at Danny. "You're kidding me."

"I am not."

"I thought you swore off."

"Two-time loser. I probably should."

"Who is she? Anyone that I know?"

Danny looked just the slightest bit embarrassed. "It's Teresa," he said.

James set the paintbrush down. "Efraín's Teresa?"

"Yeah."

All those poker games, thought James, all those meals. And not a word from Efraín, or Teresa, or Danny himself. Worse: how come he never saw it?

He said, "Teresa's a little young, isn't she?"

"Yeah, but she has that kid. Being a mother makes a girl more mature. And I like that kid. Besides," Danny raised an eyebrow, "you're one to talk." He scrubbed at a part so small it looked like he was cleaning his fingernails. "The real problem is that they're Mexican citizens."

"You can fix that."

"Teresa doesn't want it fixed. She wants to live here."

"That might not be so bad," James said. "It's a trade-off, isn't it? Worse commute, better food." He grinned again. "All the beer you can drink."

"Can I ask you something?" Patillo said.

"Sure, Danny. Ask away."

"Are you happy? Being married, I mean."

"Yeah," James said. "Mostly, I am." He thought about Mercedes, how much he loved her, how much he wanted things to work out for them. A baby, he thought.

"I'm scared," Danny said.

"There's plenty to be scared of," James said. "But you'll be okay."

All the parts were clean now. They reassembled the carburetor. Patillo hit the starter button and the generator coughed and spit and started to chug. James was screwing in the side panel when they felt the first drops of rain. Quickly, they collected the paintbrushes, the gas and loose newspaper. They carried everything back around to the patio. The campesino was inside, sitting at a table, the blanket covering his head. James stepped under the roof just as a crack of thunder split the lumbering sky. The rain came down hard, droplets pinging against the patio. The cottonwoods by the creek were shrouded in mist. James could see nothing at all of La Boom.

"Where's the light switch?" Patillo asked.

"Behind the bar," James said. "I'll get it." Blindly, he brushed against tables and chairs.

Patillo said, "I could get in a lot of trouble for this, but I've got to tell you something . . . they sent your air-pak back to the factory. Back to Scott's."

"Yard already told me."

"The report's in. But I don't think Yard has seen it. I . . . I don't know how to say this."

"Just say it," said James.

"All right. It looks like someone was messing with it."

"With the air-pak?" James was over by the bar now. "What do you mean?"

"Someone let out the air."

James felt for the latch in the gate that would let him back behind the counter. Then he ran a hand over the wall. The switch was here somewhere.

Patillo said, "I'm not making this up."

"No. Of course not." James found the switch. He flipped it, blinking at the sudden brightness. Christ, the place was shabby, dog plain, and unbelievably grimy, too many years of cigarette smoke. No wonder Efraín hated the overhead lights.

"You got any ideas," Patillo said, "who'd want to do that?"

CHAPTER NINE

One a.m. Out in the desert again, James up on his quarter-horse. The sensors were tripping like crazy in Sector 49.

Pollos in twos and threes, it appeared; but though dispatch repeatedly read out sets of coordinates, he and Leo kept missing their prey. There was no guidance from above as the choppers were inexplicably grounded tonight. And Danny Patillo never had gotten around to burning 49. Dense scrub obscured the hillsides, narrow paths snaking in and out of the rock, in and out of the brush. Thick fog swirled over the creek. The two patrols rode their eight-mile stretch nearly blind, crisscrossing every hour at the halfway.

James was tired, and achy, coming down with a cold. He had the shivers. His uniform under his jacket was damp with sweat. It took effort to keep track of landmarks: a bunched stand of old oaks, the place on the highway where headlights became visible.

Then his radio crackled to life, dispatch with more coordinates.

James had passed Leo some ten minutes back, and his partner, he calculated, should be about *there*.

He turned his horse around.

He found Leo in a clearing. Leo's chin was fallen down on his chest and he seemed, incredibly, to be sound asleep.

James trotted up beside him. He kicked a little too hard at Leo's leg.

"Hey!" he said and Leo lifted his head. "Didn't you hear? I thought you might need some help."

Leo swept his gaze over bushes and trees. "There's no-body, James."

"We should look."

"Forget it," Leo said. "I got a better idea. Let's take a break."

James hesitated. "Okay," he agreed. Maybe this was his chance to talk to Leo, to find out what had happened with that air-pak, before the report went to the boss and the consequences were out of their hands.

They walked the horses through the clearing, and the animals perked up, smelling water close by. A short trot through a break in the brush, and then the horses were jostling each other at the edge of the creek.

James slackened the reins, and his quarterhorse lowered its head to drink. James's forehead was aching from the goggles. He took them off and clipped them to his belt. All around, trees dipped their branches into the fog, the tips swallowed in white. It was ghostly quiet, the only sound that of crickets and trick-ling water.

Leo twisted in his saddle and retrieved a thermos from his pack. He removed a metal cup, undid the cap, and poured out steaming coffee. Leo drank, then poured again and passed the cup to James, who, sipping too fast, burned his tongue.

"If I had a dollar," he said, "for every time I've done that."

Leo belched. He pounded his chest with his fist. "Too much gar-lic in the spaghetti sauce. My mama's recipe takes a whole head."

"You cook?" James asked.

"You don't?" Leo said.

As a point of fact, James cooked all the time. But he didn't feel like saying so now.

"Chicks," Leo pronounced, "prefer a man who can cook."

James heard a rustling sound, snapped branches and animal snorts. A burro stumbled free of the brush.

"What the fuck," Leo said.

The burro trotted down to the stream. It looked angry, comically overloaded with fat canvas saddle packs. A frayed rope trailed from its bit.

"Somebody's lost their transportation," James said. He dismounted.

"I wouldn't," Leo said. "You might get yourself kicked in the ass."

"Watch this," said James.

Hip-deep in fog, he stepped into the creek, cold water soaking into his boots. He grabbed for the rope, but it was just out of reach. The burro's hide quivered as it bumped against him. James slid in the mud and the burro skittered away.

James waded out farther. The current ran stronger here and water burbled around his knees, the sound only gradually separating itself from an intermittent murmur of human voices. And where were the voices coming from? James peered into the fog. From here, he could see past a shallow bend in the creek. At the bank's edge circled a tiny red light. A cigarette. He made out three standing figures, not thirty feet off. Pollos in dark clothing and watch caps.

James glanced back at Leo.

How many? Leo mouthed.

James held up three fingers.

Leo gave a thumbs up. He indicated that he would go around and approach the pollos from the rear.

James moved forward slowly. The pollos were standing angled away, but he could hear bits of their conversation now, something about a sister who would have dinner waiting, even if they got in at 6 a.m.

The brush behind the pollos parted. Leo, up on his mare, in full charge. James splashed forward, thinking, *Not yet, not yet.* He was still in the water and too far away.

Leo cried, "¡Inmigración! ¡No se mueve nadie!" *Nobody move!*

"¡Alto, la migra!" cried James, and the pollos dropped into a crouch. He was almost there.

Then the three men leaped to their feet, guns drawn. A pistol was trained on James's chest. The face above belonged to Richie Serrano. El Oso Hormiguero.

"Migra fuck," Anteater said. "Throw me your weapon."

James took a step back. The creek pushed at his knees.

"Don't move, migra fuck!"

James looked at Leo, and he didn't know what he expected, but it wasn't the sight of his partner leaned casually in the saddle, gun holstered, expression serene.

"What the fuck is this?" James cried.

Leo said, "*This* is *us*, capturing pollos."

Except that James was the one being captured. He slid a hand to his holster, calculating the odds.

Anteater laughed. "Forget it! Just throw me that weapon. *Now.*"

"You better do it," Leo said.

Cursing, James pinched the butt of his Colt between forefinger and thumb. He pulled it from his gunbelt, and tossed it over. Anteater caught the gun with his free hand.

James's radio hissed at his hip. He heard the dispatcher's voice.

Anteater said, "Throw me that fucker, too."

James pitched him the radio.

And now the muzzle of Anteater's pistol tipped upward, pointed at James's head.

Leo said, "You're not going to shoot him—"

Anteater swung the gun around to Leo.

"What the fuck," Leo said, and Anteater fired. *Pop, pop, pop.* Leo slumped and then he was toppling. The black mare snorted and reared. She buckled, down on her knees.

135

James sloshed forward. A sharp report, a fiery sting, and he felt as if a blade had sliced open the side of his head. His ears were stoppered, there was something wrong with his ears. He staggered like a drunk. Anteater said, "No más, you stupid fuck," and James twisted sideways and fell and going down he wondered if Anteater was talking to him, or to Leo, or to someone else. Briefly, he thought of Mercedes, how much he loved her. He thought of their child. Hitting the creek, he told himself to roll, to play dead. He flipped himself face down and went limp. He floated in the shallows, his wet clothing sagging to the creekbed.

Dimly, he heard voices, coming closer.

He heard drumming sounds. Splashing, maybe.

He heard heavy footsteps. And then he realized it wasn't footsteps at all, but a pounding in his own head, his pulse in his ears.

One wrong move and he'd be dead for real.

There were hands on him now, a heel in his spine. He felt eyes boring into him, looking and thinking, deciding, maybe. Someone rolled him over. James slackened his lips. He fixed his eyes in a half-lidded stare. Unbuckling James's gunbelt, the someone said, "He's a bleeder. Right in the fucking head." The belt was yanked free, and James was flipped face-down again.

Splashes and thuds. Then nothing. *Nothing.*

He needed air. He turned his head a little, tilted his chin and sipped at the fog. He listened hard. Nothing.

He forced himself to stay face-down in the creek.

He'd been hit in the head. The left side of his head was grinding with pain. But it couldn't be serious or he'd already be gone. Wouldn't he? He wouldn't be able to think. And he could still think. But how long would that last? If he lost enough blood, he'd pass out for sure.

Why hadn't they shot him again? Why hadn't they noticed that he was alive?

James's face in the water was prickled by reeds. He needed air. He tipped his chin and took a breath, his lungs filling partway. He wanted more, but the water and the fog were his only camouflage. Christ, he was afraid. And how was his head? He pictured the blood in his veins, the cells red and white, animated like a movie he'd seen in high school health class, and as if in a dream, he saw the cells dancing as they journeyed up the arteries in his neck, then exited from the hole in his head. But the injury wasn't serious, he told himself. He could still think. He listened to his body, the clutch and burn of his stomach, his twisted hips. His groin ached as if he'd been kicked in the balls. His feet in his boots were cold and heavy and felt miles away. He wiggled his toes . . . but his *head*. His heart was hot in his head. He took another small breath. He could feel himself starting to panic. He had to get up. He had to get up now. Now, he thought. Do it now. *Now*. In one motion, he flipped himself over and sat up.

Water streamed down from his head. He stared at the swirling fog, and the water, flowing over his legs. He turned to one side, saw a pile of rocks bulge and recede. Gradually, they stilled. He looked up the creek's bank. There was no sign of Anteater, or Leo, or the pollos, the burro, his own quarterhorse.

But, wait—*there*. A humped shape under the cottonwood tree.

James crawled forward, then stood. He waited for a blackout, but it didn't happen. He was all right. He could still think. He struggled up the muddy bank and made his way to the cottonwood tree.

Leo was leaning against the dead horse's side. His gunbelt and radio were gone, his goggles, his pack. There was a large wet stain on his jacket.

"The fucker shot me," he said. "I can't believe he shot me." Leo stared up at James. "Creature from the black lagoon. And look at your fucking ear. There's a piece out. You're bleeding like a son-of-a-bitch."

Which James realized had probably saved him. He put a hand to the left side of his head. He felt around for a hole, but his skull was intact. Then he fingered the edge of his ear, and yes, something

was wrong there. He clamped his jaw to keep from yelping. His
hand came away red.

"Fuck it, it's nothing," he said.

"I thought," Leo said, "you were a goner."

"Thought—or hoped?"

"Fuck," Leo said.

"You tried to kill me—"

"You're out of your mind."

"—*again*."

"Actually, I saved your ass. *Again*."

"You're the one put me in the shit to begin with!"

Leo didn't deny it.

"Why?" James asked.

Leo said nothing.

James crouched at his partner's side.

"Why?" he demanded again.

Still no answer. James took Leo's wrist and felt for a pulse. A little fast, a little weak. And then Leo said, "I could've left you. I was
supposed to."

James's fingers tightened and squeezed, his anger whetted for a
confrontation that couldn't happen, not now. Leo winced, and James
threw the arm down. His mouth flooded, a taste like rusted nails. He
spit on the ground, then glanced away into bushes and trees. He
studied the creek. The water was rolling invisibly under the fog.

James heard Leo breathing beside him, shallow and quick.

"I've got to check it," he said, meaning Leo's wound.

After a long moment, Leo nodded.

James unsnapped the buttons on Leo's jacket, then undid his
shirt. He peeled the fabric away. There was a puckered hole in the
center of Leo's chest, between the second and third ribs, but not
as much blood as James had feared.

"Fuck," Leo said.

"Don't talk," said James. "I'm going to lean you forward, check
out your back." He put a hand beneath Leo's shirt, his palm in the

small of Leo's spine. "On three, okay?" Leo nodded. "One, two . . ." James slanted him forward. A low groan escaped Leo as James ran his fingers lightly side to side and up and down. Leo's skin felt hot and smooth. There was no exit wound. James lowered him back against the dead horse.

"It's still in you," he said.

Leo looked down at the hole. "Doesn't hurt much. It's not that bad."

James thought it looked bad, but maybe Leo knew better. He hoped so. It all depended on where the bullet had lodged.

"At least," Leo said, "it's not one of those sucking chest things."

"Yeah," James said, thinking that he should make a dressing. But with what? The pollos had taken Leo's pack from the black mare and James's horse had disappeared.

He stripped off his wet jacket and shirt, then put the jacket back on and ripped the shirt at the seams. He folded the back panel into a four inch square. The sides and the sleeves he tore into strips. Knotting the ends together left him with three long makeshift ties.

He said, "I have to lean you forward again."

"Okay," Leo said.

James laid the folded cloth over the bullet hole. He told Leo to press his hand against it, then passed the ties around Leo's chest and secured them with knots.

"Give me your hand," he said. "Can you squeeze mine?"

Leo squeezed. Not too bad. Half strength, maybe.

James sat back, trying to think.

Their options, he decided, were strictly limited. He could leave Leo here by the creek, run on up north on foot for help. He'd be back with paramedics in a couple of hours. Or they could both sit here and wait for someone to find them. Sooner or later dispatch would notice they hadn't checked in and send out a search and rescue team.

The problem with that scenario was that Anteater might find them first.

"Your friend," he said to Leo. "You think he'll come back?"

"He might," Leo said.

Maybe James could hide Leo somewhere, conceal him under branches and leaves. But when he suggested it, Leo said, "Fuck that! You're not burying me. I'm going with you."

"That bullet—you shouldn't move."

"I'm not staying here."

"What if I won't take you?"

"Then I'll go on my own. Don't fuck with me, James. I can't stay here. That fucking coyote ain't takin' prisoners."

Leo set his hands on the ground, either side of his thighs. Awkwardly, he scuffed his feet in the dirt.

James stood. He looked down at Leo.

Stubborn lines bracketed his partner's mouth. Elbows bent, Leo pushed upward, grunting.

James crossed his arms.

Leo said through gritted teeth, "All right! I turned a blind eye. All right, James? For money, all right?" He pushed again. Sweat beaded along his hairline and his eyes were wide, a wild light burning.

James couldn't stand to watch it. "Okay," he said and Leo dropped down hard.

"Fuck," he gasped.

"Be back in a minute," James said.

Leo groaned. "Where are you going?"

"I'll be right back."

James hiked around to where they'd first walked the horses down to the creek. He searched for the thermos and cup, finding them finally in the grass. He dumped out the last of the coffee, replaced it with water, then screwed on the lid and the cup. He stuck the thermos in the waist of his pants.

He returned to Leo.

His partner eyed the thermos's bulge. "No chicks out here," he said.

"Why don't you shut the fuck up," James said.

"Who's gonna make me?" But Leo wore the ghost of a grin.

James had to laugh. He crouched down and braced his shoulder beneath Leo's right arm. Leo draped it around James's neck.

Leo pushed his right leg against James's left. "Like a sack race," he said.

They struggled up together.

"We'll take first prize." James leaned forward to look at Leo's face. His partner was very pale.

"Press on that dressing for me."

Leo did that and James waited to see if the improvised bandage filled up with blood. The bandage was wet, but didn't seem to be getting wetter.

"How does that feel?" he asked.

"Like shit," Leo said.

"We don't have to do this. We can wait here. Someone's bound to come along eventually." But Christ, James wanted badly to go.

"Fuck that," Leo said.

"They probably think we're dead, anyway."

Leo looked at the black mare. "He did my fucking horse."

"Yeah."

"Pinches pollos. Can't get any fucking thing right."

There were almost immediately more decisions to make, because once they'd cleared the brush surrounding the creek, they found themselves faced with open desert. Out there, James thought, they'd be completely exposed. If the wrong eyes were watching they'd be picked off like flies. But it was worse to stay in one place. No predicting what Anteater would do.

Which way should they go?

North they'd hit the highway—but according to Leo, north was Anteater's probable destination. South seemed safer. They were closer to El Pilón anyway. If they kept up a pace, they might make town before noon.

James said, "How do you feel about Mexico?"

"Love it," Leo said.

James pointed them south.

They struggled along, speaking very little at first, and then not at all. Progress was excruciatingly slow. With every step they sank into the sand. It was like a dream, James thought, where the effort is tremendous but headway remains minimal. Leo, however, seemed mostly okay. His color had returned and his pulse was steady. When he flexed his arm around James's neck, James winced. He worked his head forward, complaining, "It's bad form to damage the ride," and Leo rasped, "Never did know my own strength."

But after a couple of hours something changed, and Leo was clearly suffering. He'd begun to breathe in uneven bursts. His head lolled, his feet dragged. They stopped more frequently for water and rest, and each time they got up James took on more of the weight, until he was virtually carrying Leo.

The effort cost him. But he kept his head down and tightened his grip on Leo's waist. One foot in front of the other, he thought. And for a long while there, he zoned out. He was gone, absolutely, off in some fantasyland where the sun shone gold and the sky was a depthless celestial blue; where Mercedes was stretched out naked beside him on pillows of air, her hair flowing, her breath like flowers, a sheen of sweat on her smooth skin; and he put their baby in the picture too, and why not? a gurgling child, handsome and healthy, an excellent sleeper who never needed a diaper change. But then a sudden terrifying consciousness of their predicament brought him back with a rush. He felt lightheaded, and wrongheaded, a dangerous realization flickering at the edge of his mind. To focus he began counting steps. He lost track in the seven hundreds and started over again. And again. And now he counted out loud. His own voice sounded as if someone else was speaking. When he once more lost his place, he glanced up to check their surroundings, and he saw nothing that he recognized. *Nothing*. Only sand and more sand. Mountains like a crown on the desert's great head. Were they even walking south anymore? He couldn't be sure. James stared up at the sky. A waning moon, the heavens shining, rampant with stars. He searched for the Big Dipper, but couldn't find it. He tried to pick out other constellations, and that was impossible, too. The individual lights remained just that—individual—refusing to cohere.

A giddy fear bubbled up in his chest. He'd lost his internal compass. For the first time in years he didn't know instantly and instinctively where he was and where the border was and the precise geometry between those two points.

He'd only ever been out here on his horse, strong and safe.

He thought of the five pollitos he'd found, white bones laid out on a flat rock. Those kids had run first out of water, and then out of time. And up in the mountains—there were many crossings there, too—it got cold, with snowfall even in the summertime. Illegals, dressed in T-shirts and jeans, had frozen to death in mid-July.

And yet untold numbers made it across, desire their guide. The law could guard every square inch, they could build three thousand miles of 12-foot steel fence, from the Gulf of Mexico clear to the Pacific Ocean, but those who wanted in badly enough would find a way.

Leo said hoarsely, "I gotta stop."

"Okay, buddy," said James.

He lowered Leo down to the sand, then sat beside him. James took the thermos from the waist of his pants and poured out some water. Leo grabbed at the cup, but his wrist wobbled and he dropped it. He gave James a helpless look.

"It's okay," James said.

He poured again, held the cup to Leo's lips.

Leo took a small sip before crumpling to the ground. He went down on his side, knees drawn to his chest.

The front of Leo's shirt was wet again, and the jacket, too. Spilled water, James thought, as he pressed his fingers to the stain. They came away dark. *Goddamnit.* He wiped his hand on his pants.

Leo twisted his head and stared at the sky. The stars pressed down around them. "God is a greedy bastard," he said.

James agreed.

"I'm cold," Leo said.

James took off his jacket and laid it over Leo's shoulders. Goose-bumps came up on James's bare chest. He stretched out next to Leo. His partner was shaking and he pressed against him, fitting himself against Leo's spine. The sand beneath them was cold and firm. James heard a sifting sound, the *tick-tick* of lizard feet.

"Don't leave me," Leo said.

"I'm right here," said James.

He closed his eyes, and watched himself walk through a land-scape so blindingly bright that all shape and form had been bleached into nothingness. He was following someone, he didn't know who and he didn't know why. And then the ground dis-appeared from under his feet. The air grew heavy, wet as water, and there was a chemical taste at the back of his throat. Something soft swished past his ears and Leo said, "Don't leave me, James."

James's eyes popped open. He didn't know how much time had passed, but the sky was lightening now, pale blue spreading from the mountaintops. Stars faded as the sun inched upward, halos of light extended from its white brow. The daily miracle. At least James could see now which way was east. For all the good it did them.

He sat up and looked at Leo. Blood had soaked through the front of his jacket. His teeth were chattering, his face was stone gray.

Ah, no, James thought. He'd made a fatal mistake. He should never have moved Leo; they should've stayed by the creek. He'd been in such a hurry to get away he hadn't sufficiently con-sidered the shape Leo was in.

"Get him," Leo said. "Richie—Richie Serrano. Promise me."

James said, "I will. You can count on that."

Leo licked his lips.

James poured out the last of the water. He held Leo's head, but Leo couldn't swallow. Water spilled from the corners of his mouth. "The Scott-pak—" he wheezed.

"I knew it," James said.

"—that was his idea."

"You're the one let the air out."

"I only wanted to see you piss your pants. You never treated me right, James . . . you never did."

James laid his fingertips against Leo's neck, feeling for his pulse. Leo's heart was beating too fast.

"But I didn't know he was gonna shoot you . . . believe me, old man?"

James couldn't see how it mattered much now.

"Guy's got a hard-on," Leo said, around quick gulps of air. "Richie—"

"Save your strength. We can do this another time."

"We *can't*. Listen to me. He says . . . he says you're his natural enemy."

And what, James wondered, did Richie Serrano mean by that? Was he referring to the usual antagonism between coyotes and patrols. Or was there something else?

He thought about Anteater rising up out of nowhere in these last several weeks, a name and an image and an idea, too: the long nose, the sticky fingers that could locate possessions wherever hidden.

There had to be something else.

"But where'd he come from?" James asked.

"Tijuana," said Leo. "I think, maybe . . . I don't know."

"What's he doing out here? What's he want?"

"I don't know."

James added in the van full of pollos, and a little boy crushed to death, the body placed deliberately in Desmond's field. He'd thought it was some sort of move against Des, but maybe it had more to do with himself. James thought about Anteater crashing the poker game at Efraín's. Watching him. Leo saying, *Richie wanted to meet you.* But why? And what had Anteater called James? An enemy of the people. *I know you better than you know yourself.*

James squinted out at sand and more sand. Ripples like waves. The sun was a yellow stare against a blue background that reminded him of being at sea, out where the wet surface of the earth merges into the sky.

Anteater had used Leo to get to him. The question was why.

Leo was breathing heavily now.

"Hey, buddy," James said, "you ever watch that old TV program, *Sea Hunt*? In reruns, maybe? Christ, they were reruns even when I was kid . . . Saturday mornings, my uncle and I used to tune in. I liked the star of the show. Lloyd Bridges. The character was Mike Nelson. Remember him? Nelson lived in a wetsuit, which I thought was very cool. That show had great underwater shots." James was babbling, but he couldn't stop. "Schools of fish," he said, "and shipwrecks, rocky places where people got stuck. Seemed like every episode someone ran out of air. Mike Nelson was always johnny-on-the-spot with his tank. Like you, Leonardo. Ready to share."

Leo said, "The fucker shot me." Then: "I loved her."

James knew he meant Mercedes.

"I loved her," Leo said again.

"I know," James said. The worst part was, he did.

"And you pushed right past me . . ." Leo twisted suddenly. "*You . . .*" He flopped onto his back. The entire front of his uniform was sticky with blood. In a loud clear voice he said, "You here, James?"

"I'm here. Yes." James moved closer. "I'm here."

Leo's breathing quickened. His chest and shoulders bucked in a series of short heaving gasps. His eyes opened wide. James made himself look. The sun fell on his naked shoulders. He smelled blood. He heard Leo's gut growl, the bowels emptying. Blood trickled from a corner of his mouth. To die in full daylight, James thought, completely exposed. He looked into Leo's face. He was a witness here.

Abruptly, Leo's breathing ceased. His skin was very white. His eyes shone bright and glassy, and within a few minutes, they'd flattened and dulled. The pupils dilated, swallowing light. The creases that fanned out to his temples smoothed.

The old man, James thought, that Leo would never be.

He sat with Leo's body for hours. He made a pillow of sand for Leo's head, thinking of the dead boy in Desmond's field, and rolled him onto his back. He straightened Leo's limbs.

Then he waited. He watched the sun climb. Throughout the day, small creatures visited, ants and spiders and lizards and snakes, all drawn by death.

Occasionally, birds circled overhead.

James wondered where the search party was. Where were the helicopters? The INS jeeps?

But time passed and no one came. He realized it was stupid to continue to sit. He had no water, no food. He should get up and get going. Right now. But he couldn't do it. He couldn't abandon Leo. He might never find the body again. And he was too weak to carry him out.

He heard the engine before he saw it, a low throb that carried on the desert's thin air. Some minutes passed. Then he saw headlights traveling toward them from the west. The Patrol, he thought. Thank God. He stood, his legs wobbling like a newborn colt. But as the vehicle came closer he saw it was a truck, not a jeep. A blue truck. And so probably not the Patrol. Anteater maybe, returning to finish the job.

The truck rolled to a stop, spitting sand. There were two men in cowboy hats in the cab, several others seated on benches in the bed. Those in the back wore white trousers, black hoods. James knew that meant something, but he couldn't name it just now. It didn't matter.

The driver's side door opened, and the passenger door. The men in cowboy hats got out and walked over. Thumbs hooked through their belt loops, they stared at Leo for a long time. Then they looked skeptically at James. They took in his soiled uniform, his bare chest.

The driver said finally, "¿Es su amigo?"

Just about everything Leo had ever done had driven James crazy. But, "Yes," he said. "Yes, he's my friend."

"We can put him in back."

The two men positioned themselves at either end of Leo's body. The driver lifted from under the arms; the other took Leo's feet. They carried him to the back of the truck, James following.

One of the hooded men got up from a bench and unlatched the gate. The driver fed Leo's shoulders up, pushing, while the hooded man pulled. The driver climbed up and together they moved Leo onto a blanket. But they did not cover him.

The driver put his hand down for James. James grabbed and the man hauled him up. James stumbled to a bench, where the others had already made room. Leo's body was laid out at his feet.

The driver jumped from the bed and shut the gate, and then he and his passenger walked back to the cab and got in. The truck started up.

They bounced over the sands.

A warm wind blew James's hair from his forehead.

He felt the hooded faces staring at him. He kept his head up and tried not to hide, thinking: You choose to see me, therefore, I will see you. And what was it he saw? Dark skin and Indian bones. Dusty bare feet. A few had blood on their white trousers. One reached across Leo and offered James a plastic milk bottle half-filled with water. He took it greedily. Drinking, he saw out of the corner of his eye that a youngster seated at the end of the opposite bench seemed to be growing a strange sort of mustache or beard. Then he realized that the boy's lips were sewn shut.

Penitentes, he thought.

The boy reached into the pocket of his white pants. He bent forward and passed a hand across Leo's face, then sat up again. Another man lifted a wooden flute. He started to play. The line, thin and melancholy, compelling and sweet, merged with the whistle of wind until James couldn't tell where one stopped and the other began.

He looked down at Leo, the sun throwing a beam from the coins placed on his partner's closed eyes.

CHAPTER TEN

Yard wanted him taken to the hospital in Chula Vista, but James refused, insisting he was just fine. So they cleaned him up right in the ambulance, hooked him to an IV while a medic sewed up his ear. Twelve stitches. The missing piece was tiny, the scalp wound superficial. Lucky, thought James, wincing as the bandage was applied. And with that he figured he was done here, he could go home. But he was wrong.

The conflict between him and Leo was apparently common knowledge around the stationhouse—he'd had no idea—and since he seemed to be in decent enough shape physically, they led him straight from the ambulance to a back office for questioning. And soon it became obvious that there were those who felt James was, if not entirely responsible for Leo's death, somehow involved.

Telling his story over and over again, even he could hear it: Anteater was too easy a villain, the mysterious pollos with weapons too convenient by far. What's more, there was no Richard Serrano in either the INS or the NCIC database. James knew the autopsy would show that the bullet in Leo—and Leo's horse, too—did not come from his gun; but who was to say he hadn't another squirreled away? When in desperation he finally floated the idea that this particular coyote, this Richard Serrano, was also responsible for a dead illegal found on Desmond's property, the revelation backfired, opening the door to a rant by Tommie Yard regarding a certain phone call he'd received from Detective Raymond Fricke.

"Rafael Noyez didn't do it," James said. "But I thought he'd talk to me, if I could only get him away from the jail."

"And did he?" Yard asked.

James was stuck now. If he told about the pollos in the canyon at Schiller Farms, Yard would make a call—he'd have to—and a raid would ensue. James didn't want that.

Yard said, "Maybe you were partners with this Anteater character."

James said nothing.

Yard said, "And something went sour."

"You don't believe that, boss."

"I don't know what I believe."

They stared at each other.

"In that case," James said. "Can I go now?"

Yard exchanged looks with Homicide, then nodded. But he put James on five days' leave. "Get some perspective," he said. "Some rest. And you better stay goddamn close. I mean it, Reese."

It was nearly midnight when he left the building. A patrol was supposed to be driving him home, but as soon as the guy went to the lot for his car, James set off briskly on foot. Just past the square—the fountain a gravestone, the palm trees charcoal cutouts blocking the sky—he made the turn onto Lincoln Avenue. Charlotte Murray's street. Climbing the steps to her door, he wondered just what it was he thought he was doing here.

One look at his battered face and filthy clothes and she let him in. "My God! What is it, Jamie? What's happened to you?"

"I'm sorry. It's very late."

"I'm up," she said.

Her living room was quiet and cool, the only light a floor lamp beside an easy chair. A notebook had been placed facedown on the seat, a ballpoint pen clipped neatly to its cover. James took in the glass bowl filled with M&M's on the coffee table, the *TV Guide*, the remote. An afghan his mother Marie had knitted years ago was folded over the back of the couch. Photographs covered every wall; on the floor were books and newspapers and magazines. Strings of colored beads hung in the doorway leading to the bedroom. Unbelievable, he thought. Nothing had changed.

"God, what happened to your ear?" Charlotte said.

James fingered his bandage. "It's nothing."

"You look so strange."

"I need help, Char."

He emptied his pockets onto the coffee table. Loose change and keys, his wallet, his I.D. The knife he'd taken off the captured pollo, the silver medal that Leo claimed to have found in the sand. The rock from the box he'd been carrying around since Los Angeles. And Lara's photograph, curled and cracked from his time in the creek: Emilio, and Diego, and James.

Charlotte reached immediately for the photo. She brought it to the floor lamp. Her eyes widened as she glanced from the snapshot to James and back again.

"That's your father," she said.

"Yes," said James.

"And . . . and *you*."

"Yes."

"What do you want me to do?"

"Tell me something, Char—something I don't already know."

She dragged the lamp over to the coffee table, then prowled the walls, pulling first one picture, and another, and another. Back at the table she arrayed them around James's old black and white.

All of hers were portraits of him. James was embarrassed.

If Charlotte noticed, she didn't let on. Down on her knees, she motioned for him to join her.

"I want you to read these, Jamie," she said. "See where they lead."

"Okay," he said.

Charlotte pointed at the first of her photographs.

James standing in front of the house on Seventh Street. Fresh out of the Navy, he guessed, with crew cut and blues. His gaze slid to the old black and white. But for the clothes and the colors, he and Emilio could have been the same man.

"I look young," he said finally. "I look at loose ends."

"Oh, you were," Charlotte said. "Both."

"I remember I was glad to be home."

"Were you? I'm not so sure."

Charlotte waited. When he had nothing more, she pointed to the second shot. "Try this one now."

Here, James sat on a picnic blanket in Corville's square. A corner of the fountain was visible in the background. Leafy shadows dappled his face. He couldn't tell if he was smiling or not.

"Know the year?" Charlotte asked.

"Ninety-two," he guessed. "Ninety-three?"

"What makes you say that?"

James looked more closely. "That branch, it looks pretty thin. That tree has grown since."

"Good. You remember what happened that day?"

James shook his head.

"We had a huge fight."

"I'm sorry. I don't recall. What was it about?"

"Moving in together, sharing a house. I wanted to. You, James Reese, did not."

Well, he'd won that argument. Fifteen years and they hadn't ever lived together. James had loved Charlotte, he really had. In ways, he loved her still. But she hadn't ever been *it*.

"Okay," she said. "You can move on."

James turned to the third and final portrait, a black and white in Charlotte's current style: the face tilted and overfilling the frame. The chin was lost and the top of the head, but James projected himself into the frame and he felt rather than saw the blue waters behind, a clear horizon line. He remembered where and when she'd taken this: Mazatlán, their last vacation as a couple. They'd been dark as walnuts from a week on the beach.

There were broken capillaries in the whites of his eyes, irises flecked with gray light, water in his dark face. James stared into the pupils, trying to see what was behind. Doctors did that, he thought, looked into the eyes, and through them, as a way to get to the brain.

Hidden in the pupils was a thin silhouette. Charlotte, he realized. Charlotte and her camera.

Nodding, she pointed a forefinger at James's old photograph. "Something to think about is who took the shot. Because there's always someone else there, someone who isn't in the picture."

"My mother took it." James didn't know why, but he was certain of that. "But the younger guy," he said, "that falling arm—do you think he intends to hurt the baby?"

"Not necessarily."

"'Cause it looks to me like he's going to hit him." James amended, "Hit me."

"I think he's only reaching, Jamie."

"For what?"

"Well—that I couldn't tell you." Charlotte turned. She reached up and stroked James's cheek.

"I've missed you," he said.

"Have you?" she said.

"When I started in with Mercedes, I used to feel I was cheating on you."

"Oh, me too."

"Of course, by that time you'd already given me the boot."

"You bent over, Jamie, wanting like hell to be kicked." Charlotte sighed. "But we spent a lot of years together, didn't we? I never understood why you had to take up with that girl. Younger than me. Naturally."

"That wasn't the idea."

"And then you up and married her! Took me, oh, I don't know, days to get over it." Charlotte smiled. From the pile of junk on the floor she selected the rock. She held it in her open palm. "And what, pray tell, is this, little boy?"

"Souvenir," James said.

"Of what?"

He shook his head.

"My, my," Charlotte said, "you still can't answer the simplest question. But that's all right. Can't teach an old dog, and I don't know why anyone would want to." She stretched her arms over her head. Her breasts swayed. With both hands she smoothed back her hair and James saw the faint lines like quotation marks between her brows and he thought about how Charlotte's thoughts had always been as good as her word, as clean and direct; she'd always been so easy to read. James knew he could sleep with her tonight. He saw it in her face. He felt it in her body and in his response, too. The lovemaking would be easy, familiar and good. But it wasn't going to happen, because it would mean the end of something rather than a true start. James wondered if Charlotte felt the same way, and he decided she must; and then he wondered whether he'd come to that conclusion only because it suited his purposes.

Charlotte squinted critically at the old photograph.

"Wait a minute," she said. She got up and went into the bedroom and James was left to wonder if he'd read her incorrectly after all. But she returned a few seconds later with a magnifying glass. Kneeling again, she centered it over the print.

James leaned in.

The enlarged detail revealed pinpricks of beard on Emilio's face, a mole on his neck. The white tip of a canine in Diego's open mouth.

Smiling, Emilio cradled his son. There was a pattern in the baby blanket, pale flowers maybe, or leaves. Barbed letters arched across

Emilio's bicep: t-h-e-r. *Mother*. The tattoo below that was a crude skull and crossbones. On the forearm more gothic lettering, so crowded James couldn't make out what it said. Then a single rose. Jagged thorns. Three drops of inked blood dripped to the wrist.

Christ! He jerked his head away. He'd seen this before. Where had he seen it before!

"What is it?" Charlotte asked.

James closed his eyes, pictured playing cards held in skinny brown hands. Cigarette smoke blown down, rather than up. The taste of tequila, the swing of ranchera music on Efraín's radio.

Anteater. Anteater and Emilio had the same tattoo. What were the odds? And what did it mean? Anteater had placed the dead child on Desmond's property. But why? He'd used Leo to get to James—hell, he'd tried to *kill* him. But why? Another question: Why now? It had something to do with that letter, he thought. And Lara Shipp Santana's will. Her money. And who stood to benefit if James was gone? His uncle, Diego Santana. But . . . but there was also the photograph, its written message to James. "Guilt and Innocence." James stared at Emilio's tattoo, the same one he'd seen on Anteater's wrist. Goddamnit. He'd reasoned himself in a fucking circle.

James stood. His left ear throbbed viciously. Charlotte stared up at him. "Thanks," James said, "you've been a real help."

Confused, Charlotte stood too.

"Listen," he said, "I've got to go now."

She looked at him, said carefully, "I don't like being used."

"I know that. I'm sorry, Char."

He gathered his things, until all that was left on the table was the bowl of M&M's and Charlotte's three photographs.

At the door, he paused, looking back. "What should I have seen in these pictures of yours?"

"If you don't know—" She sounded tired.

"Christ," James said. "It's you. My life with you. You're the one behind the camera. There all along."

"I have hundreds of photos," she said. "But the images capture only a few seconds of time. Incredible, isn't it? There's so much missing."

And by that he knew she meant everything, the moments before and after and those in between, those yet to come.

"All any of us ever has is right now," Charlotte said. "If you're smart, Jamie, you'll think long and hard about that."

He hopped the fence into Cruz's back yard. He'd run all the way from Charlotte's place, his heart in his throat, not knowing what he'd say or do when he arrived, only that he needed to see his wife.

He stood on the grass. The tetherball pole in its corner looked like a man with a hat in his hand. James stared at the house. Second window from the end—uncovered, as they all were—that was Mercedes's old room.

He crossed the yard, and pressed his face to the screen. As his eyes adjusted, he picked out a filing cabinet, a desk piled with papers, a blank computer screen; the room, he remembered, was used these days as an office for Ramirez & Son. But it still had a bed, pushed against the wall, the covers messed. James couldn't tell if anyone was in there. He tapped a fingernail against the window frame.

"Mercedes," he said.

A roll in the bedcovers, then her face on the pillow.

"Mercedes," he said again, a little louder, and she sat upright.

"It's me," James said. "Out in the yard."

Mercedes threw back the sheet. She padded to the window, then climbed up on the desk. She brought her face closer and stared out at James. The mesh made a fine grid of her features and he flashed on how his Tío Diego had once shown him how to copy maps from an atlas, dividing intricate shapes into small squares. You drew the contents of these, one at a time, the shape of the whole an accurate surprise.

157

James put his palm to the screen.

"Go around to the front," Mercedes said.

He went quickly, afraid she'd change her mind, afraid she wouldn't be there.

But the door was open. Mercedes struck a match as James stepped inside. She lit a candle at her father's altar, then turned to face him. Watery-looking shadows scaled the wall behind her. Dressed in an old T-shirt that came to her knees, the sight of her bare legs made James swallow hard.

"Dios Madre," she said, "you're always hurting yourself."

James said, "Leo—"

Staring at the bandage, she said, "He *cut* you—"

"Leo's dead."

Mercedes covered her mouth with her hand. "Jesus, you killed him."

"No, it was an ambush." It hurt him that she could think it, but he understood why. "A coyote . . ." he said.

Mercedes moaned.

She started to cry and he went to her. He put an arm around her shoulders and brought her to the sofa and lowered her down. Mercedes's body folded, no resistance at all. Her skin burned through the T-shirt. James felt her trembling at the core and he pulled her close. They sat touching arms and legs and sides. Gently, he stroked her hair. She turned and burrowed her nose into the crook of his neck.

She cried for a long time.

"I hate it," she said finally, coughing, a wet rattle in her throat.

James stroked her hair.

"That *job*." Then she said, "Leo was okay. He was my friend."

James wasn't so sure about that, but he said only, "I know."

The candle flickered, lighting the photo of Carlos Senior. Mercedes's father was squinting, as if into the sun, a lock of black hair dangling over one eye.

To the right of the picture frame, a flat dish held a gold wedding band.

Mercedes took James's hand and twined her fingers in his. "I ever tell you how Papa died?"

James shook his head.

"He was driving," she said, "down in Mexico. Pretty far down. I don't remember why he was there, something for business, I think. He was on one of those roads where you go for miles and there's nothing to see but dirt. What happened was that he had a massive heart attack. One minute he was rolling and the next he was dead. The truck just stopped in the road. Papa was sitting behind the wheel, hardly slumped even. That's what they told us later. Three days he was out there. Someone finally stopped, but there must have been cars that went around. When I think about that I want to bust somebody, you know?"

"Yes," James said. "I know exactly."

"How could they ignore him? Stopped dead in the road?" Mercedes sighed. "Papa always wore an old cowboy hat, and he liked it pulled down, to shade his eyes good. Maybe they thought he was napping." She shifted sideways to look at James. "When they found him, he was all bloated, you know? They couldn't get his ring off. They wanted to cut it, but Mama said no. She had them take his finger instead."

James whistled softly.

"Now it's your turn," she said. "You tell me something, okay?"

More naked than naked, that's how James felt. He swallowed. He didn't know what to say. But he had to give his wife something—something important, and true—or he was finished here. He knew it as surely as he'd ever known anything. He thought hard. Memories flared and receded, images, sounds, and his fear was like a cloud that casts a shadow over the land: eyes on the sky, he might miss it that the ground at his feet had gone cold.

"When I was a little boy," he said, haltingly, "I woke up one night to shouting in the house. My mother's voice. Not Marie—the other one."

Mercedes tightened her grip on his hand.

"She was yelling," he said. "I thought she was hurt, so I got out of bed and went downstairs and I found them in the library on the floor. My mother and father. Clothes dropped all over the place. They'd been out earlier, some sort of formal event. My mother had been wearing a sparkly dress, something very pretty, but she was in her underwear now. My father was in his long pants. His tuxedo pants. He had lipstick smeared on his neck, I remember that. I thought it was blood.

"There was a board game on the floor between them. Pretend money everywhere, and some real money, too, I think. My mother had most of it, and she was laughing, not crying at all. She was shrieking at Papi, 'Four hotels! Off with your pants!'"

"They were playing Monopoly," Mercedes said.

"Strip Monopoly."

"You come from gamblers."

James held her eye.

"My father had a girlfriend," he said. "This is the other one again—not Des. I met this girl at least once. I don't remember her name, but I knew she meant something to Papi, and I also knew we weren't supposed to talk about her, especially not around my mother."

"Yes," Mercedes whispered.

James said, "We all went to the beach. Papi and me and Tío Diego and this girl. I remember that Tío and the girl spent a lot of time in the water, bodysurfing. They went way out, at least it seemed that way to me, maybe because my father was acting very worried. The two of us waited up on the shore and he was pacing back and forth. I remember the water was white. It looked like milk. It was a jellyfish day and all up and down the beach, these weird creatures were pulled up onto the sand. Mounds of speckled goo. You could see their insides. And there was hardly anybody swimming. Everyone was afraid to get stung . . . but Tío and that girl were in. When the waves broke, they'd disappear for a couple of seconds and my father would squeeze my hand until we saw their two heads pop up. They'd ride the wave all the way in to shore. Slide on their bellies, scraping the sand."

Mercedes said, "Your parents didn't love each other."

"The thing is," James said, "I think they did."

"But the girlfriend?"

"I know. I can't explain it."

"Leo—" Mercedes said. She stopped, then began again. "Leo— he says—he *said*—he said you've been seeing Charlotte Murray."

Goddamn Leonardo, thought James.

Mercedes said, "Is that why you told me this story now?"

"No," said James.

"Is it true? Have you seen her?"

"No," he said again, thinking how he'd come to her from Charlotte's place. "Not like that, it isn't."

"Then what?"

"My father . . ." His voice was shaking now. "My father murdered the girl."

Mercedes's face went waxy and pale. "Oh, no, James—*why*?"

"I don't know. I wish I did."

She threw her arms around James's neck. She took his face in her hands, kissed his cheeks and his chin and his lips. She breathed into his mouth and he felt, for just a moment, as if Mercedes were giving him life. Relief flooded through him, his limbs weak as water. It was all right. The world was not going to come crashing down around him. Not right now. The cushions were soft, the room smelled of hot wax. He wanted to stay like this forever. Not think, not do—just sit. On an old sofa. In a candlelit room with his wife.

She took his hand, slipped it between them and held it against her belly.

The baby, thought James. He kissed the top of her head.

"Listen," he said, hating what had to come next. "I have to go to Los Angeles for a couple of days."

"No," Mercedes said.

"My mother—"

"No, James. You can't."

"I have to," he said. "My mother died."

He felt her struggling with it.

Then she murmured, "The lady in the sparkly dress."

"I have to see the lawyer," James said. "Straighten out a few things." And Alexander May Esq. seemed a likely place to begin.

"Can you stay with Cruz a little longer?" he asked.

"Of course."

"People might come looking for me."

"What kind of people?"

Corville P.D., for one. And Anteater? But no, the coyote believed James was dead.

The candle flickered beside Carlos Senior's photograph. The light shone on the ring. The black dog came padding toward them from the darkness, nails ticking like a clock against the wood floor, and James was suddenly aware of the Ramirezes, all around him. Cruz and Carlos and Rubén, asleep in their beds. It gave him more comfort than he would've ever thought possible.

"Just stick close to your family," he said.

CHAPTER ELEVEN

T he law firm of Wyatt, Seward & May occupied the entire twenty-sixth floor of a smoked-glass-and-steel office tower on Santa Monica Boulevard, in West L.A., with floor-to-ceiling panes that offered an unobstructed view to the Pacific Ocean; and James, sitting stunned in an oxblood leather wing chair, forced himself to fixate on that view, the colors so vivid—deep blue sky over deeper, bluer water—he felt them bleeding into his brain.

From the opposite side of a huge mahogany desk, Alexander May's voice was like a rushing river, all sound, no sense, although James heard a few select phrases well enough: *real estate* and *stock portfolio, capital gains, fixed rate of return*. May was detailing the terms of Lara Shipp Santana's will. Assets up the wazoo, thought James.

May rapped on the desktop with his huge knuckles, pink as pig's feet. The lawyer was eighty if he was a day. Fleshy face, a sweep of silvered wisps across a pink skull. A rumpled brown suit, buttoned awry. Peering over the tops of rimless spectacles, he said

sharply, "You understand? Your mother has left you everything."
And then, more reasonably, "I know this is shocking, James."

"Yeah." James cleared his throat. "You could say that."

"But good news, certainly."

"That all depends."

"On . . . ?"

"Well, I'd like to know the reason. If you don't mind. If you
even know."

May was clearly taken aback. "You *are* Lara's son. Isn't that
sufficient?"

"I don't mean the will."

"No?"

"I'm talking about the adoption, Mr. May."

Frowning, Alex May removed his spectacles. He pulled a handkerchief from his breast pocket and huffed on the lenses and
began to polish them. "Your mother wasn't able to take proper
care of you."

"Yes, I've heard that," James said. "The official explanation. It
doesn't mean anything."

"Lara's mental state was, as you may recall, always delicate. And
especially so at that, shall we say, difficult time in her life. You have
to understand she'd just lost her husband. Under very scandalous
circumstances."

"That's one way to put it. But let's not sugar-coat things. Emilio
was shanked."

May closed his eyes, as if deeply pained.

"They ever figure out who was responsible?" James asked.

"No," Alex May said.

"How about why?"

"No."

"Was it a racial thing?"

"I suppose it might have been. As I'm sure you're aware, prisons
in this country are hotbeds of racial hatred."

"But what else?" said James.

May sighed. "It might have been jealousy, or a grudge, or revenge. Perhaps Emilio took more than his share of mashed potatoes at lunch. . . . Do you know how many people are killed in prison each year?"

"But this was my father," James said. "Did everyone forget that I lost him, too? That should've counted for something. With Lara, at least." The muscles in his back were strung tight as piano wire. "If you don't mind," he said, "I'd like to ask you a few things about Emilio."

"Of course. What do you want to know?"

"Well, for instance: What did you make of him? Did you like him?"

If May found this line of inquiry strange, he didn't show it. Without hesitation, he said, "Yes, James, I did."

"Why?"

"Emilio was quite . . . well, personable. He had a definite, shall we say, charm." May touched his left thumb, counting off. "A fine sense of humor, and . . ." —grazing his index and middle fingers— "considering his background, Emilio was smart. More so than people gave him credit for. The police. The prosecutor. Even Lara."

"Did you think he was an evil man?"

"Evil?" May clucked his tongue in irritation. "There's an old-fashioned word."

"I'm an old-fashioned guy."

"But you understand that most people aren't evil. Even criminals, even murderers. It's the action we abhor, not the actor."

"You're a lawyer," said James. "It's your job to say that. But I don't agree." And he didn't. Terrible things happened every day, cruelties that as far as he could see could only be explained in terms of evil.

"Is there any possibility that Emilio was innocent?"

The attorney swung his chair away and James saw that the fleshy face in profile was another matter, hawkish and shrewd.

"I don't understand," May said, "the point of this sort of questioning. Why don't we stick to the will? There are problems you should be aware of."

But James persisted, "Did *you* think he was innocent?"

"What I think," May said, "is beyond irrelevant."

"Not to me."

"Yes, to you. By extension, to you."

"Did Emilio ever tell you he didn't do it?"

"No."

"He didn't tell you? Or you didn't ask?"

"I didn't ask."

"Why not?"

"Because it doesn't matter, James."

"But it has to! It has to be easier, defending an innocent man."

James's memories of Emilio were sparse enough, a few sharp notes against a hazy background, but he'd always had the idea that his father was incapable of killing anyone. Likely, he thought, all children of convicted murderers felt much the same.

"In court," James said. "What happened there? What did Emilio say?"

"He didn't say anything. Emilio never testified."

"He never defended himself?"

"No. Your father. . . . Well, he confessed. You understand? I couldn't let him testify."

James fell back in the chair. It made sense. He didn't know why he was so shocked. "How did that happen?" he asked.

"Ah, you didn't know."

"How did it *happen*?"

"When they arrested Emilio," May said, "they took him downtown. Your mother had some trouble reaching me . . . it was Christmas Eve. By the time I got there it was too late. A fait accompli."

James thought, Incompetent boob.

And then he remembered something that Desmond Reese, the good homicide cop, used to say: Confessings are blessings on the way to Death Row. Desmond hated lawyers, especially defense. In his good cop's opinion, they got in the way.

James asked now, "What does the name Richard Serrano mean to you?"

May folded his pink-knuckled hands on his chest. "Nothing," he said.

"Are you sure, Mr. May? Take your time. Think about it."

"I don't recognize the name. Should I?"

James leaned forward. "Why'd my mother send that photo to me? 'Guilt and Innocence.' Can you tell me what that bullshit *means*?"

"I'm afraid that I can't."

"Then who can?"

May pursed his lips.

The view through the window was dizzying, all that bright blue.

The blue pool, James thought suddenly. And a woman's red hair. *Red*. A red purse slung over a suited shoulder. Strings of colored lights blinking faintly in the sunshine. Out by the pool, the day of Emilio's arrest.

"The cop Emilio confessed to," he said. "The one who took him downtown. Tell me, Mr. May: What was her name?"

James had been to Los Angeles' Rampart Station just once, thirty-odd years ago, immediately following Emilio's arrest. He'd been only four at the time, but somehow he expected to remember the place. Yet no part of the station or its surroundings seemed the least bit familiar, not the neighborhood, not the street, not the building itself. And in spite of having spent years in and out of Corville Station, he was unprepared for Rampart's big-city air of disorder.

He pushed his way to the front of a line, flashed his shield and gave the desk sergeant his name, along with that of Lieutenant Louise Conti, who was expecting him—a miracle, on such short notice—and then he waited in the overcrowded lobby, squeezed in alongside a vending machine. James wasn't hungry, but he fed in quarters and made a selection. A Snickers bar dropped. He peeled the wrapping. Chewing mechanically, he studied a convex mirror placed in a corner of the ceiling, the reflection designed to give the cops at the counter a sight line to both an ATM near the door and the station's waiting clientele.

On a bench, two old men quarreled over whose turn it was to feed the meter. One held a blood-soaked handkerchief to his eye.

"You go," he said.

"No, you."

"I did it last time."

"So do it again."

One of several juveniles on the opposite bench punched his nearest companion in the arm. "Respeto, eh, Maxie? Go pay the man's meter."

"Okay," Maxie said.

James noticed the second boy didn't move.

They were gang members, he realized, in full uniform: khaki pants ironed to a sharp crease down each leg, canvas shoes, a white cotton T-shirt under long-sleeved flannel buttoned at the collar. Tattoos needled into the meat between forefinger and thumb. The first boy had a nasty gash on his wrist, and the wound seeped, a red bracelet.

One way or another, James thought, blood was the order of the day here.

There was a commotion at the desk, and the first boy hunched his shoulders and spit, watching avidly as a sniffling, baby-faced youth was led away in handcuffs. His previous command forgotten, he said to the other boy, "Lambe." *Ass lick*. "He perpetrates, I'm gonna kill that pendejo. Así es, así será." *This is how it is, this is how it's going to be*.

"He better be watching his back," Maxie said.

The first boy suddenly twisted around in his seat. He looked at James. "Hey, ugly," he said, "what's your problem?"

James felt his temper flare. But he'd be a fool to start in with this punk. He took a last bite of the candy bar, chewed thoroughly, and swallowed, and to save his life he couldn't have said what it tasted like.

The boy laughed and slapped at his thigh, satisfied he'd won something from James. A red stain spread onto his khakis. Again he spit, then high-fived as many of his compas as he could reach without getting up.

A uniform called James's name.

He followed the cop down a corridor and into a squad room, where a dozen men and women in street dress were taking statements from witnesses and penning reports, all against a background of insistently ringing phones. The room was hot, and smelled of body odor and shaving lotion, chewing gum and coffee. Something faintly putrid James couldn't name. A fat man wearing a velvet hat and a glossy fur coat sat at a desk, his hands folded on the blotter, and notwithstanding the outfit, James's first impression was that this was the boss; and then the man leaped to his feet with a blood-curdling scream, and three cops sprang forward to wrestle him into the chair.

"PCP," James's escort explained. He led James to a glass-enclosed office at the back of the room. Inside, four suits ringed a desk; outside, a ladder had been positioned beneath a hole in the ceiling. James saw the bottom third of a maintenance man, one foot on the top rung, the other swinging free.

The suits in the office appeared to be winding up business, patting pockets and tucking clipboards under their arms. The door opened and they came out single-file. Each gave the ladder a good shake as he passed, and a muffled voice called down, "Assholes."

The uniform motioned for James to enter.

They stood at the foot of the desk, watching a woman with a cloud of red hair read a blue-bound report. Out in the squad room, the man in the fur coat was shrieking again. Oblivious, the woman made a check mark in her text. The uniform cleared his throat and said, "Lieutenant?" and a hand went up in warning: thin, wrinkled, heavily freckled. No ring, James noted. The woman wore a conservative suit and a high-necked white blouse. The red hair was, he saw now, threaded with gray. Louise Conti looked more like a teacher or nun, except for her mouth, which was lipsticked bright red.

James had met her before, a long time ago: the woman who'd taken his father away.

The cloud of red hair angered him. But the face—he didn't know if he recognized her or not.

The uniform said, "You've got a visitor, Lieutenant Conti. A James Reese."

Conti looked up. "Oh, yes," she said. "We spoke on the phone." She studied him with blue eyes, pale and watery, then she blanched a little under the freckles; and then she pushed back the chair and stood. James was surprised at how tiny she was. He'd had the impression of a taller woman.

"It's good of you to see me," he said.

"Are you kidding," she said. "How could I refuse?"

The uniform had perked up at this exchange and Conti told him curtly, "Get out of here, Barnes." She waited until the door shut, then squared her shoulders and said, "Well, the years tick on by."

To cover his confusion, James stuck out a hand.

She took it and they shook, James letting go as soon as politeness allowed.

"The last I saw you," she said, "you were a birdy toddler with your thumb in your mouth." Conti paused. "What happened to your ear?"

James's hand went to his head. "A little accident," he said. "It's not serious." He wiped his face with his sleeve. It was even hotter in here than out in the squad, and the smell was worse, too.

"Terrible, isn't it?" Conti said. "A cat had kittens in the ceiling. We heard them mewling for days, different places. I thought the mother was moving them around. Hiding them. When the crying stopped, I assumed she'd taken them out. But then, yesterday, it started to stink."

James said, "She just let them die?"

Conti gestured at the window. "I'd open it, except that I can't. None of the windows open in here." She sighed. "Thirty-one years. You'd think I'd be used to that smell."

Yet another shriek sounded from the squad room. James turned to see the man in the fur coat being dragged into a holding cell, struggling with every step. James knew just how he felt.

"We can't talk here," Conti said. She opened a drawer and retrieved her purse and stepped out from behind the desk. She wore thick flesh-toned stockings, the toes and heels reinforced. A pair of black pumps had been kicked against a cabinet, and she grabbed the top edge and forced her feet in, ankles wriggling.

"Lunch?" she asked James.

That Snickers bar was sitting like a rock in his stomach, but he said anyway, "I could eat."

Conti insisted on taking an unmarked car from the stationhouse parking lot, a silver Caprice with rusted-out wheel wells, and a dented right front fender. She moved the seat up as far as possible, the glides scraping in protest, but still her nose barely cleared the top of the steering wheel.

Opposite the station, several houses sported iron bars on the windows, disabled vehicles propped up on cinderblocks in the front yards. An unseen rooster crowed and Conti said cheerfully, "Fresh eggs." She made a left, then a quick right onto Temple. James stared up at a red-and-white billboard: *Everyone has something to hide*. The Levi's logo registered in the moment just before it passed from his sight.

With a nod, the lieutenant indicated a pack of cigarettes on the dash. "You mind starting me one?"

James pushed in the lighter, glad of something to do. He plucked a cigarette from the pack, tapped the filter against the back of his hand. The lighter popped and James put the cigarette between his lips, lit the tip, and inhaled. Smoke filled his lungs. He felt dizzy, a not unpleasant sensation.

"A fellow sinner," Conti said. "I thought so."

"Used to be, but I gave it up a long time ago." James handed her the cigarette.

"Have one," she said.

"No thanks, Lieutenant Pusher."

Conti took a drag, held it in as she rolled her window down. She blew the smoke outside. "Can't do this in the office," she said. "I'm a pariah. In a population not known for lack of vice." She made a sudden left across three lanes of traffic and pulled into a narrow parking lot.

A red-roofed hut sat on the northeast corner, underneath a revolving red-and-white sign: ORIGINAL TOMMY'S. "Best chili cheeseburgers in the world," Conti said. She opened her door. Chili cheeseburgers, James thought, already sorry he'd come. But he climbed out and followed her. They got in a line that coiled around the outside of the hut.

Creeping forward, James watched the cooks behind the counter. One flipped burgers, and turned dogs on the grill, plunging baskets of fries into bubbling oil, while the other replenished condiments and collected the cash. The first cook dipped a steel ladle into a vat of viscous-looking chili, then poured it over a foot-long hot dog.

Conti ordered for them both. In less than a minute, the burgers were served, wrapped tightly in waxed paper soaked through with grease. Hot fries sat in paper sleeves. Everything was packed into a thin cardboard box. James reached for his wallet, but Conti waved him off. They exited onto a concrete patio, where they fished drinks from an ice-filled cooler. The dining area was a chest-high wooden shelf. Metal boxes screwed into the wall dispensed rough brown paper towels.

James unwrapped his burger. He took a cautious bite. Chili oozed onto his hand and he licked it off. He chugged his Yoohoo, chocolate water, basically, but it tasted good and was cold. He ate a handful of fries, then returned to the burger. Grudgingly, he admitted Conti was right. This was the best.

They ate in silence, until finally James said, "Back at the station, why'd you stare at me like that?"

Conti wiped her lips, red smears on the paper towel. "You look like him," she said. "Only . . . white, you know? But you have the facial features, the hair. Same build, too, compact but strong. Emilio Santana was strong."

"I guess he'd have to be. To kill someone that way."

"Then you know how the girl died."

"He drowned her."

"That's right."

"In the pool."

"That's right." She wiped her mouth again. "So. Not to be blunt here, but what is it you want?"

Information, thought James. The old journalist's creed: *who what when where how* and *why*. Especially *why*. That would do for a start.

Instead, he asked about something that only now struck him as strange. "How come they put a woman in charge?" He did the math: In '65, the lieutenant would've been in her late twenties, probably.

"It was a Mexican girl," Conti said, "found dead in the hills."

"Behind Dodger Stadium."

"You know that, too?"

"Yeah." He wasn't sure how.

"Identification took more than a month. I hate to say it, but no one much cared. Didn't know the case would wind up out of downtown."

"Who was she?"

"The girl?" Conti waved a hand. "Someone from around here. Santana's old neighborhood."

173

"And her name?"

Conti thought. "I'm sorry." She shook her head, the red frizz bobbing. "And after what I just said. My first real investigation, you'd think I'd never forget. Well. The more important name belonged to your mother. The Shipps."

"Sí, los ricos," James said. It came out more bitterly than he intended. "But haven't you heard? The last Shipp is sunk."

"Lara?"

"Yeah, she left me her money."

"Did she." Conti pushed back her hair.

Red, James thought. *Red*.

He said, "Aren't you going to offer condolences?"

"Well, I can't say I'm sorry."

Conti's lipstick was gone now, her mouth pale. In the bright sunlight, James saw creases around her eyes, puckered wrinkles over her lips.

He said, "I'm Emilio Santana's son."

"I know that," she said. "Nevertheless. We're on the same side."

James couldn't believe it; he didn't want to. And yet here he was talking to Conti, and eating with Conti, standing with the woman who'd taken his father away, on a street corner in Emilio Santana's old neighborhood. And it wasn't just a matter of information. That birdy toddler had grown up to put on the uniform. Being on *that side* was unchangeable now, like the color of his skin or his eyes or his hair. And so Conti's declaration felt like the truth, an irony he hadn't anticipated.

"You might as well hear this now," Conti said. "The girl was going to have a baby." She took a last bite of her chili cheeseburger.

James's food turned to paste in his mouth.

Conti chewed, and swallowed. "She was only a couple of months along, nowhere near showing yet. We didn't know. Not until the autopsy."

"Was the baby Emilio's?" James asked.

"Oh, we assumed. No DNA in those days. But it made sense, given what happened to her. But it wasn't just the pregnancy."

"The confession," said James.

Conti nodded.

"And what, exactly, was Emilio's story? If you remember."

"Oh, I remember, all right. Santana said it was an accident. Very predictable, I'm afraid. You know the refrain. 'I didn't do it, I didn't do it, okay, I did it, but I don't remember, okay, I remember, but I didn't mean it, it was an accident.'" Conti sighed. "I'm sorry. That sounded cold."

James shrugged, though his heart was thudding.

"Usually," she said, "I have to stand on my head to get them that far. But Santana—he went there right away. Frankly, I was a little surprised."

"Didn't even wait for his lawyer," James said. "Maybe that means he was telling the truth."

"No, I'm sorry, but I can't see that at all. There was evidence of a struggle. Bruises and such. The girl had a serious whack on the head. And she was definitely held under until she was good and drowned. The body was driven all the way across town and dumped." Conti crumpled her paper wrappings. "If that's not enough, there was a witness, too."

James set the bottle of Yoohoo down on the shelf. "Someone actually saw him murder her?"

"No. Not quite that. But after Santana dumped the body, he had the bad luck to run into a hiker on his way down the hill. The hiker found the girl ten minutes later. He'd gotten a good look at Emilio—they passed within feet of each other on the path—and he remembered him. At the trial, his identification was quite convincing."

James said, "Witnesses lie."

"But usually not without a reason. And this guy had none. He was a doctor from County, out climbing to clear his head after surgery."

"Witnesses," said James, "can be mistaken."

"That's true," Conti said.

James stared at the red-roofed cooking hut, the line of hungry diners, the white smoke, the revolving red-and-white sign. With each turn, for a fraction of a second, the first two letters were all he could see: *Or.*

"Okay," he said finally.

"Nothing," Conti said, "is ever one hundred percent. But on this one. . . ."

So. That was that. James sagged with disappointment. He didn't know what he'd expected. That the lieutenant would tell him they'd made a mistake?

"You do realize," Conti said, "how lucky you are? To have gotten out of that miserable house."

Lucky, he thought. He didn't feel it.

He made a show of gathering his trash, and Conti's, too, then he marched it all to a can.

She was waiting by the Caprice. James opened her door and she slid into the driver's seat, tugging her skirt down over her knees. When he saw she was settled, he pushed the door shut. He came around to the other side and climbed in and said, "Thanks for the food."

"A good cop can always eat."

"How do you know I'm a cop?"

"Are you kidding? I can smell it on you." A faint smile. "Wipe your face. There's chili on your chin."

Back at the station, they stood out on the sidewalk. James said, "Listen, Lieutenant, can I call you if I need to?"

"Sure." Conti looked searchingly into his eyes. "I'll tell you what," she said. "I'll even get you the files. They're buried God knows where, and I don't see that they'll do you much good. But if you want, I can have them copied. I'll send them down myself."

"I'd be grateful." James reached into his pocket and took out his black and white photograph. He handed it to the lieutenant, who got her glasses from her purse and put them on and studied the snapshot carefully.

"Well?" said James.

"Very very sad," Conti said.

"Turn it over," James said.

Conti did that, and read what Lara had written there. Shaking her head, she returned the picture to James. "Your mother felt guilty, giving you up."

James said then, "Emilio had a tattoo on his left wrist. You can't see it," he waved the snapshot, "not without a magnifier, but it's a rose dripping blood. That mean anything to you?"

Conti chewed on her bottom lip.

"What?" James said.

"There used to be a clica around here, back in the sixties, I think. An offshoot of Temple Street. . . . Yes, I remember. Your father was part of that. But I'm pretty sure those guys are long gone. The gangs are like corporations these days, with members in the thousands. I haven't seen that tattoo in years."

"What about someone named Richard Serrano? Or Richie, Ricardo, anything along those lines. Ring any bells?"

Conti's gaze went inward, as if she were reviewing a list in her head. "I'm sorry," she said. "You want me to run it?"

"No, I already did. I just thought that maybe—"

Suddenly, Conti's eyes opened wide. "Margarita Jimenez."

The dead girl, thought James, the girl Emilio had killed. *Margarita Jimenez*. The girl at the beach. He repeated the name to himself, rolling it over his tongue, trying to see if the shape and taste of it was familiar. It was not.

"All right," he said. "Thank you, Lieutenant."

Conti opened her purse, fishing now for her smokes. "It was time for lunch, anyway," she said.

He drove the truck around downtown for a while, right turns, and left, no idea where he was going, or how to get there, his mind occupied with all the things that Conti had said. He flipped the information upside down, and inside out, looking for clues to who Emilio Santana had been, something beyond his designation as The Murderer, which James saw capitalized in his mind's eye, like the unnamed villain in a melodrama. He was stuck in bumper-to-bumper traffic on Echo Park Boulevard for a solid ten minutes before he actually realized he was stuck—and Christ, he thought, he hated L.A! It was too big and too dangerous, too noisy, disgusting air. He hated the man-made sprawl, the dream-in-the-desert waste, the flashy clothing and cars and phony fantasy homes. Conti was right, he'd been lucky to escape.

But the first foster family he'd lived with had been down in Poway, and for an entire year, the mother there had insisted on calling him Little Angeleno. As if he carried the goddamn place with him wherever he went.

Fuck that, he thought.

He inched forward, Echo Park on the right, palm trees and picnic tables, a basketball court, two guys in bicycle shorts playing one-on-one. The lake was placid, wooden skiffs bobbing on greenish water. Emilio's old neighborhood. The house his father had lived in as a kid was somewhere close by. James wished he'd asked Louise Conti where, exactly.

The bus in front of him screeched to a stop, belching fumes and darkening his windshield. James hit the brakes just as a kid in baggy pants and a backwards baseball cap came rocketing out of nowhere on a skateboard and viciously, balletically, kicked the truck's passenger door. The driver behind him sat on the horn. In spite of the heat, James rolled up his window, sealing himself tightly inside.

Margarita Jimenez, he thought.

Drowned in Emilio Santana's pool.

He fought a mental picture: the young girl, soaked through, her dead body limp as rags.

He turned east onto Sunset Boulevard, crawled past taquerías and bridal shops, music stores—speakers blasting above the open doors—liquor stores, toy stores, surplus clothing outlets. Signs in the second floor windows advertised the local doctors and dentists and insurance agents. James noted that all the billboards were in Spanish here. All these people thronging the street, and how many were illegal aliens?

Rounding a curve, he saw the turnoff for Dodger Stadium, a sign planted at the intersection of Sunset and Elysian Park Avenue: white print on green. The hills were humped up behind. A crown of palm trees. It gave him a sick feeling, an electric tingle in his fingers and toes, because Christ, he hadn't been expecting it, the sign for the stadium and the hills right behind. Though of course, he'd known they were here, features of the old neighborhood. He was caught in a line of cars waiting to make a left onto Elysian Park Avenue. *Up there*, he thought, where the hiker had found the dead girl's body. Her pregnant body—*placed*. Up in the hills, with the foxtails and dried grass and eucalyptus. The city spread out like a picnic below. James could picture it all so vividly. But why, he wondered, had Emilio brought her there? Why go to the trouble, when there was plenty of empty country closer to home? For that matter, the whole goddamn Pacific Ocean. He tightened his grip on the steering wheel. He should make the turn, go have a look at the park, but now the traffic was moving forward again. He merged right, exhaling as he changed lanes; he'd been holding his breath. He followed a purple lowrider, the tension in his chest easing with every block, until finally he turned right onto Hill Street. Downtown proper: Bunker Hill, The Dorothy Chandler Pavilion, Angel's Flight. Skyscrapers stood like pillars of ice, their mirrored sides reflecting the sky. Just past Pershing Square, he caught a glimpse of City Hall, the only building he remembered from his childhood.

And then came the garment district. Concrete and barbed wire and metal canopies. Here, the costureras took their lunches outside, gathered on the sidewalks and in parking lots. Continuing south, the landscape became increasingly industrial, with buildings entire blocks long and semis parked behind iron gates. The occasional open lot gave him glimpses of railroad tracks. They looked compellingly familiar. He made a U-turn across double white lines, pulled the truck to the side, and sat a while, and then he got out and locked the door and set off across an empty yard littered with aluminum cans and cardboard boxes and broken glass. At the tracks, he looked left and right, surveying his surroundings: a windowless building, rails crossing and recrossing, and far ahead, an abandoned boxcar. He stepped onto the tracks and started to walk back toward downtown. The tops of the distant office towers rose shrouded in smog. The sun shone a hard hot white in the sky.

He'd been here before, a long time ago. With his father, the Christmas before Emilio's arrest. They'd come to the railroad yard to purchase their tree. He remembered acres of pines balanced on crossed wooden feet, unloaded boxcars dusted with snow. James shut his eyes, imagining the bite of fresh-cut evergreens. And then he was lifted into the air, swung onto Emilio's sturdy shoulders. James could feel it, himself the young prince, secure in the strength of the king. He'd looked out over treetops, a man-made forest in the middle of the city, while his father haggled in Spanish with a toothless old man in worn overalls and a striped red-and-white cap. Coins jingling in an apron pocket. He saw the old man shaking his head and pointing a muddy finger at Lara's Cadillac. It had been cold, he remembered, the sky red at one end, at the other, a seething dark gray. Taste of rain. James had blown ribbons of pretend cigarette smoke into Emilio's hair.

By Christmas Eve day, it had warmed enough to swim in the pool.

James's attention caught now on a dark heap puddled beside the abandoned boxcar. The heap was spread out over the tracks. Coming closer, James saw it was a plastic garbage bag stuffed to bursting, the top end torn to accommodate a gray-haired human head, eyelids swollen shut, skin bruised about the nose and mouth. He watched the head for a full minute, until he was certain it breathed.

The man opened his eyes and an arm thrust up through the opening. James took in an archaeology of clothing: waffled long underwear, grimy shirt cuffs, raveling sweater. From somewhere deep inside the bag came a merry clinking of glass.

"You got any money?" the man croaked.

"Hello to you, too," said James. But he was relieved. The man seemed healthy and alert, in good enough shape.

"You don't got any money, what do you want?"

He remembered riding his father's shoulders, loose and easy, no need to hold on. His breath steaming, made magically visible.

James said, "I'm looking for ghosts."

"Oh, that's too bad," the man said. "I don't got any of them . . . you going to hurt me?"

"Christ. Of course not."

"'Cause if you are, make it quick."

"I'm not." James's scalp itched, his eyes stung. "Aren't you hot in that bag?"

"No. This here's a mighty cold place."

Gently, James toed the plastic, setting off another chiming of glass. "You should move this," he said. "Get it off of the tracks."

The man shook his head sadly. "Trains don't come this way anymore. Everything's changed, you can see that, can't you?"

James nodded.

"You got any money?" the man asked.

He knew the ten-spot would be spent on liquor, but James took his wallet out all the same.

At four thirty he found himself again in Alexander May's office on Santa Monica Boulevard, up on the twenty-sixth floor, ensconced again in the oxblood leather wing chair. A lowering sun shone through the glass as James said firmly to the attorney, "I want a key to the house." My mother's house, he thought. My father's house. And now mine.

May stood to lower the blinds, and slanting shadows fell into the room. He ran a finger down the slats, a clicking glissando, then again took his seat. May clasped his hands under his chin.

"I can't do that," he said. "We've barely started probate, and I'm afraid settling the estate is going to be a bit problematic. Nothing that can't be resolved, but . . . this morning, we never talked about Diego. Your uncle, as I mentioned in my letter, is contesting the will."

"Does he stand a chance?"

"He's claiming your mother was mentally unfit."

"But what's that got to do with him? Why should he get anything?"

May blinked, so slowly it seemed he might fall asleep.

James was flustered; and then he was ashamed, a feeling caused by an unexpected rush of greed. He didn't want Lara's money, but he was also certain he didn't want to share it.

May said, "Diego lived with your mother for many years."

"How many?"

"Until quite recently, I believe."

And what could that mean? Lived with Lara how? As a younger brother, as family?

But it was James's family, too.

"What *about* Diego?" he said. "Why didn't he stop the adoption? He could have if he'd wanted to."

"Your uncle was still in school."

"So what!"

May stared inscrutably.

James could feel the attorney waiting—waiting for him to remember the trouble he'd caused. Fire and flood and demolition, lightning bolts hurled from his little boy's brow. What was the word? Incorrigible. *Yes*. As a child, James would bite to draw blood. He remembered that well enough.

He'd been a boy who bore watching. Until maybe it wasn't worth the effort anymore.

But he had to ask: "Who gives away a six-year-old kid?"

Alexander May shook his head.

The sun was creeping below the edge of the blind. The light dazzled and James's eyes stung.

He knew arguments could be brought to bear here, but first, he needed to think about things. It seemed obvious that Lara—and Diego—had wanted to get rid of him. They'd only been waiting for the right opportunity. Emilio was murdered in October 1967, and by December, James was in his first foster home.

May rose from his chair. He disappeared into the outer office, and a quiet settled, no sounds filtering up from the street. May returned, and sighing, flopped down. He held out a single page.

It was a photocopy of an official-looking document, with names and dates and witnesses. In the bottom right corner, the seal of Mexico. A wedding certificate, James realized.

Santana, he read. But the name of the groom was Diego Luis, and not Emilio. The bride's name was Lara Shipp Santana. He understood now. No need to change her driver's license. God-damnit! How could they?

He understood why Diego might do it. But why would Lara marry *him*? James cast his mind back, searching, and that led to an entirely different question.

"What did Lara see in Emilio?" he asked.

May smiled faintly. "What does your wife see in you?"

Fair enough. And James couldn't begin to answer.

"Your mother was a mystery," said May.

James pointed at the marriage certificate. "Any reason to think this is a fake?"

"None. But it's easy to check, if you want us to."

James stared at the date: December 12, 1967. Just days after he'd been given away.

That first Christmas in Poway, he remembered, had been a real shock, lights strung across cactus, a fake blue-and-white tree. There were a number of other children in that family, and every-

KAREN PALMER

one had opened their presents at once, screaming with laughter, wrapping paper strewn around the living room. The father had burned it all in the brick fireplace. James had received a G.I. Joe doll, but as soon as the thing was out of the box, he'd tried to throw it into the flames. The mother saw, and fished the doll out before it caught fire, scolding James.

He'd spent the rest of the morning glued to a window, watching for Lara's blue Cadillac.

Alex May held his gnarled hand over the desk, palm down, fingers closed. He opened the fingers and dropped a brass key. "For whatever it's worth," he said, "I always thought you were a nice little boy."

In the hills above Will Rogers State Beach, the streets were narrow, some no more than a single car wide, and winding. He hiked out over purple ice plant. From the top of the cliff, he watched a corkscrew of fog gather far out to sea. The falling sun was a disk that set scattered windows on the hillside afire, the kelp beds like unaccountable shadows beneath the red sky. A lone surfer rose and fell with the waves.

A hedge divided the lot from the house next door, where out on the rear deck a woman in a maid's uniform watered begonias in painted clay pots. The maid put the can down, cupped her hands to her mouth and called, "Ésta es private property, señor."

James thought of explaining that he belonged in this neighborhood; he thought of saying that when he was a boy this place had been his home. He stepped closer to the edge of the cliff, and the maid's voice climbed, but her words didn't register. He stared down at a white stucco house. A rounded front door, a red-tiled roof. Then a tantalizing glimpse of back yard: the hammock strung between two lemon trees; the bank of hibiscus in luscious full flower; wrought-iron patio furniture set beside a blue-tiled swimming pool.

Home.

CHAPTER TWELVE

Upon closer inspection, the house exuded an unmistakable air of abandonment. Cracked stucco, a walkway absent several tiles, leaning second-floor balconies with rust stains running from the old iron joints. The front window was broken, its glass reinforced by crossed strips of silver duct tape. Alexander May had assured James that someone was taking care of the yard, but the grass was ragged and studded with dandelions, the azaleas woody, unpruned. A drift of leaves and yellowed newspapers piled against the garage.

The side gate, strangled by ivy, canted crookedly on a single hinge, and the vines looked every bit as treacherous as they had when James was a boy, when he'd been forever worried by things unseen but imagined well enough: biting spiders, slithering snakes.

He forced himself to push through, hurrying along the side of the house, back to the patio. He crossed the flagstones to the pool, and stood at the shallow end.

It was all wrong, he decided finally. Too small and too narrow—he remembered a broad sparkling expanse—and the diving board was too close to the steps. The pool was three-quarters filled, leaves and a layer of green scum floating on the surface. The metal ladder at the deep end—all but the bottom rung was exposed.

James lowered gingerly to sit on the steps, planting his shoes in a quarter-inch of water. He could hear the Pacific churning at the bottom of the cliff. Watching a ladybug negotiate the edge of a sodden brown leaf, he had a sudden memory: his father dropping a shred of lettuce into a clean mayonnaise jar, poking air holes in the top with a knife. With the tip of his shoe, James submerged the ladybug's raft. But the insect took flight without so much as dampening her wings.

He thought about his father's arrest. Christmas Eve day, 1965. He'd been four years old.

He remembered pots of poinsettia on the flagstone patio, wreaths tied into the hibiscus with bows. Strings of colored lights blinking faintly in the sunshine.

Standing at the end of the diving board, he'd watched as the red-haired lady led his father away, Emilio still in his bare feet and jeans. His hands were cuffed behind his back. Blue spark of sun on metal. A huge jay had screamed down from the trees, and when Emilio glanced up, he'd said something, and the red-haired lady had smiled.

James had been reassured.

Then a uniformed officer pushed Emilio through the gate.

He remembered his mother crying as she came around the side of the pool, Lara in a pink two-piece bathing suit, the skin of her belly iridescent, like the inside of a shell. Rubber thongs slapped the soles of her feet. She'd collected her towel, then vanished behind the mirrored sliding glass doors.

Young James had locked his knees; he'd pressed his arms to his sides. He stood stiff and still for a very long time. The diving board was covered with a dense flat-braided rope, and when he bent a sore foot, his curled toenails snagged. His small testicles itched. The water below him was an unbroken blue sheet.

But after a while, his Tío Diego came out.

Jaime, he cried, what are you doing up there?

Tío, I'm stuck!

Ah, a dilemma. Tío Diego scratched thoughtfully at his chin. He appeared to be considering a multitude of options. You could go back, he suggested. Or you could jump. What fun that would be.

But you or Mama have to be in the pool. I don't have my vest.

You don't need it. I am right here.

Tío, I'm scared.

Nonsense. The pool can't hurt you.

And so jump he did, sinking at once to the very bottom. The weight of the water was a hand on his head. Pressure bloomed in his chest; he felt as if he'd swallowed his heart. Bubbles left his mouth in a thin boiling stream.

But he bent his knees, pulled his elbows in tight and pushed off, his arms steepling instinctively over his head. He rose like a rocket and, gasping, broke the surface.

Frantically, he dog-paddled in place.

Well, well! Diego said. Aren't you a brave boy.

James gulped a little water. The side of the pool looked too far away. I wish, he said, that Papi had seen.

You can show him another time, Diego said.

Tomorrow?

Perhaps.

Tomorrow is Christmas.

Yes, your Papi loves Christmas.

But the day came and went without Emilio's return.

James stood now, too quickly, catching a shadowed movement against the back of the house. His heart thumped, his hand went to his empty hip. He cursed himself, cursed also the man confronting him: dark-haired, dressed in a dark, short-sleeved shirt, dark pants. Then he realized the man was himself, reflected in the mirrored sliding glass doors. Two ancient bougainvillea framed either side and the gnarled branches strained toward each other in an oddly human embrace. James found himself mesmerized by the swagged profusion of flowers, bright as blood.

He walked back around to the front, fishing in his pocket for the key.

The smell hit him hard, a sweet fetid rot: shit blood bandages, salt, formaldehyde, dust and rust. Lara Santana had died of colon cancer, and even from the vestibule, evidence of her illness was everywhere. James flipped the switch on the inside front wall and the first thing his eye landed on was a surgical cart, its surface cluttered with scissors and paper wrappings, bottles of medicated lotion, plastic tubing. Holding his breath, he stepped around dozens of spilled envelopes—most, he saw, were medical bills—and headed down the hall to the kitchen, where a small pharmacy marched across the countertop, bottles of medication arranged crazily according to height. James found a plastic dispenser labeled with the days of the week. The compartments held four separate daily dosages, and he opened the column marked Sunday and tipped the pills into his palm: caps and tablets, assorted colors. The smell was bad in here, too, but different, with a gone-sour edge. Spoiled food. He followed his nose to the storage space under the sink and pulled out an uncovered can filled with writhing maggots. He dropped it, the muck spattering. He almost vomited, so strong was the feeling that this filth had come from inside himself.

He left the mess alone and continued on to the library.

Throwing open the wide double doors, James stepped onto polished parquet. Bookshelves stood floor to ceiling, filled with leather-bound books. Velvet drapes closed the room off from the patio, and the sun. James turned on a floor lamp, but the room still seemed steeped in gloom. At the bookcases, he selected a volume at random and spun through the pages—a collection of essays by Francis Bacon—but the words quickly blurred and he closed the book and slipped it back into place. He went to Grandfather's desk: as a child he was never to touch. He opened all the drawers, but found only blank yellow pads, loose pencils and pens, stamps and paper clips. And now he forced himself to face the hospital bed. Set in the middle of the room, it was raised to a sitting position, as if awaiting its customary occupant. But the mattress had been stripped, the linens a tangled ball shoved into the seat of an overstuffed chair. An IV stand, its empty packet of saline attached, rose up behind the headboard. James took in a second well-equipped surgical cart. A blood pressure machine, a steel-armed commode. Lara must have set up in here when she could no longer negotiate the stairs.

He walked around the bed to the stone fireplace. A portrait above the mantel showed a young Lara Shipp in strapless green silk, one hand on the banister of a curving staircase. Pale skin, pale lips. Her blond pageboy brushed gleaming shoulders. Lovely woman, thought James. But the likeness, while accomplished enough, struck him as cold, matching the chill he felt upon viewing it.

Lara's hands were too large—the one on the banister, but especially the other, held open against the folds of her skirt. Some flaw, James imagined, in the artist's perspective. He stared into hazel eyes so like his own, searching for clues to the disparity between who Lara had been and who she became.

But finally he gave up. Either way, he didn't know the woman.

He took the stairs to the second floor two at a time. He turned into his parent's bedroom and made straight for Emilio's closet. He found it empty; he'd half expected to see Diego's things. Next, he looked into Lara's closet, and this in contrast was choked with clothing: dresses and sweaters, blouses, skirts, coats, pants, scarves, hatboxes and shoeboxes and department store bags. His eye caught on a yellow shift and he pulled it from its padded hanger. He brought the curve of neckline to his face. James smelled his mother, cigarettes and oranges, and he sank to the floor. He sat very still, listening to the silence that surrounded him; and then he reached up and gave a vigorous yank and torrents of dusty fabric rained down on his head. Methodically, he began to work through the hatboxes and shoeboxes and department store bags. He was looking for something, he'd didn't know what, but he was sure he'd recognize it when it was in front of him. He lifted lids, tossed tissue paper aside. The boxes contained stiletto heels and loafers, tennis shoes and boots, derbies, turbans, berets. In a lingerie bag stashed on a hook behind Lara's robe, he unearthed a small trove of paper, printed slips that when he shook them floated gently to the floor. But the slips of paper were only receipts, evidence only of purchases.

In the master bathroom, he stood on the white tiles, remembering how he used to bathe with Emilio here. His small body placed between his father's thick legs, James would rock to set the water sloshing like a tidal wave up the tub's sides. And Emilio would hold him, saying, M'ijo, this is pool enough!

Now, stretched lengthwise in the long tub, a flexible hand-held showerhead looked like a snake with a rodent caught in its mouth. A single row of tile had been torn away to accommodate a steel handrail, the exposed drywall slick with mildew. An unemptied wastebasket held bloodied bandaging. Lara's, thought James. He backed out, careful not to touch anything.

And now he entered Tío Diego's old room, the one his uncle had occupied as a teenager. Nothing of interest here, only a twin bed, a dresser, and empty white walls: a cleric's chamber. However long Diego had lived with Lara, all traces of him were gone.

He looked briefly into three empty guest rooms. And then he came to the last door, the final bedroom: his own.

A bed like Tío Diego's, an identical dresser and chair. The dresser was walnut, with shining brass knobs. As a kid, James had carved his initials into the wood with a knife, and he'd taken a beating for it, too. Kneeling, he ran his fingers down the sides and over the top, but he couldn't find the carving. He went over the piece inch by inch, reluctantly coming to the conclusion that there were no initials. Either this was a different dresser, or Lara had had it refinished. A third possibility occurred to him: he was recalling something that had never happened.

He checked the closet. Empty. The shelves that had once held his toys were also empty. James had arrived in Poway with little more than the clothes on his back. What had they done with the rest of his things?

Defeated, he sat on the bed, and immediately he was desperate for a clean breath of air. He got up again. The balcony door was swollen, but the knob turned easily. A good yank and the door opened, groaning. James stepped out onto the balcony. A salty breeze blew his hair from his face and he grasped the rail with both hands, taking in great gulps of cool air. He felt a rush of gratitude, and then just as quickly, he was afraid. His bedroom overlooked the back of the house, the yard and the pool and the sea, invisible now under a blanket of fog, and he remembered how as a kid he used to watch the mist roll up the cliff. A malevolent force, he'd imagined it coming for him. James stared down at the pool. In the dark, the half-sunk debris was disturbing, the shapes reminiscent of—what?

How was it, he wondered, that he'd known Margarita Jimenez had drowned? Where had he picked up that particular piece of information? And how was it that he could he picture, so clearly, the view from the hills behind Dodger Stadium?

Abruptly, he left the balcony. He shut the door to his room and returned to the library downstairs. At the overstuffed chair beside Lara's hospital bed, he pitched the soiled linens to the floor, and sat. After a while, he got up from the chair and went to the drapes. A yank of the cord and the velvet panels slid to either side. A milky gleam slanted into the room. The sliding glass doors were crusted with salt. But outside the yard was an Eden, birds in the dark trees, innocent flowers. The doors squealed as James opened them, and he wondered how long it had been. For a second, he pictured Lara in her deathbed, curtains closed and lights out, hiding to the bitter end.

He went back to the mattress, and perched on the edge.

The nightstand held an empty water pitcher, a cloudy drinking glass. A book.

He read off the title: *Dark Matter*. And the subtitle: *The Search for the Missing Mass of the Universe*. An astronomy text. Then he saw the author's name: Diego Luis Santana, Ph.D. James reached for the book. He turned it over. Forthright and unsmiling, Tío Diego stared out at him. Despite a thinning crop of gray hair, Diego appeared preternaturally boyish, dressed in chinos and a pristine lab coat. Sloping shoulders, a thin, ascetic face. Sideburns, too long. Diego stood in a field of brown scrub, the rounded dome of an observatory in the background. The sky was colored an intense peacock blue, stars winking brightly.

James set the book down. He rolled onto one hip, pulled the rock out of his pocket and placed it on the nightstand. Then he got out the old photograph.

Emilio, and Diego, and James. Lara, behind the camera.

He propped the photo against the water glass.

He took Diego's book up again. On the inside flap a short biography offered the information that Santana lived in Los Angeles, that he'd published widely in scientific journals, that he taught astrophysics at the California Institute of Technology in Pasadena.

James swung his legs up onto the bed. He lay back, his head sinking into Lara's pillow.

He thought about what he knew: Emilio had killed Margarita Jimenez.

And he thought about what he remembered: Climbing out onto the balcony from his room. Squinting into a bright blazing sun.

Up from his nap, he'd heard noises outside. Splashes and laughter. Crying, maybe. At four he was small enough that he'd had to peer through the bars, and he'd looked down at the pool and he didn't know what, exactly, he was looking at, the diving board, sunlight on the blue water, and something at the bottom, down by the drain. His father and his uncle were sitting on the pool steps. Naked, which James had found very funny, but scary, too, the hair curling on his father's chest, and his tío's smooth brown skin, both with that fur between their legs and the mouse in its nest. Glancing away from the pool, Emilio said, Are you happy now? and for that second James had stopped being scared. He'd laughed and his father and uncle had looked up at him.

What came after was out of focus, mere shapes and presences. Was it a memory? Or an invention, a dream? Was it *that day*, or a day like any other? And how would he ever know?

Tío Diego, he thought.

The night of Emilio's arrest, Diego had played Santa Claus, stuffing his brother's smoking jacket with pillows and gluing cotton balls to his teenaged chin. Here in the library, with the tree lit and the stockings hung and a fire crackling in the stone fireplace, he'd lifted his nephew onto his lap.

And what, James wondered, had the boy asked for?

He opened Diego's book and started to read. He understood enough to keep the pages turning, no more. And gradually, the written words came to seem as if they were spoken as well, the voice of the speaker more real than the ink.

Fourth of July. A windy dusk, tattered clouds sweeping across a blue sky.

Jaime, Tío said, you must try to keep up.

James was—what? four years old? five? Emilio was up at San Quentin and had been for a while. But the rest of the family was celebrating the holiday in Elysian Park, above downtown L.A. Already, they'd enjoyed a picnic on the grass, fried chicken and potato salad, jalapeño corn bread. Fresh peaches, fresh plums.

Though it was mostly James and Diego who ate, Lara merely picking, with little appetite.

Now they were hiking up the side of a hill, up behind Dodger Stadium, where they'd watch the evening's fireworks for free.

A dirt path, a rising slope flecked with white-barked eucalyptus. Dried grass and dried brush, the smell of baked earth. Birdcall, and buzzing insects.

The path grew steeper and Diego stopped and waited and took James's hand. Lara followed behind.

The brush closed in on the path, tearing at their clothes and their hair. They ran up against a massive oak tree, the gnarled trunk grown straight out from the hill, its branches a low-slung canopy. Ducking, they crouch-walked single file, until they were out from under the tree. The path widened. Another few yards and they crested the hill.

The fading blue light struck electrifyingly clear. They were surrounded by air. The whole of the city was laid out below, the freeways like shining rivers, the streets like feeder streams. Traffic hummed, the breath of a lion. The buildings downtown nicked the bottoms of clouds. To the east, James saw the buckled spine of mountains; to the west, the sun hid behind a wide stroke of gray.

Diego waved an arm. Look, Jaime, there is our famous fog. He said to Lara, Right here. This is good.

Lara dropped onto the grass, into shadows cast by towering trees. James sat beside her, and Diego sat beside James. Acorns crunched underneath them, releasing a dry, medicinal smell.

But the Santanas were not the only spectators here. The hillside was dotted with couples and families and noisy teenagers. Everyone could see straight down into Dodger Stadium, where the seats were filling, more people on one side than the other.

Diego said, They don't want the sun in their eyes.

We should have gone to the pier, Lara said.

No, this is better, Diego said.

Lara's mouth thinned. She lay back on the grass and placed her pale forearm over her eyes.

Diego rubbed his hands together. He said to James, Your father and I used to come up here as boys. Smoke a little reefer, drink a little beer. In the summer, we'd watch the ball games. We could never hear the announcer, we were too far away, so we made up our own stats.

Darkness was falling. The blue light blackened behind feeble stars. Music sounded faintly.

And then without warning, *ka-boom*. A rocket shot up into the sky, followed by shivers of light, green and silver, falling away. James heard the crowd's collective gasp: *Ah-h-h-h!* A whine, and the sky filled with trailing squiggles. Pop-pop-pop, *ka-boom*. Gold-spangled flowers broke into lines. These are aerials, Diego told James. The fireworks blast out from hard paper shells filled up with little black balls, called stars. Some stars are only one color, others are rolled like jawbreakers in layers. As each burns off, a new color appears. And every kind of shell has its own name. Gold-brocade-to-red-butterfly. Red-tipped-comet. Green-peony-with-a-silver-palm-core.

Ka-boom. Whining shrieks without color or shape. Those are whistle shells, Diego said. *Bang-bang-bang.* Those are salutes. If we were in the stadium, you'd smell gunpowder now. That one, he pointed, is weeping willow. See the branches, Jaime? The stars contain a little charcoal, which makes an orange fire that lasts a long time.

Then, too soon, the finale began. Down in the stadium, the lights were shining. At one end, just above ground, a rectangle fired red, white and blue. The American flag. Every corner of the sky lit at once, the night and its stars banished. The hillside was weirdly exposed. James held up a hand, hoping to see the bones through his skin.

The sky was strobing, rings of brilliant red stars and dazzling red tips. Streams of flitter. Shells shot by the dozens. Red blue green silver gold. The light faded slowly. The silence that followed was complete and profound.

A smattering of applause from the spectators on the hill. Several stood, laughing. The excited voices seemed to come from some other place.

James turned to his mother.

Still lying on her back in the grass, Lara appeared to be sound asleep. James looked at Diego, who winked. Diego put a finger to his lips. He crawled over James, approaching Lara on his hands and knees, and positioned his head above hers. He blew a soft puff of air.

Lara opened her eyes.

James said, You didn't watch, Mama! Why didn't you watch?

Querida, said Diego, this is the place.

James tracked his mother's breath, the shallow rise and fall of her chest. He couldn't see Diego's face, but there was something in Lara's that filled him with fear. He kicked at the hillside. Let's go now, he said. Diego raised an arm, and with delicate fingers, tucked a wayward blond strand behind Lara's ear. James kicked again, as hard as he could. This time he loosened a small egg-shaped rock.

Another memory.

San Quentin, October 1967. James's final visit with his father, Emilio.

The family sat at a table in the visiting room, Emilio and Diego on one side, Lara and James directly opposite. The room hummed around them, the sounds of prisoners, their wives and children, parents and friends.

Guards lined the walls, legs braced apart. Every few minutes, they rotated counterclockwise, switching positions with smooth efficiency.

Six-year-old James sat quietly in his seat. He wiggled his toes—his shoes were too small—and studied Emilio from under half-lowered lids.

196

Months had passed since he'd seen his father last, and Emilio had changed. His eyes were sunk into plum-colored shadows; his hair clung to his skull, oily, unwashed. Emilio's neck hung wattled and loose, and furrowed cuts ran the length of his cheeks. His skin was pale from being so long indoors, and the inked blood that dripped down his wrist looked frighteningly real.

Emilio said to Diego, I thought you would not come. Visiting is nearly over. And you have classes tomorrow.

Diego said, We missed the plane by a few minutes only.

But James knew this for a lie. They'd never even made it to the airport. They'd driven all the way up from Los Angeles, hours and miles through the Central Valley. From the back window, James had watched empty fields rolling like thunderclouds to meet the round hills. He'd found himself succumbing to an odd sleepiness, lulled by the sensation of hurtling through space.

Stepping from the car, however, the cold air hit him like a slap. His hair whipped about his forehead, his shirt molded to his chest. He swayed on the asphalt, blinking uncertainly. Fresh-painted parking lines gleamed away in every direction, ghostly trailings that seemed a message of unknown origin. Heels tapping, Lara came around the front of the car, and James reached for his mother's hand, a rare demonstration of need. Diego walked ahead, whistling, a light jacket thrown over one shoulder.

The crowd at the front gate was unexpected, and scary, the homemade signs, the lumpy scarecrow tied to a stick. Someone was playing a tinny transistor radio. As the Santanas passed, an old woman in a black dress cried, ¡La familia del asesino! and Lara pressed James's head to her waist. He buried his nose in her fur coat, smelled cigarettes and overripe oranges, and underneath, something musky and dark, something that made him think of wet earth. The woman shouted, ¡Queremos justicia! Lara said to James, Ignore them. It has nothing to do with us. And then the guards were opening the gate.

Halfway across the yard, James heard shouting. He looked back. Up in the guard towers, shadows moved behind glass. Down on the ground, the scarecrow was on fire.

Emilio's eyes swept the visiting room, looking into every corner. In a low voice, he asked Diego, Did you talk to the lawyer?

Yesterday, Diego said. As you requested.

And what did he say?

What could he say? That you must wait, and we must wait.

Emilio hunched forward. You have to get me out of here, 'mano, he said. Talk to May again. Make him write a letter to the governor, the parole.

There's nothing the lawyer can do, Lara said.

Emilio glared across the table. *You.*

Lara huddled into her fur, butter-colored hair folded against her white neck.

Emilio said, You are taking care of my son?

Lara licked her dry lips.

For once, querida, you must try to be strong.

I'm sorry, she said. I'm so very sorry.

I know. But it does no one good now.

Blondie bitch, Lara said. That's what someone called me.

People don't like it, querida. White girl playing with the gardener's boy.

Lara protested, They don't know that.

They do, Emilio said. In here, they know everything.

He turned to Diego. And *you.* You are also taking care of my son?

Of course, Diego said.

You must study very hard.

Of course.

Because the stars have their secrets, just as we do. You must ask the questions, 'mano, always and forever. So it is not all a waste.

Emilio paused, as if waiting for a reply.

James waited, too. He thought about Diego's big books, filled with tiny print and mysterious symbols. Sometimes, his uncle disappeared into the desert for days, to study the heavens through an enormous telescope, and if James had no clear idea how this instrument worked, he accepted the notion that it put the stars within reach.

But now Diego said nothing. His hair hung, shining, the purply blue-black of a bruise.

Emilio stretched his arms over his head. He extended his neck and rolled his shoulders.

Diego said, There's a crowd outside, by the gate.

Sí, said Emilio, they are gassing tomorrow night.

Lara moaned.

James understood that *gassing* meant someone would die, and he wanted to ask: Do you keep your eyes open or closed? Does it hurt, and how much? Was dying like sleeping, something to be struggled against? Was it like a room you could refuse to enter?

Diego said, Do you know who it is?

We all know. Again, Emilio's gaze flickered around the visiting room. Can't you feel it, 'mano? The relief. Every man glad it isn't going to be him.

Diego said, No one in this room is condemned.

I have to get out, Emilio hissed. He stared unseeing across the table at James. Then his face softened. ¿Qué quieres, m'ijo? he asked, so gently that James thought the question had originated inside his own head.

What did he want?

James wanted to hear how much he'd been missed, wanted Emilio to marvel at how much he'd grown. But he was afraid. His father had taken a life, but James didn't understand the how and the why; no one had ever explained. So he could never quite bring himself to believe.

He wanted, he realized, to *know*.

Papi, he said. There is . . . something. He stopped. Diego was watching him. James began again. I want to know, he said. Did you do it, Papi?

Lara put a hand to her throat.

¡Chitón! cried Diego. ¡Qué pregunta!

But instead of answering the question, Emilio asked one of his own: Tell me, m'ijo, are you a good boy?

The question clanged in the air like churchbells.

James hung his head in shame. Because sometimes he stole things. And he'd run away, more than once. He'd set a fire in his room, the match held to the hem of a white pillowcase. His mother running in, his mother screaming. Diego staggering with the cooking pot in his arms. From out on the balcony, James had watched the water thrown.

Emilio stood, shunting his chair aside. He came around the end of the table to James, who cowered, certain he would be struck. A muscle twitched under Emilio's jaw. He clamped a hand on his son's shoulder. James tried not to squirm.

Gathering his courage, he asked again, Did you do it, Papi?

Emilio's fingers tightened as he looked to his wife and brother in turn. Jaime, he said, I am ashamed of many things. But I am not the only one. Dios sabe. *God knows.*

He said to James, Do you know, m'ijo, what is the job of a man? The job of a man is to protect what he loves.

Emilio dipped his head and brushed his lips against his son's temple. And James might have had an answer—except that the words were like birds fluttering soft in his ear, flown before he had the chance to capture them.

Two months later, Emilio was dead. And shortly thereafter, James was given away.

It was Diego who told him he was going into foster care.

December 1967, very close to Christmas again. But in that year of Emilio's death, no one had installed twinkling lights. No wreaths had been tied into the greenery with bows. Nephew and uncle sat on the patio in the back yard, in iron chairs. A light wind had set the leaves to whispering.

A bird chattered from deep within a hibiscus bush and James heard it hopping from branch to branch.

Drink up, Jaime, Diego urged. He lifted his bottle of Coke, threw his head back and swallowed, then wiped his mouth with the back of his hand.

James tipped his head, too. He poured in a mouthful of soda and the sweet fizz exploded deliciously on his tongue. It tasted *good*. And his uncle was in a good mood, easy and affectionate. At six, James knew enough to be suspicious of this, but today, he'd allowed himself to surrender to Tío's charm. Today, they'd had fun. In the morning, they'd looked at the daylight moon through Diego's telescope. Then they'd walked on the beach. They'd gone to the movies, *A Man for All Seasons*, which James didn't understand at all, not that it mattered, just so long as he had his popcorn and Jujubes.

Just minutes ago, they'd been tossing a football in front of the house. Heaven.

But now a word was rolling around inside his head, bouncing off corners, picking up speed. The word was *foster*. James didn't know what it meant. There was a Foster's Freeze in Pacific Palisades. They served soft vanilla ice cream, dipped in chocolate that hardened into a shell. But that couldn't be what Diego was talking about.

It is for a short time only, Diego said.

But *where* am I going? James asked.

Someplace fun. You'll like it. I promise.

An unsatisfying response. What about Papi? James said slyly. Emilio was his best weapon, his ace in the hole, reserved for those times when he needed to hurt or worry Diego somehow. Which he'd clearly done here.

Diego fixed him with a stare. What about him, Jaime?

James held his tongue.

Again: What about him?

And now James was scared. He didn't *know*.

Diego's face looked ugly, as if there was another person under his skin, struggling to escape.

Emilio was my brother, he said. I loved him very much.

The words brought on an angry ache in James's chest. The bird chattered madly from inside the bush and he screamed, Shut up! Shut up! He screamed at Diego, You are supposed to take care of me! Papi said so!

I am, Jaime.

No! You aren't!

Diego grabbed his arm and yanked him close. James smelled the oil on Tío's face. Diego's mouth was open, and there were the white teeth, and the dark tongue, the dark disappearing tunnel beyond.

You little shit! Diego shook James, then fell back, smiling grimly. Someday, he said, you will understand. Diego drew his arm back over his head and the glass bottle sailed across the pool and shattered against the flagstones. Crying, James threw his bottle, too, as hard as he could. The shards glittered like jewels.

Feels good, Diego said. Doesn't it?

It did and it didn't. At least the bird was silent. It seemed to James that the whole world had stilled.

Feeling a presence behind them, he twisted in the iron chair.

Lara stood in the opened sliding glass doors. She wore her red silk bathrobe untied, the sides skimming her shining white skin. James tried not to look at her breasts or between her legs.

Lara gathered the material and held it closed at her throat. Without speaking, she stepped back inside. The red robe billowed as she swung around. Lara floated away. There were no lights in the house, only darkness, and try as he might, James couldn't see his mother anymore.

The house seemed to breathe and sigh all around him, filled with unhappy ghosts. James heard a shushing sound, a woman's voice. But it was only the ocean, waves breaking at the bottom of the cliff. The drapes billowed and a gust of damp air swept the room.

Just past the open sliding glass doors, the yard glowed, beckoning. A slice of moon hung low in the sky, which was the color of ash, city lights reflected upward and obscuring all but the brightest stars.

James walked outside, drawn again to the shallow end of the pool. The water was a black hole, ominous and inviting. He looked at the curved stairs, the diving board, the metal ladder at the deep end.

He heard a car approaching, climbing the hill. A bluish light flashed down the side yard, crisscrossed patterns in the lemon trees.

He remembered now.

Lying in the back of the truck with his wife, making love. Making a baby, no diaphragm. God help him. That night, they'd had dinner at the Thai place on the square, and there was a young woman in the booth next to them, alone with a sleeping infant. James, drunk on plum wine, was telling Mercedes some story about Tommie Yard, when he'd been distracted by the tiniest bleat of a cry. It sounded so lonesome, he'd looked over the top of the booth, and he saw the woman take out her breast, saw her feed the nipple into the child's mouth. He could hear the baby sucking. The woman's expression as she looked down into that small, serious face, had been every bit as intent as the child's. It set James's heart to galloping. When Mercedes asked him, "What do you think?" he drew her hand under the table and placed it between his legs. She began to stroke him, softly at first, then with a pressure that made him want to scream. They didn't even make it the half-mile home. He pulled the truck over to the side of the road, under an oak, and dragged Mercedes into the back. Like teenagers, stretched out on a blanket. All their clothes off, every last stitch.

James stripped down until he stood naked on the flagstones. The air goosepimpled his skin. That night, he and Mercedes had been drunk and exposed and in love—*in love*. The occasional car had driven past them, patterns of light playing in the branches above . . . how had he forgotten this?

Well, he knew how. The missing diaphragm. He'd known what it meant.

And wasn't it what he wanted?

He stepped into the pool, syrup lapping his toes. He felt as if he were watching himself in a dream.

He took another step. The water swallowed his feet.

Another, and his calves were lost. His knees, his thighs. Another, and his genitals pulled up tight. Waist, chest, shoulders and arms. Finally, all that was left was his neck and his head. The leaves on the surface concealed his body from his own sight.

He lifted his legs and kicked a little, moving his arms just enough to take him to the deep end. There he dogpaddled for a while. With the water level so low, he saw only the sides of his containment, the scummy surface under his chin, and the sky. The pool smelled foul, algae and rotting leaves. James heard disembodied sounds, soft scuffs like footsteps surrounding him.

He slipped under. His wounded ear stung like a son-of-a-bitch. The bandage dragged and loosened, filled with water, and he pulled it off. He continued to drop until his heels scraped a shallow layer of muck, the hard tile underneath. And there he remained, his arms suspended like kelp at his sides. He opened his eyes, saw nothing, opened his mouth and let the cold water inside. It coated his tongue and his teeth and tasted like the bottom of the vegetable drawer.

He imagined himself as Margarita Jimenez. Drowned, right here in this pool.

He glided down the gentle slope to the drain.

His chest squeezed. He wondered if Margarita Jimenez had known how to swim. And what about the baby, that swimmer inside?

James's head was throbbing, pressure building behind his eyes. But he forced himself to stay down. Everything in him fought to come up, knowing he could.

Margarita Jimenez must have fought. But she'd had company in the water, and under the water, too.

Someone was under the water with her.

Emilio was under the water with her.

There was something dark in the water, down by the drain. But Emilio and Diego were sitting on the pool steps. Naked, which was very funny. James had laughed, and they'd looked up at him.

He kicked himself to the surface, and filled his lungs with air. Then he stroked backwards, legs dangling, until his feet touched the tile. He could picture it all so clearly now. His family in the back yard, a lazy weekend, or a Monday afternoon, a hot morning, a warm night. The air would be still, or breezy and smelling of salt, the sky blue, the sky gray, the sky black. The roar of the ocean was the single constant, felt as a rhythmic rumble in the chest. And everyone in the pool except Emilio.

It was Diego who'd taught James to float, to kick straight-legged, hanging onto the side. Diego who'd held two hands beneath his belly, and then one, and then none. Diego who'd caught him before he could sink.

CHAPTER THIRTEEN

James peered through a window in the lecture hall's door, looking down onto rows of note-taking college students. The seats slanted toward a small stage, a table, and podium, and a blackboard white with chalk dust, upon which Tío Diego was drawing a funnel-shaped object, his shoulder hitching beneath his white shirt. Diego stepped back to survey his handiwork, then pivoted on his heel to face the students.

The sweep of cheekbone, the shape of the ear—James was unprepared. It was like staring into a funhouse mirror, or a composite drawing: himself in fifteen years, Emilio in a future he hadn't lived to fulfill.

He heard the rise and fall of muffled speech. He glanced at his watch. According to the secretary in the Astronomy office, ten minutes of class remained. He could wait out here in the hall, or he could go in.

He created a disturbance upon entering, forced as he was to climb over a dozen legs to the one empty seat. Diego stopped the lecture midsentence and folded his hands atop the podium. His eyes followed James. He resumed speaking only when James was fully settled.

". . . and then the star collapses," Diego said, "having exhausted every bit of its nuclear fuel. Becoming ever more tiny and dense, gravity ultimately overwhelms all the remaining forces that might prop it up, and voila! we have a black hole. Where gravity is so immense that whatever dares to come near is sucked in." Diego returned to the board. At a point near the top of the funnel he drew an ellipse. "The black hole," he said, "is wrapped in an oblate zone— 'oblate' meaning only that it is flattened at the poles—and this zone delineates the event horizon. A border over which none can venture with any hope of return. Nothing escapes. Not even light.

"A journey over the event horizon, if one were to be so foolish as to attempt it, would be quite distressing. If the black hole were small, one would experience tidal effects. Gravity stretching one unbearably. Human spaghetti, human thread. If, however, the black hole were large, and by that I mean merely large enough, one wouldn't notice much of anything—at first. But one would be lost all the same. Hastening irrevocably toward doom."

Diego drew a line from an edge of the ellipse down into the bottom of the funnel. "So. We can never look this particular beast in the eye. A disappointment, eh? For the human mind desires every answer.

"Yet in the absence of definitive experimental proof, one can always speculate." He marked the funnel with a large X. "So, my good friends, what do you suppose is in there?"

Hands went up around the room.

Diego pointed at a young man with a thick fringe of red hair. "Yes, Mr. Thorpe?"

"A singularity, Professor."

"Which is what?"

"Mass without matter."

"Which is *what*?"

"I . . . I don't know."

A woman in the front row jumped in. "Spacetime," she said, "infinitely curved."

"Yes!" said Diego. "Consider this: Einstein's theory of general relativity predicts the existence of black holes. And yet within these strange creatures all the equations break down, producing infinite results. Which, by the way, very much inclined Einstein, at least initially, to refuse the notion. Because inside the singularity, space atomizes and time has no direction at all. The rules of physics appear to break down. Unsettling, no? But if you think about it, it begins to sound very much like something we've encountered before. Ideas, anyone?"

Another show of hands. Diego cast his eyes about the room, as if seeking someone in particular. The students squirmed. A long minute passed.

Gradually, James concluded that Diego was looking for *him*. He felt the blood creep up his neck. He looked at the windows, leaves brushing the glass, and blocking the light.

Diego called out, "What do you think, Mr. Reese?"

James returned his eyes reluctantly to the front.

"Sit in my classroom," Diego sang, "and you must always expect to be called upon, eh?" He folded his arms and began to whistle. Several of the students snickered, recognizing this performance and happy it wasn't directed at them.

But James said nothing.

Diego stopped his whistling. A theatrical sigh. "Anyone else?"

Eager to restore himself in the professor's eyes, the red-haired young man said, "It's like the Big Bang."

"Yes!" cried Diego.

A soft bonging sounded, bells ringing the hour. The students stood and shuffled from the rows.

Diego called after them: "Don't forget, my good friends, the exam is next week. Please bring number-two pencils for the multiple choice."

Slumped in his seat, James watched Diego shove papers into a briefcase, heard the snap of the latch as it caught. When the last of the students had gone, Diego looked up. "Ah, Jaime, you are still here."

As if he were surprised. James said nothing.

Diego put a hand in his pocket. He cocked his head. "You might as well come down," he said.

James took his sweet time.

On the stage, he turned to look back at the empty classroom. An odd perspective: the rising seats, the two doors set in the rear wall like ears. A clock ticked between them, placed where no student could surreptitiously determine the hour.

"Do you like teaching?" he asked.

"I'm good at it," Diego said. "Though I prefer my graduate students, especially those who most want a leg up on future careers. Ambition makes them . . . pliable." He sighed. "This class is a bit of a bore. Too elementary. But I am going to England for a conference next week." Diego smiled. "Shattering revelations are in store. About the nature of dark matter, eh?"

At the blackboard, he started in on the funnel with an eraser, but soon changed his mind and returned it to the tray. Quickly chalking in a series of symbols, he said, "I have an equation for you."

$$\Delta p \cdot \Delta x \geq \hbar$$

He thought a moment, then added:

$$\hbar = \text{Planck's constant}$$
$$p = \text{momentum} = (\text{mass}) \times (\text{velocity})$$
$$x = \text{position} \neq \text{zero}$$

It all meant nothing to James.

"This calculation," Diego said, "is just one illustration of the Uncertainty Principle. Important to today's discussion, inasmuch as it turns out that the odd quantum particle can in fact tunnel through the event horizon of a singularity. Showing its hairy little self where it doesn't belong."

"But you told your students that nothing could escape."

"Ah, well, I lied. Just a little. But notice," Diego underlined his equation, "that here we are given important information: a particle has both position and momentum. Meaning that it should always be somewhere, that is, have a location," he pointed to Δx, "while also traveling at a certain, theoretically measurable, speed." He pointed to Δp. "The joke, and it is a fantastic one, is that we can never know both with complete accuracy. If we measure the position, the momentum becomes unfixed. If we measure the momentum, the position is lost. In the quantum world, one of these complementary attributes may increase at the expense of the other, but the uncertainty in position *times* the uncertainty in momentum can never be less than Planck's constant." And now he circled $\hbar$.

James faked a yawn. "What is the point of all this?" he asked.

"Patience, Jaime," Diego said. "You will understand when I am finished. Now. Here, at the event horizon, we can fix the particle's position, and because of the Uncertainty Principle, it becomes possible for the particle to borrow enough momentum, for a correspondingly short time, to increase its energy sufficiently to cross. The particle has escaped the black hole!" Diego drew a sweeping arc from one side of the event horizon to the other. He put down the chalk and dusted his hands. "*Uncertainty*, Jaime, is the key concept here. Because the more we poor pitiful human beings try to fix reality, the more elusive it becomes. Ambiguity and uncertainty are inherent features of the human sphere. Wouldn't you agree? One can focus on the facts of a situation, or one can give oneself over to the feel of it. Facts cost us perspective, perspective costs us particulars. Either way, it is impossible to ever quite know the truth."

Diego picked up his briefcase. He started up the lecture hall's center aisle. Halfway, he turned and said, "I always swim after class. Why don't you come?"

There were two outdoor swimming pools, lined up side-by-side, closed in by buildings Diego termed the old gym and the new. Both pools were twenty-five meters in length, but the first ran three feet at the shallow end and twelve at the deep, while the second, of newer construction, was deep enough overall to prevent touching bottom anywhere. A polo pool, Diego explained. And in fact the women's team was in the water now, swimming vigorous laps, while the coach, a fat man in glasses, observed from the deck. The coach's neck was turtled into a blue windbreaker and he was scowling, as if having just placed a bet he was certain to lose.

James sat in one of several chairs placed near the old pool, his arms folded against the chill. The sky was overcast. The water steamed. Alone in the old pool, Diego crawled the center lane, muscles bunched in his shoulders and back. He switched briefly to a butterfly stroke, a humped undulation, then dropped under, coasting along the bottom. Stingray, thought James.

Diego broke the surface at the deep end. He hoisted up and out, slid his hands vigorously down taut arms and legs. Beads of water flew. Smoothing his hair from his face, he started back to the chairs. Diego carried no towel and James could see his genitals outlined beneath the swim trunks. It made him feel sick.

Diego dropped into an empty chair, arms and legs splayed.

Over at the polo pool, two young women were setting the nets. Each time they had one side secured, the other collapsed. The coach's voice rose with irritation: "This is college, ladies! Not kindergarten!"

"What about you, Jaime?" Diego asked. "Did you ever go to college?"

"I wasn't much of a student. I worked instead."

James cupped a hand to the side of his head. His ear felt like an animal was gnawing on it. This morning, he'd left off the bandage, but Diego hadn't so much as glanced at his injury. In fact, he hadn't seemed the least bit surprised to see James. He hadn't missed a beat in the classroom, and right here, right now, he was completely at ease. How could that be? James was supposed to be dead.

"Doing what?" Diego asked.

Small talk, thought James. *Fuck it*. He could do that. He said, "Different things." He'd been a bank teller, toiled on a road crew. He'd driven a moving van. There were other jobs, too, nothing that went anywhere. "Eventually," he said, "I wound up in the Navy."

"And you liked that?"

"Some of it I did. Mostly, I puked my way through."

"A weak stomach, eh? It runs in the family."

Family—how could he even say it to James?

The polo team was splitting in two, gathering at opposite ends of the pool. Blue swim caps versus white. On each side there was a single player in a red cap with the number 1 stenciled in white.

"The reds are goalies," Diego explained. Then: "Did you see any action? In the service."

James said, "I was too late for Vietnam. Spent some time in Japan, though, and the Philippines."

"What did you think of that part of the world?"

"Japan was strange. I couldn't get used to the food. But there are a lot of Spanish speakers in Manila. That was easier."

"And what do you do now? For a living, that is."

As if he didn't know. James said, "I'm Border Patrol."

"¡Viva La Raza!" Diego raised his arms and clapped his hands three times, like a flamenco dancer. "It is good to honor your culture, to keep ties with the past."

"It's a job," James said tightly. "Somebody's got to do it."

"Certainly."

"It's a small town. There isn't much else."

"But who ever said you had to stay there?"

Who indeed? But he'd never really considered going anywhere else.

"Do you remember, Jaime," Diego said, "how I used to take you down to Olvera Street? Mexican Disneyland. Huaraches and sombreros and piñatas, eh?"

James remembered. There was a wooden crucifix at one end of the street. He used to climb it like a schoolyard jungle gym.

"I liked that old house," he said.

"Avila Adobe. It is the oldest dwelling in Los Angeles. Commodore Stockton used it as headquarters during the American conquest. . . . You enjoyed the glassblowers, too."

Old men with their lips to an iron wand. A bubble would form at the end, delicate, but white hot. Beautiful and dangerous.

Diego said, "I'd buy you a stick of sugarcane. And taquitos. You could eat a million of them."

But living out at the beach, James had downed more doughnuts than tortillas any day. He'd seen more surfboards than santos. He'd listened in the car to American radio. The Beatles and the Beach Boys. A visit to Mexican Disneyland was always exactly that: a visit.

The net finally secured, the two teammates returned to the water.

Diego sat forward. "Jaime, watch this."

Crouched midway down the pool, the coach tossed a yellow ball in the air, caught it in the palm of his hand. Again. The swimmers poised at the ready. Suddenly, the coach lobbed the ball into the pool and both teams sprinted from their goal lines. A white cap grabbed it, pushing it between her forearms. She swam with her head above water, the ball riding the wave at her chest.

Diego asked, "Did you ever marry?"

James countered, "Did you?"

"Let me guess. You found una gabacha, a beautiful blonde. Just like your mama. Boys always marry their mamas, eh?"

"Emilio didn't. And neither did you."

Diego turned.

213

"Actually, I'm here about Lara," James said.

"Of course you are," Diego said. "Did you see the obituary in the *Times*? It was very fine. 'Beautiful socialite, many good works, terrible illness . . . unfortunate past.'"

"You can cut the crap, Tío. I've seen Alex May."

"Ah—so this is not a social visit."

"Why are you contesting the will?"

"If you've seen Alex May, you must know. I was Lara's husband. She was my wife."

"Funny then that she left the estate to me."

"A deathbed scourge of conscience. Not worth the paper it is printed on."

"It was what she wanted."

"Jaime. Please. Lara owed me."

"You!" James said. "How do you figure that?"

"I helped your mother a great deal over the years. With the house, and her investments. Things of that nature, eh? She leaned on me after Emilio was gone—"

"I'll bet she did."

"Facts of life, Jaime. Lara was rich. A beautiful blondie. And your father was just a poor little vato, pushing the lawnmower over the grass. But she wanted him. Or maybe she only wanted to push her daddy's face in it. Who knows, and who cares? Me, I came along for the ride, with my slide rule and books. . . . I can't tell you, Jaime, how lucky we felt, changing one world for another. The Cinderella brothers, eh?"

"And what about Margarita Jimenez?"

Diego waved a hand. "A little nobody from the old barrio. Una bruja. A witch, eh? Determined to ruin everything."

"Because she was pregnant."

Diego sighed.

James said, "Louise Conti provided that piece of information. You remember her?"

"Ah, yes." Again Diego sighed. "'Conti the Cunt.' That's what we called her, Emilio and I."

"Can you tell me, Tío, what happened that day?"

"I cannot. I wasn't there."

But it was obvious they were talking about the same thing. The hair at the back of James's neck stood on end. "I saw you," he said. He offered the statement as if it were true. He wanted it to be true.

"Nonsense! You couldn't possibly. You were four years old."

One of the blue caps had captured the ball. A white cap flung an arm and the ball flew in the air and the coach shouted, "Get it! Get it! Get it!" Diego leaped to his feet. The pool was a chaos of arms and legs, torsos and heads, the water churned frothy white. James thought of sharks in a feeding frenzy. He'd seen that once, off the coast of Japan. He never wanted to see it again.

James said, "You killed her, Tío."

He thought Diego hadn't heard. But then his uncle turned, and stepped in front of James and leaned down, gripping the armrests of James's chair. Diego's chest heaved slightly. He smelled of chlorine. "And what is this idea based on?" he asked. "On *feelings*? Or memories, perhaps? These things are worthless, I can assure you, Jaime. An example. I have a student, a girl here on scholarship from Fresno, who is convinced that her father molested her. She remembers his hands coming through the bars of her crib. His fingers inside her. This girl's therapist has convinced her that this horror explains some of her current sexual difficulties. Also, perhaps, her terrible personality.

"But the facts interfere. The girl's father died shortly after her birth. So perhaps we are talking about ghost fiddling, eh?"

Diego was standing too close. James wanted to smack him. He wanted to put his hands on that smooth muscled chest and shove Diego into the pool.

He looked down at his uncle's left wrist, at flattened pink scars. Then he filled in the picture: red roses, black thorns.

Diego pushed off the chair. He stepped back. He rotated his forearm for James, giving him a better look. "They do miracles with the laser these days."

James said, "You were in a gang. Papi, too." Then he waited. He heard shouting in the pool, and frantic splashing. The sounds seemed to come from far away.

"It was a lifetime ago," Diego said. "De rigeur for boys from our neighborhood. But then Emilio met your mother, and poof! We were free."

"It's not that easy to get out."

"It is when you want it badly enough."

And how had Diego kept those ties to the past? Through Richie Serrano? James wanted to ask, but it was too dangerous. He stared into Diego's eyes, a flat black that revealed nothing.

"Everything in life is timing," he said.

"Unless you're an astronomer, and then everything is gravity." Diego smiled. "You have to see, Jaime, that human beings are small. Our wants and our needs—to us they are of ultimate importance. But in the grand scheme, we do not signify."

And that, James thought, gives you license to do anything.

He said, "I read your book, Tío."

"Ah—did you?" Diego looked pleased. "And what did you learn?"

"That most of the universe is missing."

"Clever boy! You understand, however, that the mass is almost certainly there. In the dark matter. That is what gives the universe its gravity. We just don't know what it is yet, what it's made of."

"But you're going to find out."

"It is only a question of effort. And time."

"Just like policework," said James.

CHAPTER FOURTEEN

Safely off campus, James stopped at a pay phone. He dialed Rampart Station and when he had Lieutenant Louise Conti on the line, he said without preamble, "Did you ever think it was Diego instead?"

He waited through a buzz in his ears, traffic sounds, the coursing of his own blood.

Conti asked, "Who is this, please?"

"James Reese. Or Jaime Santana. Take your pick." His lips were numb. His mouth felt stuffed with cotton. But he said again, pressingly, "Did you ever think it was Diego instead?"

"Oh, God. James? What? . . . well, it was . . . it was looked into."

"Which means what?"

"Which means," Conti said, "that that case was solved. A man was tried and convicted. By a jury of his peers."

"That sounds rehearsed, Lieutenant. Like maybe you've said it thousands of times. But is it possible you're just protecting yourself? Maybe you made a mistake."

Out in the street, cars were pulling abruptly to the curb. Pedestrians stopped where they stood.

"I should have told you before," Conti said. "But I couldn't bring myself to do it."

"Told me what?"

"Diego. He had an alibi."

"Which was *what*?"

"He spent the day with your mother. The whole day . . . you understand?"

And now heads were swiveling in James's direction. An ambulance careened around the corner, the siren wailing. James stuck a finger in his ear.

". . . clerk," Conti was saying, "at the motel. He identified them. I'm sorry, but he identified them both."

James waited for Conti on a wooden bench at the edge of Echo Park Lake. Stately palm trees lined a green perimeter. Waves lapped at the shore. Out on the water, a canoe slid silently by, a bare-armed young woman working the oars. It was, James decided, very peaceful here.

A cardboard box landed with a solid thump on the bench beside him.

Lieutenant Conti walked around and sat, the box fitted tightly between them, like a child that requires supervision.

"The files," she announced.

"Yes, thank you," said James. "You found them fast."

"If you know where to look . . ."

Conti dug in her jacket pocket for smokes. She tipped a cigarette from a hard pack. Another search yielded a silver lighter. Conti lit up, inhaling deeply. She draped an arm along the top of the bench, her left ankle balanced on the opposite knee. The hem of her pantleg pulled up a little, exposing short coffee-colored nylons. The elastic drooped on her white leg.

James had been holding the egg-shaped rock in his hand. Now he placed it on top of the box. Show and Tell.

Conti picked up the rock. She turned it over, weighing it in her palm. "And this is . . . ?"

"A little something from up behind Dodger Stadium."

Conti blew smoke from the side of her mouth. "Really."

"Diego took me on a hike to the top of a hill. Lara came too."

"When was this?"

"I was about five years old."

"Why would Diego do that?" Conti asked.

"It was the Fourth of July. We went for the fireworks. Diego thought we'd have a better view from the hill."

She asked again, "Why would he do that?"

"You tell me."

Conti took another drag off her cigarette. "The last twenty-four hours," she said, "I've been thinking a lot about your uncle. Diego Santana. That boy—well, he was something of a marvel when he was sixteen. Nothing whatsoever like most teenagers. So steady. So composed. With all the commotion, the arrest, his brother in jail, most kids would've thought it was the end of the world. But Diego never seemed that distressed. He had a stupendous gift for abstraction, as I recall. Must be part of the scientific character. He passed a lie detector with flying colors."

"And Emilio?"

"His attorney wouldn't let him take it."

"No surprise there."

Conti rummaged in her bag. She took out a folded clipping. "I pulled this from the file. For the picture, mostly. Your father . . . I don't know. You might as well have a look."

The yellowed newsprint was soft and limp, coated with a powdery dust. It was an article, James noted, from a 1966 *L.A. Times*. The headline read: "Stadium Killer Due to Stand Trial."

He scanned the text. Descriptions of the house by the beach, the pool out back, the dumpsite in the hills behind Dodger Stadium.

The reporter speculated that Emilio Santana had been stepping out on his wife, socialite Lara Shipp of Pacific Palisades, that he'd drowned Margarita Jimenez to keep his infidelity a secret. There followed some background on the Shipps: rubber manufacturers who'd sold their company before the 1929 crash, and put the profits into gold. The Santanas were next: *immigrants* and *working class*. James read the disapproval between the lines. How a rich white girl had no business with a boy from the barrio. Some paragraphs down, Detective Conti was cited for fine policework. The article concluded with a *We'll-nail-him* quote from a Deputy DA.

There was no mention of Diego or James. And no mention of the dead girl's pregnancy.

James studied the accompanying photograph. His young parents stood before a curtained backdrop, Emilio tuxedoed and mustachioed, his broad face gleaming like steel. His shoulders strained the jacket, his neck rose from the collar like a tree stump. Lara hung on her husband's arm. Even in black and white, her hair cast a pale moony glow.

Conti said, "It's not in this particular piece, but you might be interested to know there was no drag trail on that path up the hill. And the lower part of the girl's body was clean. No scrapes on the heels or the back of the legs. During the trial, your father's attorney tried to make something of that."

"Meaning what?"

"Meaning that they wanted to give the impression the killer was someone else. Or rather, more than one someone else. The confession was the sticking point, of course. May tried to get it excluded, claiming Emilio was coerced. That made the press jump. It was the 60's, and the civil-rights movement was in full throttle, and there were a lot of stories out there. Black men found hanging in their jail cells. Brown men beaten by unscrupulous cops."

This possibility had not occurred to James.

"But it didn't happen like that," Conti said.

James knew the use of force was a fact of the job. For himself, and for others, as well. With some cops violence could become a kind of condiment, enhancing the flavors of righteousness. James couldn't picture Louise Conti, so small, and a woman, laying a hand on anyone, but that didn't mean someone else hadn't gone to town on Emilio.

He looked hard into the lieutenant's face. There were sagging half moons under her eyes. The wiry red hair stuck out every which way.

"I give you my word," Conti said.

James could trust her or not, but he had to choose.

"Okay." He let out a long breath. "Emilio was strong. He could've thrown the girl over a shoulder easily."

Conti nodded. "So said the D.A. Still. It's a very steep path."

James remembered.

"And Diego," Conti said, "was built small and sleek. More like a boy. So I don't see that as a viable alternative."

"Could they have brought her up there together? Maybe Diego killed her and Emilio helped him clean up."

"But Jimenez was Emilio's girlfriend. Pregnant with Emilio's child. There's no getting around that."

A priest and a little red-haired girl strolled past the bench. The priest was dressed in a clerical suit, the collar tight at his neck. He carried two fishing rods and a plastic tackle box. At the edge of the lake, the two dropped onto the grass and removed their shoes. The girl rolled her socks neatly, then dipped her bare feet in the water.

James asked the lieutenant, "You got any kids?"

"Me? God, no. I married the job." Conti sighed. "Sometimes I think it's been a bad match. All these years. The same sad story, played out over and over again."

"That's just what my father says—my dad's retired Homicide."

"I might've guessed," Conti said. "You know, right now I've got a gal, an architect who lives at the top of a hill in Silver Lake, claims

221

her husband went for a walk and never returned. It's been two weeks. There's blood in the bedroom, microscopic spatters all over one wall. God bless Luminol. This house is perfect, you understand. A perfect view, a perfect garden. One of these modern boxes with very little furniture—this gal actually gave me a lecture about negative space—but every piece exquisite. And *clean* . . . well, the blood type matches the missing husband."

"You think she did it?"

"If she didn't, she knows who did."

The priest had finished baiting one of the two fishing poles. He cast into the lake with an expert flick of the wrist. The sinker landed and ripples spread outward, flattened by the time they licked at the shore. The priest passed the rod to the little girl.

"Out by the beach," James said, "there's all that empty country. Miles and miles of it. Why do you suppose he brought the body back here?"

Conti said, "I always thought Emilio wanted to get revenge on his old running buddies. He'd made good, you see, gotten out, and they weren't anywhere near as pleased as he was. Whites weren't the only ones who thought Emilio didn't belong with Lara Shipp."

"Mexicans weren't supposed to marry white girls."

"Especially if they were pretty."

"Especially if they were rich." James thought a moment. "Do you know what happened to the girl's family? Did she have anyone?"

"Oh yes, poor souls," Conti said. "Mother and father, and an older sister, as I recall. I felt so sorry for them. They went back to Mexico after the trial. Can't say I blamed them, though it isn't as if horrible things don't happen there, too."

"I met her, you know. At least once. I remember her."

"Good God." Conti shifted on the bench. "I had no idea." She flicked her cigarette to the ground and crushed it with a heel. She bent down, picked the butt up, then dropped it into her jacket pocket. "Another bad habit." Conti's face was very red. "I forget to take them out later, too. The clothes I've ruined . . . But listen, James. I had a look at Diego's alibi. The day of the murder, he and Lara checked into the Aladdin Motel on Alvarado Boulevard. In at nine, out at six."

"That about covers it," said James.

"The thing is," Conti said, "I'm pretty sure I screwed up. The motel's still there, still owned by the same people. Or the same woman. The husband died some years ago. He was the original interview, the one who identified them, the one who testified. I went over last night and talked to the wife." Conti squared her shoulders. "She claims to remember very little of this, but I don't know. She seemed tense. Wouldn't look at me, wouldn't answer questions beyond yes or no."

"You think she was lying?"

"Hard to say. But I've got a feeling."

"That would mean that the husband lied, too. Why would he?"

"Money. Friendship. Maybe fear."

"Did they know Emilio?"

"Well, I wish I'd looked into that way back when."

"And what about Lara?" James said.

"You know," Conti said, "at the time, it never crossed my mind that your mother might lie. My own youth and inexperience were no doubt factors there. And Lara was so embarrassed. Diego was only a boy, after all. The whole idea of those two sleeping together was just so preposterous, it felt like the truth."

"It became the truth," James said grimly. "They lived together for years. They even married."

The corners of Conti's mouth fell. "I didn't know."

"They kept it secret. They had their reasons, I guess . . . and now Diego's contesting the will."

"A thousand motels in this city. Why pick that one? It's not quiet, and it's not nice, and price certainly wasn't a consideration."

James said, "I think Diego killed her."

"I know you do," Conti said. "But she was Emilio's girlfriend, carrying Emilio's child. Emilio confessed. You have to keep an eye on the facts."

"Here's a fact for you, Lieutenant. Three days ago my partner was shot. By Richard Serrano—I ran the name by you yesterday? I think he knows Diego. There's a connection there."

"Based on what?"

"They have the same tattoo."

"That's nothing," Conti said. "And you know it."

"The thing is," James said, "Richie Serrano was trying to get *me*. Leo—my partner—just got in the way. He put himself in the way."

"To protect you?"

"No, not exactly. Leo was trying to collect something, at my expense." James grimaced. "I paid Diego a visit this morning, over there at Cal Tech. Sat in on an astronomy class. Afterward, we had a conversation. And guess what? Thirty years on, he's still steady, still composed. . . . But I'll tell you something. Margarita Jimenez intended to make trouble for the Santana boys. And Diego saw an end to his meal ticket. Or maybe he wanted to help his older brother. Maybe it was even an accident, like Emilio said. I don't know. Something happened." Suddenly, James remembered Emilio's words, the last time James had seen him. *A man protects what he loves.* He said, "The brothers were together that day, up by the stadium. Emilio's the one the doctor saw, but Diego was there."

"You can't prove it," Conti said. "It's been too long."

"Look, Lieutenant," said James.

The little red-haired girl had caught herself a fish. Small and silvery, wriggling in the sun. The girl was laughing as the priest helped her reel in. The priest took the fish and carefully removed the hook from its mouth. He said something to the girl, then slipped his hands into the water and let the fish go.

He found the address inside the box, near the top of the pile, on his father's rap sheet—his juvenile rap sheet—the existence of which was something of a surprise, because James had always believed those records were sealed. But here it was in stark black and white: burglary, assault, breaking and entering. It might've been his own record, he thought, except that he'd had Desmond to wipe his slate clean.

From Echo Park Avenue, he made a right turn and climbed a low hill, and then he was in the old neighborhood. It was nicer than he'd expected. Cottages and bungalows and restored Victorians, though a few places looked as if they might be falling down around their owners' ears.

Knocking on doors, James covered ten blocks in just less than two hours. Most of the houses were empty, the owners off at work, he supposed, supporting those expensive restorations. He did talk to a handful of retirees, a couple of mothers home with young kids. All were white, with the exception of one emaciated Latino in a leg cast. Bare-chested, a gold hoop winking from his left nipple and a freshly lit joint hung from his bottom lip, he responded to James's inquiries with a shrug, his only comment a puzzling, "Pop goes the weasel."

In any case, no one had information for him. No one had ever heard of the Santana family, or Richard Serrano, or Margarita Jimenez, or the Shipps. It was as if everyone had vanished, or never existed at all.

He saved the old house for last.

Nondescript and flat-roofed, the bungalow was hidden behind a hedge of oleander. But James recognized the gate—padlocked now—from Lara's photograph. He drove past the house, found a parking spot down the block, and then walked back, skirting a grafit-tied garage and a spill of purple roses planted in a trashcan. The side-walks were deserted, but he had the distinct sense of watching eyes.

At the gate, James yanked on the lock. It held firm. He glanced right, and left, and then he hopped the fence, finding himself in a tiny yard choked with weeds. Iron bars on the curtained windows. The front door was just a few steps away, made of wide pine planking, rounded at the top edge. A square metal plate capped an old-fashioned peephole. Below hung a brass knocker in the shape of a whale. No bell. James heard voices inside. He rapped the knocker, but got no response. Again he rapped, and suddenly the voices stopped. A long wait, and then a scraping sound came from behind the door. The metal plate creaked open and a bloodshot eye appeared. Before James could say anything, the plate shut again. *Thump* and *scrape*.

The door opened a quarter inch.

A quavering voice said, "¿Qué quiere?"

"Señora." James guessed the voice to be female. "Por favor, may I talk to you?"

"¿Por qué?"

"Will you open the door?"

"¿Quién es usted?"

He introduced himself as Jaime Santana, said that he was looking for anyone who knew anything about his family. "They lived in this house a long time ago."

"Un momentito." The door shut, *thump* and *scrape*, and then opened wide.

At first, James thought he was looking at a little girl, the woman was so impossibly small; the top of her head barely came to his chest. He took in the voluminous flowered muumuu and white Nike cross-trainers. Clawed hands gripped the back of a kitchen chair, the source of the scraping sound. A white braid swept the floor at her feet.

The old woman peered up at him, her mouth gaping beneath a beaked nose. Several gold teeth gleamed.

"I am in this house from before my quince," she said.

Unlikely, James thought, since the woman was in her seventies, anyway.

She said, "My son bought it from the Santanas for me. Nineteen sixty-four."

The name and the date gave James hope. Politely, he asked the old woman who she was. She seemed bewildered by the question.

"Creía que estabas en la cárcel," she said. *I thought you were in jail.*

Did she mistake James for Emilio?

Off the top of his head, he said, "I was, but I've been released."

"They killed you, eh?"

"No, I don't think so."

"Aren't you un espectro?"

James looked down at his feet. The old woman was clearly senile, he was wasting his time. She said accusingly, "Un fantasma," and not knowing what else to do, he held his limbs out and shook them for her, each in turn, a hokey-pokey demonstration of his own living flesh. The woman laughed and he gave her his hand. She ran her bony fingers over his palm and up his arm, jabbing and prodding.

Satisfied, she said, "Okay, you are not dead and you are not a ghost. You may come in." Then she abandoned the door. James watched her disappear behind an armoire. He stepped into the swallowing gloom and followed, navigating between piles of miscellaneous junk: mildewed newspapers, rolled carpeting and disassembled furniture; pots and pans, clocks, cabinets, bags and rags. They passed from room to room, finally entering a space only slightly less cluttered. Here, sunlight filtered through sheer curtains dragging with dust. James saw a hand-woven rug, a camelback sofa, and buried beneath dozens of picture frames, a grand piano. A color TV was placed in front of the sofa, the sound of a talk show tuned low. Groaning, the old woman plopped herself down. She patted the cushion beside her, indicating that James should sit. Beneath the yellowed stuffing, he got a glimpse of rusted springs. He lowered down cautiously.

The old woman folded her hands on her thighs. "My people are from Guanajuato, México. Do you know it, señor?"

James nodded. He'd heard of the town. An old silver-mining center, somewhere in the mountains north of the capital.

Proudly, she said, "We have an ancestor in El Museo de las Momias."

James had heard of that, too: the Mummy Museum.

"We couldn't pay the tax for the grave, so they dug him up. He sleeps in a glass case. Skin like shoe leather, shrinking from the bones. He still has his hair. But no clothes." She covered her mouth with a hand, hiding a smile. "You can see his pene."

"Did you know Emilio Santana?" James asked.

The old woman eyed him suspiciously. She rocked to her feet and shuffled off, and James figured that was the end of that; but it was only a detour to the grand piano. She picked through the collection of photographs on display, gathered several frames and returned to the sofa. She spread them out in her lap.

James looked down into faces from a long-ago world. Solemn young couples. A dead teenager lying in a coffin, outfitted in finery. The old woman pointed to a baby asleep in a carriage, the photograph so faded the child's features were no longer visible. "Soy yo," she said. She indicated another picture, this of a handsome man with thick hair combed over his forehead in an extravagant wave. The man stood on a sidewalk beside a poster, ladies caught in a wild dance, cocked legs and bare arms, the fringe on their dresses swinging. "Es Emilio." James looked more closely. There was a slight resemblance, but he was certain it couldn't be. The photograph looked like something from the 1920s, well before his father was born.

He tried another tack. "Did you ever know Diego Santana?"

"¡Ay!" The old woman clapped her hands. "Your brother was so very smart!"

James nodded encouragingly. "Yes, he was."

"But those were bad boys. One of them went to prison, I think. The little one was much worse."

"Why do you say that?"

"Ay, he was sneaky! Had his pants down all over town, making little angels for El Señor. I saw him eating a scorpion in the yard."

"What about Margarita Jimenez?"

"¡Ay! A woman at the heart of every trouble. Those people! They didn't come back unless they wanted something."

"And what did they want?"

"Filthy gangbangers. Everybody dead all the time from the drive-by." The woman pulled at James's arm, turning his wrist, and he realized she was looking for a tattoo.

"Richard Serrano," he said. "Do you know him? Long nose, black hair?"

But the old woman was transfixed now by the flickering TV. Two women were screaming, eyes flashing with hate. James looked away. There was too much stuff in this room, he felt, too much buried history, and it struck him as it hadn't before that this was where Emilio and Diego had *lived*. They'd been boys here, sat in the kitchen, played in the yard.

He'd been here, too. A baby, wrapped in a blanket, posed with his father and uncle in front of the gate.

He reached into his breast pocket, removed his photograph, and showed it to the woman.

"¡Ay!" she said. "You were so young."

James pointed to Emilio. "Ése es mi padre." He pointed at Diego. "Mi tío."

The old woman said, "Los veteranos play basketball in Echo Park once a year. They come from all over, the ones that aren't locked up en la carcél. Some of them are businessmen now. Judges and doctors . . . they sell slices of cantaloupe for twenty-five cents." She clutched at James's arm. "¿Y tú? Do you play basketball?"

"Not very often," James said.

"Where are your people from?" she asked.

"From here." James's voice was a little too loud. "My people lived in this house."

"No! ¡Es imposible! *I* live in this house."

James sighed. He sat back, closing his eyes.

"They're from the border," he said.

"¿La frontera?" The old woman leaned. She put her head on James's chest, nestling in. "Such a dangerous place! Not here, not there."

After a while, he brought his arm up and wrapped it around the woman's shoulder and held her close. He understood she was listening to his heart.

"Sí, I thought so," she said. "You are very much alive."

He almost missed it, the Aladdin Motel on Alvarado Boulevard, tucked as it was between a liquor store and a laundromat. Set back several yards from the street, the place looked more like a double-wide mobile home, with its vinyl siding, green shutters, a striped metal awning that covered most of a picture window.

A hand-lettered VACANCY sign swung from the mailbox.

James pulled in and took the first parking spot, nosing the truck up against a shallow concrete step. The step ran the length of the building, forming a porch of sorts, with beach chairs set at regular intervals. James saw a few potted plants, a rusted barbecue. At the back of the property, the motel took a short L, and there a woman in a pink jogging suit leaned in an open doorway. Several shrieking pre-school-aged kids circled the lot in front of her, dizzy circles describing an unidentifiable game.

James walked around to the front office. Bells tinkled softly as he entered, but there was no one in the room. A naked bulb of dim wattage dangled from the ceiling. The wall behind the Formica counter had been fitted with a pigeonholed cupboard; underneath, a single row of hooks was hung with brass keys. A coffee pot sat on a table pushed to one side. The machine's ON light shone. The smell of burnt coffee made James's stomach flip.

He tapped the service bell and a late-middle-aged blonde emerged from behind a closed door. The blonde's skin was blotchy, like a pinto pony, the flaw showing through heavy makeup. Her left eye, James noted, was a bit of a rover. It was impossible to tell if she was looking at him.

The blonde said, "You're wasting your time." She crossed her arms on her chest. "I already talked to that lady cop. I said what I knew, which wasn't that much. Only that those two were here, they stayed the whole day. I got nothing more."

James blinked.

"You're a cop, too," she said.

"Then maybe you can tell me if you knew them or not."

"I did not."

"Had you ever seen them before?"

"Never." She pursed her lips. "My husband was the one on that day. They only showed me a picture later."

"Do you know which room was theirs?"

"If I ever did, I don't remember now."

"Think a little."

"I could think all day long and it wouldn't make a difference. Because I don't know."

"Okay." James pulled out his wallet. "I'd like a room for tonight."

"I'm sorry," she said firmly, "but we're full up right now."

"How much is a room?"

"Thirty-five. But we're *full up*, I said."

James took out five twenties and laid them on the counter.

The blonde bit her lip. Her bad eye darted and rolled.

James took out two more bills. It was nearly all that he had.

Sighing, she reached under the counter, brought up a spiral-bound ledger, and slapped it down. Licking a finger, she leafed through the pages. "Here's a cancellation. But I'm telling you now, I won't answer any questions." James shrugged. The blonde turned around and selected a key from the hook. James followed outside.

Halfway down the porch, she stopped at a door. She jammed the key in the lock, then pushed the door open. James got a glimpse of brown shag, a brown-and-orange bedspread.

"How's this?" She stepped in.

"It's fine," said James.

She dropped the key on the dresser. "Check-out's at noon. Stay any longer, I'll have to charge."

"That's fair," said James.

The door shut and the room was plunged into darkness. James turned on a lamp, then stretched out on the bed. The mattress was lumpy and soft and sagged alarmingly toward the center. He folded his arms to prop up his head. There was a hotplate on the dresser, inches from his feet; to the left of that, a half-size refrigerator hummed in a doorless alcove. People lived in these rooms, he realized.

The TV perched on a high shelf, up near the ceiling. There didn't seem to be a remote, so he sat up and swung his legs over the side of the bed. He climbed up on the dresser and switched on the set. Flipping through the channels, he saw news, mostly, a few syndicated sitcoms. He got stuck for several minutes on a silver-haired televangelist shrilling about Christ on the cross, our Savior's suffering. Nails in His hands and feet, a lance in His side. The preacher had the saddest eyes James had ever seen; he looked as if he'd gone without sleep for days. But when he suddenly switched gears and began exhorting his congregation to up their contributions, James, disgusted, switched off the TV.

He heard traffic surging out on Alvarado, the kids outside screeching like seabirds. Someone—the woman in pink, probably—yelled, "Mario! You leave your sister alone!"

He climbed off the dresser, sat again on the bed.

He didn't know what he was doing here, what he'd come here to find, what he was hoping to prove.

He decided to buy himself a six-pack of beer.

The liquor store just north on the boulevard was narrow and dark, its single window blocked with tinfoil. An old Selena song blared from two speakers set up near the register, the sound so scratchy and loud James couldn't make out the words. Oblivious, the counterman read a foto-novela. The cover featured a half-naked woman in stiletto heels, a villain menacing from the background. James trudged back to the refrigerated cases and pulled a six-pack of Bud. At the register, he waited to pay. The counterman had one cigarette going in an ashtray, another clamped between his lips, and he turned a page of his book while holding his free hand out to collect James's cash.

James stared at the hard liquor displayed on the shelves. As Selena's voice faded, he heard a pint bottle of Cuervo calling his name. He added it to his purchase.

In his absence, the motel children had surrounded the truck. He walked back up the driveway and they scattered like mice, giggling.

James sat in the beach chair outside his door. He extended his legs, popped the top on a Bud. He opened the tequila and took a swig and chased it with the beer, wishing he had some salt. Then he settled in to watch the kids play. There were two groups, a mix of boys and girls, each alternately in pursuit of the other. Some kind of tag, James thought, or hide-and-go-seek. The kids ran in and out of a couple of rooms, and then around back, behind the motel.

The woman in the pink jogging suit still leaned in her doorway.

James took the rock out of his pocket and set it on the ground. Next he got out Lara's photograph. He studied the three subjects—Emilio, and Diego, and James. He turned the snapshot over. *Guilt and Innocence. It is my fault.* It was all so goddamned cryptic, he thought. *What* was her fault? The marriage? The murder? Emilio's own death, maybe? How much guilt had Lara suffered, giving James up? *A deathbed scourge of conscience.* Yes. Why else leave him the estate? But way back when . . . had she done something specific to drive Emilio away, into the arms of Margarita Jimenez? A catalyst for disaster. James had to wonder, as well: Were the Santana brothers really so afraid of Lara that killing the girl was the only way out? *Guilt and Innocence.* He held the photo up to the light. Lara's writing bled through from the other side. The word "guilt"—backwards, here—crossed Diego's face. James wondered if that meant anything.

The sky was darkening now, lights coming up on the boulevard. Squinting, James fractured the beams, making stars. The four lanes were backed up with cars and trucks and buses and vans, and he heard shouting and horns, music pouring from the vehicles' open windows.

He tipped the tequila bottle into his mouth, then shoved the photograph back in his pocket.

A battered Chevy wagon made a right turn and bumped into the lot. The driver slowed as he passed, staring first at the truck, and then at James, slouched in the beach chair. For a second, the driver caught James's eye; then he shut his face down. James had run into that look so many times on the job. *I don't see you, therefore you don't see me.* The Chevy sped up, swinging into an empty slot back by the L. The doors opened and four men climbed out and a little girl in a frilly dress ran to the driver. He picked her up and set her on his shoulders, and all of them went into one of the rooms.

The boys were using the Chevy's right rear fender as a bunker. Down on one knee, arms stretched forward, they cocked their wrists as if they held guns. When three girls ran around from behind the motel, the boys leaped out. A classic ambush. Like Anteater, James thought. And Leonardo. *Goddamnit to hell.* How much of what had happened was his fault, how much Leo's own? He suspected he'd never know the answer.

The children were shouting wildly now, "¡Migra, migra!" For a terrible moment, James thought they meant him. He took another gulp of tequila and chased it with beer.

But no one was looking in his direction.

Then he understood that this was an immigrant's version of cops and robbers, cowboys and Indians, good guys and bad. He knew without a doubt which side, for these children, la migra was on.

Later, inside his room, he sat on the end of the bed and stared at the wall. He stared at the silent TV, at the hotplate and the refrigerator. He stared at the dresser. Wood-grained particleboard, with six drawers set two abreast. Ornate brass pulls.

Leaning forward, he opened a drawer. It was empty, of course. He ran a hand around the inside anyway, the unfinished surface sanding his palm, then he pulled the drawer all the way out and set it on his knees. He turned it to look at the back, flipped it to inspect the underside. Nothing. He tossed it to the floor. James sat a moment, trying to think. He smelled cooking smells, fried meat, something sweet. He heard a guitar softly playing, and a woman's voice. He opened the next drawer, which was also empty. He pulled it and flipped it and tossed it aside.

He was conducting a search, he realized. Just as he had at Lara's house.

It was stupid, profoundly so, but he didn't care. There was something here for him, some piece of information, he just didn't know what.

Quickly, he worked through the rest of the drawers. He unplugged the refrigerator and removed the shelves, slid the dresser away from the wall and examined the back. He emptied the nightstand, upended a small table, a chair. He dismantled the room's few objects—the hotplate, the lamps—and set about stripping the bed. He wrestled the mattress up on one end and, grunting, pushed it to the floor. The box spring was next. Inside the bed frame, he stood on the dirty carpet, light-headed, nauseous from effort and drink, his face hot, the blood throbbing unendurably in his ears, and he was thinking that he should slice the mattress—but with what?— when he heard voices again. A man and a woman. No guitar. He wanted to know what they were saying, and so he went to the wall and put his ear against it. But the voices had stopped. Tentatively, he pounded a fist. Again. The wallboard gave slightly, and he hit it harder. And harder. He was crying now, and he let it come.

Finally, he heard an answering bang.

In the time it took him to figure out that the noise came from outside rather than in, his door flung open. The blonde stood there, angrily surveying the mess that he'd made.

Good, thought James. He leaned against the wall.

"Get out," the blonde said.

James said, "Look at me."

"If you don't get out, I'm going to call the police."

"No, you won't. This place is crawling with illegal aliens."

She said through clenched teeth, "Who do you think you are?"

"Look. At. Me."

The blonde's lazy eye rolled like a pinball and then came to rest. Her shoulders stiffened as if she'd been knifed.

"I'm Emilio Santana's son," James said. "Remember him? He went to prison, a long time ago. He was killed there. And do you know why?"

The woman made the sign of the cross. She said hoarsely, "They didn't come here."

James had found what he'd been looking for. Air rushed from his lungs.

The blonde said, "They were never here."

CHAPTER
FIFTEEN

H e'd clean forgotten the box.

He went out to the truck—all quiet now, the parking lot deserted—retrieved the box from the passenger seat and carried it back to the room.

Plopped down cross-legged, he dumped the contents onto the floor.

He lifted a few papers at random and skimmed through, tossing the half-read sheets aside. He grabbed another set, and another, and he read so quickly that most of the information didn't really register. But he was afraid to slow down, afraid that if he stopped he might never look again.

He'd worked his way through a good third of the file when a few items finally caught his attention. Forensic reports, mostly: autopsy, serology, fiber and fingerprints.

Blood tests done on both the fetus and Emilio indicated that he could not be excluded as the baby's father. Odds of paternity were set at 96 percent.

No surprise there.

The autopsy report contained the standard diagrams and pathologist's narrative, but no photographs. Probably Conti had decided not to copy these. James didn't know whether to be grateful or mad.

Next was a short list of the dead girl's belongings: blue skirt, white blouse, white panties, white bra, brown leather sandals.

And then he came upon a folder that contained transcripts of the initial police interviews of the Santana family. Conducted by Detective Louise Conti, on December 24, 1965, at Rampart Station in downtown Los Angeles.

Right on top sat a copy of Emilio's confession. It looked as if the original had been written out by hand on a wide-ruled legal pad.

James steeled himself to read.

I was in the house with my son. My wife and brother were out. They were out together at a hotel. I didn't find out until later but that is where they were. My brother and my wife had left early in the day different times I think. Diego was going to the library over at UCLA. Lara ~~she~~ I don't know where I thought she was going. Shopping maybe. I don't think she said. So I was alone in the house with my son Jaime. I played with him for a while and then fixed some lunch and then I put him into his bed for a nap. He never liked to go for his nap but I made him because he was getting ~~unhappy~~ crankie. He fell asleep right away. It was a hot day and I decided to go sit by the pool and read the newspaper. I took some beers outside. I was out there for about an hour I think when I heard the voice of my girlfriend Margarita. I thought I was sleeping, that I fell asleep from the beer and dreamed her voice, but she said ~~it~~ my name out loud and I knew I was awake. I was sweating from being out in the sun but I began to sweat even more because I did not expect Margarita to come to my house. She had no business to come to my house. My son was sleeping upstairs. My wife and my brother were not at home, but she didn't know that and ~~it~~ she was coming to make trouble for me. So I was angry right away. That doesn't mean I did anything on purpose to her. Because I did not. But Margarita came through the back gate and walked around the side of the pool and stood in front of me. She took the beer bottle out of my hand and drank some. I was hot and dizzy from the beer and from falling asleep. We took off our clothes and went swimming naked in the pool. I don't know what I was thinking about doing this because I didn't know for sure when my wife and brother were going to come home. My son was sleeping upstairs in his room. We were fooling around dunk each other under and laughing and splashing. Margarita liked to go off the diving board and she kept getting out of the pool and running around the board and going off. She was a sloppy diver. Belly flops and things like that. I wanted more beer so I got up and went in the house. Sometime in between going in the house and coming back out again I decided ~~I wanted Margarita to leave~~ I had to ask Margarita to leave. But when I came out she wasn't there. I thought maybe she was hiding. The pool was ~~quite~~ quiet. I thought she was playing hide and seek. I sat on the chase lounge and read the newspaper for a while. I was sure she was hiding. In the bushes. Somewhere. I don't know. But then I began to get nervous. I got up and put my jeans on and I went around to the front of the house. Her car was still there. I went into the back yard again. And this time I saw she was in the pool. At the bottom down by the drain. I dove in and pulled her out her hair was tangled up in the drain. I had to come up for air and go back and pull really hard on her arms. When I got her out by the side of the pool I gave her mouth-to-mouth. But it was no use. I didn't call the ambulance or the police because I knew she was dead. She was not breathing and her skin was gray. I put her over my knee and whacked her between the shoulder blades and a little water came out. But she still didn't breath. I got scared then. I took her and dressed her and carried her to my car in the garage and put her in the trunk. I felt bad but I didn't know what else to do. She was all wet. I didn't want my wife to see the seat wet. Then I moved ~~the car~~ Margarita's car down to the beach parking lot. The next day I took it downtown and left it out on a street. But right then it bothered me that she was in the trunk of my car. I couldn't leave my son Jaime in the house all alone and I had to wait until my wife and my brother came home. I don't remember what I did until then. My son woke up sometime, so I was taking care of him. When Lara came back I said I had to go out. Diego still wasn't at home. I drove, I didn't know where to go. I ending up going into L.A. I took Margarita's body up to the park. But it was an accident. I didn't do anything on purpose. I didn't mean for anything to happen to her.

James set the photocopied sheets on the floor. His hands were shaking. It was beyond eerie: He'd heard his father's voice.

But the confession disturbed him for other reasons.

For one thing, Emilio had clearly implied, even if he didn't come right out and say it, that Margarita Jimenez had hit her head diving from the board. Hit her head and accidentally drowned.

James dug through the scattered papers. He relocated the autopsy report and spread the diagrams out before him. Drowning, he noted, was listed as the official cause of death, but the diagrams showed that the girl did indeed have a cracked skull. She could maybe have been injured the way Emilio said—except that there were two L-shaped contusions, above and behind her right ear. *Two*. Arrows pointed from the contusions to a small supplementary sketch. Some kind of metal joining. There was a detailed enlargement on the next page. A tube attached at right angles to a flat rectangular piece. Two Phillips-head screws. Just beneath the enlargement was yet another drawing, this one of a three-stepped ladder. Curved arms screwed into a pebbled slab. It was, James realized, the metal ladder at the deep end of the pool.

The pattern of bruising on the girl's head matched up with the joint of sidepiece to step. Not one of the wounds, let alone two, could have resulted from a bad dive. They were on the wrong side of her head if she'd been up on the board. If she'd gone in from the deck, the imprint faced the wrong way.

So someone had to have been in the deep end with her.

There were finger-shaped bruises on the girl's neck and shoulders and arms. A hank of hair pulled from her scalp. Someone had to have grabbed her—while she was trying to get out?—grabbed her, and given her head a good whack.

He could see now why Emilio had said that it was an accident. It must have seemed a plausible explanation. There would've been plenty of blood and he might not have noticed that the girl was hit twice.

In any case, his father had lied. But James already knew that. Something else was bothering him.

He read the first few sentences of the confession again.

I was in the house with my son. My wife and brother were out. They were out together at a hotel.

More lies. In James's experience, people lied to gain advantage, or to impress, but mostly, they lied to save their own skins. In this statement, he could hear Emilio doing that. But his father had also been protecting someone—he could hear that, too. Of course, he knew now what Conti had not, what the prosecutor had not: that Diego's alibi was out-and-out false.

James thought about his own memory.

Up from his nap, he'd heard noises outside. Splashes and laughter. Crying, maybe. He'd climbed out onto the balcony and peered through the bars, down at the pool. There was something dark at the bottom, down by the drain. His father and uncle were sitting on the pool steps. Naked, which he'd found very funny. He'd laughed, and they'd looked up at him.

I dove in and pulled her out her hair was tangled up in the drain. I had to come up for air and go back and pull really hard on her arms.

He remembered Emilio stalking the waves at the beach.

And he remembered everyone in the pool except Emilio. James wasn't allowed in without Lara or Diego.

Christ! he realized, Emilio couldn't swim! And if he couldn't swim, there was no way he'd killed Margarita Jimenez.

Diego, on the other hand, moved through water as if it were his natural element.

James riffled through pages until he found the transcript of Diego's interview.

Diego claimed to have spent the early hours of the morning at the university library, after which he'd driven downtown. At 9 a.m. sharp, he'd met his sister-law, Lara Shipp Santana, at the Aladdin Motel. When Conti questioned his ability to recall the precise time and date—the arrest having taken place months after the crime—Diego said that he remembered everything, always; knew always where he was and what he was up to.

Next came queries about his brother, Emilio's relationship with his wife. Yes, said Diego, they seemed happy enough. No, there weren't any difficulties in the marriage that he was aware of. Conti asked Diego what he thought he was doing in a motel room with his sister-in-law, and Diego replied that he was merely partaking in a little harmless entertainment.

Sixteen years old, and he could say such a thing.

LC: Did Emilio know about your affair?

DLS: It wasn't an affair.

LC: Well, whatever you choose to call it (. . .) your brother aware that you were sleeping with his wife?

DLS: No.

LC: What about the other side of that equation? Did Lara know about Margarita Jimenez?

DLS: There was nothing to know.

LC: Let's try this again. Did Lara understand that her husband was cheating on her?

DLS: No.

LC: And what about you?

DLS: I wasn't cheating on anyone.

LC: Don't be smart (. . .) know what your brother was up to?

DLS: I did not know the girl.

LC: That's not what I asked.

DLS: Please repeat the question.

LC: Did you know that your brother had a girlfriend?

DLS: (*long pause*) Yes.

LC: And what did you think about that?

DLS: What should I have thought?

LC: You tell me.

DLS: All right. I was not surprised.

LC: Why not?

DLS: Emilio is a man. Also . . . you can take the boy out of the barrio, but . . .

LC: I see. Do you know why he killed her?

DLC: He didn't kill her. It was an accident.

LC: If you weren't there, then how do you know?

DLC: My brother says so.

LC: Well. (*long pause*) You said before that you did not know the girl. Is that correct?

DLS: Yes, it is correct.

LC: You didn't know her?

DLS: That is what I just said.

LC: Emilio never introduced you?

DLS: No.

LC: But wasn't she from your own neighborhood? In Echo Park?

DLS: We don't live in Echo Park.

LC: Excuse me. Your *former* neighborhood. You must've seen her around.

DLS: Please. Detective. Do you know everyone who lives near your house?

LC: We're not talking about me.

DLS: *(sighing)* I did not know her.

James thought: But what about that day at the beach? Margarita and Diego riding the waves, Emilio and James waiting up on the sand. And what about what Diego had said by the pool at Cal Tech, the way he'd described Margarita Jimenez to James: *una bruja, determined to ruin everything*. What was it that nutty old lady had said? *I used to see your brother with her*. Your brother who was *so very smart*.

He continued reading.

LC: This day that we're talking about, the day of the murder, when you went off to the motel with your sister-in-law—did you know what your brother had planned?

DLS: In terms of what?

LC: In terms of his girlfriend coming out to the house.

DLS: No.

LC: Did you have any bad feelings before you left that morning?

DLS: No, I am not a psychic.

LC: And what about the little boy?

DLS: Jaime?

LC: Unless there is another.

DLS: No, we have just the one.

LC: Where was the little boy that day?

DLS: With his father, of course.
LC: Of course?
DLS: Of course.
LC: Doing what?
DLS: How would I know?

James set Diego's pages aside, nerves jumping at the unexpected reference to himself.

He searched until he found Detective Conti's interview with Jaime Santana.

Conti began by asking how old he was. According to her notes, James had held four fingers in front of his face. Conti asked him about his house at the beach. (*Thumb in the mouth.*) Did he like to swim? (*No response.*) Did his father spend much time in the pool? *No*, said Jaime Santana. The detective showed him a school picture of the dead girl. Did the girl look familiar? (*Thumb in the mouth.*)

Christ, James thought: Did she really have to do that to him?

On a normal day, the detective asked, did he usually stay with his mom? Or his dad?

I stay with Papi.

Conti asked several additional questions, and for answers received a nod, or a shake of the head, sometimes both in response to a single query.

Was he going to have Christmas dinner at home?

(*Out came the thumb.*) Papi likes Christmas.

At the bottom of the next page, there was a note to the effect that the suspect's son was obviously too young and too scared to be of any assistance in the investigation.

Too young, yes. Too scared. *Yes.* James didn't remember any of this, but Christ, he must have been terrified, surrounded by strangers in that strange place.

He turned now to Lara's interview.

Right off the bat, she admitted to being in the motel room with Diego. She'd left the house early, driven straight into L.A. Yes, it was the first time she'd slept with him. No, she really couldn't say why. It had been a mistake, naturally, one she regretted deeply.

LC: Did you ever consider that this was a minor child you were having sex with?

LSS: *(no response)*

LC: Shall I ask the question again?

LSS: *(no response)*

LC: All right. Let me rephrase it. Were you at (. . .) concerned, Mrs. Santana, that your brother-in-law, Diego, is a minor child?

LSS: You don't know Diego.

LC: That's true, I don't. What should I know about him?

LSS: *(no response)*

LC: All right. What should I know about your husband, Emilio?

LSS: That he's a good man.

LC: Do you love him?

LSS: Yes.

LC: You'd do anything to protect him.

LSS: I don't know what you mean.

LC: All right (. . .) you first learned of the murder, what did you think?

LSS: You were there. I was crying, of course.

LC: Yes. But perhaps, Mrs. Santana, you could tell me in a little more detail what you thought about it.

LSS: I . . . I didn't think anything.

LC: Really? How can that be?

LSS: Well, I was in shock. Naturally. It was horrible, horrible. But it has nothing to do with me.

LC: It doesn't?

LSS: *(30-second pause)* My husband has *(inaudible)*.

LC: Has he ever been violent with you?

LSS: No . . . I don't know.

LC: You don't know?

LSS: Emilio has a temper, but he's never hit me. If that's what you're asking.

LC: Can you tell me, Mrs. Santana, who handles the funds in your house?

LSS: I don't understand.

LC: It's a simple question. Who makes the financial decisions? Who controls the purse strings?

LSS: Well. I do, I suppose.

LC: Does your husband work?

LSS: Not anymore.

LC: What did he used to do?

LSS: (*inaudible*)

LC: Would you repeat that, Mrs. Santana?

LSS: His father took care of our garden for years.

LC: I see.

LSS: No, I don't think you do.

LC: Why don't you enlighten me.

But on that subject Lara Shipp Santana had nothing further to say. She had nothing more to say about her marriage. Conti asked: Why was the little boy with your husband that day?

LSS: I'd hardly have brought him to the motel.

LC: Does he spend a lot of time with his father?

LSS: Yes, he does. He always has. Emilio is a good father. I couldn't have predicted what he would do.

LC: Did you know the girl? Margarita Jimenez.

LSS: That little bitch. No.

LC: But you knew of Margarita Jimenez's existence, didn't you?

LSS: (*no response*)

LC: Margarita Jimenez is dead, Mrs. Santana.

LSS: I realize that.

LC: Why did you call Margarita Jimenez a bitch?

LSS: I know what you're doing (. . .) stop saying her name.
LC: Did you know she was pregnant?
LSS: *(no response)*
LC: Was sleeping with Diego your idea of revenge?
LSS: *(no response)*
LC: Mrs. Santana. Are you worried at all about what the boy might have seen? Since he was with his father that day.
LSS: *(no response)*

And there the transcript suddenly stopped. The interview was over, halted by the arrival of the Santanas' lawyer, Alexander May.

James slumped. His chin fell to his chest. The room was dead quiet.

All those years ago, when he was given away, he'd believed it was only temporary. He was to be in foster care for a short time only, and only because Lara was sick and couldn't take good care of him.

The day he'd left Los Angeles, a man from the attorney's office had driven out to the beach. The doorbell rang and James came down the staircase with a small duffel bag filled with clothing and a box in his hands. A rag doll, a kaleidoscope, a rock. The man had walked him out to a car, long and black, with tinted windows. Settling James in the backseat, he'd instructed him to fasten his belt.

And that was the end of Jaime Santana. He never saw his family again.

He wondered now: Where was Diego the day that he left? At school, probably. And Lara? Was she standing in the doorway, watching him go? In the window? The driveway? At the foot of the stairs?

No. She was in her bedroom, in bed. Hiding. Either she didn't care, or she'd been too ashamed of what she was doing to him.

James stared bleakly at the overturned furniture, papers scattered all over the floor. It looked like the scene of a terrible accident.

He began to gather everything up. He straightened the table and chair, put the drawers back in the dresser, dropped the mattress and box spring onto the frame. He began to collect loose pages of paper. Carelessly he threw them into the box. At some point, he came upon Emilio's juvenile rap sheet again. He stopped to skim the list of offenses: burglary, assault, grand theft auto.

There was ink bleeding through the paper from the other side; he hadn't noticed before. He turned the sheet over. At the top, written in black ballpoint, were two initials: *K.A.* Underneath, a list of names. James had to think about that, and then it came to him with a rush: *known associates.*

Ramón Pineda. Eloy Trask. Bennie Gutierrez. Ricardo Serio. Ricardo Serio.

The gang. The tattoo.

Richard Serrano.

Anteater! El Oso Hormiguero. It had to be.

James stood, too quickly. Blood rushed from his head, the room tilting and spinning as if he were still drunk. But he wasn't drunk. He only needed something to hold on to here.

Anteater was Diego's known associate, too.

Diego had sicced Anteater on James. Because of *money.* But James already knew that.

Except that it wasn't just the money. It was because of what James had seen, what Diego feared he'd remember, what after all these long years he was certain to tell. Lara and Diego had never stayed in this room. And Emilio couldn't swim. And James was the only one who knew that.

It was the reason he'd been given away.

Suddenly, he remembered that Penitente out in the desert, in the back of the truck. *His lips sewn shut.* And Leo, laid out with shining coins on his eyes. *See no evil.* It amazed James, what people were willing to risk, the boundaries they'd cross to get where and what they wanted: oaths, commandments, blood loyalties.

He needed to call Lieutenant Conti. She'd act fast, do whatever the situation required. He could count on her. Likely they wouldn't get anywhere near Diego, but who knew what was out there on Ricardo Serio. Ricardo Serio was the key. And if James was wrong? But he knew he wasn't wrong.

But it was the middle of the night now.

And then James thought: Fuck it, this is L.A. *Fuck it!* Anteater operated on the border now. Maybe he always had—he worked it like a rat who knows his ship inside out. But the border was James's world, too. He'd made it his. They could cross paths again and James could make it happen and he would. Sooner rather than later. Instead of waiting for Ricardo Serio to find him first.

CHAPTER SIXTEEN

J ames parked the truck a half-mile past the entrance to
Schiller Farms, then walked back and turned into the dirt
road and followed it to the clearing. There a thin mist drifted,
trees and bushes dripping with dew. The bicycle was still shoved in
the bushes, but the grocery cart had disappeared. James debated
the wisdom of going down into the ravine, and had just decided he
had no choice, when he heard engines approach; and then three
trucks bounced into the clearing, horns tooting their call. Within
seconds, the workers came bubbling up over the ridge, like a pot
on the boil. Two dozen at least. But Rafael Noyez was not among
them.

The bosses got out of the trucks, slamming doors.

James sidled over to where the workers had gathered. He
placed himself among them, aware of glances and a little muttering. He did his best to ignore it.

As they had the last time he was here, the drivers leaned against
lowered tailgates and pointed at the workers. Business was

conducted in silence. The selected men ran forward and climbed onto the stakebeds. It went very quickly.

One of the bosses pointed at James. As before, he pretended not to have seen. A sudden elbow to the ribs, and he grunted in surprise.

"¡Está loco!" Rafael Noyez hissed. "You got cojones coming out here."

James said. "We have to talk—"

"Sorry, man. No hablo inglés."

"You know what I want."

"No sé nada, señor."

The first truck was full now, and most of the second. Two men in front of James ran for the third.

He said to Noyez, "This camp could be raided at any time."

Another man ran.

James raised his voice. "You won't like what I can bring down on you."

A boss was staring at them.

"And him?" Noyez muttered. "Men like your father, what will you bring down on them?"

James said, "Whatever it takes."

The boss frowned, waiting for this inconvenient conversation to cease.

"Get away from me now!" Noyez said. "I have to work."

James said, "It's not just the little boy. He killed my partner. And—" He stopped. Christ. There was no explaining the rest.

"¡Ni madre! That is a reason for silence, not talk." Noyez loped off, selected at last. James watched him climb onto the crowded stakebed and take a seat at the back.

Slam of doors and the trucks started up. The vehicles circled the clearing, exiting onto the narrow dirt road. Noyez's was the last. He stared stone-faced at James as the truck pulled away.

Fuck that, James thought. He started to run. Ahead, the trucks were picking up speed, dust flying from under the tires. James pumped his arms; his feet pounded the dirt. The workers on that last stakebed watched him, interested in whether he could catch up. One stood, swaying.

The first truck had reached the main road. It idled there before making its turn, and the other two were forced to slow down. James ran faster. He reached up, grabbing for the top of the gate. He grunted and hurtled himself forward and the standing man obliged him by leaning down. The man yanked at James's shirt, then gripped his belt and hauled, and James was up and over, tumbling into a sea of blue-jeaned legs.

The ride into the valley was cold, bone rattling and unbelievably loud, with no opportunity whatsoever for talk. In any case, the men seemed preoccupied with individual thoughts. James watched Noyez for a while—he had his eyes closed—but he couldn't come up with anything guaranteed, or even likely, to induce the guy to speak, so he shifted his attention to the passing scenery. Lettuce and broccoli. Groves and more groves. The fog was thick here, rows of trees swaddled in white. The bright fruit hung like tiny lanterns.

Eventually, the truck got off the highway. They turned onto a graveled drive. A mile in, this dead-ended at a wood-framed house, freshly whitewashed. Behind that stood a red barn. The workers hopped off the stakebed. A line formed beside a large wooden crate and the men filed past, picking up canvas sacks, which they hung around their necks. Several tied bandannas over their noses and mouths, and gloves appeared from under their shirts. James got himself a sack and tied it as he'd seen the others do.

Around the side of the barn, a flat trailer was piled with metal ladders and hitched to a John Deere. The men mounted the trailer, the ladders shifting and clanking beneath them. A man in overalls and an engineer's hat—the foreman, James thought—climbed up behind the wheel.

Deep into the orchard they went. When they came to a place where the trees were denuded in one row, filled with oranges in the next, the tractor stopped. The workers jumped down. Each grabbed a ladder and bolted for the trees. The ladders clattered as they opened; the men swiftly climbed. James, still at the trailer, shouldered his equipment awkwardly. He looked for Rafael Noyez, but with the men already in the treetops, everyone appeared much the same.

The foreman was eyeing James skeptically. He took a clipboard from the tractor's front seat. In English he said, "You aren't dressed for this. You'll be sorry later."

James grinned and nodded, as if failing to understand.

Shaking his head, the foreman said, "Suit yourself." Then he said, "What are you waiting for? Go on now!"

James dragged the ladder into the row.

It was dim and cool between the trees. James walked on, and on, realizing now why the men had been so quick about choosing: it was a long trip back to the trailer.

Finally, he came to an unclaimed tree. He set up his ladder and climbed. The men all seemed to be working the top branches first, so that's where he started, too. The fog was lifting a little now. Above the treeline, gauzy white clouds trailed across pale blue. James copied what he could see of his nearest neighbor's technique: two-handed picking, a sharp twist of the wrist. It required balance. And attention. He'd had it in mind that he could talk to the men while they worked. But that was clearly impossible. Slowly, James worked his way down, the bag grown heavy and then heavier around his neck. When it was full, he hopped off the bottom rung and hurried back to the trailer as he'd seen the others do. He stood at the end of another line.

While he'd been picking, two longer trailers lined with wooden crates had replaced the ladder rig. The overall-suited foreman stood nearby, clipboard at the ready. James saw Rafael Noyez ahead. Noyez saw him, too, but gave no indication. James watched as Noyez hoisted a canvas sack over the edge of a crate and dumped the contents. The foreman made a note on the clipboard and handed Noyez a ticket. This disappeared into a shirt pocket. Noyez withdrew a notebook and a little yellow pencil and made his own notations. The foreman glared. Noyez continued writing. Finished, he nodded, as if satisfied. He replaced the notebook and pencil and returned to the row.

Soon enough, it was James's turn. He dumped his sack as the others had done. Frowning, the foreman peered critically at James's oranges. He seemed about to say something, but then he handed James a ticket and waved him away.

James went back to his tree. He moved the ladder a few feet clockwise and resumed his work.

Throughout the morning, the foreman paced below him, hollering whenever James fell behind, which seemed a constant state of affairs. He figured that, compared to the others, he was working at only half-speed. At one point, he was overcome with hunger and thirst, and he stopped for a minute to eat an orange, and the foreman was there to harangue him again. Each time he carried a full sack to the trailer, none of his fruit seemed to meet the man's standards, though he gave him the tickets anyway.

James was drenched in sweat. The fog had burned off; the air was hot and dusty and dry. In the midst of the trees, James was lost in branches and fruit. His arms in the short sleeves were scraped, scratched and cut. And he'd finally noticed—the air was too still. No birds, no bugs. A fine white powder coated everything. He'd thought the men wore bandannas to keep out the dust, but he realized now it was because of pesticides. James felt dizzy. He couldn't turn his head on his neck. The muscles in his shoulders throbbed, and his hands had liquidy blisters at the crotch of forefinger and thumb.

Two hands, he told himself, then a twist of the wrist. Over and over, till his palms were so tender he thought they might split.

He forgot entirely why he was here.

255

Lunch.

There was no signal of any kind. But when the sun shone directly overhead, the trees around James emptied, all at once.

Back at the trailer, the foreman passed out paper bags.

The men sat in groups of three and four, legs dangled into a shallow dry ditch. The gloves and bandannas had been tossed aside. As they ate, they spoke quietly among themselves, conversations wandering, pauses as important as the actual words. James stood for a minute and more, but no one offered an invitation, so he made his way over to Noyez and sank down beside him. Noyez sighed but said nothing. James opened his paper bag. He pulled out a sandwich, a warm can of Coke, and two crumbling chocolate chip cookies. Looked good to him. He removed the plastic wrap and had a bite of the sandwich. Baloney and cream cheese. He wolfed about half before hitting a jalapeño in the middle. He choked and sputtered. He had the sense the men were looking at him, and laughing, but trying not to show it.

The foreman had disappeared. "A la casa blanca," somebody said. "To get his hot meal."

Someone else complained about not making it home for Semana Santa. *Holy Week*. This time of year, many workers returned to their villages, the traffic at the border heavy in the other direction for once.

The man said sorrowfully, "My wife will give my new boots away."

Another said, "Unless she finds somebody else to fill them."

"She better not!"

"Send her money, compadre."

"Also—there is a new baby I have not yet seen."

"Boy or girl?"

"Boy."

"And will you bring him across?"

"It is too soon to think about that. Besides, I hope to have enough next year to go home for good."

The second man laughed. "The baby will be an old man himself before you leave these trees."

James's tongue was still burning from the jalapeño. He drank some of the soda, then transferred the can to his other hand. The aluminum was soothing against his sore palms. He said to Noyez, "Desmond told me you have four kids."

Noyez chewed his sandwich.

James said, "Back in Mexico."

Noyez got up. He dusted the seat of his pants. "I am not going to talk about my children with you." He moved away and sat somewhere else and James was again alone.

He ate his cookies and finished his Coke.

A boom box materialized from thin air, and the grove filled with sound. The dial was tuned to a ranchera station and James recognized a song he'd last heard at Efraín's. He sang along, softly at first, then with more volume. Gradually, the men stopped talking to listen to him. Though he almost never used it, James had a good voice. The song was a ballad of love lost—what else?—and he put some pathos in it, a gulping catch in his throat.

Even Rafael Noyez was listening.

When the ballad was finished, James stood. He looked at the men, his gaze shifting from face to face. He placed a hand over his heart, as if pledging something, he didn't know what.

"Señores," he addressed them. "Ese coyote. El Oso Hormiguero—"

Immediately—immediately!—the atmosphere changed. Faces shut down. It was predictable and hopeless. He was wasting his time.

"The boy who died in the van," he said. "That's a federal offense. The United States government. You understand?"

No one said a word.

"There's no reason to be afraid. It's the coyote's fault that that boy is dead. He'll go to prison for a very long time."

Someone turned up the boombox, drowning James out.

Then, one by one, the men stood. They began to wander away. All avoided James's eyes. Paper bags crumpled, thrown with soda cans into an empty fruit crate. The foreman was back now from his hot lunch—no one had heard him arrive—standing by the trailer with tickets and clipboard, a spill of what had to be ketchup down the front of his overalls.

On the way back to the trees, a man tapped James on the shoulder. James turned hopefully.

The man handed him gloves.

James worked like a demon for the remainder of the afternoon. Might as well, he thought, the day should not be a total loss. He got into a solid rhythm, and a kind of hypnosis took over: twist and pull, knees locked, legs braced, the sting of sweat in his eyes, the ache in his back, the sack like an anchor wrapped round his neck. He'd pay later, he knew.

At the end of the day, there was again no signal that they were through, only a dawning realization that the activity around him had ceased.

James dragged his ladder back to the trailer and threw it clanging onto the pile. He dumped his sack of oranges and collected his final ticket from the foreman.

They rode the trailer to the white house. The boss, the guy who'd driven them in, was waiting there, along with a woman in a checked dress and apron, blond hair in braids, like some farmwife in a painting James had seen long ago. The woman had a metal cashbox in her arms. James expected the tickets to be turned now into green. But the woman went in the house, and the boss climbed behind the wheel of the truck; apparently, this was a transaction that occurred another time.

The workers swarmed onto the stakebed.

On the ride back to the camp, they played craps on the floor, using tickets for scrip. James knelt, initially to get out of the wind, but then he shouldered in on the game, and this time no one said boo. When it was his turn, he blew on the dice and rolled, the blisters on his palms seeping blood. He lost that first roll. And the next. The men tried unsuccessfully to hide their delight. James lost every single roll thereafter. He wanted to lose, he finally realized. He cursed theatrically and smacked himself in the forehead, and the men's shoulders shook with laughter. James watched his tickets disappear. By the time they pulled into the clearing, he was flat broke. There were huge grins all around. James looked at Noyez. He had that notebook and pencil out again, scribbling away.

The driver came around and lowered the gate, and the men jumped down to the dirt. Quickly they dropped over the edge. The truck drove off, and James was left standing with Rafael Noyez.

Noyez ripped a page from his notebook and handed it over.

"What's this?" James asked.

"It is the cost."

"Of what?"

Noyez gave a short nod, as if they'd come to an agreement. Then he walked away, disappearing like the others into the ravine.

James crumpled the sheet in his fist.

Back in the truck, however, he smoothed the paper on the steering wheel. It was getting dark and he had to turn on the light in the roof of the cab. Instantly, the road outside dimmed, the landscape bleeding into shades of deep gray. He felt exposed in his tiny circle of light.

Noyez had written $1300 on the sheet.

James didn't understand—and then he did. $1300: the price of a border crossing. Underneath was a sketchy diagram and an address. The address was in Tijuana, Mexico.

James sat nursing a beer at 24-Hour Efraín's, a black night on display through the open back wall. The cantina was lit with candles, the only two customers huddled at opposite ends of the bar. James knew the other guy for a worker at La Boom. Whispering to himself and scowling into his glass, he looked as if the last thing in the world he wanted was company. That suited James fine. He was grimy from the orchard. Scalp to toenails he hurt. Three days' growth of beard needled his chin and his cheeks. He couldn't smell himself anymore, but knew it wasn't good. He should go home. He wanted to go home. He should sleep. Christ, he needed it. But his thoughts wouldn't stop flopping and flapping, whirring in his head like hummingbird wings, moment by moment too fast to nail. James sipped at the beer. He sagged a little, then sat fully upright. It was no use. Every time he relaxed, a current surged through him, and he knew he couldn't rest until somehow, someway he got to Ricardo Serio.

Efraín stood behind the counter, polishing a glass with a rag. He wore an apron and a white shirt, his thin arms poking from the loose sleeves. The radio was tuned to a talk station for a change, the sound so low James couldn't make out what was said.

He asked Efraín, "Business okay?"

"Pinche Honda," Efraín said.

The generator. James said, "I thought Patillo fixed it."

"Motherfucker blew up."

James shook his head. "Poor Danny."

"Poor Danny nothing. Poor me."

"So. How do you like him for a son-in-law?"

Efraín put the glass down, took up another. "He's honest. Makes a living."

"Firefighting's dangerous," James said.

Efraín shrugged. "Everything is dangerous, eh?"

James wrapped his hands around the cold beer. "Where's the family tonight?" He'd noticed that neither Efraín's wife nor Teresa nor the boy were around.

"Sábado de Gloria." *Holy Saturday*. "They are at church."

The worker from La Boom signaled for Efraín, who got another beer from under the counter and slid it down the bar.

Efraín said now to James, "You look very bad."

James took a sip of his beer. He wondered how much Efraín knew about the business with Leonardo. Probably more than he'd ever let on.

"You heard about Leo," he said.

Efraín lifted the glass to a candle, inspecting for spots. "Worthless fuck. But he did not deserve to die. Not like that."

"Anteater killed him."

Efraín nodded.

"Richie Serrano," James said. "You remember him."

Efraín nodded again. "Ese malvado. You should fuck him up good." He said, "Does it hurt?" He meant James's ear.

James had forgotten his ear; the mention of it now brought on a piercing ache. Still, he said, "Not as bad as everything else."

He dug into his pocket for the paper Rafael Noyez had given him, the one with the directions to the house in Tijuana, and a price. He passed it to Efraín. "A dead boy was found on my father's farm."

"I heard," Efraín said.

"He's responsible for that, too." Then, very carefully: "You have any information for me?"

Efraín was still looking at the paper. "It is a lot of money."

"Yeah." James sighed. "And I ain't got it."

Efraín wiped his hands on the rag, stuffed it in his apron pocket. He walked down the bar and went into the kitchen. The door swung behind him.

The radio clicked and popped. All at once a preacher came in loud and clear. He was discussing resurrection, Jesus' resurrection. As if in competition, the guy from La Boom raised his voice, ranting fervently about a traffic light and a dog.

The kitchen door swung again. Efraín returned to James, a bundle of gray wadded up in his hands. He laid a hooded sweatshirt on the bar.

"It gets cold in the desert," he said.

"Yes," James agreed.

Efraín pulled something from his apron. A 9 mm Glock. "You cannot use your own."

James inspected the gun. He nodded at Efraín, tucking the weapon in the back of his waistband. He slid off the barstool and pulled on the sweatshirt. He put up the hood. The edge of the fabric caught his ear and he winced.

Efraín eyed him critically. "You could be any pollo," he said. "The rest of what you need is in the pocket."

James stuck his hand in and his fingers closed around a folded bundle of cash.

He said to Efraín, "I'll pay you back."

In the candlelight, Efraín's thin face was carved and shadowed. He looked like the santos in back of the bar.

He said softly to James, "You fuck him up good."

Outskirts of Tijuana. James parked at the foot of a hill.

The street was an arroyo that cut through bodegas, tattoo parlors, panaderías and saloons, everything crooked and teetering, as if the buildings had slid down the naked hills. It was nearly midnight, but the neighborhood was hopping, overrun with children and dogs. Smells of carnitas and barbacoa, piss and geraniums, tortillas, chocolate, pan dulce and garbage cans. The nose alternately offended and seduced.

The bodega on the corner was outlined in neon. Young men loafed in front, dressed in their weekend best: clean slacks, shiny shoes, and colorful button-down shirts. They bopped to music that blared from the open doors of a Volkswagen bug. A bus-stop bench had been pushed against the wall behind them, three viejos and a bottle of tequila sharing its span. To one side sat a donkey cart painted with an image of a fierce Aztec king, likely stolen from the tourist area near Calle Revolución. The cart was filled to overflowing with cans.

In the street, two little girls sang and twirled a rope, the jumper, however, nowhere to be seen. Four boys ran around them, ducking and feinting, firing squirt guns. Plastic Uzis, lime green and hot pink. The boys' wet hair clung to their foreheads; their soaked clothing hung like a drooped second skin.

James went into the bodega, came out with a machaca burrito and some vegetable dip. He leaned against the building and ate and watched the water wars. One boy seemed to be in charge. About nine, he wore knee-high boots and a striped T-shirt that gave him a pirate's flair.

The kid, James noted, went for the face every time. And he had good aim.

James stuffed the last of his burrito into his mouth. He scooped vegetable dip with a finger. He waited to catch the boy's eye. Finally, the kid trotted over, squinting and smirking at James.

"¿Cómo te llamas?" James asked.

"LL Cool J." The boy shouldered his Uzi. He looked as if he was dying to shoot it at James.

"You live here?" James asked.

The boy pointed at a window, a dark square above the bodega's neon.

"How much to guard the truck?"

"For how long?"

"Couple of days."

The boy pursed his lips, then named an outrageous amount. James countered with an equally outrageous lowball. They haggled for a while, settling finally near the middle.

The boy demanded his money up front.

"Forget it," James said. "I'll pay when I get back." He was thinking this strategy would improve the odds that the truck would come through unscathed, but the boy wasn't having any of it. They agreed on half now, half upon James's return.

He started off on the long walk up the hill. The road was unmarked and unpaved, a narrow dirt track a half-mile straight up, paralleled by a running ditch. The smell of sewage made James's eyes fill. Here and there, flat spots sprouted tiny dwellings made of scrap wood or highway signs or tin cans hammered flat. He saw odd indications of enterprise, too, cowhides stretched and staked with bones, glass bottles stacked against a collapsed wall. Crosses made from white sticks: an improvised cemetery.

Halfway up, he was joined by a buff-colored three-legged dog. The dog loped ahead of him, then sat panting and wagging its tail, waiting for James to catch up.

They came at last to the top of the hill, where a single small house sat surrounded by chainlink and barbed wire. Steel security bars masked all the windows and doors.

The lights were out, the crabgrass knee high.

The three-legged dog sat. It lifted a paw and looked expectantly at James.

He huddled into the sweatshirt.

There was a buzzer at the front gate, a padlock with a thick metal chain. James pushed the buzzer and waited. Nothing. He pushed it again.

Now he heard voices coming around the side of the house. Two old men advanced through the dark. Both walked with silver canes. Closer, James saw that the old men were identical twins. Their foreheads were matching domes, their loose cheeks raked with matching creases. They sported identical silver crosses nestled in the wrinkled hollows of their necks.

The old men stared through the chainlink at James.

James stared back.

A minute passed.

"Quiero ir al Norte," James said.

The old men looked bored.

"Tengo dinero," James said. "Cash."

The twins perked up at that. In unison they said, "¿Cuánto?"

James knew better than to name a figure. "Suficiente." *Enough*. "Más que suficiente." *More than enough*.

The twins looked at each other. One reached into a pocket and got out a key and opened the padlock. The other yanked on the gate. James entered and the gate was quickly shut behind him, the padlock reset. Out in the street, the three-legged dog whined.

The twins said, "Ven—ven." *Come.*

James followed them down a side yard, ruts and tire tracks in gravel. Behind the house was a yard seven feet wide, the ground beyond falling off precipitously down the hillside.

A plank was set on cinderblocks, and James counted ten men perched upon it, facing into the gulch. The men sat attentively, as if before a movie screen. He noted broad backs and skinny, long-sleeved plaid shirts, a shiny green windbreaker. Four cowboy hats. Woven sacks were set in their laps, or down by their feet, along with coiled lengths of rope. Curls of cigarette smoke wafted over their heads.

The man on the end scooted, making room.

James sat. He looked into the gulch.

A short ways down, a tree grew out horizontally, with bunches of wet-looking leaves and yellow pods hung like Christmas ornaments. The roots were exposed, clods of dirt hanging from what looked like thick arms. One branch angled more sharply than the rest. It took a bend, forming a seat like a swing. There sat a young girl. Twelve, maybe. Thin legs and a sweep of dark hair. A woman— her mother?—crouched, smoking, on the hillside below. Like the men on the bench, both she and the girl stared into the gulch.

James shifted on the plank, leaning. He craned his neck. And now he saw what so fascinated everyone.

It was a rambling house fashioned from a mish-mash of materials: stucco and tile, wood and concrete, brick and tin. Set into the opposite hillside, there appeared to be no way in, not from any street. No driveway, no steps, not even a path. There was, however, a long patio ringed by banana trees, and little girls in party dresses were streaming through a doorway that shone with golden light. The girls ran all over the patio, sneaking up behind each other and cracking open hands firmly against heads. This was followed by showers of tiny white particles. Some clung to the girls' hair, more fell to the patio. Confetti-filled eggshells, James realized.

The man next to him said, "Huérfanos."

"What?" said James.

"Un orfanato." *An orphanage.*

James nodded. There were a lot of them in Tijuana, some state sanctioned, some not. The children were generally castoffs of whores or addicts, vanished illegals or prisoners at the jail. Families impoverished or too ill to provide.

A man and woman stepped out onto the patio. They clapped their hands and called to the girls and gathered them into a group. The two adults then strolled from banana tree to banana tree, reaching up into the branches. Sparks shot from their fingertips. James saw now the figures dangling in the wide leaves. For a moment, he thought they might be vultures; but they were too brightly colored. He heard sharp sputtering and snapping sounds. Skinny fizzes of light snaked upward.

Then the firecrackers exploded, one after the other, with ear-splitting bangs, and echoes of bangs, and bursts of light that rapidly chased round the patio. Debris fluttered and rained. The little girls screamed and huddled together and covered their ears. At the same time, there was a furious howling and barking of dogs. Bats flew into the sky.

The men on the plank applauded and whistled and stamped their feet.

Down the hill, the girl in the branch-swing kicked her thin legs. The mother pressed her hands to her cheeks.

"Justicia," said the man beside James. "The burning of Judases." Papier-maché figures painted to represent Judas Iscariot, or the devil, or unpopular politicians—then ignited and blown to literal bits. A triumph of good over evil, in preparation for the resurrection of Christ.

Sábado de Gloria. James kept forgetting what day it was.

But something in the scene was tugging at his memory. *The flaming scarecrow outside San Quentin's front gate.* It was the last time he'd seen Emilio. There'd been no fiesta that day. And in spite of firecrackers and laughing girls and confetti that blanketed the ground like soft-fallen snow, there was no fiesta here. Not for him, not tonight.

All through the hills, untold numbers of dogs were going utterly nuts, their frenzied barking now closer, now farther away. Hard to believe these were the same beasts that during the day lay pathetic, and motionless, in the dust of the streets.

"Los perros de la noche," James said.

His neighbor nodded. "Everything is different at night."

The twins informed them that the crossing would not take place tonight. They should all settle in for a sleep. No one would be allowed inside the house or outside the fence, not even to piss— there was a ditch for that.

Uncomplaining, the men lined up against the back wall, belongings tucked between their legs. Cowboy hats and baseball caps slid forward, faces covered to allow for nodding off unobserved.

The woman and her daughter walked around the side of the house.

James felt for his money; he felt for his gun. He stared at the sky. Then, in spite of his intentions not to, he dozed. He drifted in and out of a flickering dream, voices garbled and action unclear, like a TV plagued with staticky snow. At one point he said to himself, *Bad reception.*

A sharp report woke him. He thought it was a gunshot and his hand flew to his waist. But it was only the house's screen door. The old twins were outside in pajamas and robes. A few of the men stirred, collecting their belongings. The hillside was quiet, the sky still dark. But the air smelled of dawn. The twins made their way down the line, kicking with leather slippers.

James heard a low rumble, the crunch of gravel. A van nosed past the end of the house. The driver cut the engine.

Someone said, "Fíjate." *Check this out.*

The woman and her daughter appeared. The woman held two paper sacks and her daughter's hand. The girl was rubbing sleep from her eyes. Something about her reminded James of his wife, the long legs, the wide mouth, the sharp bones. At twelve, Mercedes must've looked much the same. It gave him a pang, and he had to look away.

The van, he noted, was dark blue, not tan.

The driver strutted around back to open the doors. Too young, James thought with disappointment. The guy wore shit-kicker boots, yards of thick silver chain wrapped around his neck. Impatiently he gestured at the passengers. He ran a hand over buzz-cut dark hair, then stroked the Fu Manchu mustache beneath his button nose.

CHAPTER SEVENTEEN

He stood in line with the others at the back of the van, shuffling forward as the mustachioed young man collected their fees. The process was orderly. Everyone seemed to possess correct change. James focused on a bumper sticker, CHOOSE LIFE; and then the young man was poking him in the biceps. He handed over his $1300, climbed into the van, and sat on the floor.

With each additional body, the space closed in around him. He drew his knees to his chest, to his chin. The woman and her daughter were the last aboard. Then the doors shut on them all. There was a short, low-voiced conversation outside, and the van started up. They backed up a little, stopping again. The front passenger door opened and someone got in. The door slammed. And who, James wondered, was in that front seat?

They rolled off down the hill.

Stop and go, stop and go. With each turn, the passengers fell against each other. But no one complained. No one said much of anything. It was quiet in the driver's compartment, as well.

After a while, they got onto a highway, and there were no more stops. The van picked up speed, the road smooth beneath the wheels.

The two windows in the cargo area had been blocked out with foil, the only light that which leaked through a square of mesh in the wall dividing them from the driver. James figured they weren't headed either north or south; the light was angled incorrectly for that. It shone directly ahead. They were driving east.

Time passed, two hours and more. Then the van started to climb, up and up, very gently. And now there were sweeping curves in the road. The driver was going too fast, swinging wildly. The road straightened for some miles, then curved again. The air in the cargo area had grown hot and stale and the girl was whining. James heard the strangled sound of vomiting, the mother murmuring reassurance, the men nearest them groaning in protest of the smell.

The girl cried.

James maneuvered himself to a half-stand. Curve left, curve right; but the packed bodies held him mostly upright. He yanked at the foil and pushed the window latch. Fresh air rushed inside. The girl had vomited into a sweater, and the garment was passed quickly forward. The van was descending now. James peered through the window at crags scraped bare above dizzying drops. He flattened sideways, trying to get a look at what was ahead. Desert, of course. They'd long since passed Corville and El Pilón. North were the salt lake and the valley, orange and lemon groves, lettuce and broccoli. The van took a wide curve and the guard rail disappeared and James saw kinked metal glinting at the bottom of a ravine.

He thrust the sweater through the window, twisted to watch it flutter out behind them.

From the driver's compartment came a voice: "¡Ciérrala!" *Shut it.*

James froze. He'd know that voice anywhere.

He did as he was told.

The van was stifling, swelteringly hot, filled with a stink of fertilizer and rubber and ripening sweat. James couldn't get enough air. He breathed through his mouth and wondered when it would end. Periodically he tried to estimate where they might be, but he'd lost track of time, and the heat and the darkness canceled whatever clues his body usually took in. When they finally turned off the highway, no one was prepared. The pollos knocked against each other, groaning as the van bumped over what could only be a dirt road. Then they very suddenly stopped.

The front doors opened and shut. There were footsteps outside. The back doors swung open and the pollos tumbled gasping and blinking into brilliant sunshine. The temperature was preposterous, the air so dry it scraped in the nose and the throat. All around them, ocotillos stood on the sand like men with arms outstretched.

To the north, escarpments cut against the blue sky, sheer treeless rock that ran east to west.

James knew where he was now and he was afraid. Even the Patrol left this area mostly alone. He couldn't believe they were going to cross here.

The young driver stroked his mustache. He rattled the chain at his hip and said, "It's fuckin' hot."

The pollos milled about on the sand.

Some yards away a makeshift tent was set up, a few sheets sewn together and stretched over poles. An old man crouched in the shade. James counted a dozen plastic milk jugs, one blue-and-white cooler, one char-encrusted grill. A small woven basket was filled with Tootsie Rolls.

"Club Med," Anteater said.

James kept his head down. He watched Anteater from under his hood.

The pollos walked to the tent, the girl and her mother lingering behind. They looked around in distress. The girl shifted from foot to foot, and James realized they needed to relieve themselves.

Anteater realized it too. Grinning, he said to the woman, "The desert has no secrets." He swept an arm expansively. "You may shit or piss anywhere."

Horrified, the woman shook her head.

Safely under the tent, one of the pollos risked a question. "What do we do now?"

Anteater said, "You wait."

Heat and tedium. Sweat evaporating on the skin so rapidly that all that was left was a layer of salt. For hours, they waited under the tent, until eventually, the sky went up in flames, the sun's radiance intensifying before it withdrew. Dusk was palpable, the hot heavens distilled.

Then the light was gone and the travelers were off.

Twenty-two miles to the escarpment, the first leg of the journey: they should make it before dawn. Each carried his or her belongings, along with two candy bars and a milk jug filled with water. Even here, in the moonless dark, in the middle of nowhere, there were in the white sand human trails to guide them, braided tracks of tennis shoes and huaraches and boots. Some fresh, James saw, and some weathered at the edges, some so shallow as to be nearly invisible. But all pointed north, the way marked also with empty peanut butter jars and cigarette butts, soda cans, tuna cans, plastic bags, rounds of black ash where campfires had burned. And each small sign of those who'd crossed before them was both a comfort and a warning. Because human beings were an afterthought here; the landscape, vast and indifferent, had existed unchanged for millennia. Sand, rock, and stars. It was the same desert James had worked for seventeen years, and yet he didn't feel the same within it, but rather a version of himself reduced to essentials. Blood and bone. An element in a larger body: the pollos moving north.

Anteater was the head of that body, and as such he set the pace, everyone else threaded out behind him. The young man with chains and mustache brought up the rear. James stayed some-where near the middle, walking most often with the mother and her girl. But he kept his eyes on Ricardo Serio. Anteater carried a black backpack that made of him a creature top-heavy and humped, and a white cowboy hat that floated like a buoy in a dark sea, and James had a sudden memory of being in the pool at the house in L.A., an orange life vest strapped to his chest. He remem-bered bobbing like a little cork in the deep end, his family up on the patio. Emilio and Lara and Diego, so far away, but all eyes on him.

James stumbled over a pile of white stones.

He saw the dried carcass of a coyote beneath an ironwood tree. He heard the screech of an owl.

These things seemed to be omens, of what he could not have said.

And yet those first miles were covered in good spirits and decent time. There was laughter, and cigarette smoke, and eager walking feet. Every hour or so the group stopped for water and rest, then pushed off again quickly, impatiently, as if renewed pur-pose had been breathed in with the parched air.

As time passed, however, the terrain grew more difficult. It became harder and harder to see. The desert floor dipped into shallow culverts filled with mesquite and tamarisk, and the travel-ers dodged ratholes and clumps of black creosote. James's arms and legs hurt. He felt seared, inside and out. He was very tired, and worried now about his perceptions and reflexes. He heard the mother panting and stumbling behind him and he stopped to wait, then told her to follow closely, stepping wherever he had stepped first. He was glad enough to slow down.

The girl, who since leaving the van had showed more energy than anyone, called forward, "And where will you live in El Norte, señor?"

The mother shushed her daughter, seeming to think this ques-tion was rude.

But James answered, "San Antonio." He'd never been there, had always wanted to go.

The girl said, "Texas?"

"Yeah, Texas," James said.

"Then this is a really dumb place to cross."

The mother shushed her again.

"It's all right," James said. "She's right. . . . You've done this before?"

Shyly, the woman said, "Sí." And sighing, "Four times."

"You should swim the river," the girl said. "You'd be closer."

James said, "You're right."

And now the mother ventured, "Do you have work that is waiting for you?"

"Family," James said. "And you?"

"Also family," she said. "In Phoenix, Arizona."

The girl said, "Better watch out, señor. You're drinking too much water."

He'd been sweating like a dog, slick streams down his chest and his back. His hairline was soaked. But he couldn't remove the sweatshirt, couldn't lower the hood. James checked his plastic jug. The girl was right again; he'd been hitting the water too hard. He thanked her. She seemed about to say something more, when there was a disturbance ahead. The men had stopped and were gathered into a hushed circle, some standing, some crouched. James saw the beam of a flashlight. He hurried to catch up, elbowed into the circle to see what they were looking at.

A shed snakeskin glittered on the sand, perfect and complete, the faceted scales like diamonds. James thought: every one of these men had seen snakes before, but this one was different, compelling, unique.

Anteater lifted his hat. "You are in America now." He looked from pollo to pollo. No one said a word.

A new-risen moon was a sliver of pumpkin perched on the bluffs. A sideways smile.

James felt Anteater's eyes. He ducked his head, shrugged himself more deeply into his hood. For the first time, it occurred to him that he did not have a plan.

The entire party was dragging now. When they stopped again for a rest, several wanted to make camp and call it a night, but Anteater insisted they keep on. They had to reach the escarpment before the sun rose, or they'd be swept up by the migra helicopters and jeeps. Some of the pollos seemed dubious. For hours, an ominous curtain of rock had loomed straight ahead, close enough, but somehow never closer. Anteater assured them it was less than an hour away.

The pollos drank water and chewed on their candy bars. Then they got up again.

As promised, they arrived within the hour at the base of a cliff. The wall appeared unbroken here and James didn't see how they were going to get in.

Two of the pollos suggested they walk around.

"Go on," Anteater said. "Next week, I'll see you in Tijuana. Get your money again."

Persuasion enough. There were no more recommendations from the pollos.

Anteater led them west along the rock wall until they came to a narrow fissure, hip high. He instructed the pollos to get down on their knees. Apparently they were meant to crawl through.

The passage was less than fifty yards long, but tight, and crawling, James saw nothing but the thighs and rear of the man in front of him. The walls closed in and scraped at his sides, and at one point, the ceiling lowered so much that he was forced to wriggle forward on his belly. When he was nearly through, someone back down the line started to yell and that set everyone off. Voices echoed fiendishly. James crawled faster. He felt a thin waft of air, and then he emerged from the pandemonium with ears jangling.

He stood in a narrow canyon, sheer rock, levered and buckled, as if disgorged from the underworld. To one side, an over-hang capped a shallow cave, a heap of dirty linens piled against the back wall.

"Your suite," Anteater said.

The last of the pollos had made it through the passageway. Everyone made a beeline for the blankets. They spread out under the overhang.

James grabbed a yellow bathmat and set himself up against the back wall. Acutely aware of the bones in his feet, he took his shoes and socks off and checked for blisters. He rubbed his sore calves. He picked thorns from the front of his sweatshirt. Leaned against the wall, he saw a scorpion crawl across a tiny ledge. He got his shoe, but before he had a chance to take aim, the scorpion disappeared into a crack.

Outside the overhang, Anteater paced. James watched from under his hood. He wondered what was on Ricardo Serio's mind. But finally Anteater gave up. He stretched out flat on his back.

The patch of sky paled. James slipped down, the rock hard and cool against his spine. Beside him, the girl and her mother were already asleep. And then he was gone, too.

It was late afternoon before he awoke, sweating and disoriented, the words *get him get him get him* chugging like a train through his head. He sat up. The sun shone into the canyon at a violent slant, the walls stained red as if splashed with blood.

And where was Anteater?

Still asleep. Stretched out in full sun on the scorched rock.

But several of the others were up and about. One group crouched in the near-useless shade, talking about their families and their plans, dream vehicles, and preferred jobs. Work hard, play hard, send some money home.

The men smoked cigarette after cigarette, blue smoke pooling under the rock. A radio appeared from under a shirt. Nothing came in but static, but the volume was set on high anyway, the fierce crackling like an invisible fire. Someone announced, "I'd like to see snow." Someone else said, "Wisconsin. Good factory work and eight months of snow." One man, James saw, was very drunk, a glass bottle tucked like a baby in the crook of his arm. Another had taken money from his sock; he counted the wad of bills, then slipped them back in. Another whittled a piece of wood with a knife. Yet another had a length of rope in his lap. He tied a few fancy knots, admired them, then undid his handiwork and began again.

The woman and her daughter were no longer by James, having moved a short distance away from the group. The mother was pretty, he decided—he hadn't noticed before—and younger than her child's age would predict. She sat cross-legged, palms on her knees, as if meditating. But the girl was fidgety, wanting to get up and play. The mother leaned over and said something to her. Then she pulled an apple from her sack and gave the girl sips of water from the milk jug.

Anteater was awake now, sitting with the guy in the shit-kicker boots, their heads together in a way James didn't like. But there was nothing he could do now. He'd have to wait until everyone was safely across, then jump the guy at the first opportunity. James had his gun, and the element of surprise, and that would have to be enough.

He got up and went over to the girl and her mother and sat down beside them. Into the silence, the girl announced that she'd never seen the ocean. The mother clucked her tongue, and James said, "It's important. You have to go." At that, the mother leaned forward and said firmly to James, "Phoenix, Arizona."

To kill time, he taught them the word game Ghost. One letter from each and keep going around. The first to spell a word loses and takes the letter G. The girl wanted to play in English. James won six rounds, lost two. Then lost again, spelling the word "close" when he was thinking of "closet" instead. But he was distracted now, trying to eavesdrop on Anteater, who was talking animatedly, just under James's ability to hear.

"Pay attention," the girl said.

James said, "I think I've had enough." He heard Anteater saying, *in the end . . .*

"You can't quit," the girl said. "I don't have Ghost yet."

James said, "You get Ghost by losing."

"I know," she said. "I don't care." She looked him in the eye. Her face was plain, knife-edged, and infinitely pleasing to James.

"All right," he said.

The girl said, "You start."

"A," said James.

The girl thought and thought, as if the next letter would settle her fate. "L," she said, drawing it out.

"B," the mother said.

James thought this might be a word, but he wasn't sure, so he didn't say so. He closed his eyes and "albacore" formed itself in his mind. He was certain neither of them would get it, which didn't seem entirely fair. But he couldn't resist.

"A," he said.

"T," said the girl, so quickly that James became suspicious. He studied her, but picked up no clues. This kid would make a hell of a poker player some day. Did she have a word? Or did she not?

Finally, he said, "I challenge you."

"Albatross," the girl said.

James stared. "You've got to be kidding." He looked at the mother, who shook her head and shrugged.

They walked single-file, Anteater in the lead. And if the open desert had been eerie, the canyons were more so, intensely claustrophobic, the walls radiating a diabolical heat. Very little light filtered down from the stars, and the floor was crisscrossed with cracks and loose stones, and they had to step carefully. Supposedly, they were continuing north. Two miles, and then they'd be out in the desert again, with the last leg before them: five miles to the Interstate and freedom. But James sensed that they were instead heading west, tracking just inside the canyon's outer wall.

They'd just passed a huge rock shaped like an anvil when he became aware of voices. It wasn't the pollos. And he wasn't the only one who had heard. The group slowed, and stopped. The voices were faint but growing louder. The pollos began to whisper among themselves. Someone said, "La migra, sí," and an air of panic set in.

Remembering Anteater's MO, James thought it was more likely to be bandidos.

And now an argument broke out about which way to run, and where to hide. Everyone looked to Anteater, except that Anteater wasn't there.

"¡Nos ha dejado!" *He's left us!*

James pushed forward. It was true. Anteater was gone.

"Relax," said the guy in the shit-kicker boots. "He's scouting ahead."

James hesitated for a moment only, then took off in pursuit.

The way was clear at first, a narrow strip that wound between towering rocks. Then he came to a fork. James took out the Glock. He clicked off the safety. He inspected surfaces, but saw no disturbance, no snagged threads, no shed hairs, no footprints. He started off to the right. Rounding a curve, he nearly tripped over Anteater's pack, precisely placed in the middle of the path. And how to interpret this? Was it meant to lure him on? To send him back? James didn't know what to do. But the left path was closer to a possible exit from the canyons, so he decided to return to the fork and go the other way.

Within a few minutes, he came to a jutting outcrop that blocked both progress and view. He stopped, listened, heard nothing at all. He pulled the Glock to his chest and slid around, extending his arms, prepared to shoot. But he'd entered an empty rock room. Smooth walls rose like a basin around him. The path continued on the opposite side. He crossed the open space, feeling exposed.

Again, he pulled the Glock to his chest. He swept around the edge, into another chamber of rock, this one small and square.

Anteater was waiting, his gun also drawn.

"I killed you once already," he said, his voice echoing weirdly, the words repeating a half second behind.

James sighted down the barrel.

"Traitor," Anteater hissed, "in a fucking disguise. But migra fuck, I knew it was you—you look just like him."

Emilio. *Yes*.

Anteater said, "I saw you with those little birdies, you know, shooting them out of the trees. I saw your heart bleed."

"I'll shoot you," James said, "And feel nothing at all."

And then Anteater vanished.

Goddamnit, thought James.

He strode the few yards to where Anteater had stood, discovered yet another wall with a slender entry behind. James held his breath and came around. This time the path led to a dead end. He saw nothing, but sensed movement above. A small stone fell to his feet. He looked up. A shadow was scaling the wall. James raised his arm straight overhead, aiming the Glock. But he didn't shoot. He couldn't shoot. The space was too tight. A bullet hitting rock would ricochet. *Goddamnit!* Gun still in hand, he started to climb. Feet and fingers in crevices, scrape of rock at his cheek. But he was gaining, and then Anteater turned sideways and kicked at him. He kicked at James's arm, and his head. Undeterred, James scrabbled up a few inches more. He grabbed onto Anteater's foot. Anteater thumped his caught leg against the rock wall until James dropped the Glock. James looped his arm around Anteater's calf. Anteater slipped. He bent down, swatting at James, and his gun also clattered to the ground.

James let go. Anteater tumbled down on top of him and they fell together. They hit bottom with thuds and grunts and terrible groans.

James had the breath knocked out of him. His ears were ringing. He was banged up; his shoulder felt wrenched from the socket. But more important, where was his gun? Where was

Anteater's gun?

James heaved to get Anteater off of him. He rolled and sat. He couldn't see anything. He ran his hands over the ground. Nothing.

Anteater was beginning to stir. James scooted around behind him, yanked him backward, and pulled him up between his legs. He threw an arm around Anteater's neck.

"My partner." He spoke into the side of Anteater's head. "That gets you a date with the needle. But listen. *Listen*. This might be your lucky day. All you have to do is sing."

Anteater wheezed, "Fuck you, migra fuck!"

"You know the words—"

"Fuck you!"

"Tell me about Diego."

"Fuck you!"

James tightened his hold. He whispered harshly into Anteater's ear: "Poor Ricardo Serio. The guy fell—not even that far—and broke his fucking neck. What a freak thing."

"Fuck you!" Anteater gasped.

James said, "Diego killed Margarita Jimenez."

And Diego would pay. He had to pay! For Margarita, and Leonardo, and the dead boy found on Desmond's property. For Emilio, shanked in his bunk. And for young Jaime Santana, heart-broken, lied to, erased.

He felt Anteater's shoulders starting to shake. Perfect! The fucker was crying—except that it wasn't crying, James realized, but laughter instead. Anteater clawed at James's arm. He said, "Diego would never dirty his hands. Tight-assed fucker. Chasing that gabacha bitch, just like Emilio." He choked and spittle flew from his lips. "You Santanas think you're better than anyone."

He said through clenched teeth, "It was your mother, you stupid fuck."

"Liar," James said. "Liar!" But his mind was racing.

Emilio and Diego on the pool steps. Naked, which James found very funny, the hair curling on his father's chest, and his tío's

*smooth brown skin, both with that fur between their legs and the
mouse in its nest. Glancing away from the pool, Emilio said, Are
you happy now?*

And who had Emilio been talking to?

Not James, up on the balcony, peering down through the bars,
but Lara, hidden directly below.

His mother. She was the one. How could she be the one?

James's grip weakened.

"Everybody knew," Anteater said. "How she slammed that little
girl . . . and put her under . . . and Emilio tried to pin it on us! Bring-
ing the body back home. Fuck him!"

That dead boy had been placed on Desmond's property. Placed,
exactly as Margarita Jimenez had been.

Anteater jammed an elbow into James's ribcage.

James grunted and fell back hard on the rock. He hit his head
hard and bit his tongue and his mouth filled with blood. But he
didn't let go. He dragged Anteater down. Anteater thrashed and
kicked and James locked his legs around him. His chin dug into
the top of Anteater's head. He could see the thin strands of black
hair and the bumps in his skull; he could smell the guy's scalp.
James snorted in disgust. He rolled his eyes skyward. The rocks
stood around him like jagged teeth. He felt swallowed. And then
he was sinking, spiraling down. The sky above him narrowed and
closed. It was so far away. He was trapped at the bottom of something and he'd never get out.

But the sky—the sky!—it was a color he'd never seen in his life.
Blue blue blue, purple black, pinpricked in white, as if there was a
great shining behind.

A man protects what he loves.

Emilio had betrayed his blood, to protect what he loved.

"Emilio," said Anteater, "got what he deserved."

As hard as he could, James rammed his forearm up into
Anteater's neck. He'd kill the fucker, right here, right now! There
was a roaring deep in his head, a high-pitched whine in his ears,

and then the sounds suddenly seemed to be outside of him, rather than in, and he thought it was Ricardo Serio, squealing and screaming, except that the only noise Anteater made was a labored inhaling and exhaling of breath.

Another wail cut the air, high-pitched and thin. The sound echoed and multiplied. A female voice, James realized.

The pollos!

James let go of Anteater's neck. He booted him forward, then scrambled to his feet. The rocks bulged, the stars heaved.

Then he found his footing and everything stilled.

He looked down at Anteater.

The fucker was grinning! But he didn't get up. And James saw then what he hadn't before, that Anteater's leg had broken in the fall. His foot was twisted and faced the wrong way.

James saw his Glock now, as well, kicked against the rock wall. He swept down and retrieved it, came up aiming at Anteater's head. *Do it*, he told himself, his finger on the trigger. *Do it now*.

Another scream. It was like a knife to his heart. *Goddamnit to hell!* He lowered the gun. Anteater was still grinning at him. He knew that James would run back to the pollos, into the arms of the thieves. Gun or no gun, they'd get him. Then they'd come and collect Ricardo Serio. And who knew what would happen then, nothing good, surely, the only certainty being that one way or another Anteater would be lost to James.

Fuck that, he thought. He'd take Anteater with him. Use him as a hostage.

He crouched down and grabbed Anteater under the arms and hauled him up. Anteater didn't fight. But when James began to drag him backward, he shrieked as if being eaten alive. James turned around, humped Anteater up onto his shoulder. He stumbled into the small, square space, then around the edge of the wall and into the basinlike room. Christ, the guy was a load. Carrying him was going to kill James. He stopped for a second to catch his breath. He stood very still.

There were shadows moving along the rock walls, a dark pouring into the bowl.

"Compadres," Anteater cried, "I am here!"

The shadows did not reply. James saw eyes in the darkness. Too many eyes. He heard the scuff of footsteps on rock.

The shadows moved in like a wave. And Anteater was keening, babbling now, saying that James was a bad man, a betrayer, a sneak, and first and always their natural enemy. James stooped under Anteater's weight. It took effort to lift his own head, his neck like a thread that surely must break. But he wanted to see. He had to *see*.

Broad chests and skinny chests floated toward him, encased in long-sleeved plaid shirts. He saw a shiny green windbreaker. Some number of cowboy hats. He saw the girl's mother, and then the girl. The girl was coming toward him. She was saying something but he didn't know what, because Anteater's voice was soft in his ear, familiar as the beating of James's own heart. He concentrated on the girl's mouth. Anteater slipped down his back and James reached around and grabbed at him, but the guy continued to slide. James concentrated on the girl's mouth. He read the girl's lips. *Put him down*, she was saying, *put him down, you can put him down.*

CHAPTER EIGHTEEN

The pollos carried Ricardo Serio out. Everyone else walked, including the two bandidos, arms roped to their sides. The mustachioed young man had been stabbed in the shoulder, his chains confiscated and a blood-soaked T-shirt tied round his wound; and the pollo who'd done this took on the responsibilities of an unofficial escort, the tip of the knife used to prod the young man forward, as necessary.

The party went back through the canyon the way they'd come in, crawling on hands and knees. The bandidos had ridden in on a truck, which waited nearby on the sand, and the pollos, excited over this find, decided to continue northward on wheels. Everyone piled in. For a mile or two, they hugged the white cliffs. Then they shot around a jutting finger of rock. They were out in the open now. They could just make out the headlights on the Interstate when they heard the faint whopping of chopper blades. White glare, a deafening mechanical wail. James's first response was, *Ah, shit, no;* his second, *thank God.* And then bright lights shone directly ahead. Jeeps were rolling at them like tanks on a battlefield.

At a turnout on the Interstate, Anteater and the bandidos were handcuffed and loaded into an INS van. A second vehicle carried the pollos. The driver was a guy James had gone to Patrol School with in El Paso, way back when, though it took convincing before he accepted James's identity.

"Well, you look like shit, Reese."

"Yeah," said James.

"Man, I heard about your partner." The driver was chewing gum, snaps and pops issuing from his mouth as if he had a cap gun in there. "That's some bad fuckin' luck."

James climbed into the front passenger seat, where, theoretically at least, he belonged.

The driver came around, got in, settled himself behind the wheel.

"You stink, Reese," he said.

"Yeah," James said again.

Back at the stationhouse, James called his wife. He called Des and Marie. He called Lieutenant Louise Conti up in L.A.

And then he stood in a doorway, watching the pollos as they marched from the processing room to a holding tank. They went single-file. The girl and her mother were being taken to a separate cell and they passed directly by James, close enough to touch him.

He waited for them to turn, to say something, to catch his eye. But it didn't happen.

James knew that as witnesses to a crime, they wouldn't be deported just yet. He also knew that the inevitable was, by sad definition, inevitable.

He felt a tightness in his chest.

He went after the girl and her mother, caught up just before they entered the cell. He had a business card in his hand and he held it out to them, feeling like an insurance salesman. The mother folded her arms. James got a pen from the patrol, turned the card over and quickly scribbled his number at home. Again, he held out the card. The mother raised an eyebrow. But the girl took the card and looked at it and slipped it into the pocket of her jeans.

Meanwhile, in a back room, Anteater sang.

James waited for Mercedes by the fountain in Corville's square. He sat alone on a bench. The sun was down now, but the light not yet gone. Trees and bushes were draped in deep blue shadows.

The park was filling for the evening, a scene he'd witnessed thousands of times. There were elderly couples from the retirement home, and bored-looking vatos in pressed chinos and Pendletons, and teenage girls with big hair and red lips; and young families, too, men in work clothes, or sweatpants, women with blankets to spread, carrying coolers that promised sodas and fresh fruit and sandwiches. There were diaper-babies, and a group of kids tossing a baseball. A blond girl played with an orange Hula Hoop, her skinny hips sending the plastic ring into orbit.

Two boys, nine years old tops, huddled in a hollowed-out hibiscus bush, with lit cigarettes and pleated paper bags that surely hid liquor bottles.

James watched for Mercedes to come from the direction of her mother's house.

But as always, she surprised him. One moment, he was alone; the next, her hands were on him, her fingers caressing his face and his hair. He stood her between his knees and closed his legs and held her captive there. He wrapped his arms all the way around her waist. The day's accumulation of heat rose from the pavement. He could feel it through the soles of his boots. Promise of a hot summer. But then, what summer was not? James laid his face against his wife's belly. He felt floaty and loose-limbed, as if he were adrift on a soft-rolling sea. But he wasn't afraid.

After a while, Mercedes gently freed herself. She kept his hand in hers as she lowered down beside him.

They watched a line of sparrows perched at the fountain's edge. Tiny heads dipped over the rim, tail feathers in the air. The birds were looking for water that wouldn't be there for months.

"Do you think they remember?" he asked.

"Of course they do," she said.

"I wish they'd turn the fountain on now. Water the birds. Cool things off for the humans, too."

Mercedes sighed. "The city doesn't work that way, James." She said, "I guess you'll just have to wait for Christmas. Good things come at Christmastime, eh?"

The baby, he thought. *Yes.*

"Everything," he said, "will be different by then."

"Everything, corazón, is different right now."

All around them, lights were coming on in the square. The glass storefronts, eye-burningly reflective during the day, now allowed anyone who wanted to to see in. There were people in the lingerie shop, and the Thai place, and the stationers, a huge flag pinned on the brick wall behind them. This could be any town, James thought, anywhere in America. But he didn't really believe it. Because the border was like no place else. It was a no-man's land, gritty and violent, heartless and holy, an invention, a dream. The native language here was neither English nor Spanish, but desperation.

"That dead boy," he said to Mercedes, "no one is ever going to come and claim him." The child had no parents, and he'd been so far from home. The poor kid. James wanted to apologize. But who was there to apologize to?

God, he was tired.

"We can do it," Mercedes said. "We can bury him."

Gratefully, he kissed the side of her head. "That feels right," he said. Mercedes's hair smelled like coconut, her skin like warm sand. The tip of her ear was soft, but firm.

"But you have to understand," she said. "You can't fix everything."

"I know that," he said.

"Do you?" she said. "Do you really? You've worked so hard. Trying to keep the world in order, everything and everyone in their proper place."

"Someone's got to do it," he said.

"But it's impossible. You see that, don't you? You have to decide what's worth the effort." She leaned against him. "These people, you know? They're so anxious to come here, to give their kids a chance. They leave their families and their culture. They break the law. They break their backs. And this country sucks them right up. Because we want their labor. Their bodies, their hands. But their *souls*, corazón. What about their souls? Not everyone is a criminal, James."

In all his life, he'd never really trusted anyone. He'd had his reasons.

"I don't know, honey," he said. "Can't teach an old dog."

Laughing, she said, "Oh, yes, you can."

The sparrows by the fountain rose in a flutter of wings.

"Who are you?" she said. "And who do you want to be?"

The birds circled above the treeline, flying first in one direction, then another.

He heard the *thwock* of a baseball hitting a glove. A baby crying. Rap music blasting from a boombox on the other side of the park.

"Everybody," Mercedes said, "is only looking to find them a home." She squeezed his hand. "This," she said, "is your chance."

Lieutenant Conti invited James to Diego's arrest.

He declined. He had work to do.

In the weeks since the capture of Ricardo Serio, Alexander May had loaned him a sum of money, an advance of sorts on his coming inheritance. He used some of the funds to pay Des and Marie, wiping out his debt and then some, he hoped. The rest was bailout for Ramirez & Son—on the condition that he be allowed to labor alongside the family. Having quit the Patrol, James wanted a hammer and he wanted nails. He wanted to make something with his own hands. He liked the lingo, too: spans and plates, plumb cuts, soffits, studs and joists. He made a point of being on the site bright and early each day, of being open to instruction and aware of just who was boss. One moment, James would catch Carlos giving him a version of Cruz's fish eye; the next he'd be demonstrating how to estimate supplies. How to mix concrete, how to measure and cut, how to frame, how to install windows and put in a floor. They got the second house in the development built in July. By mid-August, they were roofing the third.

Mercedes, in her fifth month of pregnancy now, worked down on the ground. She sat in a director's chair under a canvas canopy, counting copper pipe. The black dog kept company.

These days, James's wife was sleek as a seal, her sharp bones padded with baby fat. Her belly button had popped. James was looking forward to the birth. He liked feeling the baby move inside his wife, watching the small kicks and somersaults and trying to identify different parts. He'd been to all the doctor's appointments so far, and he'd seen an ultrasound of his child. A miracle. He and Mercedes gave one copy to Cruz, who seemed to think it indecent somehow, another to Desmond and Marie. Up at the farm, the picture, gold-framed, hung on their living room wall, an honored position above the silent TV.

The baby was a girl. James was glad of that, and a little relieved, though he could not have said why.

Up on the roof, the plywood decking was mostly in place. All that remained was a final course beneath the ridge plate.

Rubén slid a four-by-eight sheet up the rig and James grabbed it and carried it to his end. Heavy son-of-a-bitch. He heard another sheet going up behind him, Carlos taking hold of that one.

Resting before heading up to the peak, James lowered the plywood onto one edge. A relentless sun beat down on his head.

Sweat in his eyes, he glanced at his watch: twelve fifteen. It was possible that Lieutenant Conti was at this very moment knocking on Diego Santana's door. James pictured his uncle's look of surprise, Conti reading his rights, the handcuffs jangling.

The more he'd thought about it, the greater Diego's crimes seemed. He hadn't killed Margarita Jimenez, but chances were he'd wanted her dead. He'd wanted James dead. And for what? James had to wonder as well: Had Diego understood the danger Emilio was in, had he suspected Emilio was going to be killed? Maybe he'd loved his brother, but how willingly and easily he'd stepped into his life.

James had thought a lot about Emilio, too, about love and loyalty, misjudged and misplaced. Maybe Emilio had been greedy, too happy to escape the old neighborhood. Or maybe, with Margarita Jimenez, he'd discovered that there was no escape, and that when push came to shove he didn't want it anyway.

Then again, maybe not. Because Emilio had protected Lara. It was, James decided, his shame and his saving grace.

And Lara Shipp Santana? What did it mean to him that his mother was a murderer? Instead of Diego. Instead of Emilio.

Lara had killed that girl out of passion and jealousy; James was sure of it. And she'd let her husband go to prison for her. She'd taken up with her husband's brother and given away her own child. But was she an evil woman? In spite of everything, he couldn't decide. The truth was too complicated, filled—as Leo might have said—with all those nice shades of gray. Diego's Uncertainty Principle seemed to be working here, too. There were facts, and there were feelings. Giving up one for the other came with a price. *Guilt and Innocence*. And James was her blood. Had she ever loved him? Was that deathbed gesture of hers fear of damnation, or proof of remorse?

It was possible, he thought, to be two things at once. The past might be the past, but it was the future, too. And Diego was wrong:

human beings weren't small, but so large they made their own universe.

James took up the plywood again. He struggled with it up to the peak. There he looked down. He could see through the rafters, straight into the house's interior. Walls and windows, cutouts for doors.

Then the plywood slipped from his hands. It clattered against the decking, slid away before he even registered it was gone. Down it went, scraping, then straight over the side, landing with a splintery crash on the hard dirt below.

"¡Cabrón!" Rubén shouted up at him. "Be careful, eh!"

James swayed. The sun was blinding. He was off balance here.

Mercedes had walked out from under the canopy, the dog at her side. She shaded her eyes and stared up anxiously. And, Christ, James thought, he was a lucky man.

From the other end of the roof came Carlos's drawl: "It's dangerous, I warned you, ese. And workman's comp don't mean a thing."

Rubén called up, "Not if you break someone's neck!"

Carlos said, "It could be your own."

James put his arms out to steady himself.

He said, "I'm not going to fall." He looked over at Carlos, who was grinning now.

Rubén, too, who said, "Come back to the rig, James. I'll get you another, okay?"

He was all right.

He waved at his wife. She waved back, ducked again under the canopy.

He looked all around. The bird's-eye view was fantastic, and humbling. The desert, the mountains, a bank of fat clouds in a field of bright blue.

Rubén passed him up a fresh sheet. James dragged the plywood up, and up. Carefully, he set it in place, making sure there was proper spacing at the edges, to allow for swelling after it rained. As if it ever rained.

He retrieved his nail gun from where he'd left it. Down on one knee, he stared into the house. For just a moment he wished he didn't have to close in the roof. He'd like to leave it like this, open to the sky.